Safe Passage Guaranteed

Pete Torrey

Fiction/Sports

Available from Amazon.com
and other retail outlets.
Available on Kindle and other devices.

While inspired by true events, this is a work of fiction. Names, characters, places, and incidents either are the product of the author's imagination, or are used fictitiously. Any resemblance to actual persons, living or dead, events, or locales is entirely coincidental.

Copyright © 2021 by Pete Torrey

All rights reserved, including the right to reproduce this book or portions thereof in any form whatsoever.

This book is dedicated to my wife Jean,
my inspiration,
and the true love of my life.

Acknowledgements

I never in my wildest dreams ever thought that I would really write a book, but the story of the mid-1970s Indiana high school basketball players was so compelling that I couldn't get it out of my mind-even after nearly fifty years! My wife's cousin, Dr. Leah Haygood, the author of the exciting Claire Ghest mystery series of books, would not let me just talk about it. She even wrote the first couple of sentences to get me started, and then said "go!" No question about it, if it hadn't been for her, I probably would have just talked about it for the rest of my life, but never would have attempted it.

What always held me back was putting this story in the proper context. Do I wrap it around a mystery or political narrative, or how about romance and history? I eventually decided to use several events in my short ten-year broadcasting career as a backdrop, at the risk of it being labeled by critics as a "vanity project." Hopefully, readers may find the twists and turns of my broadcasting career to be funny and entertaining, but I really want them to be touched and moved by what these 1970s Midwestern teens accomplished. I know I was.

In addition to Leah, I have numerous other people to thank for their input, criticism, and friendship. So here goes:

My good friend Steve Dini, a San Jose State classmate and a screenwriter, offered many helpful suggestions as did my other college pal Hal Ramey, a Bay Area Broadcasting Hall of Fame member. My high school friends, Marilyn and Kent Muhlker, also contributed greatly with their hard work "proofing" some of my manuscript. Nancy Parker, published author and family friend, also chipped in with some sage advice as did my cousin Jody Hodges, a former book publisher. I sent chapters to a diverse collection of readers who gave me their invaluable feedback and encouragement. They included Tom Walker, Alan Spiegelman, Vicki Hughes, Pete Katches, and Bobbie deRuiter.

I also would like to thank my broadcasting friends whose lives connected with mine at some point in my career. Each one of them contributed to this story. They include J Webb Horton, Steve Corona, Ian Pearson, Stenn Bowman, Tony Vignieri, Kathy Kerchner, Dave King, Ken Kurtz, Roger Mann, Ron DeHart, Russ Coleman, Reid Chapman, Mike Cohen, Francis Conway, Al Wright, Paul Barys, Jim Brunner, Hilliard Gates, Marvin Simmons, and Hoshang Moadelli.

I need to give a shout out to the 1974 Indiana State Champion Northrop High School Basketball team for their inspiration, as well as Tim Smiley, former 1970s Fort Wayne Elmhurst High School basketball star, who told me he played in a series of secret summer games like those depicted in this book. I can't forget my two Burlingame High School English teachers from the 1960s, Marshall Umpleby and Robert Palazzi for being great motivators and encouraging me to keep writing.

Last, but not least, I want to thank my wife Jean, for whom this book is dedicated, as well as my adult kids, Zack and Andrea for their love and encouragement. I am sorry if I have left somebody out, but thanks to all of you for making this dream project come true!

SAFE PASSAGE GUARANTEED

1

JULY 1976

Early Saturday morning the phone rang waking both my wife Rochelle and me out of a sound sleep.

"Nick Cunningham," the voice said, "Get up! It's time to play some b-ball, brother!"

I had forgotten about my plan to join A.D. and his buddies for some "roundball." Every Saturday in July and August Arthur Daniel Webster (to us, he was just "A.D.") arranged a game at one of the Ft. Wayne Unified School District gyms. He was the human relations director for the school district and had the keys to all of them.

The purpose of the gatherings for us wasn't just to play a competitive full court game of basketball, but to bring adults and kids from different backgrounds together in an environment where they could get to know one another. This was the brainchild of A.D., who felt strongly that sports was one of the few venues where performance mattered more than connections, race, religion, or social standing. These games usually featured at least one high school varsity player on each side. A.D. tried to make sure that these players came from different areas and environments. He also tried to bring in athletic public officials, many times with opposing viewpoints. I remember a new housing plan for the city, for a long time a subject of acrimony and mistrust, getting resolved over a post-game pizza and beer lunch. There was also a bit of selective mentoring of the teenagers who took part. The kids got to see how the adults interacted with one another, and during game breaks the kids were encouraged to ask questions about anything that was on their minds.

I was included in these events not because I was a good basketball player, but because I was the local TV sports anchor in 1976 for WFTW, the CBS-TV affiliate in Northeast Indiana, Northwestern Ohio, and Southern Michigan. The kids all knew who I was because my shows-5 minutes in each of two newscasts five days a week- featured lots of local high school sports stories. The fact that I had a "baby face," and was the youngest TV sportscaster in town helped them identify with me. The teenagers would frequently emulate my "on-air" appearance- '70s leisure suits and "puka" shells around my neck-part of my California background. But what really gave me credibility in the eyes of the kids and school officials was my close professional and personal relationship with A.D.

Arthur Daniel Webster was raised in an upper middle-class neighborhood of Hartford, Connecticut by African American parents who were both public school teachers. Richard and Harriet Webster were the first of their families to graduate from college, and they were so determined that their three children continue the trend, they gave them monikers to remind them. Arthur's younger sister Phyllis also had a literary name, Phyllis Wheatly Webster (named after the 18th Century African American poet) as did the baby of the family, Frederick Douglas Webster. All three siblings went to top New England colleges, with Arthur attending nearby Trinity.

At Trinity, A.D. was a relatively good student who played varsity tennis and basketball. He was legendary at fraternity parties as a guy who could really "work the room" conversing with everybody and remembering everybody's name, whether they were a guest or a frat brother. A.D.'s active social life was probably the reason that he was a "B" student and not an "A" student like his younger siblings, much to the dismay of his parents. After getting his liberal arts degree young Webster decided against graduate studies or law school. He wanted to get out of the classroom and work with people, particularly the younger generation.

With his parents' encouragement he decided to send out resumes to school districts all over the Northeast in hopes of landing a job in the area of counseling and human relations. While no real opportunities near home came his way for several months, he heard about a job in the Midwest with the Fort Wayne Unified School District. He took an Indiana road trip, met with school officials, and got the job in 1971, not knowing the past history of racial strife in the community. The job was created for him in hopes that he could bring about a better and more open relationship among black and white students, teachers, and school officials. A.D., who had never lived in the "inner city," was truly a deer in the headlights at first. He was in a position of not only having to win the trust of mostly white school system employees, but also skeptical inner city black families as well who looked upon him as an elitist outsider.

Webster knew the only way he could be successful at this job was to be himself- to be genuine. He also knew the way to win favor of the parents of all races would be by winning over their kids. A.D. regularly attended sporting events, pep rallies, spelling bees, graduation ceremonies, and chaperoned numerous junior and senior proms, most of the time with a lovely lady at his side. He always had numerous girlfriends of all races. It was a shock for many Fort Wayne area residents in the 1970s to see a 6-foot 3-inch black man dating a white woman.

In 1972, Webster and I became acquainted as competitors on the tennis court in the Fort Wayne City Tournament at Swinney Park, where he beat me in a very competitive second round match. We both enjoyed the match and discovered we had a lot in common, as we both were new to the community and both had a keen interest in sports. He and I also knew that we could really help each other out with our jobs. A.D. could give me the inside scoop on the local prep sports scene, and I could help publicize school activities on the air.

He became the first African American to join Fort Wayne's new indoor tennis facility in 1973, the Times Corners Racquet Club. A.D. stood out at the club for obvious reasons, but so did I because I had come from California and was a local TV personality. In the winter months with snow on the ground, my wife Rochelle and I would even keep the Club open until 3am during the week so that local members who worked during the day could get their tennis "fixes." This was a period in history when tennis was booming, thanks in no small part to the likes of Chris Evert, Jimmy Connors, and Arthur Ashe, among others. I would frequently head out after the 11pm newscast and meet A.D. for a midnight tennis match. I would sleep in until 11am the next morning, but A.D. would somehow be on the job by 9am. The guy had two speeds:100 miles per hour or dead stop! He even fell asleep on our sofa watching his beloved Arthur Ashe playing in the men's semi-finals of the U-S Open. The two of us had just moved the heavy sofa-bed from the back bedroom to the living room with Rochelle's promise that she would fix us bacon, lettuce, and tomato sandwiches (A.D.'s favorite) for lunch. In the process of the move, the damned thing turned itself into a "bed" pinning A.D. against the wall, sending all of us into hysterics. With Rochelle's help, I extricated our guest, and we completed our mission, but later A.D. jokingly told others about being attacked by the Cunningham's deranged sofa-a story that got better over the years.

It was 10am when I arrived at Ben Geyer Junior High School for our Saturday game, and I was greeted at the door by A.D. who told me about the two prep basketball players who were joining us for the game. They were Greg Jordan of Eastview High in Kendallville, a rural, predominately white community north of Fort Wayne, and William Isiah "Whip" Perkins of Roosevelt High, an inner-city Fort Wayne school. Both were star players as juniors, and both had high expectations for the coming '76-'77 season. My hope was that playing with us did not set their games back. What struck me during our morning game was the fact that the two seemed to be very familiar with one another. Perkins referred to Jordan as "Hops" and Jordan to Perkins as "Whip," as the two joked and trash talked the whole morning. A.D. thought, as did I, that he was bringing kids together who did not know one another and had little or no personal contact. I knew something about Perkins as I had interviewed him and several of his teammates during Roosevelt's excellent playoff run in the '75-'76 season before they were stopped by Marion High School in the round of the final sixteen.

There was still another connection. Jackie Knight, one of Perkins' teammates and good friends on the '74-'75 team, was an intern at WFTW. Knight made sure that I had all the latest news on the Roosevelt team-what they ate for breakfast, their favorite TV shows, girlfriends, and, in some cases, their goals in life. Jackie was also a big reason that his former teammates trusted me.

My curiosity was killing me, so I approached the kids who were sitting on the bench together laughing and joking. I just rudely jumped into their conversation.

"So how do you two know each other? It's obvious that today's game was no introduction."

Perkins said," We know each other from playing hoops, man."

"Come on Whip," I said, "You guys are from different leagues twenty miles apart, and I know you didn't play each other in the state tournament last year or the year before that."

Perkins turned to Jordan and said" Do we tell him?" I could see the hesitation in their eyes, especially Jordan's. Perkins continued to lobby Jordan, saying "He's ok. He can keep a secret. We know this guy." I had no clue that I was about to hear the best "feel good" sports story of my career, and these kids didn't know that in less than a year their teams would be battling it out for a spot in the Indiana High School Basketball Final Four. But the story was much bigger than basketball. It was truly uplifting and "network worthy," but I could not go public with it, at least not yet.

Before these kids tell us their story, I need to tell you my own.

SACRAMENTO

When I arrived at San Jose State University in the fall of 1967, I didn't know what to expect, but I did know that I wanted to get into sports broadcasting. I also did not expect to meet the love of my life, but fate and destiny stepped in.

At State I was directed to "the man" in sports broadcasting, Hank Ramsey, who was raised on the San Francisco Peninsula right near where I grew up in the San Mateo/Burlingame area. We hit it off immediately, and he took a chance on me as his color commentator for the SJSU basketball games on KSJS Radio, the student station at the school. I learned so much from Hank, who was a marvelous play-by-play man. My job on the air was to provide background information on the players and coaches, as well as do live interviews. Ramsey had formed a great partnership with Mark Brinson, a technical genius, who was the producer/director of the broadcasts. Together the three of us traveled up and down the West Coast covering an exciting Spartan basketball team for KSJS radio as if we were professional broadcasters. It was a great gig and a lot of fun, but of course, it was really a fantasy world for us because we weren't getting paid. It was time to graduate and get real jobs.

Hank was hired by a major market San Francisco radio station as a sports show producer. His career took off as he became the voice of University of Oregon football and basketball, Stanford football, San Jose Earthquake Soccer as well as many other big-time sports events. Eventually, years later, Ramsey would be inducted into the Bay Area Broadcasting Hall of Fame, an honor that he richly deserved.

While I was determined to be a sports broadcaster, I had no idea where I was going in the romance department until I met Rochelle Wildi, a beautiful and popular brunette with a congenial personality and the patience of Job. She spent many a night listening to my broadcasts when she could have been out on a date at an exclusive restaurant with another guy. No question I was smitten-sportscasting and Rochelle, or rather Rochelle and sportscasting.

I landed a job at KCBG-TV in Sacramento in March of 1970 and Rochelle and I were married in November. It was a beautiful ceremony at an older church in Alameda followed by a memorable reception at the Blue Dolphin Restaurant nearby, all arranged by Rochelle and her family. Immediately after the wedding we headed by cab, accompanied by my best man, Jimmy McGregor, and Rochelle's maid of honor Rhonda Agnost, to the San Francisco Airport where we were to embark on our Hawaiian honeymoon, a gift from my parents. "We've Only Just Begun" by the Carpenters was playing on the cabbie's radio which was to become "our song" for that chapter of our lives. Jimmy and Rhonda wanted to see us off at the terminal, but when we got to SFO the two of them were enjoying each other's company so much that those plans were scrapped. After a quick good-bye they zoomed off to an unknown destination.

By the time we got to Honolulu it was 8pm Hawaiian time and 11pm Pacific Coast time-we were both tired and hungry. We checked into the huge Reef Hotel at Diamondhead and hurriedly dropped our luggage off in the room. I had promised Rochelle that I would take her out to dinner at the Willows Restaurant in Honolulu which had come highly recommended by her friend and former stewardess, Jean Pederson. We both had the specialty of the house, fresh Mahi-Mahi. It did not disappoint to say the least. When we got back to our room, we opened the drapes hoping to see a romantic view of Diamond Head by night, but instead got the wall of the neighboring building. I got on the phone with the front desk and complained bitterly but was told we would have to wait until tomorrow to plead our case for a better room because all the supervisors had gone home for the night. The next morning, I went down to the lobby, asked for the manager, explained that we were on our honeymoon. That was all he needed to hear, and we were immediately moved to a 10th story room with a spectacular Diamond Head view.

Then it was off to the beach for some sun and surf. As I lay on the beach on my towel, I overheard a discussion between a man and his wife regarding a broadcasting job offer from the Cincinnati Reds Baseball Team. I looked over and saw the same guy whom I had watched on the 11pm local Honolulu news show the night before-a young fellow by the name of Al Michaels. Yes, that would be the same Al Michaels who would become the voice of the Reds and San Francisco Giants, not to mention numerous Super Bowls, and the "Do you believe in Miracles? "Olympic Hockey classic broadcast.

That night we went to the Don Ho Show which was also recommended by some good friends. I made the mistake of telling the waitress that we were on our honeymoon. Big mistake! Next thing we knew Rochelle and I were both on stage with Don and his harem of scantily clad beach babes. While Don sang and encouraged Rochelle to play his piano, I was having my shirt removed by the beach babes who hung my tie around my forehead. Don dubbed us the "All American couple, "gave me the mic, and had me sing "God Bless America" as Rochelle accompanied me on Don's piano while his harem of honeys cozied up to me on stage. With apologies to Kate Smith and the many talented artists who have recorded that beautiful song, I was awful, although Rochelle's piano effort kept me from getting booed off the stage.

After declining Ho's post show invitation to visit him and his harem backstage, Rochelle and I headed to Maui the next day where it was very quiet and romantic. The memorable honeymoon was over too soon, and it was time for the two of us to head home to the real world in Sacramento.

My job title at KCBG was "studio operator," which meant that I was basically a "do everything" gopher. It was a non-union shop, so I was promised an opportunity to go "on air" and do some reporting in the field. In the meantime, I was running a studio camera, setting up lights, and putting microphones on the "talent," as the on-air personalities were called. I can also remember some less glamorous chores like going to the dog pound to pick up the "dog of the week" for one of our shows. Many times, that dog did not want to leave its friendly confines and get into my waiting van. The pooch would show its resentment by depositing a big turd on the floor of the van. On other occasions "Rover" was too enthusiastic, jumping all over me as I attempted to navigate the streets of Sacramento back to the station in KCBG's van. I nearly wrecked the van more than once. I really did wonder if cleaning up dog crap was going to lead me to a successful broadcasting career.

Then I caught a big break when I was befriended by Caldecott "Cal" Samuels who was the station's long-time sports anchor. Samuels was an ex-minor league baseball pitcher for the Reno Silver Sox in the 1950s, who blew out his arm and ended up on television. He was a bigger than life personality with jet black hair who was on a first name basis with a number of sports legends like golfer Arnold Palmer, baseball players Willie Mays and Willie McCovey, as well as many 49er and Raider football players. Because I was an ex-jock and a knowledgeable sports fan, he liked me and would occasionally allow me to write his sports show when I wasn't setting up cameras and lights in the studio. Cal, who was married five times, also was a favorite of the ladies- that is, the ladies who were NOT his ex's.

Cherry, one of his ex-wives, obviously peeved about Cal's philandering, showed up one night just before the 6pm news wielding one of his prized possessions, a baseball bat given to Cal by 1940s Cubs' slugger Phil Cavaretta, who later managed the Silver Sox in the 1950s. She went down swinging, as they say, but not before she took out meteorologist Owen Storke's weather set with its maps, and high- and low-pressure systems. Storke, a kindly and buttoned-down fellow in his 60s, was so shaken that he locked himself in the men's room and said he couldn't go on the air. Cherry's target was her ex-husband, but Cal like one of his pro football buddies, famed 49ers running back Hugh McElhenny, ran all over the studio dodging cameras, lights, and studio personnel, trying to elude his "Ex".

Cherry, who was in hot pursuit, was screaming "you lyin', cheatin' son of a bitch!" She would have gotten him had it not been for studio operator Melvin Baker, a burly African American former all-city linebacker from the mean streets of Cleveland, Ohio. Mel tackled her moments before we went on the air, shaking up the on-air talent and the entire production staff.

As anchorman Ted Dorsey was doing the headlines, a shooting at a nearby park and a bank robbery in Placerville, the viewer at home would hear the background noise of a studio struggle and screaming obscenities as the police arrived to take Cherry away. Those folks tuning in to see the news might have thought Ted was in the middle of a violent attack. It got even more complicated as the police originally put the handcuffs on Melvin, thinking he was the culprit. This allowed Cherry to have another "go" at her man as Cal headlined his story about Giants' pitcher Juan Marichal's injury. It was a surreal scene as a quick-thinking Sacramento police officer, realizing his mistake, took down the ex-wife a second time as she slammed the bat on the news set counter as we went to commercial.

We had to clear the studio and regain our composure during the two-minute break. Apologies were made to Mel Baker who later told me that he felt like he was "back home" in Cleveland. Mel and I worked the same shift and got to know each other quite well, talking sports, politics, and life in general. His views would have a profound effect on me going forward. While I had several casual friendships with African American teammates on football and track and field squads at San Mateo and Burlingame High Schools in the 60s, I never really had any deep conversations about social and political issues. Mel would challenge me when I asked him a dumb question about race. "Nick, there is no way you can understand what being Black is all about," he said. "I am reminded of my Blackness every day of my life in everything I do. Are you reminded of your Whiteness?" I said I didn't even think about it. "There you go," said Baker. "I would like to feel that way someday, but I don't think that day is coming anytime soon."

Mel pointed out subtle racism that was right in front of us at the station that I had not noticed. For instance, when the janitor and receptionist would call upon us to perform maintenance chores when we were not tied up in the studio, they would refer to the three African American studio operators as "boys," and when they spoke with the rest of us it was "young men." Baker said, "Have you ever noticed that the station never has two or more Black studio operators in the studio at the same time during a live telecast? It's always one Black and two White during a live telecast, or all White." I got to thinking that he was right as I never saw two African-Americans working the studio together during a live telecast for the two years I worked at the station. There were also no women among our ten studio operators at KCBG in 1970.

Cal Samuels had a motorhome which he positioned in the station parking lot 24-7, despite the fact he was violating local parking and zoning laws. Cal was buddies with the police and local authorities who were not about to bother him because many of them were guests at his motor home soirees. It was there that he would entertain his lady friends before, between and after the 6 and 11 o'clock news shows. One of his "parties" lasted a bit too long – the rocking motor home was a bit too festive. Spent and hung-over, Cal did not want to get up for his early morning appointment at the Oakland Raider training camp in Santa Rosa.

I got a call at 1 am from the news director. "Could you meet cameraman Matt Stokes in Santa Rosa tomorrow morning and shoot some interviews with the Raiders? We can't pay you but think of the great experience!" said the news director Lloyd Brennan. Remember, we were a non-union shop, which had its pluses for opportunities and minuses for compensation. I was paid $105 a week as a "studio operator", but nothing as a sports reporter.

So, I was up at 5am and off to meet Matt in Santa Rosa by 8am. Stokes was the head of our Stockton bureau, a one-man department. He was a free-spirited guy that I really admired for his ballsiness and hutzpah. He came out of the University of Pacific with degrees in philosophy and in journalism, but a very limited experience working with "sound" news film. So, he essentially embellished his resume, "aced" the face-to-face interview with the news director and got the job right out of college. He told me "just tell them you can do it and learn on the job. They didn't want to fire me and try to find somebody else. Besides, who really wants to live and work in Stockton?" I must admit that I envied him and admired his courage. His first couple of news stories looked like Buster Keaton movie comedies from the '20s with fast and slow-motion action figures, and people talking with no sound. But eventually Matt got the hang of it and became a helluva reporter with guts and conscience.

When I pulled up to Raiders Training Camp at the El Rancho Inn in Santa Rosa, I was surprised that the parking lot was not overflowing. Matt pulled in right behind me, got out of his car, and said "Where the hell is everybody? Nick, are you sure we are in the right place?" I told him that this was the place and time that our news director gave me, based on Cal's information. So, the two of us grabbed our cameras and mics and headed to the football field behind the El Rancho.

Safe Passage Guaranteed | 13

There it was, my "Field of Dreams," the Oakland Raiders in full uniforms running through some non-contact drills, and we were the only media folks in the place, save for one "cubbie" newspaper reporter from the Santa Rosa Herald. Matt and I were stunned to say the least. Did Cal have a Raider "insider" set this up for us? Did the Oakland P-R guy screw up, and not inform other news outlets about the team's availability on this Saturday morning? I interviewed all the 1970 Raider Legends-Daryl Lamonica, Fred Biletnikoff, Dan Connors, Ben Davidson, and of course Hall of Fame Coach John Madden. In all, Matt filmed me doing 21 interviews- I was having the time of my life. Not getting paid for any of this didn't bother me in the slightest. In fact, I would have given KCBG-TV everything in my paltry checking account in exchange for this opportunity. Interviewing media-savvy professional athletes, I discovered, was a lot easier than trying to extract comments from nervous college athletes. I remembered the training that Hank Ramsey gave me at SJSU. He stressed the importance of preparation-doing the "homework in advance." As I made the early morning two-hour drive to Santa Rosa, I thought about everybody I could remember on the Oakland roster, and what questions I would ask them.

Matt and I had been at it for about two hours and were beginning to run out of film when Coach Madden came up to me and said, "Nick, can you do me a favor? I have this homesick rookie quarterback from Alabama. I think it would help him feel more connected to the team if you did a short interview with him."

Jeez, John Madden was calling me by my first name, and asking me to do HIM a favor. "Be happy to, Coach," I said. Matt was frantically waving at me, indicating that we didn't have enough film left to do much of anything. So, Madden brought over his homesick Alabama quarterback, Ken Stabler, who six years later would become an All-Pro and Superbowl Champion with the Raiders. I think the coach could see that Stabler and I were about the same age and in about the same position in our careers. Ken was trying to make the team as a quarterback, and I was trying to make the TV news team as a sportscaster. We hit it off from the start. Stabler spoke very softly and measured his words carefully. I remembered that he was left-handed, and that would require adjustments from the Oakland pass receivers who were used to Daryl Lamonica's right-handed delivery. That was my angle on the interview. I even got Coach Madden to bring over Hall of Famer Fred Biletnikoff to comment on the adjustments he would make in catching Stabler's throws versus Lamonica's. This piece was our best work of the session, but it would never get on the air because we ran out of film after 30 seconds. Matt and I both knew it, but we wanted to keep going because of our promise to Coach Madden, and to help this young quarterback feel less homesick.

We packed up our gear in Matt's news van and headed into the dining room of the El Rancho for lunch. I was talked out after all the interviews but felt that this was an opportunity to get some "industry tips" from Stokes. What I thought was going to be a "quick bite "turned into a two-hour conversation about our pasts and our future plans. Stokes was raised by a very religious single mom in Modesto who made sure that he went to church every Sunday. Mary also made sure that he had a good sense of right and wrong and knew the value of a good education. You could tell even then that eventually Matt was headed out of the TV news business and into politics. When I told him that I wasn't getting paid for our work in Santa Rosa he said" Yes you are! I'm splitting my overtime pay for today's job with you. "I protested, but he wouldn't back down. Matt picked up the lunch bill and sent me an envelope a week later with $150 cash in it. The guy was the "real deal."

I remember being very excited as I drove home to Sacramento thinking that I had just gotten my big "break." I had done 21 Interviews with the Oakland Raiders, had gotten to meet some of my football heroes, and Coach Madden had called me by my first name. This euphoria literally reminded me of my first trip to Disneyland when I was eight years old.

Safe Passage Guaranteed | 15

Cal used all of my interviews on the air, as it made for less work and more party time for him. The Raiders even requested that we send them to several Jacksonville, Florida stations to help promote a pre-season game with the Dolphins.

Then the opportunities to get out in the field and do some sports reporting became more frequent. I did a series on Little League Baseball called "Learn It from the Pros," where I would show the kids making some good plays and bad; running into each other on the bases, dropping fly balls, and forgetting the number of outs, plus "overly-amped "parents trying to instruct and "encourage" their kids. We inter-cut with" b-roll" the "mad-cap" film of the youngsters with instruction commentary from legendary Giants' players Wille Mays, Willie McCovey and Juan Marichal. "B-roll" is a piece of action film that illuminates what the on-camera subject is saying. In this case, Willie Mays was talking about how to properly run the bases while we showed the kids making all the wrong moves- a great juxtaposition. The piece worked so well that film cameraman Roy Wright got an Associated Press Award for editing.

Later Roy and I took a sports reporting road trip to Stanford to visit Coach John Ralston, another pal of Cal Samuels, during football practice as his team got ready for the "Big Game" with rival Cal. David Bachman, a long-haired and free-spirited defensive back on the team, was a guy I had played against in high school. We also knew each other socially as he was a friend of my sister Pat at Stanford. After I interviewed the coach, David lined up several of the top players for interviews, telling them I was his best friend from high school, a huge exaggeration. But Bachman delivered a biggee, Indians' quarterback Jim Plunkett, a shy, reserved fellow who rarely gave interviews. Cal was thrilled that I had gotten so much out of Plunkett, who would later win the Heisman Trophy, two Super Bowls, and eventually overcome his shyness to be a successful broadcaster when his playing days were over.

Because of David's help, I decided to interview him even though he was not a "star" on the team. I suggested something for our "future file," as journalists like to call it. I asked him to jump forward a month and" imagine" that Stanford was invited to the Rose Bowl to face top-ranked and undefeated Ohio State, which seemed like a long shot, but still possible.

David thought it was a great idea, looked right into the camera and commented," The big bad Buckeyes don't scare us. We are a passing team, the likes of which they haven't seen this year. I guarantee we'll beat them!"

This was truly "stomping on Superman's cape," a la Joe Namath and Muhammed Ali. I told him I would destroy the interview if the Stanford-Ohio State match-up did not materialize. When the Indians got the bid to face the Buckeyes a month later, David was not only the star of KCBG news at 6 and 11pm, he became somewhat of a national celebrity as news outlets from all over the country picked up the comment. It was Bachman, however, who had the last laugh and, as it turned out, a whole lot more.

The Stanford Indians, after their surprising loss to Big Game Rival Cal 22-14, were a three touchdown Rose Bowl underdog to the mighty Buckeyes. It looked like the oddsmakers were right when Ohio State took the opening kickoff and marched right down the field until the inexplicable occurred. Buckeye Coach Woody Hayes, the man who said only three things can happen on a forward pass and two of them are bad, called for a pass play on first and goal from Stanford's five-yard line. David Bachman made a diving interception in the end zone stopping the Buckeye drive. As he got up, he pointed at the Ohio State bench as if to say, "I got you!" From that point on, momentum changed, MVP Jim Plunkett put on a record setting passing display and led Stanford to a convincing 27-17 upset win.

After the game, reporters seemed as interested in Bachman as they were in Plunkett. Who was this unknown free safety who poked fun at Ohio State and predicted the upset? David, never at a loss for words, gave them all the good quotes they needed. "I am just a hippie-dippy Rolling Stones fan from the sleepy little town of Millbrae, California," he said from behind his granny glasses, long hair, and sideburns. Bachman, an English literature major at Stanford and a true Renaissance man, punctuated his comments with quotes from Shakespeare.

The press corps ate it all up, conjuring up headlines like "Hippie Beats Buckeyes," "David Moonbeam No Goody for Woody," and the Millbrae Sun, Bachman's hometown newspaper with "Millbrae's David Slays Goliath!" I must have seen my film clip of his run numerous times during KCBG-TV newscasts. Actually, it ran more after the game than before because it was so prophetic. If they only knew David made these comments way before the Rose Bowl bid or the loss to Cal! After his bout with fame, Bachman would leave his football heroics far behind. He would marry his college sweetheart, move to Florence, Italy, and become an English literature professor at a local university.

LIVE TELEVISION

My reporting in the field led me to my first live on-air sportscast on New Year's Eve of 1970. Cal was on the "party circuit" that night so I was scheduled to do the six and eleven o'clock news shows with anchorman Ted Dorsey and meteorologist Owen Storke.

It was a big night for me, and I was very excited and nervous. I was going to be in front of thousands of viewers "live." I had been on live radio in college doing basketball broadcasts with several hundred listeners on a good night, but this was the big time-what I had been working for. I really wanted to perform well!

Back in the early 1970s we did not have teleprompters which carried the script on the expanded camera face, allowing the on-air talent to look right into the camera. So, in those days newscasters and sportscasters had to read their scripts on their desks, looking up periodically for emphasis. Their goal was look into the camera as often as possible so the viewer at home would get the feeling of intimacy. Generally, the more experienced the on-air talent, the less he or she looked down at their scripts on their desks. Production problems would occur when on-air talent would get too "cocky" and go off-script, throwing the control room into chaos, a Cal Samuels' specialty.

Samuels would occasionally go off on a rant about an athlete or an event that was not in the script, leaving the control room director and production staff dumbfounded. Our scripts were used to "cue" visuals, particularly film interviews which were spliced together in a master reel for each newscast, commonplace in those days. If one film clip was missed or malfunctioned, then the entire film portion of the newscast could collapse like a house of cards. Though it rarely happened, there were times when we were without film and had to "read" our entire news and sportscast. I can remember operating a camera with the studio director telling me in my headset to signal Cal that he was out of time, and we were not going to get his film interview with Vikings' quarterback Joe Kapp on the air, due to Cal's rambling. When we went to break, Samuels headed straight for the control room to confront the director. The battle was on with profanities flying with just a minute and 45 seconds to go before we were back on the air. Fortunately, no blows were struck, and even Cal understood that during live television, it is generally the control room director who calls the shots, like it or not. In the commotion, however, the interview with Joe Kapp, who was very upset about losing the Super Bowl to Kansas City, was still cued up on the master reel. When anchorman Ted Dorsey called for a comment from the mayor on better relations between the police department and the inner city, he instead got Joe Kapp saying, "I don't give a damn about the Kansas

City Chiefs! To hell with them!" Sometimes our newscasts seemed more like" Saturday Night Live" with Dan Ackroyd, John Belushi, and Eddie Murphy!

I remember going into the dressing room to read my script in preparation for my first live on-air sports show. I practiced looking up at the mirror emphasizing what I thought were the major points. My thoughts wandered back to my years at San Jose State and the live radio broadcasts when there was no script to rely on. Hank and I back then could fill vast amounts of time shooting from the hip with nuggets about the Spartan basketball team. This should be easy, right? Maybe not, because in my mind my career as a TV sports anchor was on the line.

Most of the on-air personalities, both male and female, would wear make-up, not just to enhance their looks, but to prevent the perspiration from running down their faces during a 30 minute or 60-minute newscast. I rarely wore make-up for a couple of reasons. I was only on for five minutes maximum and I favored the heat of the lights. They would help me relax on-air and get into a rhythm. I would focus on the camera as if it was a friend of mine who really wanted to hear the sports information I was spewing forth. I was essentially "selling" the information I was reporting on to the viewers, and I had to believe that my subject matter was of the utmost importance. At that moment in time, I had to believe it was my universe. It was also very important that I knew my subject matter, as the viewers could spot a "phony" in a heartbeat. I studied up on my material as if I were preparing for a final exam in college. If I was to mispronounce the name of the Toronto Maple Leafs goalie, I would lose all my credibility with the audience.

I felt I was prepared for my big moment. My headline was the New Year's Day Rose Bowl. I had a short network video tape preview of the game featuring the two coaches, Woody Hayes of Ohio State and John Ralston of Stanford. That would be followed by my narration of the network video tape highlights of the

Astro-Bluebonnet Bowl from Houston. Then came the scores of a couple of NBA and NHL games. My final segment would be a local film piece on an annual charity football game played between Sacramento firemen and policemen held at Hughes Stadium. I timed my segment out at 4 minutes and 38 seconds which was comfortably under my five-minute allowance.

Anchorman Ted Dorsey introduced me as "our new sports guy," much to the excitement of my fellow $105 a week "studio operators" who were on the floor and in the studio at the time. The 6pm show went quite well until the end when I had to "throw it" to Owen Storke, our meteorologist. I blanked on his name, but covered well by saying, "Here he is, surrounded by his maps, cold fronts and warm fronts-THE weatherman!" Mel Baker, who was running a camera, was falling down in hysterics, trying to control his laughter. But the viewer at home wouldn't have noticed my screw-up, except that Storke called attention to it by saying "Nick is new to the business. It is understandable that he forgot my name." Jeez, thanks Owen!

Being a perfectionist, I couldn't hide my disappointment. I called Rochelle, my new wife of 45 days, to ask her how the show looked. She, of course, said she thought it was great, and that the viewers at home could not care less that you forgot "that old goat's name," to use her words. In college, she always knew the right things to say after a "dicey" broadcast to help me renew my confidence. Her comments at this moment were timely too. My 11pm sportscast went very smoothly, and I did remember Owen Storke's name. The crew surprised me by making a video tape of my show, which I could use later on when I applied for other on-air jobs. I got complimentary calls from a number of friends and fellow news reporters who saw the shows, including Matt Stokes who said "Nick, I want to be your agent!' You're on your way!" Matt and I had gotten to be close after our Santa Rosa-Raiders adventure, and I really valued his opinion. So to repeat a phrase my mom often used, I was on "cloud nine," thinking my career was about ready to take off.

I then was given other on-air assignments like co-hosting the Noon News with Samantha Dawes when Ted Dorsey took a week off during his kids' Easter break from school. Samantha Dawes was a runner-up in the Miss Texas Beauty Pageant of 1962. She went on to get her journalism degree from the University of Texas and was determined to be a news anchor in a major market. Outside of Barbara Walters, there were very few female anchors or even "hard news" reporters in the late '60s and early '70s. Samantha, now in her early thirties and still single, was determined to get to the "Big Time." She knew that would mean postponing marriage, family, and kids. She also kept her private life "private," and did not date anybody at the station, even though she was constantly asked out by many male employees at KCBG, including Cal Samuels.

Her full name was Samantha Dorothy Dawes which made her the butt of jokes behind her back. Lecherous weekend anchorman Bill Harrington who was always trying unsuccessfully to get her to go out with him referred to her as "Sammy Double-D."

Harrington, who was my least favorite person at the station, was continually in Sam's face with innuendo and inappropriate comments, trying to get her alone even though he had a wife and two kids at home. It was truly sexual harassment, but this was the 1970s and management, along with the rest of us, did nothing. My relationship with Bill Harrington who was ten years my senior and had a massive ego did not go well from the start. He would pick on the studio operators and TV production personnel repeatedly, criticizing their appearance, job performance and personalities. Harrington took issue with my camera work on my first day on the job. "Hey, college boy," he shouted at me in front of the entire KCBG studio crew, "didn't they teach you anything about framing at San Jose State? And your set lighting sucks! It looks like I'm doing my show in a closet!" I will admit that I spent most of my time in front of the camera or microphone at SJSU, and not pointing cameras or setting lights. To take this shot from one of the on-air anchors on my first day really was humiliating, and an event that I would not forget.

It was a year later that I would be joining Bill on the weekend news as a temporary weekend sports anchor replacing vacationing Rob Nevels. Harrington showed up at the station that Saturday afternoon not feeling well, questioning whether he was capable of going on the air. A call went out to news director Lloyd Brennan who said that Samantha was out of town and unable to fill in. Brennan suggested that Bill could write the show and that I could do the entire newscast solo, including my sports segment. The prickly and insecure Harrington did not like that idea at all and said he would "gut it out for the team even though my stomach is in the midst of a civil war." I watched him consume several cans of 7-up as he put the newscast together in hopes they would alleviate his stomach ache. What was he thinking?

We hit the air at 6pm with Harrington, good lighting or not, looking pale and ill, and fighting off "burps." I tried to sit as far away from him on the news set as I could so as not to contract his ailment. We did the headlines and got through the first break with no problems but then Bill started to stumble and slur his words. The director and the crew were so worried that they wanted me to stay on the set, and not go back to the newsroom to collect updated sports news for my show. Their fears were soon realized when Harrington in the middle of serious story exploded on the air with a loud "burp" and then vomited on the set. I heard one of the cameramen say on his headset to the director "Oh shit, Bill has puked all over himself. He is gassed and done! "If we hadn't been so shocked, we all would have laughed our butts off. The director then "faded to black" and went to commercial. The viewer at home who was really paying attention got to see "live" television at its most comical. It really looked like another sketch from "Saturday Night Live" with Harrison playing the role of Chevy Chase.

Now we had another mad dash during our two-minute break. We had to get Bill off the set, clean up his mess, and insert me in his place, reading the script (which I didn't write) cold turkey. The smell almost made me sick, but I collected myself and positioned myself in the anchor chair. The red light on the camera came on and the floor manager cued me. "Unfortunately, Bill Harrison has become ill, and I'll continue with the newscast. My name is Nick Cunningham," were my confident words. I stumbled a couple of times but got through the newscast, did the weather segment as we did not have a weekend weather anchor, and raced through my sportscast as I did not have a chance to update the information.

The unscheduled break when Bill got sick put the timing of the show in chaos, and because the sports segment came at the end it got "hacked," as we were running long and had to meet network exactly at 6:30pm. Somehow our "wing-it" production all worked out, and I was lucky enough to hit the network right on time. "Now we go to the CBS Evening News Weekend Edition with Dan Rather" was my live toss to the network. The show was not my best work, but the studio crew including the director were all complimentary. The studio operators whom I regularly worked with behind the camera crowded around me on the set and were gleeful.

"You got the best of that arrogant asshole," was Mel Baker's comment referring to Bill Harrington.

I thought back to my first day on the job when Bill had picked me out for public ridicule in front of my co-workers. To be able to take over for him on the air in a time of need and to watch the studio personnel clean the vomit off him was sweet revenge. From that day forward Harrington treated me and the other studio operators with much more respect and civility. But to me the most exciting and memorable moment was" passing the baton" to CBS Anchor Dan Rather, the man who would eventually replace Walter Cronkite as network kingpin, at the end of our show. When I got home to our $200/ month apartment off Arden Way in North Sacramento, Rochelle greeted me with a big hug and kiss, telling me that I was great. "So, it's you and your buddy Dan Rather now is it?" was her remark as we laughed about the crazy day I had just endured at KCBG. "It's not just anybody who gets introduced with a burp and a barf" was her next salvo, making sure that I did not get too cocky after my performance. We both knew that in the TV business, disappointment, like momentary success, could come at any time as I would later find out.

One of the most exciting stories I got to cover was the Ali-Frazier championship fight of 1971. I covered it by going to the old Alhambra Theater, watching the closed circuit telecast, and interviewing some of the folks who paid $20 a seat to see a black and white screen with Don Dunphy, Archie Moore, and Burt Lancaster (of all people) describing the action. Cal Samuels got me two tickets and I invited Mel Baker, a big Muhammed Ali fan, to go with me. The country was very divided over whom to root for due to politics more than anything else. Both fighters faced harsh and unfair criticism- Ali was called a traitor and a draft dodger and Frazier was called an over-rated Uncle Tom. Mel and I had a great time needling each other as the fight progressed. Going into the 15th round, the fight looked dead even until Frazier landed a thundering left hook on Ali's jaw, knocking him down. "Oh no!" shouted Mel as his hero fell. The auditorium crowd went silent as Ali got back on his feet at the count of eight and fought gamely the rest of the way. Frazier won the unanimous decision, but not in the eyes of Mel and most of the crowd.

Samuels had given me his complimentary tickets for the fight as a payback for doing some of his" dirty work." Several weeks before the fight Cal sent me out on a story that he did not want to do. Vikings quarterback Joe Kapp was in town visiting one of his girlfriends, and Samuels wanted to get a comment from Joe on his recent Super Bowl loss to Kansas City. Cal knew that Joe took that loss personally and would not want to discuss it any further, nor did he want to get bothered while he visited his girlfriend. I kind of felt as though I was invading Kapp's privacy by going on this mission for Cal. So, I collected photographer Roy Wright and we went to the young lady's apartment. I knocked on the door and heard a gruff voice on the other side saying, "Who's there?"

I responded with "Hi, I'm Nick Cunningham, KCBG Sports. I work with Cal Samuels!" The new NFL schedule is out, and you play your Super Bowl opponent, the Kansas City Chiefs in your opener this season. How will your game plan differ from that of the Super Bowl?"

Joe opened the door clad only in his jockey shorts and said "First of all, Samuels is a gutless motherf...er for not coming here himself and asking that question. Second of all, I don't give a shit about our season opener. It's a long way off! Thirdly, you and your camera man better get off Mimi's front porch before I kick both of your asses!"

He slammed the door and Roy said, "I got all of that on film!" We had to do a lot of bleeping and editing if we were going to use any of that on the air. Frankly, I didn't blame Joe for being mad, and I didn't like what Cal had sent me to do. To Samuels credit he did go back to "interview" Kapp and got a terse one sentence sound bite. Cal had an ego too and he didn't like being called gutless, but he did not get much more out of Joe than I did.

I didn't realize it at the time, but there was a movement afoot to unionize KCBG. The wages of our news reporters, studio and production personnel were way behind the other two network affiliates in town. In fact, the situation came to a head when the National Labor Relations Board was called in to investigate a charge against the management of KCBG for "unfair labor practices." That sent the NLRB to Sacramento to set up a meeting at the local Hilton for all station employees, except management. It turned out that my job description versus what I was actually doing came under NLRB scrutiny. I was called up to the front of the meeting by an NLRB official who questioned me about my duties at the station. I told him my job ranged from pointing cameras and setting lights to picking up nervous dogs at the local pound, to anchoring the newscast. He was stunned when I told him what I was paid, as were many of my other co-workers at the station. I also had to explain my lack of payment for my Oakland Raider interviews in Santa Rosa with Matt Stokes, who was in the audience. I explained that Matt insisted I share his overtime pay for that event which got Matt some high fives and a smattering of applause. I also told the federal official that for many of us newcomers to the TV business that the opportunities we were given outweighed the issue of low pay, and if we complained about the low pay, we feared that our opportunities would be limited.

"That's the oldest game in the world, and clearly not right," uttered the NLRB representative. And so, with the NLRB's guidance, the folks at KCBG were about to undertake the long and somewhat painful process of unionization. The good news was that we were going to be paid considerably more, but I worried that my days of reporting and doing on-air work would be curtailed, due to union rules.

The other piece of bad news was that now KCBG was going to be a hotbed of political turmoil pitting pro-union supporters against management. I definitely had mixed emotions and felt that my days at this station were numbered. I wanted to be a sports anchor and reporter, and I felt I was ready to take my career to the next level. I wasn't going to replace a fixture like Cal Samuels, so it was time to "hit the road" and find the right sports anchor position.

Also, I was anxious to get Rochelle out of her unpleasant job as the assistant director of a convalescent hospital. Her boss was a red-neck bully who puffed away on smelly cigars and could not care less about the well-being of the patients in his charge. Rochelle would come home with tales of racism and her clothes smelling like White Owl cigars, but she made more money than I(and we needed it) so she soldiered on.

My friends at KCBG helped me make an audition tape with several of my interviews and on-air work which I could mail or deliver to TV stations that may be looking for a sports anchor. In the early 1970s there were only 205 television markets in the country, ranked in terms of size, which equated to very few on-air jobs for the thousands of applicants. Typically, a young up-and-coming television personality would start at a smaller market station and work his or her way up the ladder, with the goal being a top ten market position in a Los Angeles, Chicago, New York, or San Francisco network affiliate. The pay scale difference between a television anchor position in the 205th market-Bozeman, Montana- versus the same job in number one New York City was amazing. The guy in Bozeman, likely in a non-union shop, would make $7000 to $10000 annually in the early '70s while his counterpart in the Big Apple could make $500,000 or more with longer union contracts including medical coverage. To say the broadcasting business was and is top-heavy with a lot of turn-over would be a huge understatement. The industry would force up-and-comers at smaller stations who were trying to create a better life for themselves and their families to be constantly looking for new jobs "up the ladder." Contracts for television on-air personalities in small and even medium markets were frequently for thirteen weeks to six months. A television personality was only as good as his or her latest rating book. Low ratings meant a small audience which was unattractive to advertisers. The easiest fix, even in some of the larger markets, for a poor rating book is to fire the on-air personnel, a very common occurrence. The other easy fix is to hire a new general manager who may come in, clean house, and hire his buddies from his previous station. This industry phenomenon made "settling down" in one community, buying a home, and raising a family very difficult.

Hank Ramsey and I had talked about this at length back at San Jose State, but we had no idea the extent to which our broadcasting careers would create hardships for our wives and children. Rochelle said she was on-board with the insecurity of television broadcasting business and thought of it as an "adventure." I worried that her "adventure" would turn into a nightmare if her husband was fired. We promised each other that the business would never come between us.

RENO

     Every month when my Broadcasting Magazine arrived, I would turn to the back and find the "help wanted" ads for available jobs in this enigmatic industry. I sent out numerous letters with resumes and even video tapes beginning in the Spring of 1971 with no results. The feedback and encouragement I was getting from my co-workers was terrific, but where were the job offers? Then, out of the blue, I got a call from one of my old friends from San Jose State, Dean Stevens, who earlier in the year had landed a job at KWOO-TV in Reno as the weatherman and host of the afternoon movie show. Dean, who worked with Hank Ramsey at SJSU on college baseball broadcasts in the late 60s before being drafted and sent to Vietnam, was a very witty and creative guy. After telling the military about his broadcasting skills, the Army decided to give him a wireless radio and send him behind enemy lines. Dean had the very dangerous job of tracking and reporting on Viet Cong troop movements. Ultimately, he was wounded in action, was given several medals, and was sent home for rehabilitation. During rehab he had the opportunity to audition for the small market ABC affiliate, KWOO. Dean, feeling relaxed and happy to be alive after his Vietnam experience, aced the audition and got the job. Now, he was calling me with the news that Evan Downing, the sports anchor at the station, was taking a similar position in Portland, Oregon. The job was not going to pay much, but the cost of living in Reno was very low, and would I be interested? Wow! He put me in touch with the general manager, and we made a date for me to drive up to Reno and cut an audition tape.

So, I got up early on a beautiful June morning and drove to Reno for my 11am meeting. I was armed with a video tape of some of my work and a film reel of interviews with Heisman Trophy winner Jim Plunkett and Oakland Raiders' quarterback George Blanda. My friend at KCBG, Roy Wright, put "leader" on the film interviews so it would be newscast- ready for the production folks at KWOO. I had prepared a ten-minute show with the interviews inter-woven into the segment as if it were a live telecast. I was prepared and confident. This was a job I wanted to win. Probably the biggest factor working in my favor was that I was already performing in a mid-level market, Sacramento, and I already had on-air experience with a larger audience. The gorgeous two-and-a-half-hour drive to Reno was a breeze.

When I arrived at KWOO I was welcomed with a bear hug by Dean, who took me in to meet the general manager, Bob Storin, a neatly dressed man in his early '60s, smoking a large cigar. Storin's office was impressive with autographed pictures of show business personalities, some with affectionate notes to Bob. I didn't have to say much because Dean was selling me hard to the guy. Storin suggested that Dean give me the tour of the station while the studio and production staff prepared for my audition. He was impressed when I handed him a copy of my script plus film reel, and I added, "The film has leader on it-it's ready to go. I will cue the sound bites in the script." He smiled and said he would make sure the director understood. KWOO was about half the size of my current place of employment, KCBG-TV. It had just one studio to handle everything: news, live interviews and public service programing, and commercial production. Dean introduced me to Evan Downing, a former USC football player, the current sports anchor.

"Dean tells me that you're the guy that will be taking over for me later this summer!" was his opening comment. I was a bit taken aback, but said I was certainly interested in the position if and when he left. Evan explained that "all the T's haven't been crossed and all the I's have not been dotted yet in the Portland deal," but he took the time to explain to me what covering the sports scene in the Reno/Lake Tahoe area was all about. He explained that I needed to know something about skiing and stock car racing because they were the big winter and summer local sports. I did not know much about either, but I remembered that Matt Stokes had told me earlier, "Just tell them you can do it and learn on the job." Downing went on to say that he made some extra money doing commercials for local businesses, announcing the skiing competition in Lake Tahoe, as well as doing the public address announcing of the stock car races in Carson City. Jean Claude Killy was the only skier I could think of, and Richard Petty was the lone stock car driver that came to mind, but I was ready to do my homework.

Dean then took me into the studio to cut my audition tape. I looked around at this small studio with its "bare bones" news set and thought "This is going to be my new home, my own shop." The red light came on the camera, the floor manager cued me, and away I went with my prepared show. The studio director in the control room did a good job of hitting all of my film cues and the audition went very smoothly. I could not resist a little twist at the end of my show by saying, "Now, to take a look at Reno's ever-changing weather, here is meteorologist Dean Stevens!" I wasn't sure if Dean really was a meteorologist, but I thought it sounded good, and so did Dean.

He bounded out of the control room, gave me a high five, and said, "You aced it! It will be great to be working with you very soon. I know Bob liked what he saw on your audition and wants you to join him in his office."

When I got to Sorin's office we were joined by news director Ike Forbath, a long-time broadcast veteran who, it turns out, was a friend of my current news director, Lloyd Brennan.

Apparently, Forbath had spoken to Brennan about me at length a week earlier. Both the news director and general manager Bob Storin were very complimentary about my audition, and both wanted to talk about my future employment at KWOO.

Talking money and contracts was a very new experience for me. I had no training in this area at all, and, in the exhilaration of the moment, I had not bothered to talk with Dean about what to expect. I was ready to accept whatever they offered me because I really wanted this job.

Storin said, "Evan hasn't signed his Portland contract yet, but we suspect he'll do so within the week. Ike and I would like you to be able to start no later than August 15th, and we'd be willing to pay you $800 a month. This would include a standard thirteen-week contract with a renewal clause, which is what Downing has, and he's been here four years. I think Evan told you that he's able to make extra money with personal appearances, commercials, and announcing jobs like The Carson City Stock Car Races. Once Evan signs his new contract, we'd like to finalize our arrangement with you to be the next sports director at KWOO. Sound good to you; do we have a deal?"

He extended his hand which I instinctively took in mine. I was stunned and speechless. Rochelle and I had jokingly talked about living in Reno and I knew she supported me in that endeavor, but I was not prepared to agree to all those details at that point in time. I probably should have said" I am flattered by the offer, but please let me think about it." But I had just "shook on it" which means I felt I was committed. Obviously, the news director and general manager were anxious to replace the departing Evan Downing, and I was recommended to them. They just needed to see me deliver the "goods." Could I have asked for more money and better terms? Possibly, but their offer was almost twice what I was making as a studio operator at KCBG. I had been told that thirteen-week contracts were normal in small "fluid" markets like this one. Bob Storin promised to get back to me within a week to set up our next appointment, which would mark my "official" hiring by KWOO. I gave Dean Stevens a big thank-you hug and bought him lunch before heading home.

He winked at me and said," We're going to have fun here, just like we did at State! I'll send you some information on housing so you and Rochelle can get started – I have some suggestions. This place is really cheap compared to California!"

Before I headed home, I put the top down on my 1964 Skylark convertible, a college graduation present from my parents. It was a brisk early June day in the mountains, but I was feeling like I was hot stuff, so the "top-down with the shades on" was the look that matched my mood. I couldn't wait to tell Rochelle, my family and my friends my news. Just like the Santa Rosa adventure with Matt Stokes, I was styling!

When I got home that afternoon, Rochelle greeted me excitedly and asked how the trip went. I said, "They offered me the job of sports director at $800 a month and they want me to start no later than August 15th!" Then she gave me a big hug with tears in her eyes and said "Wow, you have to be proud! You deserve this!" and I responded with "No, we deserve this! Now, after I call Mom and Dad, let's go out to dinner to celebrate."

I took Rochelle to our favorite restaurant in Sacramento, the Coral Reef, where we talked about our future over a nice bottle of "Lancers" wine. She reminded me that we had a little more than sixty days before I was on the job in Reno, and we had many loose ends to tie up, like giving our landlord and current employers notice. There also were the issues of where we were going to live in Reno and where was Rochelle going to find a job. It was only until late in the evening of celebrating that I sheepishly told her that my hiring was not official until the current sports director signed his Portland deal within the week.

"Maybe we hold off the rest of the celebration until you're officially hired. Nick, you warned me about how crazy this broadcasting business is. We need to hold on notifying anybody until you are signed, sealed and delivered," Rochelle proclaimed.

When I came into work at KCBG the next Monday morning, I was determined not to say a word to anybody, and just to keep my head down. The station was a rumor mill already with the union issue dividing sides. I was shocked to find out that nearly everybody was aware of my Reno trip and possible move to KWOO to replace Evan Downing, who apparently had talked to Cal Samuels about me. Ike Forbath of KWOO had informed news director Lloyd Brennan that I was being hired, so the" cat was out of the bag," so to speak. I was trying hard not to be overconfident, but I was constantly having my co-workers, particularly the other studio operators, congratulating me on my new job. Mel Baker in particular was really happy for me.

"I'm going miss you, Nick," said Mel. "Guess I'll have to find another white boy to beat up!" I quickly responded with "Yeah, just like Ali beat up Frazier!" We both had a good laugh about that exchange. I was going to miss this guy who had taught me about a world that I never knew before. I hoped that I had the same impact on him.

A week went by with no call from Reno, but I vowed not to call the KWOO people because I didn't want to seem too anxious. Rochelle was understandably impatient, and by day six she said, "Nick, do these people know we have to make a lot of elaborate arrangements for you to be on the job by August 15th! Where's the phone call?"

I held out until day ten when I finally gave in and asked Lloyd Brennan if he had an update from his Reno counterpart. Brennan swung into action immediately, calling Forbath who was unavailable and "in a meeting." By this time, I was getting really nervous, but Lloyd calmly said, "Relax Nick, these people really want you. They've been really busy with a small news team covering the big Tahoe casino scandal and closure. I'm sure this will all work out for you." I appreciated the advice from our news director, but I was growing very uneasy about the possible move.

One hour later I got the call I had been waiting for, but it was Evan Downing on the line and not KWOO general manager Bob Storin. "Nick, Evan Downing here. Bad news for you and me. The Portland guy that I was replacing didn't get the L.A job, which means I didn't get his. So, I'm staying here after all. I'm so sorry to put you through all this. I know Ike and Bob are really sold on you, as am I. When I do leave this job, it will be yours." I thanked him for the call and my heart sank. I reminded myself again that the broadcast business has its highs and lows.

Dean Stevens called me a bit later to offer his "apology" for the disappointing turn of events. I thanked him for setting me up for a great opportunity which, through no fault of his, did not work out. "This was a great experience, Dean," I told him. "Next time I won't wear my heart on my sleeve. I'm still a rookie in this crazy business." Even though I was putting on a good show with the philosophical stuff I was hurting. It would be difficult telling my KCBG friends that I was not going to Reno, but the worst task would be telling Rochelle and our families. Moments after hanging up the phone with Dean, I ran into Mel Baker in the studio setting up the lights for the Noon News. "Looks like you have to beat up this white boy for a while longer," I whispered.

Mel was shocked that my dream job in Reno did not materialize, and said, "Those assholes never should have called you until Downing had signed his contract with the Portland people!" It turns out that Ike Forbath had told Lloyd Brennan my sad news earlier in the day, shortly after my phone call, so the whole station was buzzing. My day was filled with well-meaning co-workers wanting to know what went wrong and offering their sympathy. Even Bill Harrington, of all people, commented, "You didn't deserve that, Nick. But your time is coming." His comments were both surprising and heart-warming. But my exhausting day was going to get even tougher. I was heading home to face Rochelle, whom I purposely did not call from the station.

She was cooking her famous pork chops and rice dish, one of my favorites, when I walked through the front door. I did not have to say a word as she saw the concerned look on my face. Rochelle, who could read me like a book, said, "Something happened to the Reno job, didn't it Nick?" Holding back the tears, she gave me a big hug as I told her my sorry saga. "I know you're very disappointed Nick, but it wasn't meant to be. There will be plenty of other opportunities, and maybe something far better than Reno. We both have jobs and friends here in Sacramento, so we will be just fine. Just get back up on that horse and send out some more tapes and resumes," was her reassuring advice.

Rochelle seemed to always have a great insight in seeing the "big picture." So, amidst the rancor in the air over the union issue, I spent the next few months keeping my head down, doing my job and chasing job leads.

CAL'S RANT

Because of the union issue, I had not been doing as much sports reporting and on-air work until Cal Samuels threw one of the worst tantrums I had ever seen at the station. He had done a lengthy film interview with former 49ers football star and good friend, Hugh McElhenny, who had just been elected to the Pro Football Hall of Fame. The entire interview had been "lost in the film processor," an unfortunate occurrence that was more common when station monies were not spent on regular maintenance of equipment. It was 5pm and I was in the newsroom gathering up some of the early sports scores for the 6pm sports segment, when Cal stormed into the newsroom. He spewed forth an impressive stream of profanities and threw a video tape across the room hitting the large TV monitor and cracking the screen.

"This is the cheapest f---king station I have ever seen. Management can kiss my ass!" With that he walked out the front door of KCBG, presumably leaving no one to do the 6pm sports segment. The good news was that I had written most of the show, and I could substitute a national news video tape for the lost McElhenny film interview. But the bad news was that I was dressed for my studio operator duties, not going on the air. I had no dress shirt, coat, or tie. Fortunately, anchorman Ted Dorsey was about my size and had plenty of shirts, ties, and coats to choose from. Local clothing firms would provide on-air anchors with an abundance of clothes for free provided they got a plug in the closing credits.

I must admit that I was a bit nervous going on the air that evening. I had not done much on camera work in recent weeks and with less than one hour to prepare, I was feeling rushed. But this was another opportunity that I had been hoping for, so suck it up, Nick!

As we were getting ready to do headlines Ted Dorsey looked over at me wearing his clothes said with a chuckle "Nick Cunningham, studio operator by day and sports anchor by night. You are KCBG's Swiss Army Knife!" My response was, "I prefer the baseball term of utility infielder."

Then Mel Baker barked out "Stand by in the studio!" pointed his finger at Ted to cue him, and away we went. Not my best show but not bad under the circumstances. They brought the weekend guy, Rob Nevels, in to do the 11pm news.

The big question was, "Where was Cal Samuels?" Did he just quit, was he fired? He was not in his "party central" motor home in the parking lot, either. The next day news director, Lloyd Brennan, announced that Cal had gone on vacation for a week, and that I would be doing the weekend sports while Rob Nevels would handle Cal's position. KCBG was going to pay me overtime on my low studio operator's salary for doing the weekend sports, which wasn't even close to what they were paying Nevels. They could not ask me to do it for free with the National Labor Relations Board looking at the possible "unionization" of the station. Who was I to complain? I would get some more tapes of my work, "air checks" as we liked to call them.

      Cal's absence gave me another surprising opportunity. KCBG sent cameraman Roy Wright and me to the San Francisco 49ers training camp in Santa Barbara at the UCSB Campus, where I had spent the first two years of my college career. Our assignment was to get as many interviews as we could and to film a 49er live scrimmage at Gaucho Field in Goleta, a familiar place. The really fun part of the trip was the fact that we would stay in on-campus housing with the team for three full days, eating meals and visiting with them. The press corps was also invited to take part in the team's table-tennis tournament, which was far more physically taxing to the players than the coaches could have imagined. John Brodie, the team's 36-year-old veteran quarterback, was not only the leader of the squad, but the best table tennis player in camp. My good friend Hank Ramsey, who was there representing KLIB Radio, goaded me into challenging Brodie to a match billed as the "Press vs. the Players." Much to the delight of the 49ers, he beat me easily just as he had beaten all of his teammates. Brodie, San Francisco's top draft choice out of Stanford in 1957, was one of the most intelligent and competitive athletes I have ever seen. He took a bad Stanford football team and made them mediocre, and he took a mediocre 49ers team and made them good. He single-handedly" moved the needle," as they say. After his playing days in the NFL were over, he became a successful pro golfer, even winning a tournament on the Seniors Tour. Later, he became both a golf and pro football commentator for NBC. It is a travesty that he is not in the Pro Football Hall of Fame. Dick Nolan was the San Francisco head coach, but all the players knew that Brodie was the real leader and the heart and soul of the team.

The trip was productive and a lot of fun, except for one big mistake on my part. On the night of the scrimmage, we were allowed to be on the sidelines filming. This was a new experience for me as I had not seen these big, fast, and gifted athletes so "up close and personal." Sure, I had played high school football, but this was another level entirely when it comes to speed and power. Roy told me before he began filming that he would be following the action through his lens, and he could not see the whole field. He pleaded," Nick, if those big guys are coming my way, I need you to look out for me-got it?" I said," sure," as I was captivated by the hard-hitting going on right in front of me. I was so captivated, in fact, that I did not see fullback Ken Williard put a crushing blindside block on 245-pound linebacker Frank Nunley, who was knocked air-borne into my cameraman. Roy and his camera went flying, while an incensed Nunley went after Williard claiming he was given a cheap shot. Fortunately, Wright was not hurt, and his camera was not damaged. As a field TV reporter, I had made a rookie error by not protecting my cameraman. I spent the rest of the trip apologizing to Roy and carrying most of his equipment. Needless to say, I would not make that mistake again.

A month later, Roy Wright and I had another exciting adventure together at the 1971 National League Playoffs in San Francisco, when the Giants hosted the Pittsburgh Pirates. Just minutes before game one, Roy and I walked right on to the field and interviewed Pirates' manager Danny Murtaugh. I think he mistook us for the NBC-TV crew which was doing the national telecast. When I asked him how he was going to deal with the Giants' powerful lineup of Mays, McCovey, and Bonds, he gave me a long-winded answer which I followed up with another question about his inconsistent starting pitcher, Steve Blass. As he answered with his very deliberate style, I heard an argument going on behind me.

Apparently, NBC-TV's Tony Kubek, a former Yankee shortstop, was upset with the fact that I was doing the interview with Murtaugh when he was scheduled to go "live" with the manager just before game time. Kubek, who was paired with Curt Gowdy on the national telecast, was giving the Giants' publicity guy an earful as I droned on with Murtaugh.

When we finally finished, I heard Kubek utter, "Christ, we're not going to have time to do this! Pack it up. I've got to get up to the booth."

He gave me a dirty look and stormed off after apologizing to a dazed and confused Pirates' manager. I turned to Roy and said that we may have screwed up NBC's pre-game show. It was definitely time to leave before we did any more damage. The proper media protocol would have been to defer to the live network telecast, but we were not made aware of the situation until it was too late. So, Tony Kubek's planned pre-game show became our one-on-one interview with Murtaugh on both the early and late news.

It was the fall of 1971 and I was getting impatient. I was getting positive feedback from viewers and station personnel, but where were the job offers? I wondered if I had chosen the wrong profession. With my frustration building, I had asked several of my co-workers, friends, and, of course, Rochelle to be super critical of my work. What came back from them was helpful. The consensus was that I had a "baby face" and I looked very young. Also, it was pointed out, that I did not have a deep broadcast voice. I decided that I would grow a moustache to go with my black hair to look older, and that I would slow my delivery down slightly to improve the quality of my voice.

"You're better on the air than Rob Nevels, and you look more like an athlete which is what the audience wants. It's hard to believe a sports reporter who looks and sounds like rock-jock Bobby Sherman on Hullabaloo" was Rochelle's very biased critique in reference to me versus Nevels. Ironically, she gotten to know '60s rock star Bobby Sherman when she was sixteen years old. Rochelle, as a representative of Fremont High School of Oakland, was part of a teenage journalistic delegation that held a press conference with Sherman in order to publicize his upcoming appearance at San Francisco's Cow Palace. Bobby had invited her up to his hotel room for an "in-depth" interview, which she thankfully turned down. I jokingly never missed an opportunity to remind her of a missed opportunity to get to know Bobby Sherman.

Cal Samuels finally surfaced after a week and was immediately asked to meet behind closed doors with general manager John Blake and news director Lloyd Brennan. The station was abuzz with rumors. Was Samuels getting fired and, if so, who was going to replace him? There was no way a newcomer like me or a rock jock like Nevels was going to replace him in a market of this size. After a long two-hour meeting, Samuels appeared in the main reception room, looking very sheepish, standing beside Blake and Brennan. The general manager had come on the KCBG loudspeaker indicating that Cal Samuels wanted to address all the station employees. Cal was very humble and contrite, stating that he has had anger issues his whole life and is trying to deal with them as best he could. He apologized for his actions of the past week and said they will never be repeated. The story is that GM Blake had read Samuels the riot act on the phone when he walked out of the station just prior to the 6pm news. Blake wanted to fire Cal but the Corinthian ownership of the station in New York City liked the audience that Samuels brought to KCBG. As a result, Cal was given a reprieve, much to the dismay of the GM.

This incident added to the drama in the place which was already in an argumentative mood over the union issue.

Meanwhile, my moustache was beginning to fill in and Rochelle and I decided that she would take some pictures of the "new" me to include with the resumes I sent out to potential employers. With my new "stash" I resembled one of my favorite TV heroes from the 50s, the Cisco Kid. Video tapes would be sent upon request, and sometimes not upon request. We were spending a lot of time and money at the post office sending "air checks" all over the country. Finally, in February of 1972, I got some exciting news. Texas native Samantha Dawes of KCBG recommended me to a station in San Antonio. They were looking for a weekend sports anchor who would double as a news reporter Wednesday thru Friday. They liked my tape and wanted to talk to me before flying me to Texas for an audition.

Carl Harkins, the General Manager of KXGX, the NBC TV affiliate in San Antonio called me at home so we could talk privately, and he got right to the point. "Sammy Dawes has some very nice things to say about you, and we like what we see on your air checks, interviews and field reporting. How do you feel about reporting on hard news stories including crime and violence?"

I remembered Matt Stokes' advice; "Tell them you can do it and learn on the job." I wasn't surprised at the question because many sportscasters and feature reporters want nothing to do with crime and violence. As a news reporter three days a week in San Antonio, I knew I would see plenty of bank robberies, shootouts, and ugliness, but that would be a small price to pay to be the weekend sports anchor.

"I have done some hard news coverage here in Sacramento, and I even co-anchored the Noon News with Samantha for a week recently. I can handle hard news reporting," was my confident response.

It did occur to me that picking up the "Dog of the Week" for the Morning News at the local kennel did not count as hard news. We talked some more about the job and the demographics of his station's San Antonio audience. Carl asked me if I spoke Spanish. I thought about my two years of Spanish in Senora Gulla's Burlingame High School Class in the 1960s, and said, "A little bit, but I would not call myself fluent by any means." He went on to say that it wasn't mandatory that I was fluent in Spanish, but that I should "bone up on it a bit" before I come to San Antonio. The job was going to pay a base salary of just under $900/month with overtime available too, double what I was currently making. I wrote that number down on a piece of paper and handed it to Rochelle who was carefully paying attention to my conversation. She quietly mouthed the word "WOW!" and both of us were getting excited. But then Harkins added," There's one final requirement. We would like you to take the on-air name of Nicolas Espinoza. Is that going to be a problem?" I was really taken by surprise by this question.

"I don't know. Can I discuss this with my family and get back to you tomorrow?" was my response. He said yes and we agreed to talk at the same time on the following day.

"Holy shit, Rochelle! They want to trick their market and maybe the FCC by hiring a fake Latino--me!" was my exasperated comment to Rochelle when I hung up the phone.

When I told her, they wanted to give me a Hispanic name and essentially take the job away from a qualified minority candidate, she just could not hold back her frustration.

"Don't these people at KXGX have any sense of fair play, right and wrong or morality? If they really want you, they will accept the real you with your real name!"

I was prepared to tell Harkins that we were interested in the job offer but there was no way I was going to change my name. Rochelle and I talked about the possible move to San Antonio late into the night and continued the topic at breakfast. I was becoming uncomfortable with the fact that KXGX was prepared to mislead its audience. What if Harkins agreed to let me keep my name and offered me the job? I had about twelve hours to think about it before my evening phone call.

Ironically, it was my turn to do the "Dog of the Week" pick up at KCBG that morning. It was humbling to go from talking about a sports anchor job to picking up a nervous beagle puppy at the animal shelter, who decided to empty his bowels in my company van. Mel Baker, who was my studio operator partner that morning, was in hysterics. I had given him a bad time several weeks earlier when he had to clean up after a large poodle mix who "could not hold it" during his van run. "Karma is a bitch, isn't it Nick?" was Mel's good-natured jab at me. I felt I had to tell him my story of the last 24 hours in order for him to fully appreciate what cleaning up dog crap meant to me this morning.

When I told him about the possible anchor job and name change request, he said he wasn't surprised at all. "You're not going to do it, are you Nick?' was his response.

"Of course I am NOT going to change my name, but the fact that they asked me to, makes me uneasy with the station management and ownership," was my comeback.

We talked about the job offer and name change request all morning leading up to the Noon News with co-anchors Ted Dorsey and Sam Dawes. "Nick, the eyes of Texas are upon you!" was Sam's first comment when she saw me, referring to the KXGX offer which she apparently knew all about.

I quickly responded with "They want to me to change my name so I appear to be Hispanic. I just can't do that Sam! But I really appreciate you recommending me to them."

Ted Dorsey, overhearing the conversation, chimed in with, "You gotta go with the opportunity. You can change your name back later if you want. If they want you to be Jose Gonzalez, do it! Get the job and show them what you can do. By the way, my real name is not Ted Dorsey; it's Theodore Andrei Dorchinski." Mel and I just looked at each other in amazement as we cued Ted and Sam for the news headlines.

When we went to break Samantha started in on me. "There is no such thing as the perfect job in this crazy business, Nick. You have to grab at all the opportunities you get. With your love of football, you are a perfect fit for Texas. Don't let this slip away!" I appreciated the fact that she was pushing me hard on this opportunity, particularly considering what she was having to endure in order to climb her career ladder.

That afternoon I had a long conversation with Mel Baker about the job offer. By this time Mel and I had spent a lot of time together on the same shift and had come to respect and even seek out each other's opinion on current issues and events.

"If they don't require you to change your name, you have to take the job, Nick. I know you don't like the management's intent on trying to get around hiring a minority, but KXGX is like a thousand other organizations trying to do the same thing. If you want to effect a change in attitudes down there, you'll get your chance. From what I've seen change usually occurs from the inside out rather than the outside in, "was Baker's well thought out advice.

His comments really struck home to me. I wasn't going to San Antonio to be a crusader; I was going to be a sportscaster/news reporter. But if I could help change attitudes by just being myself with my news reporting and on-air performance, then I was good to go.

When I got home that evening Rochelle and I again discussed the San Antonio offer, and we agreed that if KXGX would drop the name change requirement, we would take the job. At 7:30pm the phone rang, and I answered. "Hi Nick, Carl Harkins here. What did you decide about our offer?" No beating around the bush; he wanted an answer right now, as if he had a back-up plan waiting in the wings if I said no.

"I really appreciate the offer and like everything about it, except I'm not comfortable changing my name. If I can keep my name, you have a deal." There was a long pause on the phone. My father, who trained young insurance salespeople and was a great negotiator, had taught me that "silence is golden" at a moment like this.

Finally, Harkins said "Well, I must admit I'm surprised by your answer. We feel the name change issue is not negotiable. Have you talked to Sammy about this? You would be missing a great opportunity to cover prep, college, and pro football in Texas. Football is a religion down here!" He was not going to budge, and neither was I.

"Mr. Harkins, I realize the opportunity I may be passing up, but I just can't change my name. I would be living a lie." There was really nothing more to say. We politely said goodbye to one another and hung up. Rochelle went on a brief rant about the TV business, but the two of us agreed that we had made the right decision. There would be other opportunities down the road, and we had to be patient, as difficult as that seemed to be for two kids in their mid-twenties who had come so close to two attractive TV jobs.

The next day at the station was exhausting as I had to explain to my friends and co-workers that I was not taking the Texas job. The only folks that I thought knew anything about it were Ted Dorsey, Sammy Dawes, and Mel Baker, but apparently "news" travels fast in the news department of KCBG. Everybody seemed to have an opinion about my decision not to take the job because of the name change requirement. Ted and Sammy thought I had made a big mistake, while Mel felt that I had made the right decision. Meanwhile the union issue was becoming more divisive every day. The general manager as well as news director Brennan hinted to me that if KCBG became a union shop, my on-air sports work would be limited or possibly eliminated. Mel Baker was told that if he wanted to be sitting in the producer or director's chair, unionization at KCBG would greatly slow up that process.

FORT WAYNE

About a month had gone by with no opportunities for me either on-air or in reporting. These are skills that I wanted to keep sharp, and I felt that the inactivity would hurt me should I be given another opportunity to cut an audition tape like I did in Reno. In early March of 1972, when I was feeling pretty discouraged about my TV future, Lloyd Brennan called me into his office. He had returned from a Corinthian news directors meeting in Houston where he had spent time with his old friend and colleague Stan Sheets, the news director of WFTW in Fort Wayne, Indiana. They had been young news reporters together at a Chicago radio station in the late 1950s. Stan was lamenting the fact that he had just lost his sports anchor to the ABC affiliate in Indianapolis, and now he was going to have to go through a "million" tapes and interviews to find the right replacement. Lloyd told me that he recommended me for the job, and that Stan would be calling me this week. Brennan said Sheets, although a bit quirky, was among the best minds in the business with a "nose for news. "He went on to say that I would learn a lot from his friend Stan Sheets, who, as Brennan described it, was from the "Edward R. Murrow School of Ethical Broadcasting."

Wow! Another opportunity! Where the hell is Fort Wayne, Indiana? Rochelle and I got out the atlas and found it on the map in northeast Indiana, less than a four-hour drive from Chicago, two hours from Indianapolis, and 2 1/2 hours from South Bend, the home of Notre Dame Football. Our research told us that Fort Wayne was Johnny Appleseed's farthest venture into the "West," and it hosted the first night baseball game, lit by gas lamps. The city was the home of Magnavox Electronics, International Harvester, Lincoln Life Insurance and Lays Potato Chips.

Safe Passage Guaranteed | 47

It had a minor league hockey team, the Fort Wayne Komets, a five-star restaurant, Café Jonell, and a hunger for local sports events, particularly high school basketball. The only relative that Rochelle and I had anywhere near Fort Wayne was an aunt of mine in Dayton, Ohio, whom I had not seen in ten years.

At KCBG we had an engineer, Ken Sturbridge, who came to us from WFTW where he had worked in the late '60s. Ken was very helpful to me and explained how the state of Indiana is "totally mad about basketball," and that during the state basketball tournament my sports segment would be the most watched portion of the newscast. He also waxed on wistfully about the "friendly Midwest folks who would give you the shirts off their backs." Ken explained that he thought that Fort Wayne was far enough away from some of the bigger cities like Chicago, Cleveland, Indianapolis, and Detroit so that it had its own identity, and would not be overpowered by the larger TV markets. He added, "Because the city is within a day's drive from the big markets, it is easier to be seen and hired by general managers and news directors from major network affiliates." That point really got my attention as I remembered Dean Stevens had told me the same thing about Reno.

The next day at work I was summoned to Lloyd Brennan's office about 1pm. He said he had Stan Sheets on the phone who wanted to speak with me privately. Lloyd handed me the phone and left me in his office alone to have a long chat with the WFTW news director. Sheets spoke at length about the great attributes of the city of Fort Wayne, and the fact that WFTW wanted to get younger looking broadcasters and reporters on the air to improve its ratings. They were not only looking for a sports anchor, but they wanted to hire a younger reporter as well.

"I can offer you a starting salary of $800 per month with some overtime potential," he said, "and you can keep all your vacation credits with Corinthian because you'd be going to a sister station. We'll also cover your moving and travel costs, plus you won't have to change your name. What do you say? And please call me Stan."

He added that I would be the sports director in a one-man department, writing, producing, and performing ten shows a week plus two Saturdays a month on overtime, plus I would do some booth announcing. This guy was direct to say the least, and it looked like Lloyd had told him my story about the Texas job.

"I appreciate your offer, Stan," I said," but before I can say yes, I need to discuss this with my wife. When would you want me to start?"

Sheets did not hesitate. "We would like you on the job by June fifth. Nick, we have seen your tapes and you come very well recommended by Lloyd and others at KCBG. Is it possible to give me a call back tomorrow?"

I felt beads of stressful sweat forming between my eyebrows and said, "Absolutely, I'll call you back tomorrow with my answer." I thanked him and hung up the phone with my mind racing. June 5th was a little over two months away- and I was considering a move of 2300 miles away to a place I have never seen. WFTW was prepared to hire me without an in-person interview or audition based upon tapes and good words from my friends and supporters here at KCBG.

Brennan returned to his office as I was about to leave and said, "I think you'll be a good fit for WFTW, Nick. It's a great place to begin your sports anchor career." I must have thanked him two or three times before he interrupted me and said, "Just go out there and make us all proud.!"

That evening, Rochelle and I discussed the pros and cons of the job far into the night. We both felt, in the big picture, that this was the right position at the right time. The tough part was going to be leaving behind our immediate families living in the San Francisco Bay Area. Albert and Pauline Wildi, Rochelle's parents, were in their late 60s and had lived in Oakland nearly their entire lives. I knew that being 2300 miles away Rochelle would worry about them, but I reminded her that she'd still worry, even if her parents were only 90 miles away. My parents, Doug and Evelyn Cunningham, were almost 20 years younger than Rochelle's and had been transferred to different communities several times during my dad's insurance career. My two sisters, Pat and Grace, were both California girls. Pat was a young mother supporting her husband, Brett, as he worked toward a potential medical career at UC Berkeley and Grace was a junior at Woodside High School. Rochelle's older brother, Earl, living in nearby Fremont with his family, worked as a printer in the newspaper business. It was going to be difficult to leave all these people behind, but we knew that this was an opportunity we could not pass up. We were going to a place where we did not know a soul, and we knew this move would test our marriage as well as our job skills.

I was anxious to get to the station the next day to finalize the arrangements for my new job. I didn't want to jinx myself by talking about it too early. The bitter taste of the Reno disappointment was still in my mouth. As Mel and I set up the microphones for the Morning News, I was unusually quiet and reserved. "You're going to take it, aren't you Nick?" was Mel's ice-breaking comment. I responded with the lyrics from a popular song, "Indiana wants me!" Never mind that the song was about an escaped convict. "Mel, I need to be hush-hush about this until I talk to the news director, Stan Sheets, later today. Hopefully, they want me as much as they did yesterday!" The Morning News with Sam Dawes went off without a hitch, and it was time to make my call to the Midwest.

I caught the eye of Lloyd Brennan in the newsroom and asked if I could use his office for an important phone call. "Is it a go, Nick?" Lloyd asked.

I told him, "Yes," and that Rochelle and I were excited about starting our new life in Fort Wayne. Brennan loudly congratulated me in the newsroom, causing some of my reporter pals to chime in with their best wishes. Finally, I was able to pull away from my premature celebration and call Stan Sheets, who had not formally hired me yet.

"Hello Stan, this is Nick Cunningham and I'd be delighted to be your new sports director at WFTW!" were the first words out of my mouth when he picked up the phone.

"We can't wait to have you here and be part of our team," was his equally enthusiastic response. Sheets went on to explain that there would be an announcement in Broadcast Magazine and local newspapers about my hiring. As such, he wanted a little more background information on both Rochelle and me for the press release that WFTW would be sending out. We talked a while longer about details of the move, and he reminded me that I would be on the job by June fifth-less than nine weeks away! My mind was racing as I thanked him and hung up the phone.

When I emerged from Brennan's office I was greeted with more handshakes and hugs-the "cat was really out of the bag." The party continued for a few more minutes until Lloyd soberly announced, "Get to work everybody! We have a Noon News to put together!"

I worked the floor with Mel on the Noon News which featured Sam and Ted Dorsey in the anchor chairs. They even worked in a "breaking news headline" as they put it, and announced my move to WFTW in Fort Wayne, Indiana. As they did so, Mel Baker swung his camera around and got a shot of me. I must admit I was touched by all the hoopla and good wishes.

Rochelle and I now had to tell our families and friends about my new job as well as make arrangements for our cross-country move. We had become close friends with our neighbors,

Mike and Joanne Ferris, who lived across the hall in the Arden Oaks Apartments. They had both become our regular tennis partners and good friends during our two-year stint in Sacramento. The Ferrises were both huge racing fans and vowed to join us at the Indy 500 in 1973. Both sets of parents were excited about our new job, but sorry to see us go. "Why can't Nick just be a garbage man in Milpitas?" Pauline Wildi famously commented when she heard our news. I must admit that there were times when I thought the garbage business had more appeal than the crazy broadcast industry.

The next few weeks flew by, filled with moving plans, congratulations, good-byes, and best wishes from many surprising sources. The head of the Radio-TV department at SJSU, Dr. Charles J. Frick, sent me a nice congratulatory note after he saw the announcement in Broadcast Magazine. I also heard from my SJSU pals Dean Stevens and Hank Ramsey. KCBG had a going away luncheon for me at the Hong Kong Café down the street from the station. General Manager John Blake presented me with a framed caricature of me with the KCBG logo in the background which had been signed on the back by all my friends at the station. I must admit that I was touched and surprised that the KCBG brass would make such a big deal about one of its lowest paid employees moving on to greener pastures. The cynical part of me thought that all the fuss over me was a good public relations move by management in light of the upcoming union vote.

It was hard to say goodbye to my two best friends at the station- Matt Stokes and Mel Baker. While I did not see Matt that often because he was the Stockton Bureau Chief, I would regularly hear from him by phone with words of encouragement. Whenever he was in Sacramento, he would make an effort to get together. Because of his keen interest in cooking, he was always one of Rochelle's favorite dinner guests. Sadly, he would die as a result of the Jonestown massacre with religious zealot Jim Jones in 1978. Matt was taken in by Jones "one world utopian philosophy", and left KCBG to become his public relations/media director in 1975.

Stokes could not get out from under Jones' spell. In a bizarre twist, he took his own life at a Modesto, California press conference, apparently despondent after the recent Jonestown tragedy. With many of his friends and former co-workers present, he excused himself to go to the bathroom where he proceeded to end his life with his .38 caliber pistol. When I heard the news about Matt, my jaw dropped, and my heart sank. I tried to remember the twinkle in his eye, the terrific sense of humor and the great day we had together in Santa Rosa in August of 1970.

Mel Baker and I had each other's backs for two years and were great sounding boards for one another on many subjects, including unionization and career advancement. "Go get 'em Nick, you're gonna do great!" were his parting words as he gave me a hug.

"Your time's coming too, Mel- sooner than you think. I know you'll be ready!" was my comeback.

I can't say that I had the impact on Mel that he had on me, other than I got him to appreciate the Beach Boys music and the comic madness of Jonathon Winters. He made me a fan of several African American groups like the Drifters and the Temptations. Rochelle and I even took a trip to Reno together with Mel and his girlfriend Margueritte to see "Little Anthony and the Imperials", a popular singing group from the 1960's. Baker would go on to be very successful in the area of TV production. He did this despite having nothing more than a high school education because he was very observant and a fast learner, two qualities he needed to survive growing up in inner city Cleveland. Mel would become the first-ever African American producer/director at KCBG in 1975, after the station voted for unionization a year earlier.

Saying goodbye to family was even more difficult, especially for Rochelle who was born and raised in the Bay Area. Her mom, Pauline, spent her whole life living in Oakland and even attended Rochelle's high school, Fremont, in the 1920s. Albert,

Rochelle's dad, left the family farm in North Dakota and hopped a freight train heading west, settling in Oakland prior to the Great Depression. Before we pulled away from the Wildi home in Alameda, Pauline gave Rochelle a California poppy and told her this flower would bring us back to the Golden State, a wish we all shared. The next day we would leave Sacramento heading east toward Fort Wayne with our hearts full of excitement, hope, and wonderment.

2

AMERICA'S HEARTLAND

With the radio blaring the popular hit song "It's Too Late to Turn Back Now" by the Cornelius Brothers and Sister Rose, which seemed "apropos" for the time, we began our journey in Rochelle's 1965 Comet. My 1964 Skylark convertible, a college graduation present from my parents, did not seem to be practical for the cold winters we would encounter in Indiana. With the help of my parents, I got $500 for the car from a Stanford professor-money we really needed to help fund our trip. We were not sure how far we could go on our first day, but it looked like Elko, Nevada would be a reasonable goal. It was a beautiful spring morning as we headed up I-80 toward the Sierras, very much like the day almost a year earlier when I was traveling this same road in hopes of landing the Reno job. As we passed the state line leaving California, Rochelle turned to me with tears in her eyes and said, "Nick, do you think we are ever coming back?"

With a shrug of the shoulders I said, "I sure hope so!"

Later in the day, as we got into eastern Nevada, the landscape changed from gorgeous trees, flowers, and views to desert and desolation. We pulled into Elko, Nevada in late afternoon and checked into a hotel which was also a casino. We enjoyed a relaxing swim and a nice dinner, but with the excitement of the trip and the noise from the enthusiastic gamblers, both Rochelle and I had trouble sleeping. At one point in the early hours of the morning she rolled over and said to me, "Is this trip really happening or am I dreaming?"

I responded with "You aren't dreaming Baby; we are headed to Indiana!"

We were up early the next morning, got a nice and inexpensive breakfast (love those food prices underwritten by the gambling industry in Nevada), and headed out into the badlands of Nevada toward Salt Lake City, Utah. We made great time and pulled into a Chevron station in Salt Lake around mid-day to fill up our tank and to get some lunch.

After we gassed up, I turned the key to start the ignition, and NOTHING HAPPENED. The young gas station attendant who didn't look more than 18 came over to check out our car.

"Sir, I think it's your starter. I have a rebuilt one here that I can slide in for you at a good price- 40 bucks plus $25 for labor-have you outta here in an hour," said the attendant whose badge said "Duke." Rochelle and I looked at each other knowing we didn't have much choice.

" Let's do it, Duke! My wife and I will be across the street getting a bite to eat." We headed over to Mary Jean's Café hoping that our new buddy knew what he was doing. After we came back from lunch Duke had just completed the installation and said, "Sir, why don't you fire this baby up?" Much to our relief, and to the seeming surprise of Duke, the old Comet purred like a pussy cat. I paid the young man, and off we went heading east, hopefully as far as central Wyoming.

As we pulled away Rochelle said, "Did you see the look on his face when you started the car? That didn't inspire confidence. What happens when we're in the middle of nowhere and it doesn't start?"

I winked at her and said, "Didn't I promise you an adventure when I asked you to marry me? Well, this is it. We're going to be just fine!"

About 20 minutes east of Salt Lake we were in the "middle of nowhere," but the scenery was a dramatic improvement over eastern Nevada and western Utah. The afternoon sun gave a majestic hue to the Rocky Mountain Range as we climbed in altitude. We made our way into Evanston, Wyoming, where we stopped at "The All American" gas station adorned with four huge American Flags. The '65 Comet started right up, and we made one final late afternoon push eastward to the rodeo town of Rock Springs, Wyoming.

We found a Rock Springs Howard Johnson's Motel that looked decent in Rochelle's AAA book and decided to stop for the night. We were told that when the sun goes down in the "middle of nowhere" (where street lights are a rarity) it gets really dark. Clarence, the inn keeper, recommended the Purple Sage Country Club for dinner, located up the winding road about three miles out of town. Clarence insisted that the place was worth the drive and welcomed travelers. The little town was "hoppin" and decorated with rodeo signs and posters in preparation for the big event scheduled for tomorrow. Some of the posters saluted the skills of the competing cowboys, while other signs were supportive of the animals. One hilarious sign especially caught my eye-it was a picture of a huge angry black bull blowing steam and snot out of its nose with a caption "Beware! Tarantula will kick your butt!" It kind of reminded me of ancient times in the Roman Coliseum when the gladiators fought lions and tigers, as most of the enthusiastic spectators rooted for the animals.

After a short walk around town, me in my tennis shorts and Rochelle decked-out in her yellow sundress, we decided to have a leisurely swim at our motel. We both looked out of place in this rodeo town. It wasn't until early evening that we headed out on our breath-taking drive on a dirt road to the Purple Sage Country Club. As the sun was going down it lit up the golden Rocky Mountain Range with the lush late spring foliage- a spectacular sight that I had never seen before. The dinner we had was every bit as good as we were told it would be, including the bottle of Charles Krug cabernet which Rochelle and I totally consumed. We were in a celebratory mood, feeling like this trip was sort of a second honeymoon. By the time we finished dinner it was totally dark and driving back to our hotel was going to be a challenge, plus I noticed our gas gauge was on empty. I had not filled up our gas tank since Salt Lake City! Oh Shit! What was I thinking- or not thinking? I don't think I was totally aware that it takes more gas to climb up the mountains than to go down-a lesson that I would have a hard time learning.

Ten minutes into our drive back, we ran out of gas. It was very dark except for the rising moon, it was getting cooler by the minute, and we were really in the middle of nowhere with no gas station in sight. We were dressed in our good clothes with Rochelle in high heels-she wasn't about to do any walking and I was not going to leave her there. She was not happy about running out of gas. The second honeymoon was definitely over.

"Nick, why didn't you gas up when we pulled into Rock Springs?" she said with an irritated stare.

I gave her my standard comeback when I knew I "f'd" up and said, "I was distracted by your beauty!" That annoyed Rochelle even more.

Fortunately, we did have a flashlight in the glove compartment, and I decided that our best course of action was to try to flag down a car- that is, if a car would come by at 10pm on this lonely road. After nearly an hour of waiting in vain for any cars to appear, we decided that our best options were to walk back to the Purple Sage or to sleep in the Comet until help arrived. All of a sudden, we heard the pounding of hooves. Silhouetted against the moonlight appeared to be a team of horses pulling a stagecoach- a stagecoach like from the Old West? I asked Rochelle if I was dreaming, and she confirmed what we were seeing. I grabbed the flashlight and flagged down the stage- I felt like John Wayne.

"You look like you're in a peck of trouble, pahdna!" yelled the driver as he pulled the reins on his team and brought the horse drawn coach to a halt in front of our Comet. I explained our predicament and the driver said, "You're in luck, young fella. We're headed to a gas station down the road to pick up a rodeo super star. It's going to be a tight squeeze, but I think we can give you a lift if your lady sits on your lap."

Since I felt like I was John Wayne I shot back with "Much obliged, thanks!" Rochelle and I were sandwiched with five other passengers in a coach that was designed to seat six, all of whom were dressed in cowboy and cowgirl outfits-Dolly, Candy, Kathy, Buck, and Billy. All five of these folks, who in the next half hour were to become our new best friends, were carrying and openly displaying firearms.

It turns out that this was the annual "Moonlight Stagecoach Ride Extravaganza" held in conjunction with tomorrow's rodeo. All five of these other passengers were stars who were going to perform at the big event. They were on their way to pick up gas station attendant Bronco Greenly, who was the local rodeo hero. Their final destination was to be Jerry's Saloon in Rock Springs where the pre-rodeo party was scheduled to be going strong all night. We explained to our fellow passengers that we were a couple of California kids headed out to Indiana where I was going to be a TV sportscaster in Fort Wayne.

"The hell you say!" exclaimed Buck. He went on, "So you are in TV sports? You know we have a Wyoming boy that played in the Super Bowl a couple of months back."

Now I had these people, and I fired away, "You, of course, mean the great Jim Kiick, Miami's fifth round draft choice in 1968! Local sportswriters have just nick-named Kiick and fellow Dolphins' running back Larry Csonka "Butch Cassidy and the Sundance Kid!" Rochelle looked at me and just rolled her eyes. I am sure glad that Cal Samuels let me do some of his research. Butch Cassidy and the Sundance Kid are still heroes in this part of the country due to their "Robin Hood outlaw exploits" of the late 19th Century. The recent movie with Paul Newman and Robert

Redford about the two bandits helped to fortify the legend. We talked television and sports the rest of the way until we reached the Hudson gas station which was closed except for a light in the office.

Andy, the stage coach driver, hailed the local cowboy/gas station employee. "Bronco, I got a nice young California couple on board who've run out of gas a mile or two up the road. Can you give 'em a hand?"

Greenly, looking like Hopalong Cassidy in his black outfit and hat with two holstered silver pistols around his waist, did not hesitate saying, "Sure, be happy to. I will meet the rest of you cow-punchers at Jerry's!"

I asked Andy if I could pay him for the coach ride and he said, "Nah, happy trails you two!" as he cracked his whip on the horses and rode off in the moonlight.

Bronco turned out to be another one of our Rock Springs heroes as he took us back to our car with a gas can, and then lead us back to the Hudson station. The facility was technically closed, and the rodeo star was going to be late for his party, but he took the time to fill us up and get us back on the road again. He let us take him to Jerry's so he could catch the stagecoach ride back home with his friends when the party ended in the early morning hours. Bronco explained that the locals did a lot of betting on the rodeo, particularly when it involved their famous bull, Tarantula, who got his name because of his "arachnid-like" running style. Nobody, even our star passenger, had been able to stay on the ornery beast for seven seconds since the bull became a rodeo celebrity in 1969. It turns out Tarantula even had a local fan club called the "Giant Spiders," who openly bet on the bull to "throw" local cowboys. Bronco went on to explain that it could be worth hundreds, and possibly even a couple of thousand dollars to him if he could stay on Tarantula for the full seven seconds at tomorrow's annual rodeo. We reached Jerry's Saloon, thanked Greenly for all his help, and politely turned down his invitation to the party. Rochelle was silently mouthing the words, "No Way!"

Fortunately, our Howard Johnson's Motel was right around the corner. Rochelle could not hold back any longer and blurted out, "Tonight was much more of a rodeo country adventure than I bargained for! Jim Kiick! How did you come up with that one?" I explained that Kiick was no native Wyoming boy at all, having grown up in New Jersey. I was effusive as Rochelle groaned.

"Too much information! I am sorry I asked and I'm exhausted! Hopefully tomorrow will be less exciting. Boring would be nice!" exclaimed my young wife as she kissed me good night.

The next day we were up early and hit the road east. We were coming down out of the Rockies as we went through Rawlins, Laramie, and Cheyenne before crossing over into western Nebraska, which looked a bit like the San Joaquin Valley of California. Rochelle wanted "boring", and she got it with this part of the trip as we passed through an endless list of small towns like Sidney and Ogallala, before finally stopping for the night in North Platte. The day wasn't that boring for me, as I was able to listen to Mark Donohue's victory in the Indy 500, with the incomparable Sid Collins at the mic. "Stay tuned for the greatest spectacle in racing!" was his signature introduction to the big event. I could not have imagined it at the time, but I would be having dinner with Collins at the Indy 500 Press Party less than 18 months later.

The Econo Lodge at North Platte, Nebraska was where we landed for the night-a mediocre place at best, but it served its purpose. The motel recommended Jill's Coffee Shop for dinner, which was right across the street. We were too tired to do any exploring in quest of a dinner destination, especially after our Rock Springs adventure. Much to our relief, Saturday evening was a quiet one in this Nebraska town, so Rochelle and I slept well, even on a lumpy bed.

We were up early the next day, hoping to get as far as eastern Iowa, another state I had never visited before. We dodged several thunderstorms as we drove through Gothenburg, Kearny and Grand Island, Nebraska. As we got into the outskirts of Lincoln the thunderstorm warnings turned into a tornado watch. Say What? Never had I heard of one of those! Rochelle, whose father had grown up in North Dakota where these weather issues are common, later reminded me that a tornado watch only means that conditions are right for a "twister," but that one has not actually been sited. If that happens, then a tornado watch turns into a tornado warning, which can be a bit unnerving especially for a couple of California kids. Fortunately, the weather cleared, and we made our way through Omaha and across the border into a green and lush new state- Iowa. We passed through Des Moines and Iowa City before we got weary and elected to stop in Davenport, Iowa. We found a decent motel with a Shakey's Pizza Parlor across the street. Pizza and beer sounded great to me for dinner. Rochelle and I noticed what appeared to be some nice tennis courts right off the highway as we drove into Davenport. Once we got settled in our room, we decided to bring out our tennis gear, see if we could find the courts we passed, and hit a few balls.

With little trouble we found the public tennis facility, which was in a small canyon surrounded by a tiny but well-manicured park. It was a balmy late afternoon and there was nobody on the courts except us. Rochelle and I were really stiff from four days of driving, but it really felt good to bang the ball back and forth and hear the loud echo through the canyon as we exchanged ground strokes. After a good ninety minute workout it was definitely time to cool down with beer and pizza at Shakey's. But to our dismay, there was no beer, or any alcoholic beverages served on Sundays after 5pm in Davenport, Iowa in 1972 due to Blue Laws, which had been on the books for over 50 years.

Day five of our trip got off to a slow start as Rochelle and I got a really good night's sleep and didn't hit the road until 10am. With any luck we would arrive in Fort Wayne by late afternoon.

For the first time on our journey, we left Interstate 80 just south of Chicago and took Indiana's highway 30 toward our destination. We both were excited to finally be in our new home state. It was exactly as I had pictured it-very green and very flat with farm after farm, as we passed through Valparaiso, Plymouth, Warsaw, and Columbia City. It seemed like every barn we saw had a basketball hoop on it, which was my first hint that this place truly was the "basketball crazed state" I had been promised by my new boss. Rochelle and I drove slowly through these sleepy yet charming Hoosier towns which made us feel as though we were going back in time to the 1950s. This place sure did not look like Hayward, Milpitas, Oakland, or San Mateo. At 5pm we pulled into the Hospitality Inn in Fort Wayne, a place that WFTW news director Stan Sheets had recommended.

Fortunately, our room at the Hospitality Inn was clean, roomy, and comfortable because this was going to be our home until we found an apartment. It was Memorial Day, and our dinner choices were going to be very limited, so we made our reservations at the hotel dining room for 7pm. I couldn't wait to see the WFTW 6pm news which turned out to be a big disappointment. Stan Sheets, the news director and anchor, did a decent job but had an annoying facial twitch which was very distracting. He was no smooth talking Ted Dorsey, that's for sure. The newscast had very few local stories with film, and a disturbing number of black and white still pictures either full screen or behind Sheets in "chroma-key," which was a blue backdrop used to insert another picture source. At least they had "chroma-key!" Thank-you, Jesus! Stan also did the weather segment, and the weather map looked like it came out of the 1950s. The sports segment was being done temporarily by a general news reporter who must have stumbled over every name in the sports world who happened to be newsworthy that day.

I looked at Rochelle and opined, "That was an awful newscast. What did we get ourselves into? They need a lot of help!"

She snapped back with, "That's why they brought you in, Hot Shot!"

The dining room was packed, which was comforting to the two of us. We did a lot of people-watching to check out our future audience. We were surprised to see a lot of younger couples who looked like us as well as older folks who looked like our parents. We felt confident we could fit in here as we clinked our wine glasses to celebrate our arrival in the "Summit City", as Fort Wayne is often called. It seemed hard to believe that Fort Wayne, Indiana is one of the highest cities in an otherwise flat state, with the local Soap Box Derby Hill topping it off.

After a nice dinner and some unpacking, we watched the ten o'clock news which was nearly a repeat of the 6pm version. In fact, they could have taped the early news and re-run it at ten. Ugh! Tired from our five-day trip, we both dropped off into a deep sleep until we were jolted awake by what sounded like a huge explosion. I really felt I was sent air-borne when the deafening noise hit us. Turned out it was not a terrorist invasion or a Russian nuclear attack, but just an "ordinary"(according to the hotel desk clerk) local thunderstorm. This was going to take some getting used to for a couple of Bay Area kids.

I really wanted to get into the station and check out my new "digs", but our first order of business was to find an apartment as our moving van would arrive in a couple of days. We had given ourselves plenty of time to get settled and do some exploring of our new community before I hit the air on Monday, June 5th. Apartment hunting was made even more difficult that day because it was raining "cats and dogs", and we did not bring any bad weather gear. We made a quick side trip to Hook's Dependable Drugs where we picked up a couple of umbrellas, and off we went to find our new home. Between newspaper ads and guidance by Stan Sheets, we found two decent places priced within our budget, which could accommodate our Thursday move-in date. North of town we liked Sherwood Forest, a large complex with a Robin

Hood theme, and in the area southwest of the station we were impressed with the Colony Lake Apartments. Both had pools and tennis courts and seemed like good fits for us. Ultimately, after deliberating over an excellent lunch at Hall's Gas House, a restaurant recommended to us by Stan, we decided on Colony Lake because it was near Times Corners, a quaint hamlet that seemed to speak to us.

The Thursday move-in to our new furnished apartment was easy because we didn't bring that much personal property from Sacramento. By mid-day we were set up nicely in our new place and I asked Rochelle if she did not mind if I drove into the station to meet my new boss and co-workers. She knew I was anxious to get started even though officially my first day on the air was four days off. The drive to the WFTW-TV studios from our apartment could take anywhere from ten minutes to 30 minutes depending upon the train schedule. I would find that would vary even more during the winter with snow on the ground. It was a scenic trip by way of the graveyard on Lindenwood Avenue and over the railroad tracks.

WFTW-TV, CHANNEL 18

The station was just like I pictured it-looking like a smaller version of KCBG-TV in Sacramento. But unlike my previous place of employment, it was set back in a woodsy area behind a huge grass field. I stopped the car and stared at my new work-place thinking, "This setting looks very nice but how long will I really be here?" I parked my car in the visitor lot and walked in the front door of the station.

"Hi, my name is Nick Cunningham and I'm here to see Stan Sheets in the news department," I announced to the receptionist.

"Nick Cunningham! We've all been looking forward to meeting you, but didn't expect you in until Monday. I'm Vivian the receptionist, or as I like to call myself, the lobby hostess. Let me page Stan for you."

Vivian was an attractive well-dressed woman in her forties who seemed smart and friendly. She made a very good first impression to visitors coming to the front desk of the station. I was also amazed that she knew who I was and when I was expected in town.

Stan greeted me with a warm two-handed shake. "We're so glad you decided to join our team, Nick. We didn't expect you to be in today with the move and all, but let me give you the quick tour before I'll need to get working on the 6pm news. We're also expecting another young reporter to join us Monday. He just graduated from Indiana University, and his name is Tony Silva."

Stan's tour was interesting as I got to meet a number of people I would be working with when I would arrive officially on Monday. Getting introduced to my co-workers now as opposed to next week would make my first day on-air day less hectic, so I was all for it. The station had one all-purpose studio which was being utilized to shoot a clothes commercial with the on-air host of the afternoon movie, Dedrick "DJ" McQueen, who was the main studio voice for the station. He was a long-time broadcast veteran in his early 40s, who had a nice deep voice which he told me was given to him by his 30 year smoking habit. I was told you could hear DJ's voice on radio commercials all over Northeast Indiana and beyond. He was a popular prankster who liked to laugh and didn't take himself too seriously, or anybody else for that matter. He recently caught Stan Sheets by surprise by nailing his shoes to the floor. Sheets would roam around the station in his stocking feet until just before going on the air. McQueen's nailing job put the staff in hysterics when Stan slipped into his shoes and made like the "leaning tower of Pisa," as he tried to dash into the studio. Sheets was a good sport about it and laughed off the episode. "DJ" knew he was the most popular on-air personality at WFTW, so he had no fear of being fired. This guy was going to be fun to be around for sure.

The news room was small with four desks with typewriters on them as well as TV monitors on the walls and an Associated Press teletype machine behind a glass enclosure- a very familiar layout. The AP teletype would go all day and all night with news from around the globe. Beside it was a video version of the AP machine that would send black and white still pictures of major events as well as human interest stories. In Sacramento we rarely used any of the pictures because we preferred network film coverage as well as live coverage of major events. I remember Lloyd Brennan at KCBG wanting to ditch the device in favor of another news film cameraman. My current news director, Stan Sheets, was totally infatuated with the black and white photos with human interest stories, and made a point of asking all the news personnel to mount pictures on easels for future use if they found themselves with free time. I got to thinking that a good newsman should be spending his free time sniffing out stories rather than mounting pictures. So there was a huge pile of mounted back and white pictures stacked up next to the teletype machine, making passage in the small glass enclosed room nearly impossible. A spark from the overheated AP machine could set the whole station ablaze. I was warned that my new boss, while being civil and professional, was quirky-his black and white picture fixation was one of many.

I was introduced to two long-time reporters in the newsroom. Bill Weeks, a short stubby fellow of about 50 with a booming(if not somewhat affected)voice was working on our lead story about a new overpass that was being constructed on Interstate 69 just north of the city. Wally Whiteman, another 50ish looking reporter, was busy mounting pictures. I was told by a member of the film crew later that Wally kept his job by "kissing up" to Sheets, not by his investigative journalism skills. Weeks and Whiteman would serve as anchors for the noon news as well as alternates on weekends, giving the newscasts a 1950s look- not good when the station needed solid ratings to attract sponsors to pay the bills. It was easy to see why the station was a distant second in the ratings department behind the local NBC affiliate, but still ahead of the local ABC affiliate which was in the process of re-tooling its news staff.

Sitting in what was soon to be my sports director's desk was the guy who had managed to mispronounce just about everybody's name in the first sportscast I had seen when we reached Fort Wayne. Gavin Brown was a feature reporter who admittedly knew nothing about sports, but had landed a job with a CBS station in Boston beginning next week. Gavin was friendly and gracious, but anxious to be done with sports and move on to his next position. He even asked for my input on his show. I made sure I correctly pronounced all the newsmakers in his five minute segment as we discussed his content.

Next Stan took me into the film room where the photographers hung out with their old film processor which needed constant service and repairs. The senior member of the crew was an old-timer in his 60s by the name of Howie Hartman, who I later would come to find out never missed an opportunity to criticize and undermine Stan Sheets behind his back. Rob Satterfield, who had his country music going full blast, was another veteran photographer of 60 plus years. Both Hartman and Satterfield had been with the station since it came into being in the 1950s. The third member of the staff was a young Vietnam vet by the name of Rick Cassidy, who had been recently hired. Cassidy was still carrying shrapnel in his legs and the effects of Agent Orange in his lungs, but I would come to appreciate the fact that he was a really hard worker with a great attitude, who never bad-mouthed anybody. He felt he was lucky to be alive, for obvious reasons.

Leaving the station, I was able to navigate my way back to our apartment easily, going over the train tracks and past the graveyard on Lindenwood Avenue. This was going to be a very familiar trip for the foreseeable future. By the time I arrived at our new Ft. Wayne home, Rochelle had already made a couple of new friends, who were barbecuing an early dinner on the patio behind our apartment building. Our new neighbors, Tim Watters, and Joan Mann, were a young couple about our age just a week away from getting married, and with whom we felt we immediately connected. Tim was a Ball State graduate who was recently hired by a local engineering firm, and Joan, a Ft. Wayne native, was a local elementary school teacher. Both had great inside knowledge about stores, restaurants, and activities all over Northeast Indiana, and it turned out that both were huge local sports fans. When they learned that I had just been hired as a sports anchor at WFTW, they started giving me the crash course on Fort Wayne sports history- information that I would find invaluable going forward in my new job. Tim even remarked, to my surprise, that he had seen my picture on a freeway billboard and on milk cartons promoting my entry into the local TV market. They insisted that we join them in sharing their barbecued chicken, and we provided a bottle of 1964 Christian Brothers Cabernet, a going-away present from our Sacramento neighbors, Mike, and Joanne Ferris.

When the evening ended, we exchanged phone numbers, vowing to get together again in the near future. When Rochelle and I got in the elevator to go upstairs to our apartment, I noticed that she had what appeared to be tears in her eyes.

"What are you upset about, Rochelle?" I remarked. "I thought the evening went very well and we've made some great new friends!"

"That's just it, Nick, it was perfect!" was her response. "We've come all this way to a strange place where we have no family or friends, and we stumble upon really nice people like Tim and Joan immediately. After you left and went to the station, I ran into Joan in the laundry room, and we began talking non-stop until Tim started barbecuing shortly before you returned. We found we have so much in common. It's as if this move was meant to be, and I'm just a bit exhausted, emotional and overwhelmed."

I told her about my informative visit to the station, and that I agreed with her completely. So far it appeared that all the pieces were falling into place with our relocation to "America's Heartland." Aside from the fact that I hadn't even been on the air yet, we still had lots of work facing us, such as finding Rochelle a job, locating doctors, dentists, barbers, etc. But it was also very reassuring to me to know that we had new friends downstairs who were ready to share their local knowledge, and to be available to Rochelle in the evenings when I was on the air if a need should arise.

Rochelle went for a job interview in the morning while I found a tennis game at the Colony Lake Courts. A small Fort Wayne construction firm was looking for a part-time bookkeeper, and they were impressed with Rochelle due to her excellent resume and great interview. The only stumbling block to getting the job was Rochelle's request that she work afternoons instead of mornings, so she could more closely conform to my broadcasting schedule. When she came home and we started having lunch, our phone rang. The owner of Eagle Construction made an offer to Rochelle that she could not refuse, and agreed to her afternoon hours.

As we headed out for our Friday afternoon sight-seeing adventure in Fort Wayne, we ran into Tim and Joan in the lobby of our apartment building. They invited us to join the two of them, and the Mann family Saturday at their Kinderhook Lake home for a day at the beach and a barbecue dinner. The Mann's lakefront estate is officially located in Coldwater, Michigan- about an hour north on Interstate 69. We accepted their invitation immediately and were excited about seeing another new state and visiting again with our new friends.

We were up bright and early on Saturday morning as we followed Tim and Joan's directions to Interstate 69. It appeared according to our map that they took us the long way around to the freeway, which we would later find out was on purpose. Right at the on-ramp to I-69 North was a big billboard(visible in both directions) with a picture of me and a caption that said, "New Sports Director Nick Cunningham joins WFTW Channel 18 on the 6pm and 10pm News Monday June 5th!" That was really cool! So cool, in fact, that I almost crashed the car on the side of the road looking at it.

The day on the lake with Tim, Joan and the Mann family was a lot of fun. Joan's teenage younger brother Scott was a self-proclaimed sports nut who not only was familiar with the stars of today, but also the sports heroes of the past. He and I tried to stump each other with trivia questions throughout our visit. After some beach time and a nice cool swim, Joan's parents gave us all a sightseeing trip around the lake on the family boat. We got back just in time as a brief thunderstorm hit the area in the late afternoon. It cleared out just in time for Joan's dad Bill to grill us all some great steaks and some corn cooked in the husks on the B-B-Q. We had never seen that before. Joan's mom Marge added a delicious lemon meringue pie to top off a memorable meal. Rochelle took note of the lemon meringue pie as it was also her mother's specialty back home in California. I think I saw a brief moment of "home sickness" in her eyes.

The Mann's insisted that we spend Saturday night in their guest bedroom. Sunday morning Tim, Scott, Bill, and I played golf while Rochelle, Joan and Marge went exploring in the quaint little town of Coldwater. We really got a taste of true "Midwestern Hospitality," and felt like these folks were going to be our family away from home.

On the ride home Sunday afternoon we could not stop talking about our wonderful weekend. We also took a bit of a detour so we could get another glimpse of my freeway billboard, which reminded us that tomorrow was going to be a big day.

On Monday Rochelle dropped me off at the station right after lunch with a brown bag sandwich packed for dinner. That was to be our weekday schedule for the time being. We would flip-flop lunch and dinner, with lunch being our big meal of the day which we would enjoy together. I checked the AP machine to see what national stories were brewing as well as what was going to be on the CBS network feed at 4pm. Nothing major was going on that day nationally, other than a Cubs-Reds game at Wrigley Field, so I asked Stan Sheets if he knew of a local feature story I could do. His eyes lit up and he said, "I have just the thing! A local realtor in town by the name of Floyd Cotton just won the National Senior Trap Shooting Title last week in Louisville. He has a big ranch with his own shooting range up in Auburn about 40 minutes away. I think the sales department has his private phone number because he has run real estate commercials on our station. Let's go see Colin Jamison, our sales manager, who can get you that information."

Colin was a smartly dressed fellow of about 45, who greeted us both warmly. "Nice to meet you, Nick. We've all been looking forward to your arrival here. You look like a good fit for our sports department," were his encouraging words. Stan explained that we were trying to reach Floyd Cotton, and Colin checked the rolodex on his desk where he found Cotton's private home phone number.

"You'll like this guy, Nick. He's been a real estate success story in the greater Fort Wayne Area since the 1930s. He's done it the right way too-shows up on time, tells the truth, and treats people fairly. You'll see the Cotton Realty signs everywhere. Floyd is also a wizard with that shotgun of his."

After thanking both Stan and Colin for their help, I called Floyd Cotton, who said he would be delighted to meet me at his ranch at 3pm. Stan assigned film cameraman Howie Hartman to me for the afternoon, assuring me that Hartman knew how to find the Cotton Ranch in Auburn. On the way up Howie asked me if I wanted to stop for lunch, and that it was going to be free because he had a company credit card. I remarked that I was not hungry, and I just wanted to get the story put together in time for the 6pm news. Howie turned and gave me a look which said, "This California hot shot is going to have me working too hard!"

As we pulled into the circular driveway of the Cotton estate, Floyd was there to greet us, bellowing, "When you fellas say 3pm you mean it!"

Howie smiled at him and shot back "We're in the TV news business. We have to be on time." It turns out Hartman, who took care of the introductions, knew Floyd as he had done some camera work for him during a commercial filming session earlier in the year. We set up for the interview right on Cotton's front porch overlooking his huge corn field.

Not knowing a thing about trap shooting, I asked a couple of general questions. Floyd, who was very relaxed on camera, gave me several long and descriptive answers, helping my cause immeasurably. I didn't want to try to come up with 20 questions on this subject with a camera shy, inarticulate news source. This guy with the booming voice was just the opposite, as well as being modest and friendly.

"You know, you guys are the first Fort Wayne TV station to do a story on me since I won the title last week," Cotton remarked as he led us to his shooting range, "and that includes my old buddy, Herman Yates."

Yates had been a fixture in Fort Wayne sports broadcasting since the early 1950s, and had been doing the play-by-play of the Indiana High School Basketball Tournament since the 1940s when it was just on radio. Not only was Yates the Indiana

Sportscaster of the Year on ten different occasions, but he was also the general manager and sports anchor of our competing TV station, the ratings leader-WKHG-TV, Channel 35. Yates was going to be the guy I was going to go up against in the nightly news. My friends at KCBG in Sacramento had warned me that I would be competing with a sportscasting legend, so I had to plan my strategy carefully. I would pick out stories that Yates wouldn't take the time to cover, like the champion trap shooter, whose real estate commercials also ran on Yates' station. I also knew I had to appeal to the younger audience if I was going to cut into his ratings' advantage. It would be a lot more fun being "David" rather than "Goliath."

Cotton's shooting range was behind his barn about 150 yards from his home. This is where we would get some film of him demonstrating his skills with his shotgun. Floyd even had his own clay pigeon launching machine which he could activate with one hand while he cradled his gun in the other. The guy was amazing, particularly for someone in his mid-70s, hitting ten clay pigeons without a miss as we filmed. Then he turned to me, handing me his 12-gauge shotgun, and said, "Why don't you give it a try, Nick?"

This sudden turn of events had really caught me by surprise. I had never fired a shotgun in my life. I remember shooting a 22 caliber rifle at Friendly Pines summer camp as a ten year old, but this was quite different. "Just yell 'pull' Nick, and I'll release the pigeon," Cotton said as he showed me how to position myself with his gun against my shoulder, and warned me about the "kick" of his 12-gauge. Howie Hartman thought this event was going to be some "good theater" and got his camera rolling. I meekly gave the command, not knowing what to expect, and Cotton released the target. I raised the gun and fired-Pow! To the shock of all of us, mostly me, I hit the clay pigeon. Floyd explodes with "Wow, great shot, Nick!"

I sheepishly said, "Trust me, that was really beginner's luck." I proved it by missing all of his remaining nine targets, much to the delight of Howie, who filmed it all.

We thanked Floyd for being available on short notice and headed back to the station in hopes of putting a nice story together for my first show. "If I can get this in the processor by 4:15, we have a shot at getting it on the 6 o'clock. If not, it will have to be the late news," Howie explained as he picked up speed in the WFTW-TV van. Clearly my cameraman had some enthusiasm for this story too as we came tearing into the station parking lot at 4:10, taking the turn off State Street on two wheels. Howie and I were determined to get this story in the 6pm news broadcast.

The race was on to put together my 6pm show, as I had to write and produce the entire four to five minute segment, which I really wanted to be eye-catching on my first night on the air in the Fort Wayne market. I had some network video of the Cubs 3-1 win over the Reds, thanks to a Ron Santo home run and Milt Pappas' complete game pitching performance, along with some film of the high school playoff baseball game between Bishop Luers and Columbia City. I would lead with the Cubs story, followed by the prep baseball, then I would read a couple of sports news items with visuals behind me to support my content. I would finish with my Floyd Cotton piece, which Howie promised would make it in time. My thought on the Cotton story was to do a voice over lead-in to show the Cotton Ranch and shooting range, then go into the interview with Floyd, cutting in with b-roll of him hitting all the clay pigeons. I would finish with me hitting the first clay pigeon and missing all the rest. My feeling was that my audience would like the fact that I was actually getting involved in the story that I was reporting on. I didn't realize it at the time, but that was the inspiration for my "Who Can Beat Nick?" series of sports stories where I would compete against local high school tennis stars-boys and girls, bowl with the women's city champ, and numerous other future challenges. On one occasion, I must have lost my mind, and wrestled a 600 pound bear in front of 5000 hockey fans, most of whom were pulling for the bear(more on that story later). If I was going to cut into Herman Yates' audience at WKHG I was going to have to do some things I knew he couldn't or wouldn't do.

By 5:15pm, I had my show put together, thanks to Howie Hartman, and met with the studio director Steve Watson for the first time. Watson was a smart young guy with a calm demeanor who didn't look too much older than me. He also was a big sports fan who immediately understood the content and pacing of my 4 ½ minute segment. Steve and I thought a lot alike and hit it off right from the start.

By 5:30pm, I went to the dressing room to make sure my tie was straight, and my hair was presentable. I ran into Tony Silva, the new reporter just hired out of Indiana University, who was also starting his first day on the job. We agreed to meet after the 6pm News and get a bite to eat together.

I walked into the studio at about 5:50pm and introduced myself to the studio cameraman, Ralph Beevor and Gary Hausman, who both had been with WFTW for several years. We needed to get in our positions for the headlines with our microphones checked prior to going on the air. The crew checked mine with plenty of time to spare, but where was Stan Sheets, the anchor? We were going to be on the air in one minute! Suddenly Stan burst into the studio, grabbed his mic, said "test 1,2,3" and was ready to go. Gary Hausman, who doubled as the floor director, bellowed, "Stand by in the studio!"

The red light on the camera came on and Gary pointed his finger at Stan who said, "Thousands flee their homes due to toxic chemical spill in Topeka!"

Ralph Beevor then cued me and I said, "Pappas pitches another gem at Wrigley, but was it enough for a Cub victory?"

Then back to Stan who said, "Those stories and more coming up next on the Channel 18 6 o'clock News."

My 6pm sports segment went well, but I mispronounced several of the prep baseball players' names(got a phone call from a parent), and I was a little behind the action in my narration of the playoff game highlights. But the kicker at the end of my segment, the Floyd Cotton piece, appeared to be very well received. The studio crew howled when they saw Floyd's reaction when I hit the clay pigeon the first time. I was going to have to repeat this story, or at least part of it, on the 10pm News.

After the news I got a couple of nice phone calls from viewers who enjoyed my show, and liked the fact that I literally got actively involved with my sports story. My favorite call came from Rochelle who tried to disguise her voice by saying, "Who is the new sexy sports guy from California?" I recognized her voice immediately, and told her the "new sports guy from California was the man of her dreams, whom she needed to pick up after the news." We shared a laugh and agreed that the Floyd Cotton story was an "attention getter," and should make a good impression with new viewers.

Tony Silva grabbed a sandwich at the deli down the street and met me and my brown bag in one of the sales department's conference rooms for dinner. He had grown up in Gary, Indiana where his family owned and operated a very successful Mexican restaurant. The Silva family consisting of mom, dad, Tony and his three brothers and two sisters, who had their hands on every aspect of the restaurant business. Tony's mom, Maria, for whom the restaurant "Maria's" is named, is the head chef, and the kids assist in the kitchen, wait tables, and handle the cash register. Antonio, Tony's dad, a former WWII tank gunner in General George Patton's 3rd army, is in charge of the books and buying supplies. When Tony graduated with a degree in broadcast journalism from Indiana University in May, he became the first of his family (but not the last) to obtain a college diploma. Having lived in the

Hoosier state his entire life and being a huge sports fan, he was going to be invaluable to me as a resource for Indiana sports history in general, but particularly the high school scene. Although we came from different backgrounds and different places in the country, Tony and I immediately realized how much we did have in common the more we talked. We both came from supportive families, our dads were both WWII vets, our moms were both gourmet cooks, and our college broadcasting experiences at SJSU and I-U were very similar.

"Do you think they brought us in here so they could look a bit younger on the air?" I remarked jokingly.

"It's no wonder they are struggling in the ratings," he responded. "They haven't been able to get the younger audience. You're right, Nick, that's why you and I are here. Sheets had me do an on-camera "stand-up" on the freeway overpass story that Bill Weeks has been working on for months." Tony continued, "It had to piss off Weeks, but I think they wanted to work my face into the news on my first day on the job."

"What do you think of the newsroom?" I asked.

"I think it isn't much better than the I-U radio station, which surprises me," he added. "Sheets had me mounting black and white photos from that old AP machine most of the afternoon. I would've much preferred to be out in the field doing a lot more work than just the freeway overpass stand-up. By the way, have you met Stan's wife, Jimmi?"

"No Tony, I haven't had the pleasure, but I was warned by my Sacramento buddies that she was a bit odd."

"I was warned too," Silva chuckled. "But I didn't expect to get my ass grabbed on the first day on the job."

We both had a good belly laugh and agreed to meet as often as we could to share stories and observations regarding our new jobs and co-workers. I had been advised that Stan's wife Jimmi had taken a liking to the previous weekend sports anchor. The rumor was that they had an affair which caused his firing and an elimination of the position altogether. In the fall, the plan was to move me from Monday through Friday to Tuesday through Saturday because of the local prep sports scene as well as college football. For now, WFTW was going to pay me overtime to work every other Saturday until early September.

Tony and I could not stop talking for over 90 minutes. We touched on our families, our college broadcasting experiences, and how we ended up together at Channel 18. I almost forgot that I was supposed to meet "DJ" McQueen at 8:15pm so he could show me how to record the booth announcements. Apparently, WFTW wanted another voice in addition to McQueen's smooth baritone approach saying "WFTW, Channel 18, Fort Wayne." This was an annoying job between newscasts, as it kept me away from going out in the field for evening stories. I eventually complained to Stan about it, and he said he would take it up with the general manager, but never did. So, after I had received several compliments from management on my sports segments, I came up with my own plan for the booth work. If I had to do it, then I was going to do it with my impersonations of John Wayne and rock and roll Disc Jockey Casey Kasem.

For a week I alternated between Wayne and Kasem and NOBODY said one word to me. Finally, Stan called me into his office and said that the station has decided to take me off the booth assignment so I could concentrate on producing my show. Apologies to John Wayne and Casey Kasem. I also had to apologize to McQueen who would then have to pick up the extra duty and be paid handsomely. "DJ" was fine with the additional booth work, and he even thanked me. "No problem Nick, I can work five extra minutes and get paid for two hours of overtime."

Between time spent with my new pals, Silva and McQueen, I was left with very little time to prepare for the 10pm

News. Fortunately, I did have plenty of baseball scores both from the majors and the local high school regionals. I also re-used a shortened version of my Floyd Cotton story. The show went fine except for the fact that cameraman Ralph Beevor had his dog, Archie, in the studio, who started barking when he heard the background music to my baseball scoreboard. The viewer at home might have thought that the barking was part of the production to my show because Archie really cut loose when I gave the winning score for the Carroll Bulldogs. I couldn't resist the comment, "Listen to the Bulldogs celebrate their 6-3 win over Homestead!" Bark away, Archie!

My first week on the job was all about digging out local stories, but with the high school year ending there was very little to report on from the prep scene. There was a local youth basketball camp that was run by a former high school and college hero, Bobby Short. He had led Fort Wayne's Central High School to the 1964 state finals only to foul out on a controversial call in the final seconds, and watch his team lose to East Chicago Washington, 50-49. For eight years all the local prep basketball fans could talk about was the charging foul called on Short that deprived Fort Wayne of a state champion. To Bobby's credit, he was never bitter, and went on to become an All-American at New Mexico State University, leading the Aggies into the NCAA Basketball Tournament. After graduation and a brief stint in the NBA, he returned to his hometown to become a teacher and coach. I would come to find out that most of the top prep basketball players in the area had honed their skills at Short's camp. Bobby, an African-American, didn't just attract inner-city kids to his camp, but also "country" white hoopsters would attend as well. In addition to giving a very good interview, he was helpful in giving me a preview of what the 1972-73 high school basketball season was going to be like.

"Just you wait," he warned. "This place will go bananas when the state tournament begins again next February. If a local team finally wins, it will be like Jesus Christ himself walking across the Maumee River!"

When I used that sound bite on the air it lit up the switchboard with both positive and negative comments. I knew it would be something that Herman Yates of Channel 35 would not run on his show. Despite the fact that the quote spiced up my sports segment, I was cautioned by General Manager Whitney Thompson not to offend the local religious community.

The high profile sports event each year in Fort Wayne, outside of the state basketball tournament, was the Sons of the Summit City Foundation Celebrity Golf Tournament, which occurred in late June. This was a three day party featuring local and national celebrities, which culminated in an 18 hole golf match between two touring PGA pros followed by the presentation of the "Man of the Year" award, given to a deserving current or former Indiana resident. In 1972, the award went to astronaut Neil Armstrong, who grew up in Wapakoneta, Ohio, but spent his collegiate years at Purdue University in the Hoosier state. The featured golf match pitted good friends Jerry Heard against the game's rising star, Johnny Miller. I was very familiar with Miller, who like myself was a former San Francisco Bay Area resident. I had watched him perform as an 18-year old from Lincoln High School in the 1966 U.S. Open at the nearby Olympic Club. The master of ceremonies for this event was comedian Phil Harris, who had a drink in his hand and a lady on his arm for the entire time. He even called Bing Crosby at his home in Hillsborough, California, woke him up from a nap, and put him on speaker "live" for the entire dinner crowd of several hundred folks. Crosby wasn't too thrilled about it either, especially when Harris invited Bing to sing "Blue Moon" with him.

The Sons of the Summit City Foundation had a party that was very popular among former athletes and minor show business celebs, mainly because of the free booze and lodging as well as the "companionship," and I don't mean with each other. Bill Spruett, who ran a local advertising agency, also had an "unofficial" escort service which provided "dates" for the incoming visitors. No question about it-the draw for this event was booze, sex, socializing, and golf, in no particular order. I was told that when two of Spruett's ladies presented themselves to Johnny Miller and Jerry Heard the two golfers told them that they were happily married and declined intimate companionship, but they wouldn't mind playing pool with them (to justify the fees that Spruett had paid the ladies in advance). Both Heard and Miller "ate up" our country club golf course, shooting a pair of six under par 66s, much to the delight of a huge throng of fans following them around. Afterward, I did interviews with them both, remarking to Miller that my Burlingame High classmate, Charles "Chuck" Mack, had once tied him for the first round lead in a junior 2-day tournament at Pebble Beach. Johnny remembered Chuck and said, "We were hot that day, and both shot 68's on a really tough course. The next day it was windy and foggy, and our scores skyrocketed." What the modest soon-to-be golfing legend didn't say was that he won that junior tournament easily, a harbinger of a great PGA career to follow.

A year later I was invited to the Sons of the Summit City Foundation awards dinner. A late arriving guest plopped himself right down next to me and introduced himself.

"Hi Nick, I've become a big fan of yours and watch you every night. My name is Dan Quayle, and I'm with the Huntington Herald Press," he said, holding out his hand.

"Thanks Dan. It's nice to meet you," I remarked. "I'm glad that we are coming through loud and clear in Huntington."

"I'm not too informed on the sports news," he went on. "Do you mind me asking who's that bald fellow sitting across from us?"

I whispered softly, "It's Charlie Finley from Laporte, Indiana, the owner of the World Champion Oakland A's, and the man we are about to honor as Indiana's Man of the Year."

Quayle sheepishly said, "Oh, I guess I should've done my homework before I came to this event. It's fortunate that I have you sitting here to tell me who's who."

We both quietly chuckled. It didn't say much for his journalistic skills if he didn't know who Charlie Finley was. Come to think of it, it didn't say much for my communication skills either. This was a guy who supposedly watched me every night, worked for an Indiana newspaper, and he didn't recognize one of biggest names in Hoosier sports for 1973. Who knew that Huntington's Dan Quayle, the man who would become the Vice President in 1988, was sitting right next to me?

WRIGLEY FIELD

One of my next exciting broadcasting experiences during those first two months on the job was the opportunity to take a trip to Wrigley Field to see my beloved Chicago Cubs. I fell in love with the Cubs when I lived in Phoenix in the late 50s and the team had spring training in Arizona. Photographer Howie Hartman and I went up to Chicago on a Saturday in July to see the Cubs take on the Dodgers. There were a couple of interviews I knew I had to get-Ernie Banks of the Cubs, my favorite player growing up, and broadcaster Vin Scully of the Dodgers, who I thought was the best in the business. In fact, it was listening to Scully's broadcasts that made me want to go into his field. The other hot persona of the day was Cubs' centerfielder Rick Monday, who, in the middle of a game, recently stopped a war protester from burning the American flag in the outfield at Wrigley. Howie and I got some good interviews from Banks, Monday, and several other players. But I let time slip away prior to the first pitch of the game, and was unable to interview my favorite broadcasting legend. I knew I had to make an effort to tell him how much I have admired his work.

I waited for Vinny to sign off his pre-game show on the field, and went right up to him and said, "Mr. Scully, my name is Nick Cunningham, and I am the sports director for WFTW in Fort Wayne, Indiana. I just want to say that listening to your Dodger radio broadcasts convinced me to go into this business. You have been a true inspiration to me as well as many other young broadcasters, and we are all so very grateful."

"Thank-you, Nick, for those kind words," was his response. "I wish I had more time to talk to you, but I have to get to the press box in two minutes to go on the air. I'm sure you understand. And, by the way, call me Vin." I was definitely starstruck. Vin Scully was and still is the "Holy Grail" for all sports broadcasters and journalists.

Another fun event during the summer of 1972 was the Fort Wayne City Tennis Tournament at Swinney Park, in which I was excited to play. Our Sales Manager, Colin Jamison, knowing I was going to be playing in the tournament, suggested I use my appearance as a kick-off for my "Who Can Beat Nick?" feature in my sports show. He reminded me how well the audience responded when I took part in trap shooting with realtor Floyd Cotton on my very first show. Colin's idea, as a way to cut into Herman Yates Channel 35 sports audience, was that I actually participate and compete in some of the events I covered-something that Yates wouldn't do. So, thanks to a very bright sales manager, "Who Can Beat Nick?" was born.

With the cameras running, I took on a local insurance executive by the name of Dan Coats in the first round. He was a good player who was not fazed by the cameras at all, but I was able to win in straight sets. Little did I know at the time that this was the same Dan Coats who would later become a United States Senator, an Ambassador to Germany, and the National Intelligence Director.

I had my confidence dashed in the second round when I ran into A.D. Webster, who was to become one of my best friends. Webster, who relished the camera coverage, showed everyone "Who Can Beat Nick?" by taking me out in three hard-fought sets. My TV audience loved the feature in great part because I lost. That seemed to give me more credibility with my viewers, who realized that this was not a "set-up," and was, in fact, real.

As Californians, Rochelle and I were very familiar with earthquakes, but had no idea about the severity and danger of tornadoes. We were told that Fort Wayne was protected by an old Indian legend that maintained that a tornado would never strike where three rivers converged, precisely where our new home town was located. July of 1972 changed the legend forever, as tornadoes wreaked havoc on Fort Wayne and the surrounding area. It was very frightening as we in the newsroom listened to the police, state troopers, and fire fighters on their radio bands describing the twisters as they touched down. When we saw the news film showing the extent of the damage, we couldn't believe that there was only one fatality and fewer than 50 injuries. In that 1972 series of storms, tornado insurance was either unavailable or far too expensive for many local residents who climbed out of their cellars to find that their homes were gone. WFTW-TV was knocked off the air for almost 48 hours, but nearly all of us at Channel 18 were out in the field filming the damage and interviewing the survivors. My young California wife and I, while a bit rattled by the tornado season, felt very lucky to get through it unscathed.

The summer was racing by and Rochelle and I were settling into a routine with her dropping me off at the station on her way to work around 1pm. Then she would come and pick me up at 10:30pm (or 11:30pm in the winter months) after my last show, having to drive by the graveyard on Lindenwood Avenue. After the graveyard, Rochelle sometimes would be stuck for long periods in the dark at a railroad crossing while an endless freight train passed by. Neither one of us was comfortable with that situation so within six months we would buy a new car, a small Datsun "super-sport" with a four-speed stick shift. I was advised to get a stick shift because of slick driving conditions on snow and ice, an experience I had never faced before.

MARK SPITZ

In September, the 1972 Munich Olympics captured the headlines, not so much for the athletes and their events, but for what became known tragically as the "Munich Massacre." A terrorist organization calling itself "Black September" captured and later executed eleven Israeli athletes and one West German policeman during a failed rescue mission. So, understandably, this terrible event seemed to make the amazing 7-gold medal performance of swimmer Mark Spitz from my old hometown of Sacramento, California merely a footnote in history.

Shortly after the Games ended, my phone rang at Channel 18.

"Hey, Nick, it's Cal Samuels in Sacramento. Are you anywhere near Warsaw, Indiana? Because if you are, I've got a hot tip for you. It might get you a network story."

"Hi, Cal! Great to hear from you. Warsaw is about an hour away from Fort Wayne. Tell me about the hot tip!"

Samuels went on to explain that Spitz was making a personal appearance in 24 hours at a dedication of a Warsaw public pool, which was to be named in his honor. I remembered that Cal was good friends with the Olympian's coach Sherm Chavoor, who worked with Mark recently in Sacramento while he trained for the 1972 Munich Games. Chavoor had apparently told Cal about the appearance which Spitz, who is Jewish, wanted to be "under the radar" due to security concerns relating to recent events. After he gave me the time and place, I thanked Cal and promised I would send him my film interview with Spitz, if he didn't get it from the CBS network first. I was excited!

The next day photographer Rob Satterfield picked me up at 10am so we could be at the Warsaw pool in plenty of time for the noon celebrity ceremony. Rob was thrilled to be making the trip as his favorite 50,000 watt country music radio station, "WPIG, the Country Top Forty," was based in Warsaw. I must have heard Hank Williams' version of "Your Cheatin' Heart" at least ten times on the trip. The WPIG disc jockey was playing requests, and some nut case from nearby Plymouth kept calling and requesting that same Hank Williams song, so they played it over and over and over.

When we arrived at the pool before the dedication, we started to set up our cameras, and we were immediately confronted by Ross Gannon, Spitz's publicist. Gannon seemed surprised to see us and instructed us that Spitz "would not be answering any questions about the Munich Massacre, but would be happy to talk about the pool dedication and the sport of swimming in general." I acknowledged his instructions with a nod and then winked at Satterfield. My ace- in- the- hole for getting Spitz to talk about Munich was Cal Samuels and his relationship with Mark's coach. We were the only TV station at this event, and I was not going to lose a chance to talk to this Olympic champion about what really mattered to our viewers, and the American public in general.

When I introduced myself to Spitz it was like looking in the mirror. The two of us looked very much alike, dark hair and moustache, about the same height and weight. I remember Cal Samuels telling me that we looked like brothers. Interestingly, Spitz's girlfriend at the time, Susan Weiner, had a startling resemblance to Rochelle, which led to some unexpected benefits. When we visited a bar at Carmel by the Sea in California several years later, the bartender was convinced that I was Spitz and Rochelle was Susan, despite our denials. He provided free drinks for the evening, and a bottle of very expensive champagne, over our weakening objections.

"Mark, you made us all proud in Munich with your seven-gold medal performance," I bellowed. "Cal Samuels and your Coach Sherm Chavoor tipped us off about today. Until four months ago I worked with Cal in Sacramento at KCBG-TV."

He gave me a long stare and then said, "I remember you! You were Cal's assistant and did that funny story about the little league baseball players."

"That's right! 'Learn it From the Pros' was the feature you are referring to."

I knew I was going to get my "Munich" interview now despite the instructions from Spitz's publicist, but I needed to act quickly. I signaled photographer Rob Satterfield to roll, and we began the interview talking about the easy stuff, the Warsaw Pool dedication. He explained that it should have been back in May, but that training for the '72 Games had to take precedence. Mark wanted it to be known that he was making the appearance on behalf of Nike which was trying to encourage more youngsters to take part in competitive swimming. I don't know if Mark, who was a California resident, realized that by early September most public pools in Indiana are closed.

With the camera still rolling, I switched gears and asked him if he "feared for his own life when the Black September terrorists kidnapped and ultimately killed the Israeli athletes." Spitz hesitated, but then said "Yes," and launched into a spell-binding story that sounded like a script from a James Bond movie. He explained that he followed the hostage taking with great concern on TV, but was so exhausted from his competition that he went to bed, knowing the West German police had guards on every floor of his hotel. He was awakened in the middle of the night by a pounding on his hotel room door. It was a heavily armed United

States Marine saying it's time to go-NOW. Mark threw on his clothes and followed the Marine to a waiting car which he was told would take him to the airport. Mark said he and his new Marine friends changed cars three times on the way to the airport, where he would catch a plane to London. He was then told about the failed rescue mission and the deaths of the Israelis. The U.S State Department felt Mark might also be a target and decided to act quickly to protect him.

Spitz said that he had been scheduled to meet his father that next day in Stuttgart, Germany, where he was going to be presented a new Mercedes Benz, in an elaborate ceremony honoring his Olympic performance. He was surprised and relieved to know that West German Chancellor Willy Brandt sent his private helicopter to pick up Spitz's father in Stuttgart and deliver him to London to link up with Mark. From there Spitz and his dad hopped on a jet at Heathrow full of Marines and State Department personnel, and flew directly to Los Angeles. Mark could not have been more appreciative of the actions of the U.S. Marines, the State Department and Willy Brandt.

Wow! We had a story! I looked over at Satterfield who gave me a thumbs-up, indicating he got it all on film. After thanking Mark Spitz and his publicist, I told Rob to get some quick footage of the Warsaw ceremony and shoot a "stand-up" of me doing a sign-off in front of the facility in case we made network news. "This is Nick Cunningham reporting for CBS News in Warsaw, Indiana." We still had an hour drive to the station, and it was after 1pm, so we needed to get going. I wanted to have plenty of time to put this story together so it would have the greatest impact.

Even with Hank Williams and Buck Owens music blaring from the radio accompanied by Rob Satterfield's off-key vocal enhancement, I was able to put my thoughts together on my 6pm news piece. I would do a voice-over film of the dedication ceremony explaining why Spitz was in Warsaw leading into my interview with the Olympic champion. I wanted my viewers to see

Mark telling his compelling story in his own words without interruption, all two minutes' worth. I would leave in my follow-up question, "When did you feel safe?" This would make it harder for CBS to edit me out should they want to use all or part of it. Mark said that he didn't feel completely safe until he was on American soil. He even quoted Dorothy from the Wizard of Oz movie saying, "There's no place like home!" which I felt was a nice dramatic exclamation point at the end of the piece.

When we got back to WFTW, I went right into Stan Sheets' office, told him about the mind-blowing interview, and said I needed extra time.

"I think we lead the 6pm news with it!" were Stan's supportive words. "Let's go with a five minute segment at the top, leaving us about two to three minutes to discuss how you got the story and your thoughts on meeting Spitz. I can plug your interview during my headline portion of the Fran Bologna Show in about an hour." For years, Fran had been hosting a popular local afternoon talk show on Channel 18, the only one of its kind in the market.

"That's great, Stan!" I responded enthusiastically. "Wait until you see this interview when Rob gets it out of the processor! I have a couple of baseball scores and some college football news, but I think I will need only about three minutes for the actual sports segment. The Spitz film lead will probably run about two and a half minutes, which will include my voice-over."

The whole station was "abuzz" about my interview with the Olympic champ after my news director headlined it during Fran's show. But by 4pm, I was starting to get nervous because I had not received word from Satterfield that the film was out of the processor and ready to edit. I could not wait any longer, so I went back to the film room where I was greeted by Chief Photographer Howie Hartman.

"Oh Shit, Nick! You are not going to like what I am going to tell you," he said forebodingly. "The chemical balance is on the fritz in this old processor, and it essentially ate your interview. Rob, who is losing his mind over this, was just about to go down the hall to tell you. I am really sorry. We told Sheets weeks ago that this might happen."

I was stunned and speechless, but I had a show to put together, minus my lead story. When I told Stan what had happened, he could not hold back his anger and disappointment .

"I have been telling Whitney about that damn processor for weeks, and now it bites us in the ass at the worst possible time! He's been waiting for approval from the Corinthian boys in New York in order to buy a new one. "

I had no doubt that both my news director and my general manager had appealed to the station owners to replace the old processor. My friends at KCBG in Sacramento were constantly complaining about Corinthian's lack of responsiveness in replacing the old equipment, and their lack of trust in their general managers to make the purchases on their own. Corinthian owned five TV stations nationwide, including Fort Wayne, Sacramento, Tulsa, Houston, and Indianapolis, all apparently with dated equipment and pissed off employees.

"Nick, we're going to make lemonade out of lemons," Sheets announced." I still want to lead the newscast with you and I talking about that compelling Spitz interview, and we're going to be honest with the audience about why we don't have the film. We deal with the unexpected in the TV business, and sometimes technology just F—king fails. Your film was not the only victim of our processor. We also lost all of our Lima tornado damage footage that Howie shot this afternoon. Tonight our newscast is going to look like the 1950s, but our audience is going to know why."

I admired Stan for his no-nonsense, straightforward attitude. But I wasn't so sure that the "Boys in New York" would appreciate that much honesty if they got word that we shared our "processor fiasco" story with the audience.

While Sheets was a quirky fellow, he was a good, honest newsman who knew his audience. Our show that night, without any local film, went quite well and the viewers appreciated it, as did several local TV critics. Stan, doing his Edward R. Murrow impersonation, interviewed me at the top of the newscast and I was able to relay much of what Mark Spitz told me. I even got a call from several newspaper reporters who used some of my quotes in their articles the next day, but I could not hide my disappointment at the lost opportunity. It hurt even more two days later, when ABC-TV's Howard Cosell got Mark to tell the same story on the "Wide World of Sports."

After our 6pm news, I called Cal Samuels in Sacramento and told him about the lost film in the processor, knowing it probably would send him into orbit. Cal did not disappoint, firing off a profane rant that must have incorporated all the noun, verb, adverb, and adjective forms of our favorite cuss words. The cleaned-up version of Cal's comments was that Corinthian Broadcasting, the entity which owned us both, was made up of a bunch of "know-nothing, cheap bastards," to use his less-offensive words.

While driving home after the late news, I thought back to when I lost the Reno job, followed by the shady San Antonio offer that I turned down, which led to the opportunity in Fort Wayne. I knew when I went into the broadcast business that there would be many high and low moments that I could not control. I would have to learn patience from my wife Rochelle, who knew all about my disappointment at the lost Spitz interview. She reminded me that, as we have seen from the past, there would likely be other big story opportunities in our up-and-down TV world.

"Thanks Rochelle. I know you're probably right," I responded, "but it was such a letdown to lose this opportunity to present this interview, particularly when the stars seemed to line up for me with the tip from Cal. We're all trying so hard to cut into Channel 35's ratings. It will be interesting to see what happens when the rating books come out in November."

NOTRE DAME

Because of our Northeast Indiana location, we had big-time college football games at Purdue, Ohio State, Michigan, Michigan State and Notre Dame within easy driving distance. Purdue even sent me two season tickets and two press passes for every game. Rochelle and I would take the Watters to a couple of games. The ladies would get the 50-yard line seats and Tim and I would be in the press box where no women were allowed (except for the pretty coeds serving food and beverages).

In the middle of October I got a call from my old San Jose State broadcast partner Hank Ramsey, who said he would love to fly into Fort Wayne for a visit. He indicated that he would really enjoy a Notre Dame football game. I called the Sports Information Director at Notre Dame, Roger Valdiserri, and arranged to get two press passes and two locker room passes. I knew Hank would bring his portable recorder so he could get some interviews for his radio show at KXRS in San Jose.

When Hank flew in Friday night Rochelle picked him up at Baer Field International Airport in Fort Wayne and brought him directly to the station so he could watch my show in the studio. It was fun to introduce my college roommate to my new friends and co-workers at Channel 18. The weekend figured to be a sports bonanza as it featured the opening of the World Series in Cincinnati between the Reds and the Oakland A's, as well as college football on Saturday and the NFL on Sunday. It was my weekend to do the Saturday Sports, but Tony Silva agreed to trade shifts with me so Hank and I could enjoy the visit and have that day free. Tony and I would normally alternate every other Saturday doing the sports segment on the news, both getting paid overtime to do it.

It was an unseasonably warm day in South Bend on the campus of Notre Dame, perhaps the college football center of the earth. The famous "glowing" Golden Dome, bathed in sunlight, and the prominent "Touchdown Jesus" were even more impressive in person than they were on television. As Hank and I walked through the campus on the way to the stadium, we could see that the place was rocking with excitement and anticipation. The opponent for the "Fighting Irish" that day would be a mediocre Pittsburgh Panther University squad that had no idea what was in store for them. I know we didn't either when we took our seats in the stadium press box of this historic venue. The Panther team filed in first to a thunderous chorus of "boos," with Irish fans dressed as leprechauns brandishing signs proclaiming that "the Panthers suck" and my personal favorite, "Irish stew needs Panther meat!"

Then the Notre Dame team led by quarterback Tom Clements, emerged from the tunnel in the endzone and the place went crazy with the band playing the legendary fight song " bom-bom-bom, bub-bom, bub-bom." Hank and I exchanged worried glances as we literally felt the whole place rocking. We had our fingers crossed that this old press box was going to hold together. The two of us had covered a lot of sporting events for a couple of broadcasters in their late 20s, but we had never seen anything quite as intense or as intimidating as this. The Pittsburgh team had to feel like gladiators from ancient Rome being thrown to the lions. They played like it too, as Notre Dame hammered them 42-16. The score was 35-16 late in the fourth quarter when the Irish, instead of running out the clock and ending the game, decided to throw the ball and get another, seemingly unnecessary, touchdown. Hank and I realized that Notre Dame Coach Ara Parseghian, who was roundly criticized for playing for a tie against Michigan State in 1966, was very conscious of the ranking of his undefeated team. To beat Pitt decisively would help his case for being ranked number one in the nation. We were to find out that the Panther coaching staff, fans, and Pittsburgh press were extremely angry with Parseghian for "running up the score."

We made our way to the locker room after the game to hear the Notre Dame coach address the media, and to give Hank a chance to get an interview with Parseghian. The first question was asked by Drew Gallaway, the sports editor of the Pittsburgh University student newspaper, who was proudly wearing his identification badge.

"Coach, you were up 35-16 with less than 5 minutes to play in the game and you elected to pass the football," the young editor opined. "Are the rankings so important that you have to humiliate an out-manned opponent?"

Parseghian exploded in front of all of us, players, press, and several local "men of the cloth."

"Who the hell is this guy Roger?" Ara bellowed as he turned to the Notre Dame Sports Information Director Roger Valdiserri. "How did he get in here? He's just a kid who obviously doesn't know a f--king thing about football!"

The coach continued his rant in front of his stunned audience as Hank turned on his recorder. I wished I had brought my own film crew.

"I am sick and tired of this God damn bullshit I get every week from people who don't understand the game! I will say this one more time for you press folks who didn't hear me two weeks ago. This is not about the rankings. My back-up players deserve a chance to play, and I need to see who I can call upon, should my starters go down. I did not recruit them to take a damn knee and run out the clock. Jesus Christ, how many times do I have to say this?"

The silence in the room was so deafening you could hear a pin drop until my courageous friend Hank stepped up with his portable tape recorder with a large KXRS radio label on it.

"Coach, overall how would you rate your team's performance today?" Ramsey politely asked.

The paranoid and confused coach stared at Hank's badge that said WFTW-TV Fort Wayne, but his recorder was labeled KXRS radio, indicating a possible West Coast news outlet.

"Who is this guy? Maybe a USC spy trying to get me to say something stupid? Who let you in here?" growled Parseghian at Hank as he turned and stared again at the poor Notre Dame Sports Information Director. I could not stay silent any longer, so I jumped in and told a bold faced lie.

"Coach, he is with me!" I implored as I held up my WFTW-TV badge and stepped between the two. "He is with our sister station in San Jose, California and has nothing to do with USC."

There was no ownership connection between my employer and Hank's, but it was the only remedy I could think of to de-escalate the situation. It seemed to work as the suddenly relieved Parseghian relaxed as he talked about his team's strong running game, but felt the Irish pass defense needed to improve. As it turned out, the coach had reason to worry about USC, which would blow out Notre Dame later in the season en route to being the top-ranked college football team of 1972.

Hank had enough material on his portable recorder to fill a week's worth of sports shows in San Jose, as well as possible network credits. The two of us could not stop talking the whole way home about what we had just witnessed. We would recount the story in great detail to Rochelle over dinner at the Summit Club, an exclusive restaurant on the 26th floor of the Fort Wayne National Bank Building. I would find out later that Ara Parseghian was not the most paranoid, boorish coach in the Hoosier state. That title would be reserved for Indiana Basketball Coach Bob Knight.

The Fall of 1972 had a number of "firsts" for Nick and Rochelle. We both saw it snow for the first time in our lives on October 25th. For a couple of California kids who never went skiing at Lake Tahoe, we got a big thrill seeing snow actually come down from the sky. We experienced our first Thanksgiving away from our families in November, but our new friends Tim and Joan included us in their festivities with the Mann family.

The television ratings came out in November, showing only a slight improvement for both the 6pm and the 11pm news. Tony, Steve, and I were disappointed in the numbers, but our news director and general manager were pleased. We would change from the late news at ten to the late news at 11pm when most of the country would go off daylight savings time. We were on Eastern Standard Time year round where others in our viewing audience could be on Central Daylight or Eastern Daylight at different times of the year. It was all quite confusing in the Hoosier state with Indiana cities near Chicago being on Central time and cities around Fort Wayne and Indianapolis being on Eastern time. On one occasion I can remember, a prep football team from one time zone showed up an hour late for a playoff game at another time zone. They were told by the home team's athletic director to get off the bus and play without any warm-ups, or face a forfeit. Finally, after a heated argument, they agreed to start the game an hour later. After hearing that story, I became very conscious of the start times of events I would be covering, particularly if I was going anywhere near Chicago.

The first Christmas season away from the Bay Area was particularly difficult for us, not just because we missed our families, but because the weather got cold, REALLY COLD! Rochelle and I were warned but we never could have imagined what sub-zero temperatures felt like, especially when we went shopping for our Christmas tree. It was a Sunday morning when we had to scrape our car's windshield after we had run it for nearly 20 minutes in order to loosen the ice which covered our auto. As bundled up as we were, we still could not withstand more than ten minutes in the outdoor cold "tree shopping." As usual, Rochelle was really "picky" as to which tree to buy, even in minus-16 degree weather.

Knowing that most of the WFTW News Team had family and friends much closer than us, I decided to volunteer to work both Christmas Eve and Christmas Day. This allowed Tony Silva to make the two and a half hour trip up to Gary to stay with his family over the holidays. He had covered for me when Hank came to town in October.

I also worked New Year's Day because of all the college football games. The 1973 Rose Bowl Game pitted USC vs. undefeated Ohio State with the national championship on the line. It was a good West vs. Mid-west matchup. Buckeye Coach Woody Hayes bullied and shoved a Pasadena newspaper reporter who was asking questions the coach didn't like. Sounds familiar doesn't it? It reminded me so much of the Ara Parseghian incident that Hank and I had witnessed at Notre Dame that I could not stay silent. I ripped old Woody a good one on the air. In truth I came close to stepping over the line even though I had never met or interviewed Woody Hayes. After USC drubbed Ohio State 42-17, I could not help myself from taking another shot at Hayes. Little did I know that Woody's sister was watching my show in nearby Angola, Indiana. She called me right after the show and read me the riot act, claiming she was going to come to the station and "kick my ass!"

To no avail, I tried to be polite and reason with her on the phone. The following afternoon she showed up in the parking lot

Safe Passage Guaranteed | 99

of WFTW-TV, telling anyone who would listen that she wanted me to come out and meet her face to face "like a man!"

"You're not going out there, Nick," commanded news director Stan Sheets. "This woman could be unstable and may be carrying a weapon! I am going out there right now to tell her to go home or I will be calling the police."

Stan marched right out to the lot and had an animated conversation with Woody's sister, who was determined to wait out my appearance "no matter how long it takes." Finally, after another hour passed, WFTW jack-of-all trades announcer DJ McQueen called out his state trooper buddy, Fred Boomerhaus to defuse the situation. "Boomer" as he was affectionately called, was able to get the woman to calm down and eventually drive back to Angola. I would find out in the coming months that this was not going to be the last time that "Boomer" would come to the aid of Rochelle and myself.

In fairness to Woody Hayes, I must say that two years later I would get a chance to interview two-time Heisman Trophy winner Archie Griffin, who would greatly change my opinion of the OSU Coach. The affable Griffin explained that Hayes, who acted as a surrogate father to him, promised Archie's mother that he would graduate from Ohio State. This was a promise to his mom that Archie shared with his coach and ultimately fulfilled. Griffin insisted that Hayes' public and private persona were very different.

"I owe my life to that man! He was always there for me, and still is to this day," pleaded Archie in a long interview that I ran on the air, in an effort to be fair. Sadly, Woody Hayes would be fired from his long-time OSU coaching job after he punched an opposing player during a bowl game in 1978.

PHINEAS T. ESKRIDGE

I had really enjoyed covering high school sports in the first six months on the job at WFTW, and I could see that the people of this proud midwestern city as well as the rest of our viewing audience were really passionate about the competitors and the results. I had no idea that the local interest in prep football, baseball, track, and other sports would pale in comparison to the fervor generated by Indiana high school basketball. Hoosier sports fans literally went nuts for the state tournament which led to the term "Hoosier Hysteria." What made the tourney so special was the fact that every school was eligible, no matter if a team was undefeated or had lost every game in the regular season. All the schools were thrown in one big pot for the tournament pairings based on geography. Beginning in late February, we would have sectionals, regionals, and semi-states all leading up to the four teams in the state finals in late March.

I couldn't believe that the state basketball tournament draw determining who would play whom was the lead story on the 6pm News. I accompanied my visuals of the brackets with several interviews with local coaches, who A. D. Webster had introduced to me earlier. My news director reminded me that the Czar of Indiana High School sports was Phineas T. Eskridge, whose actual title was Commissioner of the Indiana High School Athletic Association. The 70 year old Eskridge, a former teacher and coach, was a native Hoosier and the son of a Baptist minister who ruled prep sports with an iron fist. It was his way or the highway. In 1964, after a player fight led to a full scale fan riot at a tournament basketball game between Muncie Central High School and Anderson High, Eskridge suspended both schools for a year from any post-season activity in all sports. His decision, which was praised by some and vilified by others, was final with no hearings or appeals. That meant that a baseball, football, or track athlete from either of those schools (even if they were not on the basketball team) would not be eligible for the state championship games or events. College scholarships were undoubtedly lost by the athletes from Muncie and Anderson. This led to lots of resentment from the Muncie and Anderson folks as well as death threats aimed at the controversial Eskridge.

It was interesting that the Commissioner, who was known as "Ty" to his friends, would be having a press conference at the Fort Wayne Elks Club just before the basketball tournament got underway. He was not going to do individual interviews, but he was going to answer questions after an opening statement. Rick Cassidy was my scheduled photographer that night, but he got diverted to a bad train accident in Waynedale, which pre-empted my news conference. Eskridge did not say anything new at the press conference, but at the "smoker" afterward he let go with a bombshell as he talked with his "friends" in the press.

"Fellas, I have to tell you that the State Supreme Court is challenging our IHSAA rule forbidding married athletes to compete in sports events. That rule, which I agree with 100%, has been in effect for at least 50 years for good reason. Married athletes have knowledge about sex which makes them different from the other boys. That could foster un-clean locker room conversations which could lead our boys to have pre-marital sex. Our athletes are looked at as heroes, setting examples for others to follow. A star basketball player who is married sends the wrong message and could encourage immoral behavior."

I was stunned at the Commissioner's comments, thinking I was back in the 1930s. This almost seemed like a scene from the movie classic "Inherit the Wind," with Eskridge assuming the Fredric March role as William Jennings Bryan. Nobody in the room had a live camera going to record these comments, and nobody questioned him on them, including me. I wish I had done my homework on this issue and had a camera crew with me that night. I vowed to follow this story, especially on the eve of the big tournament.

Unfortunately for us at WFTW-TV, Herman Yates' NBC affiliate WKHG, Channel 35, purchased the rights to televise the local games as well as the state finals, with Yates behind the mic. In 1972, there would be 25-30 radio stations simultaneously broadcasting the game along with Yates' TV play-by-play. In fact, it was Herman who called the famous "Milan Miracle" game of 1954 in which tiny Milan High with just 161 students defeated mighty Muncie Central on a last second shot by iconic Indiana hero Bobby Plump. This game, with the "David and Goliath" theme, was the basis for the movie "Hoosiers" in which Herman Yates would play himself.

Because our General Manager Whitney Thompson was a close personal friend of Herman's, and, like Yates, was a member of the Sons of the Summit City Foundation, WFTW-TV would be allowed to show same night highlights of the tournament basketball games. The agreement meant that we had to make sure that the WKHG broadcast was over, and we had to make sure to give on-screen credit to Channel 35. It was also interesting that we at Channel 18, a CBS affiliate, got first pick of the NBC shows like Bonanza, Colombo, and Sanford and Son, that would be pre-empted by the basketball games. I always wondered if the top brass at these networks had approved what Thompson and Yates had agreed upon.

I knew that I would be playing "second fiddle" to Yates in covering the tournament, so I needed to go after the tourney coverage in a different way, by focusing on the players and coaches. Sure, we would have scores and highlights, but we would do some in-depth reporting on the characters who made up this huge state-wide event. The issue of married students being ruled ineligible by the IHSAA was still gnawing away at me.

With the help of Channel 18's Tony Silva, I was able to track down a star basketball player from Berne, Indiana who missed his senior year of eligibility because he married his high school sweetheart at Thanksgiving. 18-year old Caleb Graber was part of the Amish community that embraced the tradition and lifestyle of the past which included wearing 19th century clothes, using horse and buggy transportation, and getting married at a very early age. He and his wife didn't realize they would be sacrificing his basketball career and a possible college scholarship by "tying the knot." During his junior year Caleb was an all-conference guard at South Adams High with a number of schools looking at him despite his small stature of only five foot ten.

Getting in touch with Graber was not going to be easy, as nobody knew if he had a telephone. I thought I would contact his coach at South Adams, Preston Dille. Dille said he expected to see Graber at his team's opening tournament game against Norwell High in a couple of days. While the youngster was not eligible to play, Preston had made Caleb an unofficial assistant coach and inspirational leader. Sadly for Dille, Graber and the South Adams team the 1973 State Tournament was a "one and done" affair after a one-sided loss to Norwell. I got a phone call from the coach after the game.

"Hello, Mr. Cunningham, this is Coach Dille of the South Adams Starfires. Unfortunately, we lost tonight to a very good group of Norwell Knights, but if we would have had this young fella sitting beside me firing his patented jump shot it might have been a different story."

The coach handed the phone over to a very modest and shy 18-year old Amish kid. I explained to him that I wanted to come down to Berne and do a story on him, which he had a hard time believing.

"You want to come down here and talk to me? What about? I didn't even play this whole year. I bet you want me to talk about the eligibility thing when I married Ashley?"

"We want the viewers to get to know you, Caleb," I answered, "and to give you a chance to tell your story in your own words. By doing so you may help other kids by encouraging the IHSAA to take a hard look at some of its antiquated rules."

It took some convincing by both his coach and me, but ultimately Graber relented, and we agreed to meet at the South Adams gym after school at 1pm on Tuesday of following week. Normally he would get out early that day so he could work in his family's "Country Bargain Store" in Amishville.

I let photographer Howie Hartman take me out to lunch that day to a nice restaurant in Markle, a quaint little town on the way. Of course, Howie announced to the waitress that he wanted the most expensive item on the menu, since he was using Stan Sheets' credit card. By the time Hartman had finished his prime rib, mashed potatoes, corn, and imported beer, we were going to have to hustle to make our 1pm appointment at South Adams. I don't think I ever saw Howie drive that fast through all the back roads to little Berne, Indiana, but we made it on time.

We were greeted by Coach Dille who said that Caleb, who was in the gym alone shooting baskets, was nervous and was having second thoughts. I thought the best course of action at that point was to go into the gym, shoot some hoops with the youngster and just talk basketball with him so he could relax. That strategy worked well as he seemed to loosen up, and he didn't miss a shot. I figured it would be best to talk to Coach Dille first, knowing that he would speak glowingly of his star player, as well as the unfair ruling which cost Graber his senior year of basketball. I could see that Caleb was getting emotional as he listened to his coach talk about the hardship and gut-wrenching effect that the IHSAA ruling has had on him. By the time I put the mic in front of Caleb, he could hardly talk and was choking back tears.

"Like every little boy growing up around here, I had dreams...dreams of leading the Starfires into the State Finals," he moaned. "Then I married my high school sweetheart, the woman I love, and my basketball dream got taken away! Why?"

He then dissolved in tears. He had said it all right there. No more words were necessary. I could see it on his face and in his body language. The next step was to get some footage of Caleb working in his family's Amish gift store, where his new wife was the cashier. If this story was going to be meaningful to the viewer at home, Caleb needed to be personalized, not just be seen as some unlucky Amish prep basketball player.

We didn't get away from Berne much before 3:30pm which meant we wouldn't get back to the station until 4:30 at the earliest. I made Howie promise me he would not "lose this in the film processor." Fortunately, I had told news reporter Tony Silva that I would need some help with the 6pm show because of our road trip. Stan Sheets gave the "ok" so Tony could basically write and produce my show. With "Hoosier Hysteria" in full swing, Tony had no problems filling my five minute segment. We would use our feature story on Graber the following evening when we didn't have time pressures, and I would have Tony's help to co-produce it.

We started the story with my on-camera background lead-in followed by my voice over stock high school basketball footage with the crowd roaring, intercut with shots of Caleb shooting baskets alone in a dimly lit, deathly quiet gym. The juxtaposition of those two pieces of film, even to us, was stunning as it pointed out what this kid didn't get a chance to experience. We then went into our interview with Coach Dille talking about Graber, not just as a good player but as a solid citizen. As the coach spoke, we had some shots of Caleb at the family store greeting customers and stocking the shelves. We concluded with Graber's powerful short statement and tearful plea of "Why?" The camera came back to me and all I said was, "Why indeed!" We then faded to black and went to commercial. Studio director Steve Watson had pushed all the right buttons at just the right moments so that the piece flowed perfectly.

The telephones at the station blew up with mixed feedback. Most viewers, like myself, were outraged that the IHSAA would take away this married kid's eligibility. But there were others who felt that I had taken a very prejudicial and one-sided view of the story.

I got a lecture from one viewer who called in and let me have it.

"We have the best state basketball tournament in the country with rules to protect the kids. We don't need some young long-haired California sportscaster with a necklace coming in here telling Hoosiers how to run our own home-grown event. Why don't you just go back where you came from?"

I wondered if this call came from Woody Hayes' sister in Angola who wanted to run me out of town several months earlier.

After we ran the story, Stan sent the tape to CBS-TV in hopes they would run it on their "Four Feed." That was a network feed that was sent out at 4pm weekdays to network affiliates all over the country. Those affiliates would have the option to use whatever they wanted on their local newscasts. Rarely, but sometimes, these stories would make their way on to the prime time CBS News programs. We didn't make the "Four Feed" or the CBS Evening News, but Tony Silva sent the tape to his Indiana University Journalism buddy, Jack Briner, who was an assistant assignment editor at our sister station WIND-TV in Indianapolis. Jack was able to get it on both their 6pm and 11pm Newscasts.

Now we had a big time basketball human-interest story that was going to compete with the State Tournament itself just as it was going on. After WIND-TV, a major market top-rated station, ran the story twice, the news department at CBS in New York took notice. The network sent its top sports journalist, Heywood Hale Broun, to Berne, Indiana to do a feature story on Caleb Graber. The 20 minute in-depth news piece, done masterfully by

Broun and his production crew, appeared on the CBS Sports Spectacular on Saturday afternoon. After a shortened five minute version ran on the Sunday CBS Evening News with Roger Mudd, the humble Amish kid from Berne was a national celebrity!

It would be three years before the Indiana State Supreme Court struck down the marriage disqualification rule, in great part because of the notoriety of the Caleb Graber case.

The story did have a happy ending, however. After we ran our original version, I got a call from A.D. Webster telling me about a June "Try-Out" camp that Fort Wayne basketball hero Bobby Short would arrange for local high school seniors. These were non-scholarship basketball players who were either injured, ineligible or "under-the-radar", but were deserving of a second look by college coaches.

"I talked to Bobby about this hard-luck Amish kid," A.D. commented. "He wants to invite Graber to his tryout camp to see just how good he is. We all want to see how he performs under pressure against the brothers with college hoop coaches looking on."

As it turned out, Caleb did not let his fans and supporters down by more than holding his own at Bobby Short's camp against some of the better players in the Fort Wayne area. He was so impressive, in fact, that Manchester College Coach Brian Hey offered Graber a "grant-in-aid" scholarship which would allow him to go to school and play for the Division Three Panthers. This was not the same as a full ride basketball scholarship to Purdue, but it was a great opportunity to go to a school, get a degree, and provide for his family. One of my great thrills in broadcasting, which I shared with Tony Silva, director Steve Watson, Bobby Short, and A.D., was the heart-felt letter we got from Caleb, thanking us for helping him get a second chance.

"Dear Mr. Cunningham,

I couldn't believe all the fan mail I got from people who were pulling for me from all over the country-people that I have never met and probably never will! My family and I are truly overwhelmed by their kindness and support. You and your news team at WFTW were the first folks to call attention to my story-you started it all. I can't thank you enough!

May God Bless You, Caleb"

That letter, combined with improved ratings for our news shows, helped us get through a winter that seemed unending with ice, snow and freezing temperatures until the middle of May. We even got rained out at the Indy 500, not once but twice.

The sad part was that our friends from Sacramento, Mike and Joanne Ferris, had flown back to visit us and see the race. All we got to see for two days of waiting was the start of the 500 with a terrible crash that ended the race before the drivers hit the first turn. It would take two more days before Gordon Johncock would win the rain-shortened event. By that time, our disappointed friends had gone home, vowing to return next year. They did return in 1974 and the four of us enjoyed an exciting race together under fair skies with 75 degree temperatures

I had noticed that, even with the ratings boost, News Director Stan Sheets was not a happy camper. The equipment failures, especially in the photography department, had him really frustrated, particularly when the parent company, Corinthian Broadcasting, didn't seem interested in spending any money on upgrades. Stan was pressing and testing the patience of the studio crew by asking them to make visual and copy changes just before air time.

Stan had gotten into the habit of being late in presenting the visuals and the script for the newscast to the studio director, Steve Watson, whose job it was to make us all look good on the air. Steve had told Sheets that he needed the script and visuals by 5:15pm in order to properly set up the 6pm newscast. Stan, in an effort to make his newscast even more timely, would make changes up until 5:30pm and beyond. Finally, Steve laid down the law.

"Listen Stan, I'm going to say this for the last time. I want your show in my hands by 5:15-in special circumstances by 5:30 at the latest. If I don't have it by then, you're going to do the show with no visuals-that means no film, tape, or slides-you're going to have to read the whole damn thing!"

It wasn't two days later that Sheets presented the script to Watson at 5:40pm. Steve calmly took it and said, "Looks like tonight is a reader!" Stan just laughed dismissively, and a few minutes later, started the newscast with a lead-in to what he thought would be a film interview with the police chief.

Steve faded to black, turned Sheets' mic off, and flipped on the studio loudspeaker.

"Stan, remember you have no visuals tonight! Got it?"

The director then cut back to Sheets on the camera who still didn't get the message.

"We appear to be having some technical difficulties. Let's see if we can now go to what Chief Rhodes had to say about the latest crime statistics."

Again director Watson faded to black, turned off Sheets' mic, and forcefully addressed the news anchor over the loudspeaker.

"Damn it Sheets! You need to understand that there will be no film or visuals of any kind tonight because you were too late in giving me the script. You were warned weeks ago about this. Stop acting like a spoiled kid and read the news!"

Before Sheets could respond, Steve put him on camera, opened his mic and cued him. By this time Stan was so angry, he was looking like an overripe tomato ready to explode.

The camera crew and I were watching this battle closely to see what would happen next.

Finally, after silently staring into the camera for what seemed like a full minute, but was probably ten seconds, Stan moved on.

"I guess we are having serious technical issues tonight, so I will be just reading the news."

From my off-camera seat at the news desk I could hear Steve talking with the camera operators on their headsets.

"Now, I think that asshole finally gets it. This might be my last night at WFTW. It's been great working with you fellas."

I was really worried for Steve, as he was a terrific studio director and had become one of my closest Indiana friends. We did have visuals on the late news because Sheets got the director the script over an hour before air-time, but I knew there would be trouble the following day.

When I got to the station at about 1:30pm the next day, I immediately went into Steve's office to see him sharing a good laugh with studio announcer DJ McQueen.

"Looks like rumors of your Channel 18 demise were greatly exaggerated, Steve," I said.

"You won't believe this," Watson responded. "The old man actually backed me up and re-stated the chain of command. That is, when we go on the air, the studio director is in charge. And, thanks to General Manager Whitney Thompson, we now have a rule that the news script needs to be in my hands at least 45 minutes before air time."

DJ and I, along with the control room and camera crews, were all relieved to see that we were not going to lose the station's best director. Down deep I felt that Stan Sheets, despite this flare-up with Steve, was also relieved that the skillful Watson wasn't sacked.

By the end of July of 1973, Rochelle and I were really excited because we were headed back to California for a two week vacation to visit our families, who we hadn't seen for over a year. We were so proud of what we had accomplished in carving out a new life for ourselves in Indiana, and we couldn't wait to tell the folks back home all about it.

3

TOP OF THE WORLD

We excitedly awoke to a warm and beautiful Saturday morning in August, and we drove off to I-69 to head south to Indianapolis. From there we were going to catch our TWA flight to San Diego, where we would visit with my side of the family first. My mom and dad had rented a house for the whole family at the popular beach community of nearby La Jolla, a favorite vacation spot for the Cunningham clan since the 1920s. In addition to visiting with my mom and dad, I was really looking forward to seeing my sister Pat, her husband Brett and Brooke, their 3 year old daughter, as well as my other sister Gracie, who had just graduated from Woodside High School. Rochelle and I had been away from our home state and families for over fourteen months, and it seemed like a lifetime. On the radio we kept hearing the Carpenters' new hit song, "Top of the World," which reflected our upbeat and positive mood.

When we touched down in San Diego my parents were there to greet us. My mom was very emotional as she hugged me tightly, and said, "My boy!"

My dad just winked and shook my hand, and uttered, "We're proud of you two!" I must admit that I had a lump in my throat too as I greeted them. As they hugged Rochelle, I could see that they did look older to me. I worried that living over two thousand miles away would hamper my ability to help them, should a need arise, a fear that Rochelle and I both shared about our parents.

The plan was to spend the first part of our vacation with my parents in their southern California vacation home. We would then fly up to Oakland and join Rochelle's parents, where we would have another emotional reunion. Because I had been with Corinthian Broadcasting for over three years, I was now entitled to two weeks of paid vacation instead of just one. Fourteen days seemed like an awfully short period of time to visit with our family and friends, but somehow we managed the "reunion" marathon. Everybody wanted to know when and if we were coming back to California-a question neither Rochelle nor I could answer.

The fortnight was a blur visiting family and friends, and it was suddenly time to say good-bye and head back home to Indiana. We landed in Indianapolis amidst a powerful thunderstorm with hail that caused the plane to skid as it tried to brake. Finally, as it spun around, it came to a halt with no damage done, except maybe to our hearts as the big jet lurched off the runway, throwing overhead luggage into the aisles. I turned to Rochelle and said, "Remember the definition of a good landing, according to the bomber pilots of World War II, was any one that you can walk away from!"

I encountered a storm of a different kind when I returned to my job at WFTW in mid-August. The newsroom was in a state of shock over the sudden resignation of News Director Stan Sheets, effective September 30, 1973. In his fifteen years at Channel 18, Sheets had hired just about everyone with the exception of the two older photographers, Satterfield and Hartman. Stan was offered a lot more money to take the news director job at a Lexington, Kentucky CBS-TV affiliate. Lexington is the home of the University of Kentucky, which had particular appeal to Sheets' wife, Jimmi, who was pursuing her masters' degree in art history.

With Sheets leaving in just over a month, we all felt a little insecure about our jobs. Frequently, in the television news business, when a new news director is hired, he will "clean house" with the existing staff and bring in his own people. This is especially true for a news team that is not top-rated in the market. We had been making gains on Channel 35, but we still were number two, with the ABC affiliate gaining ground on both of us. I thought, "Holy Shit, just days ago I felt on top of the world. Now, with Sheets departing, I could get sacked!"

Tony Silva, who was feeling equally as unnerved, met with Rochelle and me at our apartment after the late news. We asked director Steve Watson, a ten year Channel 18 employee, to join us, even though his job did not appear to be in any immediate jeopardy. Unlike on-air personalities, job security was much better for studio personnel, particularly talented directors like Watson. We discussed our futures and what the station might do about hiring a replacement for Sheets. Steve said he expected that general manager Whitney Thompson would take his time in finding a replacement; probably naming Wally Whiteman or Bill Weeks interim news director.

"Neither of those boobs should get the top job, but it's the safe play for now," Watson explained. "Whitney does not want to feel he has a gun to his head. He has some equipment issues here he needs to iron out, particularly in the photography department. The Corinthian Broadcasting brass in New York has been hesitant to spend the money to replace the outdated film equipment with ENG gear. More than anything, that's what chased Stan away."

Steve was referring to electronic news gathering gear, better defined for the layman as video tape and portable video tape cameras. ENG gear was going to be a big investment for Corinthian, and would mean retraining old dogs Satterfield and Hartman. No other station in the market had gone to ENG yet, but nobody had an older group of photographers or film equipment than us. Steve went on to say that he didn't expect we would attract a top news director until we had the new gear. Watson's comments were comforting to a degree for both Tony and me, who were still new to the business.

"You guys may have been hired by Sheets, but Whitney Thompson, his boss, had to agree. You're both doing great, and Whitney knows it. The ratings are on the rise in great part because of the younger look on the air. Just sit tight for now," were his reassuring words.

To Stan Sheets' credit, he was no "lame duck." He continued to work hard at his job, sniffing out news stories until the day he left. I did get a chance to thank him for hiring me and to wish him good luck. I tried to pry into his reason for leaving, but he guardedly said, "It was a great opportunity with more money and more educational options for Jimmi."

He parted with, "Nick, you'll continue to do just fine here, and I'm confident that Whitney will hire a good replacement," which was politically correct under the circumstances.

JANE PAULEY

Before Stan left, he did tell me about the "best press freebie you will ever attend." He was referring to the Indy 500 Press Appreciation Party in October of every year. The owner of the Speedway, Tony Hulman, would greet, feed, and provide gifts for 500 sportscasters and writers as a thank-you gesture for covering the Indy 500. This was a party that I wasn't going to miss.

Tony Silva set me up to meet with his college pal, Jack Briner, who worked at our sister station, WIND-TV. Jack arranged for me to spend the evening at this gala event in Indianapolis with the WIND-TV news team, after a tour of the studios and newsroom. This place was very impressive, as it dwarfed both my Fort Wayne and Sacramento stations. While touring the station, Jack introduced me to sports anchor Thad Copping, a little guy with a big voice, who went out of his way to compliment me on my Caleb Graber basketball story in the spring. Then Copping, a New Englander with a Boston accent, introduced me to the new intern at WIND-TV from Indiana University, Jane Pauley. Yes, that Jane Pauley, who would later become a national celebrity as a network news anchor at both CBS-TV and NBC-TV. At the dinner I think she felt very much like me; lucky to be there. As we went through the reception line together, we were greeted by the host himself.

"Thanks to both of you for attending our party and for covering our race," said race track owner Tony Hulman as he handed me a gift box. He didn't give one to Jane, possibly thinking the two of us were a couple. Before I started to say something, Jane, who had been quiet as a church mouse, fired back at Tony.

"Oh, Mr. Hulman, we are not together, we are not a couple!"

"That's fine, little lady, then you get one too," Tony said with a smile as he handed her a gift box. The box was filled with eight glass tumblers that had all the winners of the Indy 500 neatly etched on them. Rochelle and I made very good use of those drink glasses until we finally broke the last one in the 1990s.

The dinner was nothing short of spectacular, just as Stan Sheets had promised. We had duck and shrimp appetizers from Louisiana, steaks from Omaha, all the desserts one can imagine, and an open bar. But my focus was not on the food and drink, but on "working the room." Still feeling a bit insecure about my job, I thought it might be a good idea to meet and greet as many television and radio people as I could. I was told by Ted Dorsey in Sacramento several years ago," In the broadcast business you are always looking for your next job." With that thought in mind, I made sure I was seated next to long-time WIND news director Len Childs, who was a good friend of my former boss. He and I chatted for quite a while regarding the future of television news, specifically how the industry will change when the new ENG equipment would become even more sophisticated. For the most part, I listened and tried to ask intelligent questions as he held court.

"You are going to see more and more live news reports that are actually on the scene of the event, rather than filmed talking heads backed up with filmed b-roll," Childs opined. But then he blurted out, I think by mistake, "We're scheduled to get our new ENG gear from Corinthian by the end of the year and be ready to roll with it by January first."

That was a very interesting piece of information, because if they were getting the new gear, then we were probably not far behind them. Indianapolis was ranked in the top thirty for television market size, while Fort Wayne was number eighty seven. That would also mean that we may not have a new news director at our station until next spring. I would make sure to share this information confidentially with only Tony and Steve at WFTW, as I didn't want to pre-empt the official announcement by our general manager.

I was strategically placed at the WIND-TV dinner table, with my new best friend Len Childs on one side of me, and the Voice of the Indy 500, Sid Collins, on the other. Sid was a very interesting fellow who I admired for many years. Collins, whose real name was Sidney Kahn, told me the story of how he got the first Indy 500 live radio broadcast on the air in 1952. He not only produced and anchored the broadcast, but also sold commercial time on the event as well. The Indy 500 broadcast, with Sid at the mic, consistently had the largest world-wide radio audience of any event for decades, and 1973 was no different.

I saw Sid again nine months later when he attended the Sons of the Summit City Foundation Awards Dinner at the Fort Wayne Country Club. I had left Rochelle alone at our table for a short visit with Marc Boileau, the head coach of the Fort Wayne Komets. Marc had just led the Komets to an International Hockey League championship. When I returned to my seat at the table, I could see that Rochelle had found a new friend, Sid Collins.

"Nick, I should've known the prettiest lady in the place would be your wife," he said. "And she knows a lot about racing too!" Sports news was not Rochelle's main interest, but having to watch my show ten times a week did make her a knowledgeable and conversant fan.

After I told him how lucky I was, we then proceeded to have another enjoyable visit. Sadly, the 1976 Indy 500 would be his last broadcast as he contracted ALS, better known as Lou Gehrig Disease. Rather than put his family through the ordeal of his deteriorating health, and despondent over being replaced as the Voice of the 500, he took his own life with a single gunshot wound on May 2, 1977.

TIMES CORNERS TENNIS CLUB

The sport of tennis was growing in popularity to such an extent that folks in Fort Wayne were clamoring for a place to play indoors when the winter snows hit. Former tennis touring pro Roy Olynski, now a successful builder of indoor tennis clubs in the Midwest, contacted me in the spring of 1973. Knowing that I was very avid tennis player, he knew that I would probably give his new club more media coverage than my competitor Herman Yates at Channel 35. We filmed the groundbreaking of the new Times Corners Tennis Club on Hadley Road, complete with interviews with Olynski and the architect. The project was finally completed in late November with the grand opening set for the first week of December 1973.

Olynski definitely had some connections as he was able to get Indiana Lieutenant Governor Robert Orr and his actor friend, William Windom, to play in a celebrity tennis match. Both the Lieutenant Governor and Windom, who was in Indianapolis performing in the play "Our Town," were avid tennis players. Windom had gained national television fame in his 1960s sitcom, "My World and Welcome to It."

The Orr/Windom doubles team was matched up against me and the Fort Wayne women's city champ Donna Morandini in the first event following the grand opening's ribbon cutting. Several local politicians, business owners, tennis enthusiasts and the mayor, Ivan Christoff, were also on hand to take part in the gala affair.

I figured the match was going to be a polite "hit and giggle" affair, but like my partner, I felt the pressure to win. After all, my record on my "Who Can Beat Nick?" TV news feature would be at stake. Donna, who cruised through the city tennis tournament without losing a set, was even more intent on winning. She was a life-long Democrat who had worked hard unsuccessfully to defeat Lieutenant Governor Orr, a Republican, in the last election. Donna showed no mercy on our opponents, hitting hard passing shots, powerful serves, and deft volleys that Orr and Windom couldn't handle. When the dust cleared after just 25 minutes, we had beaten them in 6-0, 6-0. I actually tried to convince Donna to temper her ferocity and let them win a game. "Not a chance! I couldn't beat Bob Orr in the last election, but tonight I am going to kick his butt!" was her curt response. The audience also got to enjoy a more competitive three hour battle in the featured match between touring pros Tim and Tom Gullickson.

The event, which I covered thoroughly on my sports shows, was a big hit with the community. Memberships in the Times Corners Tennis Club took off like a rocket, riding the wave of tennis popularity. The co-managers of the new club were the husband/wife team of Kyle and Mary Ellen Muhlker, who had recently started a successful tennis club in Grand Rapids, Michigan. The Muhlkers made Rochelle and me an offer we could not refuse. They gave us a free membership with unlimited court time, provided that we hold the club open two nights a week from 10pm to 3am (or whenever we wanted to close it). As a result the Times Corners Tennis Club (known affectionately as the "TCTC") became our home away from home, especially after the late news. The club was also a great meeting place for many of our friends including the Watters, A.D. Webster, Steve Watson, and Tony Silva, as well as Rochelle's new-found tennis partner, Donna Morandini.

Donna, a young widow in her late twenties, had lost her husband recently to cancer in Dayton, Ohio. She had moved to Fort Wayne three years ago to be near her parents and to get a fresh start. It turns out that she attended the church in Dayton where my Uncle John Harvey was the minister. My Uncle John and my Aunt Ann Harvey helped Donna deal with the grieving process by encouraging her to pursue social activities like church gatherings and tennis. Both athletic and attractive, Donna emerged as a popular figure at the TCTC. She also became my wife's good friend and doubles partner.

The indoor tennis club also gave me a chance to host Corinthian Vice President Curt Temple when he would fly in from New York to check out our newscast. Temple, an avid tennis player, contacted me for a match at the suggestion of my old KCBG-TV pal Ted Dorsey in Sacramento. I remembered that Ted had said jokingly that he could never be fired because the V.P. did not want to lose his West Coast tennis partner. Temple, who appeared to be in his late forties or early fifties, was a good player and a nice fellow, but more importantly he was my "boss's boss." We both were very careful about talking business, but we would enjoy a spirited match at the TCTC every six months or so when he would make his rounds. I felt that my association with Curt Temple was my connection with the "big boys" in New York, and would not hurt me in the "job security department.".

Two weeks before Christmas, I got a call from my Aunt Ann, my mom's sister, asking me if Rochelle and I would like to spend the holidays in Dayton with the Harvey family, whom I hadn't seen in over ten years. My sisters and I had grown up playing with the five Harvey youngsters as kids. After all, they were my nearest relatives-normally just a two and a half hour drive from our apartment, and Rochelle's closest family member was much farther away in North Dakota. I was able to get Christmas off plus the weekend, thanks again to Tony Silva. We had a frozen turkey, a holiday gift from WFTW, sitting on our balcony for the past week in the cold weather because it wouldn't fit in our refrigerator. It was the perfect Christmas gift for the Harveys. The drive to Dayton turned out to be a five hour white-knuckle affair as we went through blowing snow and icy roads. The trip was worth it as I got to re-connect with relatives during the holidays and introduce them to my young wife. It helped to offset the homesickness that Rochelle and I both felt during the Christmas season.

Just before New Year's Day, I was summoned into the office of WFTW's general manager, Whitney Thompson. I wasn't quite sure what to expect, but I realized that we had not talked about my salary or my continued employment at the station in over 18 months. I knew the ratings were up until Stan Sheets left at the end of September, but had taken a dive in November with acting news director Wally Whiteman and Bill Weeks sharing the evening anchor position. Was Whitney going to tell me that he has hired a new news director, or was he going to announce that we were going to the new ENG gear and phase out film? The general manager came right to the point.

"Overall Nick, we're pleased with your work and we'd like you to continue here as sports director at Channel 18. As you know, there are going to be some changes around here. As of March first, we're going to the new electronic news gear which will require some training on how to properly use it. That old film processor of ours should've been replaced years ago. And I'm going to work hard to find a permanent replacement for Stan as news director and anchor as soon as possible."

I nodded approvingly and was just about ready to ask about my salary when Thompson beat me to it.

"We'd like to offer you a new agreement whereby you would be paid a straight salary of $10,000 a year and work a five day week. You won't need to submit a time card, and nobody will be keeping track of your hours. You can come and go as you please as long as you continue to produce and perform top-quality work. This will give you the opportunity to make extra income on the side from personal appearances and commercials. We'll also continue to operate with a gentleman's agreement and a handshake rather than a 13-week contract. What do you say? Do we have a deal?" He then stood up and held out his hand.

My head was spinning as I tried to evaluate his offer, which sent me mixed signals, to say the least. Rather than leave him awkwardly standing there with his hand out, I shook it and said, "Yes sir!' The existing agreement I had with WFTW would allow me to leave anytime if I found a more lucrative position. I felt this job was going to be transitory from the day I started, but I didn't figure that Rochelle and I would enjoy the people and place so much. I made almost twelve grand in salary my first full year including overtime, so the flat salary Thompson was offering was a step back. The idea of charging schools for personal appearances at rallies, dances or fund-raisers did not appeal to me in the least. My agreement with the station would let me do TV and radio commercials, but only with the approval of WFTW management. I was too busy with my sports show to chase after sponsors to do their commercials. D.J. McQueen was the master in that department, as he "voiced" countless TV and radio ads, as well as being an emcee at numerous beauty contests and ribbon-cuttings. With the exception of the top sales people, McQueen probably made more money than anybody at Channel 18, when you counted his outside income. After talking with D.J., I decided that I would accept a fee for personal appearances only if offered one, but I would be ready to negotiate a generous fee for doing commercials, whenever that might happen.

I really felt unprepared for my meeting with the general manager. The upward movement in the ratings had given me some leverage with management, but thanks to Whiteman and Weeks sharing the news anchor spot, that was changing. What if the new news director wants to bring in his own sports guy? It was time to start putting together some tapes and sending them out. I had heard that there was a TV talent agent in New York by the name of Shirley Barish who would only take a fee if she placed you in a new position. I tracked Shirley down, had a nice conversation with her, and sent her a video tape of one of my shows. That was the extent of my new job searching for the time being. In my mind I could do more for my broadcasting future by producing the best possible sports show and let the offers, if any, find me.

VICTOR

In February of 1974, the Fort Wayne Memorial Coliseum played host to the "Sports Vacation and Boat Show" with a special appearance by Cincinnati Reds baseball star Pete Rose. He turned out to be a very good interview, and he was very popular with the local fans. In addition to Rose, the show was going to feature "Victor", a six hundred pound black bear, who was going to wrestle with several of the Fort Wayne Komet hockey players on opening night. Sales manager Colin Jamison came up with the idea of me wrestling the bear as a great promotional event, in addition to adding to our news feature of "Who can beat Nick?" I learned that the bear was de-clawed and would be wearing a muzzle so he wouldn't bite me. "Victor" had recently wrestled with several members of the Cleveland Browns football team, and they were "no worse for wear," or so I was told.

I agreed to the challenge, and we promoted it for a week before the event. I even was interviewed by local radio stations and newspapers prior to the match. Rochelle thought I was crazy, and argued with me vehemently to cancel. She made it clear to me that she would not be in the audience to see her husband get "beaten up by a wild animal." But it was too late; if I backed out now, I would probably lose the respect of my audience, and lose hard-earned viewers to the competition. So I did my 6pm news show sports segment, and ended it with, "Get ready, Victor, you big ugly bear, I am coming to get you!" Director Steve Watson then got a close-up of me going "GRRRRRRR!"

Photographer Howie Hartman drove me over to the Coliseum where Victor and I were going to open the show with our match, followed by the Komet hockey players getting their turn with the bear. I could not believe it when I walked into a sold-out arena of nearly eight thousand customers, most of whom I am sure were rooting for Victor. The bear's handler, Rudy, came over to me with a "hold-harmless" document for me to sign. He said this was very customary for events like this, and that if I followed his instructions "everything would be fine."

"Just put your arms on his shoulders and make like you are dancing with him. The music will play, and he will just move around the floor with you like a big teddy bear. Do not poke him in the eyes or sneak up on him. Be deliberate with your moves and this will be simple and safe," Rudy reassured me.

I signed the "hold-harmless" agreement, took a deep breath, and stepped into the ring, which was next to a large above-ground pool used to display canoes. I engaged the bear just as his handler had told me to do, and the bear put his paws on my shoulders. Victor's breath was awful; he was blowing snot from his nose all over me, and his icy stare told me he would show no mercy. Thank God he had a muzzle on! As I looked into his wild eyes, I asked myself, "Why am I doing this?" I thought I might survive this episode unscathed as we danced around the ring in tune with the music, but the crowd started hissing and booing. They wanted action, and being young, arrogant, and dumb, I wanted to give it to them. Years ago I had learned several judo moves, and I had used them successfully on my friends and foes as a teenager. Why not try them on Victor? I could give the crowd a thrill and be a hero. Very bad idea!

My serene "foxtrot" with the semi-patient bear came to a screeching halt when I tried to trip the "big fella." Most of Victor's six hundred pounds were in his huge legs and belly, making his center of gravity much lower than most humans. My quick judo moves surprised and enraged the animal. He picked me up and literally threw me around the ring like a wet dish rag, much to the delight and approval of the huge crowd. The handler quickly came to my rescue, placing himself between the beast and me. Rudy had a handful of sugar cubes he was jamming in Victor's mouth in an effort to calm him down. This gave me a chance to escape to safety, and to check to see that I was still in one piece. Meanwhile, as the music continued to play, Rudy tried to get the bear to resume his peaceful dance. The annoyed bear would have none of it and threw the handler into the pool, causing many in the crowd to gasp with horror or to break into side-splitting laughter. To this day I am not sure if the "pool toss" was an act or was done out of frustration. As I exited the arena amidst cheers, catcalls and "boos," I ran into several of the Komet Hockey players who were not pleased with my antics in the ring. They were due to wrestle the irritated bear next.

"Gee thanks, Nick, you asshole!" uttered Komet goal keeper Bobby Steele. "Now Victor is going to beat the shit out of all of us just before our game with Saginaw tomorrow. What were you thinking?"

"Sorry Bobby! Don't do what I did. Just follow Rudy's instructions and dance with the bear. You haven't lost to Saginaw all year," I said sheepishly as Howie and I made the mad dash out of the Coliseum and back to the station. We had to get the film in the old processor so we could get it on the late news.

Howie's film was terrific, and we put together a nice self-deprecating news feature that ran on all three newscasts-the 11pm, the noon news and the 6pm the following day. I must admit that the promotional value of this event went way beyond my wildest expectations. It seemed like everybody saw my bout with Victor, and I got additional exposure on local radio stations and newspapers. As Colin Jamison had predicted, my "Who Can Beat Nick?" news feature was now well-known in Fort Wayne, but my competitor Herman Yates at WKHG-TV didn't seem too concerned. He was busy doing the television play-by-play of the state basketball tournament, Indiana's premier sporting event.

Finally, by mid-March of 1974, General Manager Whitney Thompson hired a new news director. The new head man was Raymond Gann, a seasoned news veteran in his early 40s, who had been a news director in Madison, Wisconsin. He was also our new anchor for the 6pm and 11pm newscasts. Gann was given a one year contract with the promise that electronic news gathering gear would be in place by April 1st, and fully operational by April 15th. We were all surprised and disappointed to find out that we would be the last in the chain of Corinthian stations to get the new gear which finally arrived in June. Corinthian did promise the incoming news director that he could hire two more reporters, after the resignation of long-time anchor/reporter Bill Weeks. Ironically, Weeks was hired by Stan Sheets in Lexington, a man that Weeks was constantly criticizing behind his back at WFTW-TV.

Ray Gann's game-plan to help our ratings was based on more stories with more visuals, more film, and later, video tape. He had obviously spent some time watching our newscasts before he took the job, to see what our strengths and weaknesses were. Ray could see that Steve Watson was the only studio director who could keep up with the pacing of his newscast. God help us all when Steve had a day off or went on vacation! Gann also had to deal with the older photographers, Hartman and Satterfield, who performed well only if they "liked" the event they were covering. I always would try, with mixed results, to sell my story to these two before they would shoot it. In that way I might get them "invested' in what I was covering. No question about it, Satterfield and Hartman were going to test Gann's patience, especially as they tried to learn how to use the new video gear.

I wasn't sure what to expect when the news director called me in for our first meeting. He told me that he liked my work, but he was cutting my sports segment to three and a half minutes from what had been four and a half to five.

"Nick, I've got two new aggressive reporters coming in here to do stories for a fast paced newscast. We want the viewer at home to feel that these news events and stories are happening in real time now, in front of them. We'll all need to share the 23 minutes of actual air-time. There may be days where you have a big story and you'll get more time, and there may be days when a big news event may pre-empt you altogether. One more thing, the boys in New York want us to be wearing coats and ties on the air; no more necklaces or leisure suits. While I don't like them telling us what to do, I think it'll make us look more professional."

I wasn't going to complain because I liked this guy's no-nonsense attitude, and his plan to become the top-rated newscast in the market. Also, there were no other offers for my services on the table, and I hadn't heard a thing from my New York talent agent. Ray went on to explain that we were going to get new coats and ties provided to us at no cost by Meyer's Men's Wear, a local clothing firm, who would get video credit at the end of the newscast. I didn't know it at the time, but I soon would be making some extra money doing commercials for Meyer's Men's Wear, which would sponsor my sports segment.

Gann's two new reporters, Francis "Frankie" Napolitano of La Crosse, Wisconsin and Katie Mosher from Pittsburgh, Pa. were both "good fits" for our increasingly youthful news team. Frankie Napolitano, an experienced investigative reporter in his late twenties or early thirties, brought his young wife and twin girls to Fort Wayne. He had worked with Gann briefly in Madison where Ray had been impressed with Napolitano's work ethic and his ability to sniff out a good story, like a bloodhound following a familiar scent. Katie Mosher would become the first female news reporter and part-time anchor in WFTW-TV's history. Because of

Katie's extensive academic background not only in broadcasting, but in history and English as well, she would have a very flexible role. She would not only be a feature reporter and do hard news, she would also anchor a news segment in the Fran Bologna talk show during the afternoon. I really wondered how all these changes and new faces were going to affect my friend Tony Silva, who had become the "jack-of-all-trades" for the news department. During one of our dinner meetings between newscasts, we finally got a chance to talk privately.

"Just like you, Nick, Gann called me in to his office and explained what he had in mind for me. He wants me to continue to do weekend sports, which you know I like doing, and he wants me to get more involved in city politics and school board issues. I've always had good relationships with both Fort Wayne mayor Ivan Christoff and school superintendent Lawrence Gladden. I'm excited about this new opportunity, plus I'm glad to get out of anchoring the news on the Bologna show. Gann is going to have Whiteman anchor the weekend news for the time being, which is fine with me. I don't feel threatened by the addition of Frankie and Katie at all. Quite the contrary, I think they'll help us kick WKHG's ass in the ratings."

Tony, Steve Watson, and I were all worried about the interaction between our new news director and the sub-standard WFTW-TV engineering department. The three of us felt that Herb Moreford's engineers, which included the photographers, would not share Gann's "gung-ho" attitude of "let's beat WKHG!" They were protected by their union, and it was just a matter of time before we had a blow-up.

It did not take long before Gann got his first look at an engineering screw-up. In the middle of an episode of the top-rated TV show, MASH, we were supposed to be showing a promotional announcement for our new anchor. Instead, the boys in the WFTW control room mistakenly interrupted a national Kotex commercial which made the promo sound like this: "For the best in feminine protection, join Ray Gann on the 11pm News!" I was watching MASH in the newsroom with newcomer Katie Mosher at the time. We laughed so hard that we had tears running down our faces. We both hoped that Gann didn't see this, but unfortunately, he did. Ray took it well, saying that the "Kotex connection" was nothing new because he was already called a "c—t rag" publicly when he did a story on the corrupt city treasurer of Madison.

On another occasion, WFTW-TV was running the movie, "Test Pilot," with Clark Gable, Spencer Tracy, and Myrna Loy. The control room crew got reels two and three mixed up, running them on the air out of order. One of the few people watching that night was Rochelle who told me that this 1938 classic came out looking like an "Andy Warhol avant-garde film done in flashback." It was ironic that we only got one complaint call from our viewers. Either very few folks were watching, or the viewers liked the new version of "Test Pilot" cooked up by our engineers.

HANK AARON

The big sports story of the spring of 1974 was Hank Aaron's breaking of Babe Ruth's career home run record of 714. Hank finally hit number 715 for his home standing Atlanta Braves on Monday April 8, 1974 against the visiting Los Angeles Dodgers and pitcher Al Downing. The event carried huge historical and sociological implications in great part because Aaron was black and Ruth was white, but also because it occurred in the deep south. As a result, Hank was under immense pressure and scrutiny from both those who wanted to see him break the record, and from those who hoped he would fail. I remember checking the Braves' schedule and noticed that they would be in Chicago facing the Cubs at Wrigley Field on Friday, April 12th at 1pm. Here was my chance to interview the all-time home run king. Since we were on the Cubs' TV network and carried all their games, I figured our sales manager Colin Jamison through his contacts might be able to help arrange it. Sure enough, Colin was on a first name basis with the long-time television voice of the Chicago Cubs, and Hall of Fame broadcaster Jack Brickhouse.

"Nick, I talked to Jack about your request, and he's more than willing to help get your interview with Aaron. He wants you to meet him on the field before Atlanta takes batting practice and he'll try to set you up. He did say that so many media folks from all over the world were requesting interviews that the Braves were limiting access to Hank. Jack told me to make no promises to you, but he would try his best."

I thanked Colin and promised to meet Brickhouse and follow his instructions.

My new news director Ray Gann was very supportive of my plan to go to Wrigley even though it meant that he would lose a news photographer for most of the day, and that he would have to pull Tony Silva off his political beat to cover my early sports show on the 6pm news.

By the time photographer Howie Hartman and I got to Wrigley Field that Friday, the Braves had already started taking batting practice, and I was worried that I would miss Jack Brickhouse. Fortunately, Aaron had not hit yet and Jack was standing right by the batting cage. I walked up to him and introduced myself to the venerable long-time announcer and Chicago legend.

"Hi, Mr. Brickhouse! I'm Nick Cunningham, the sports director of WFTW in Fort Wayne. Colin Jamison told me that you're the man to talk to about getting an interview with Hank Aaron. I can't thank you enough for helping us out."

"Nick, please call me Jack. Thanks to you and my old friend Colin for carrying our games and for being long-time members of the Cubs' television network. I must tell you that getting an interview with Aaron is going to be tricky. Your timing has to be perfect, and you'll need to be lucky as well."

Brickhouse pointed out that Hank did not want to be bothered by any media attention while he warmed up or while he was in the batting cage. Jack explained that Aaron's power came from great timing and quick wrists which he would work on in the cage and during warm-ups. If somebody were to try to engage him in an interview before he had completed his routine, Hank would ignore him completely. I was instructed to wait until the home run champ had finished his warm-up swings, completed his hitting in the cage, and concluded his preparation by swinging the lead bat precisely three times.

Brickhouse advised, "When Hank drops that lead bat after three swings you come in with the mic, not before. Don't wait too long either; you have to be quick, or he'll head back in the dugout. Good luck, son."

I instructed Hartman to film Hank in the cage and while he swung the lead bat as well, so that when the right moment came, I would just come in with the live microphone, and ask my question. There were several reporters hanging around the batting cage trying to do the same thing, but they had not gotten the "timing" instructions from Jack. When Aaron dropped the lead bat my moment had arrived.

"Hank, how has breaking Babe Ruth's home run record changed your life?"

He looked at me for a split second and then he went on a tirade.

"Jesus Christ, everywhere I go people are putting a mic in my face, and I'm sick of it! All of this attention has been very hard on not just me, but on my family and my team. I'm getting threatening phone calls and letters; trash is being dumped on my lawn at home. My life has been hell! I'm just a ballplayer. I'm not trying to make some kind of statement. I have nothing against Babe Ruth or his family. He was a great player. I'm just trying to help this team win ballgames. That's all, nothing more. Now will all you media people please let me do that?"

As Hank was speaking, microphones were coming from everywhere-over my shoulder, under my arm, around my waist. I pushed back to protect my photographer from the crowd surge of overly aggressive media folks, remembering that I did not protect Roy Wright at the San Francisco 49ers training camp three years earlier. Before I could spit out a follow-up question, Aaron was suddenly gone-retreating into the Atlanta dugout (which was off-limits to the media), much to the disappointment and frustration of a horde of radio, TV, and newspaper reporters. Through a" sea of bodies" I spotted my photographer.

"Did you get all that, Howie?"

Hartman shot back through the crowd, "Sure did! Got it all! If the old processor doesn't screw it up, we might have something special!"

I had already thought about how to frame my story whether I got my Aaron interview or not. I would try to talk with Braves' manager and Hall of Fame third baseman Eddie Mathews about the impact of Aaron's pursuit of Ruth's record on the team's performance. I also needed a player on the Atlanta team who would feel comfortable enough to speak candidly to me on the same subject. I remembered that one of the San Francisco Peninsula's top prep baseball stars in the mid-1960s was Serra High School's Danny Frisella, who just happened to be on the Braves' pitching staff. Serra was a rival school for my nearby alma mater, Burlingame High, so it was likely that he had pitched against several of my good friends. The "friends in common" plan had worked earlier in getting Olympic hero Mark Spitz to open up to me, so I felt it was worth a shot with Frisella.

Eddie Mathews was not a good interview. He gave me a lot of short "yes" and "no" answers, and seemed very uncomfortable on camera. You could just see the stress on his face and his bloodshot eyes, not to mention the strong smell of alcohol on his breath. Sadly, it was no surprise that he would be fired by the Braves in mid-season.

When I introduced myself to Danny Frisella explaining our rival high school connection, he smiled and really opened up to me about the effect of Aaron's home run chase on the team's performance.

"Yeah, it has literally been a circus atmosphere on this club. Everywhere we go we're hounded by the media. I really feel for Hank. He's a good fella who never figured chasing Ruth's record would stir up so much crap. He also had no idea that his journey would cause so much grief for his family and teammates. As a team we're just not playing very well, but Dusty Baker is off to a great start this season, and he is getting little or no attention. Dusty would be all over the national news had it not been for the focus on Aaron's home run chase. You'd have thought that once Hank had broken Ruth's record, this craziness would let up. Well, it hasn't, and we're all tired as hell of it, especially Hank!"

I asked Frisella a couple more questions about how he was going to pitch to several of the Cubs' hitters since he would be the starting pitcher for Atlanta on Sunday. He explained that his game plan would depend on whether the Wrigley Field wind was blowing in or out. I figured that we could use that sound bite on our Saturday night newscast.

All we needed now was for us to film Hank Aaron hitting a home run. After going hitless in his first three at bats, Aaron hit a long drive off Cubs' pitcher Burt Hooten that rode the wind over the left field fence in the 8th inning. We got our wish, and even Howie Hartman got excited as he zoomed in on the slugger as he crossed home plate.

It was just past 4pm when we left Wrigley Field and headed back. There was no way we were going to make the 6pm news, but we were going to be able to do a nice piece for the 10pm show. After I let Howie treat me to an expensive dinner on the way home with the company credit card, we pulled into the station at around 8:30pm and immediately got the old processor fired up. I was getting excited thinking about how I was going to structure the story. We would lead with me setting up the piece by doing a voice-over the film of Aaron taking batting practice, cut to the interview with Aaron, then go to the film of the home run which we could use as a bridge leading into the short interviews with Mathews and Frisella. The whole story would go two to three minutes, which would leave me little time for anything else in my sports segment. It was a big sports night with the NBA playoffs, Major League baseball and a full schedule of prep sports events. No question about it, I had to ask my new boss, who was also our news anchor, for more time.

"Nick, it sounds like you got something new and exciting out of Hank Aaron?" inquired news director Gann. "That's the most enthusiastic I've seen Hartman about a story since I came here. Come to think of it, that's the only time I've seen him enthusiastic about anything! How about I block you in for five full minutes on the late news? Let's keep our fingers crossed that the old processor will come through for us."

Thankfully, the film made it. Howie did a great job keeping the camera steady under stressful circumstances as he got jostled by other media types. He zoomed in on Aaron's face to show the pained expression and body language. The piece worked out even better than I imagined.

After the newscast, Ray Gann turned to me and said: "I think you have yourself a network scoop, Nick! I'm going to call my old pal Ed Doran at CBS right now and tell him we will overnight it to him. Ed and I were interns together many years ago at WCBT-TV in Appleton, Wisconsin. The guy sifts through news items and features from CBS affiliates to see what to use on the network shows, and what to send out on the afternoon news feed. Plus, Doran NEVER sleeps- he is news 24-7. He'll answer the phone now; you watch!"

Sure enough, Ray got right through to his old friend in New York and appeared to sell him on my interview. Doran said he would look at it, and it would be under consideration for the Saturday CBS Evening News, the Saturday CBS Sports Spectacular, the Sunday Morning CBS News, and the Monday afternoon affiliate news feed. Wow! I was impressed that Gann was so well connected at the network. I couldn't wait to tell the story about my exciting day.

That Saturday Rochelle and I took time away from our tennis matches to watch a lot more TV than we normally would do, hoping to see my story. The two-hour CBS Sports Spectacular focused almost entirely on the international ice-skating competition. Much to our disappointment, my Aaron interview never made it. Rochelle, always the optimist, brightened my spirits with a clever comment: "Don't worry, Nick, your old buddy Dan Rather will include your story on the CBS Evening News. New York probably didn't get it until mid-day anyway. Besides, Rather owes you for that snappy introduction you gave him several years ago when you did the weekend news in Sacramento!"

But sadly, it was a no-go on the CBS Evening News as well. But I did make the CBS Sunday Morning News with anchorman Hughes Rudd, the network's lowest rated newscast. Neither Rochelle nor I saw it because our station would run it at 6am before the Farm Report. Fortunately, the much maligned engineering department recorded it for me so I could see it when I came in on Monday. I made sure to thank everybody in the control room, my news director and photographer Howie Hartman, especially. I also wrote a long thank you letter to Cubs' broadcaster Jack Brickhouse. In the network piece, you didn't hear my voice and only saw the side of my head, but I did get name credit from

Hughes Rudd. My piece also made the Monday afternoon news feed which went out to affiliates all over the country, which they could use on their local newscasts. That meant that sportscasters in Austin, Texas and Portland, Oregon, for instance, who used my interview would have to lead into it with something like: "Hank Aaron of the Atlanta Braves says his life has been hell since he broke Babe Ruth's home run record, as he explained to Nick Cunningham of Fort Wayne, Indiana's WFTW-TV."

Apparently, an ABC- TV sports reporter from Peoria, Illinois wrote our general manager and complained that I physically prevented him from getting his interview with Aaron. Whitney Thompson called both Howie Hartman and me in to his office to hear our version of events before he responded to the complaint. When I told him the story of how I got the interview with the help of Colin Jamison and Jack Brickhouse, Thompson responded reassuringly. "That sounds like good preparation and good reporting to me. I'll tell that jealous Peoria reporter that he needs to work a little harder to get his story next time."

Howie chimed in with, "When Hank started talking, if Nick hadn't protected me from the crush of all of those reporters, my view-finder might have been permanently embedded in my eye socket!" Then the three of us shared a good laugh.

The following week I got letters and phone calls from old friends and relatives from all over the country, including Cal Samuels in Sacramento, Dean Stevens in Reno, and Hank Ramsey in the San Francisco Bay Area. I also thought that this network credit would be a big step forward in my broadcasting career, so I thought that it might be worthwhile to check in with my "agent", Shirley Barish in New York.

"Honey, that's great news!" she said. "Send me the tape and I'll include it in your package. With so many ex-jocks going into your field you'll need something to show that you can be a reporter as well as an on-camera talent."

I felt very uncomfortable sending the tape to Shirley as I liked our recently hired news director and rejuvenated news crew. In fact, if it hadn't been for Ray Gann pulling some strings at CBS, I probably wouldn't have ended up with a network story. Shirley was going to have to wait as I made the decision not to send the Aaron tape, at least not now. There was also a personal factor for Rochelle and me when the subject of moving came up. With the exception of the never-ending cold winters, we were beginning to really enjoy the community, our lives, and above all, our new friends. In addition to our WFTW-TV family, we also had our Times Corners Racquet Club friends. Saturday nights would usually find us at the nearby Ramada Inn listening to the music and dancing to songs like "Love Train" by the O-Jays, "I'll be There" by the Spinners, and "Listen to the Music" by the Doobie Brothers. Rochelle suddenly didn't mind being called "Rocky" by her Fort Wayne friends, a nickname she hated growing up in Oakland. She also enjoyed her new job working as a bookkeeper for an entrepreneurial businesswoman by the name of Jan Sharp, who would become a life-long friend and mentor.

We continued to chip away in the TV news ratings game, getting closer to the top spot which Herman Yates' Channel 35 still owned. It was now a three horse race as the local ABC affiliate, WPTV, channel 23, brought in a big-time anchor from Detroit, a voluptuous blonde weather reporter from Miami, and a young sportscaster from Indianapolis. In addition, WPTV hired my good friend A.D. Webster to host a Saturday morning show focusing on the African American community, the first of its kind in the market. A.D. promised me that his affiliation with WPTV would not affect our personal relationship, our rivalry on the tennis court, or my dependence on him as an exclusive news source. We had expected that when we finally got our new ENG gear in June our competition would be left in the dust. To our surprise, our competitors were less than 60 days behind us in getting the same equipment.

The transition to the new gear was a difficult one as our long-tenured photography department had to learn how to use it. There were some real growing pains during this process, which put a real strain on the relationship between the news department and the photographers. WFTW didn't make it any easier when the Corinthian brass in New York decided to expand the building at the same time to accommodate a larger news department. That meant we were forced to move our newsroom temporarily to a trailer in the parking lot. The work which started in June was not finished until December of 1974, which meant we would have to dash from the trailer through an uncovered parking lot to the studio, sometimes encountering rain, snow, and sleet.

We ended up getting visits from both sets of parents in 1974; Rochelle's came in June while mine arrived in September. It was fun and exciting to show our parents the life we had made on our own in the Midwest, and to introduce them to our new friends. Between their visits Rochelle and I took a two week trip in August to the East Coast to visit extended family and friends. We got to see the battlefield at Gettysburg, the beauty of Nantucket Island, the mountains of Vermont, and the majesty of Niagara Falls.

NICK'S PICKS

In late summer, sales manager Colin Jamison called me into his office, claiming to have an idea for a program that he wanted me to host.

"Why don't you do a five minute football and basketball prediction show on Friday night after the late news? I'm sure I can get my friends at Fort Wayne Clutch to sponsor it and pay you a $50 talent fee per show for putting it together and performing it. You could plug it on the early news by doing a couple high school football predictions for Friday night games. We could call the show Nick's Picks."

I thought it was a terrific idea, and agreed to begin at the start of the prep and college football seasons right after Labor Day. I collaborated with both Steve Watson and Tony Silva regarding production ideas. Because our sponsor was Fort Wayne Clutch, a local automotive repair firm, we came up with the idea of offering a clutch of the week award for the team that was the biggest disappointment the week before. The viewers, particularly the teenagers, might really love it if I gave myself the award for a bad pick on a local high school game. Steve got one of the engineers, Ike Simmons, who had a deep raspy voice, to come up with a shaming "raspberry" audio track to go with the award as we announced it on air. The guttural-like noise Ike made really added to the craziness of the show, and also made him an unseen celebrity as the "Voice of the Clutch of the Week." The show was meant in good fun, but knowing the sensitive nature of teenagers and their parents, we made sure that no high school team ever got the award.

"Nick's Picks" was a huge hit right from the start of the football season in September to the end of the basketball season in March. Even Ike got paying offers to appear at local high school and college gatherings provided he do his "Clutch of the Week" voice. My record the first year was remarkably good for somebody who was just offering educated guesses as to the outcomes of games. It was so good, in fact, that I started getting calls from professional gamblers asking me to give them tips. I remember getting one call from a guy who identified himself only as Vince. He needed to know if the Chicago Bears were going to beat the New York Giants on Sunday by more than seven points. I explained to him that I had no inside information and that he should go with his best instinct, just as I was going to do. "Nick, I don't think you understand," he pleaded. "I HAVE to be right. My life might depend on it!"

I didn't quite know how to respond other than to say I was sorry that he had so much "riding on this game." When I told him that I had Chicago winning 23-10 he seemed relieved. The Bears ended up winning 16-7, making Vince such a big fan of mine that he would call me weekly for "tips." The calls stopped coming the following year when the law of averages began to catch up with me, and I started losing with regularity. I always wondered if Vince lost more than his shirt betting on my errant picks.

Several years later, I did have a couple of memorable predictions that got me recognition from viewers and local sportswriters. The Indiana University basketball team had an undefeated 1975-76 season on their way to winning the national championship. The Hoosiers' biggest test in the regular Big Ten campaign was rival Purdue University, which featured former Concordia High School basketball star Eugene Parker of Fort Wayne. On my show I picked the Boilermakers to upset Indiana 73-72, with Parker hitting the winning basket in the final seconds. What really happened was stunning. With the Hoosiers leading Purdue 72-71, Parker took a long jump shot with five seconds left that rattled in and out. Indiana's Tom Abernathy got the rebound, was fouled, and hit two free throws to make the final score 74-71, thereby preserving Indiana's undefeated season. There was no three point shot in college basketball until 1986. That meant that if Parker's shot would have gone in, I would have hit the score on the nose while also predicting the shooter. My "near-miss" might have made an even bigger splash had I been more accurate on my other picks. But I had another pick in 1977 that turned out to be a winner. More on that later.

The fall of 1974 gave us another big local sports event when pro tennis stars Ilie Nastase of Romania played an exhibition match against teenage sensation Bjorn Borg of Sweden. They arrived amidst much fanfare and held a press conference at the Times Corners Racquet Club the day before their event. Borg spoke no English, so Nastase, the "bad boy" of the sport, did all the talking. He had recently lost a match in Canada where he had berated an official so badly that he was disqualified. I questioned him on camera about that match and Ilie responded without hesitation. "When I play tennis, I do it with passion. I pour everything I have into it. The line judge was not paying attention, making bad calls, and seemed to not give a sh--! I felt I owed it to the tennis fans and fellow players to take a stand!"

Nastase, who was clearly going to be John McEnroe's future role model, sought me out after the press conference. I think he picked me out because I was the youngest looking media representative in the room, and because I was dressed in a green leisure suit with a puka shell necklace(which I could no longer wear on the air). He really surprised me with his request.

"I've heard that this is a great party town," Nastase said. "I want to show Bjorn a good time tonight, so we need a couple of nice blonde ladies who will take care of us, if you know what I mean. Can you help us out?"

I explained that I was not the one who could fulfill his request, but I pointed out local ad agency mogul Bill Spruett, the "go-to" guy for the Sons of the Summit City Celebrity Golf Tourney. Spruett seemed to make his way into every celebrity event in the city. He provided the kind of entertainment that Borg and Nastase were seeking. As a result of their after-hours activities and the overall rigors of the pro tour, the two tennis players put on a very uninspired match with Borg winning 6-3,6-4. The real highlight was a pre-arranged argument between A.D. Webster, the chair umpire, and Nastase, which the crowd adored. The realistic-appearing spat, especially A.D.'s performance in it, impressed the two pro players so much that they invited Webster to join them for beers after the match. The likeable Webster would remain friends with Nastase and Borg for years to come, getting free passes to their matches whenever he wanted them.

In November, we received word that our rent at the Colony Lake Apartments was going to be going up to $220 per month, a $25 increase. This did not sit well with Rochelle or me as we had already been reprimanded by the manager for making too much noise late at night. Because of our work and tennis schedules, we rarely went to bed before 2am, which disturbed several of the neighbors who were up at 6am and in bed by 10pm. One of them even wrote a letter to WFTW general manager Whitney Thompson complaining about our late night "showering and carrying on." The writing was on the wall; it was time to move.

In December, Rochelle explained our situation to her boss, Jan Sharp, who had built her own successful "temporary help" business in Northeast Indiana. Jan really believed in the investment potential of the Fort Wayne community and encouraged us to buy a home while the prices were still among the most affordable in the country. She explained that our monthly mortgage payment might be less than our rent, which didn't even factor in the beneficial tax write-off. The thought of having our own home with privacy and a nice yard had a lot of appeal to both of us. I knew the next step was contacting my old friend, Floyd Cotton, the trap-shooting realtor I had previously featured on my show. He echoed Jan's advice.

"Nick, this is the perfect time of the year to be a buyer," Floyd explained. "There are a lot of folks who don't want to shop for a home during the holidays and others don't want to battle the weather. There are also sellers who know they've missed the selling season and are very motivated. I can refer you to a good young agent who does a lot of business in the Times Corners area. You know I'm always here if you want to talk real estate, or if you want to come back out here and see if you can shoot another clay pigeon."

I thanked Floyd for his advice, and before Rochelle and I knew it, we were meeting with Jon Shreve in the Times Corners Cotton Realty office. We explained that we wanted a three bedroom home in the neighborhood with a nice yard for under $25,000, a price range that fit our budget and savings. A week later, we braved a snow storm with Jon who showed us three homes, the last of which had just been reduced in price from $24,900 to $22,800. The home was just five minutes away from our tennis club and ten minutes away from the station. It was love at first sight for Rochelle and me! After conferring with Floyd again, who assured us that the property was a very good investment even if we had to sell it in the near future, we went ahead and purchased our first home. With $22,800 purchase price and an $800 down-payment our monthly FHA mortgage payment was just $195-less than our rent. We were both proud of the fact that we could do this on our own without financial help or guidance from our parents. Rochelle and I agreed that our parents probably would have advised us against the purchase because they would have felt that buying a new home would further tie us to Fort Wayne, and short circuit our return to the west coast.

We closed escrow with the snow on the ground in the middle of January 1975. We rented a big truck, and all our friends came to our moving party to help us transport our belongings the mile and a half from our apartment to our new three bedroom one bath home built in the 1950s. We immediately got to know the neighbors-Al and Mayro Miller on one side of us and the Stennett family on the other. Al and Mayro were an older retired couple who would be a great source of advice and would become, in essence, our Midwest adopted parents. The Stennetts on the other side were the All American Family consisting of parents Bill and Bonnie, plus their kids, 8 year old Will, 12 year old Jaime and 16 year old Mary Beth.

For two weeks Rochelle and I were enjoying our new home "honeymoon" even in the cold Indiana winter until our peace and tranquility was suddenly shattered. I arrived home after doing the late news to see an Indiana State Police car in my driveway with the red light flashing. I raced into the house to find my new neighbor Al Miller and state trooper Fred Boomerhaus both comforting my shaken wife. Rochelle had been a victim of a peeping tom, who apparently had climbed up on one of the patio chairs in order to watch her take a shower. She had chased him away by threatening to shoot him with a non-existent gun.

"You have a brave wife, Nick," Boomerhaus' told me. "She did the right thing-make a lot of noise and threaten to shoot the bastard. These incidents can be unnerving, but they generally can be traced to some neighborhood kid with too much time on his hands. Also, everybody knows you're not at home because you're doing the news. I'm going to leave you my card, and I want you to call me if anything like this occurs again. As you know, I work the night shift and the dispatcher can get me on my two-way radio. Nick, don't be thinking about doing any vigilante work. That can get you in big trouble. Do you understand me?" I nodded. "And, if you do have to shoot somebody," he added," please drag the body into your home before you call me."

I couldn't tell if he was serious. But his words "everybody knows when you're not at home" really hit me hard. Was this the price for being a local TV personality? I suddenly felt responsible for what happened to my wife, and I was determined to take action. Rochelle and I talked about what it would take to make her feel more comfortable while I was away from home. Although neither of us had grown up with guns in our households, Rochelle admitted that having one in the house might help her relax when she was alone. We ended up buying a .22 automatic rifle from Mr. Wigs Department Store on their President's Day Sale for $49.95. It was light and easy to handle, plus it could fire off sixteen shots without reloading. I prevailed upon my Channel 18 photographer Rick Cassidy, a Vietnam War veteran, to show Rochelle and me how to use it. In fact, despite my trap shooting experience with Floyd Cotton and Cassidy's Vietnam battle action, Rochelle was a much better shot with this weapon than either Rick or me.

"Rocky, you have nothing to worry about," Cassidy commented. " If Mr. Peepers comes around again you can put five bullets in him before he knows what hit him!"

While his compliment of her shooting skills was meant to be comforting, neither Rochelle nor I had any desire to shoot anything other than old beer cans. Even with the gun purchase and the lesson on how to use it, I was still seething over what happened to my young wife. If I wasn't playing tennis, I found myself cruising around the neighborhood late at night when I would finish the news broadcast, hoping to catch the peeping tom in the act.

I got lucky in late February when I came around the corner toward our home, and spied somebody standing on a lawn chair peering in the bathroom window of the Stennetts' house next door. I had to stop my car to get a better look, but he must have heard me and hopped the fence into MY YARD. Now the race was on! I jumped out of my car and sprinted into my back yard from the other side, hoping to cut off the intruder as he made his way toward my back fence. At the same time I was yelling at the top of my lungs for Rochelle to call the police, thereby waking the whole neighborhood up. I never would have caught up with the culprit had he not stumbled over our picnic table that was covered in snow. Here I was in my stylish on-air clothes from Meyer's Men's Wear, rolling around in the snow throwing punches and trying to subdue this asshole until help arrived. Suddenly two shots rang out! My combatant and I both froze!

"Don't move a muscle or I will shoot!"

I recognized the voice and disengaged myself from the perpetrator. Rochelle was standing there in her nightgown with a smoking gun. I hoped she hadn't actually shot the guy, who looked like a scared young man in his late teens. My neighbor Al Miller immediately called the state police when he heard all the commotion. Fred Boomerhaus was on the scene in less than ten minutes, accompanied by our own WFTW personality DJ McQueen, who would frequently ride with him late at night, after the news. Boomer handcuffed on the young man, who said nothing, and put him in the back seat of his squad car. He then took statements from all of us as to what had just occurred.

"Good work Rocky!" he said to my wife. "Looks like you get the collar on this one. I'll be in touch with you and your neighbors as to what happens next. For now, I'm going to take this guy to the county jail."

McQueen couldn't resist chiming in. "Looks like we have our own Annie Oakley right here in Times Corners. This could be the lead in tomorrow's newscast!"

"No way DJ! Please keep this quiet," I quickly pleaded. I knew I could trust him to do so.

It turns out that our peeping tom was 18-year old Connor Meeks, a high school dropout, who lived with his family in a home right behind us. He was a troubled young man who had attempted suicide after he lost his mother to cancer in 1972. To make matters worse, Connor apparently had become more despondent when his girlfriend, Mary Beth Stennett, broke up with him during the Christmas holidays. Karl Meeks, the young man's father, pleaded with both the Stennett family and us to give his son a second chance and not press charges. He said Connor was getting professional help and planned to join the military. Personally, I was fine with letting this go, knowing the publicity would not do any of us any good. Honestly, I found myself feeling sympathy for the kid, as I know how devastating failed high school romances can be, not to mention the crushing loss of one's mother. I also believe in second chances, especially for teenagers who are often children in adult bodies making life-changing, dumb mistakes. I hoped Connor would not fall into that category. It took some convincing, but finally Rochelle and the Stennetts agreed to drop the charges on the condition that young Meeks would never set foot on our property or the Stennetts' ever again, and that he agreed to not stalk or harass Mary Beth Stennett in any way.

The good news that came out of this upsetting episode was that we got to know and trust our neighbors-the Millers and the Stennetts. We also earned the respect and gratitude of Karl

Meeks and his family who lived behind us. Connor made use of his second chance when he joined the United States Army six months later. He became a career military man, and was part of the American ground forces in Operation Desert Storm in the early 1990s, making his family and his community very proud of his success in turning his life around.

4
A TIP FROM THE FUTURE V-P

I got a call from Dan Quayle of the Huntington Herald Press, who I had met at the 1973 Sons of the Summit City Celebrity Golf Tournament.

"Nick, I have a tip for you that might work out to be a nice feature TV sports story", explained Quayle. "We have a college basketball player down here whose setting scoring records and running a six hundred acre family farm at the same time. Sam Pratt is doing it all while keeping up with his studies and supporting his wife and two kids. We did a newspaper story on him here which, frankly, didn't do the guy or his accomplishments justice. You need to bring your cameras to Huntington and see for yourself."

Helping Dan navigate through the Sons of the Summit City Awards dinner several years back when he didn't know a soul was about to pay dividends. I thanked him for giving us the heads up and contact information for Huntington College's high-scoring basketball star. Sam Pratt turned out to be one of the most amazing people and stories I would come across in my time in broadcasting.

Photographer Rick Cassidy and I made arrangements to meet Sam and his family at his Huntington Farm at 10am on a Wednesday which allowed us to video Pratt feeding his pigs. He usually fed them at 8am, but delayed the chore two hours to accommodate us.

It made for a terrific video with hungry pigs jumping all over each other to chow down on home grown corn-husks, cobs, stalks, kernels, and all. Nothing was left.

The 26 year-old 6-foot five inch Pratt had been a local basketball phenom at Huntington North High School, but turned down numerous college scholarship offers in order to run the family farm. After four years, at age 22, he was offered another basketball scholarship after dominating local recreation leagues. This time it came from by nearby Huntington College, a small NAIA program. With the school just ten minutes away from his home, Sam figured he could handle his studies and the farm, as well as the basketball. What he didn't figure on was his wife giving birth to their two kids while Sam was setting scoring records on the court. How could one person do all this? That's why Rick Cassidy and I saw this as much as a human interest story as a basketball story.

After the feeding of the pigs, we interviewed him in his living room, getting a shot of Pratt with his infant daughter, Isabel, on his lap, wife Connie and 4 year old son, Sammy junior, sitting beside her. Then we went back to his barn where he had a basketball hoop mounted over the double-door with a nose of a tractor visible inside. I did my "stand-up," a reporter's on-camera summation and sign-off, right in front of the barn with Sam shooting hoops in the background. It looked like a scene from the movie "Hoosiers" which would not come along for another 20 years. Rick and I were excited about our story. We felt we had something special if we could tie it all together with the right timing and production.

We would start with my voice over the video of the pig feeding, segue into footage of the basketball action complete with supporting statistics, go to the interview with Sam pictured with his family, and finish with my stand-up - all in less than one minute and thirty seconds - hopefully. Here is a sample of my voice-over introduction:

"It's a cold February morning in Huntington, Indiana and Sam Pratt is feeding his hungry pigs, but the story doesn't end there. Pratt, along with two part-time hired hands, farms six hundred acres. In addition to his farming chores Pratt finds time to play basketball at nearby Huntington College where he is the nation's leading scorer."

We would then cut to the basketball video, and from there to the shot of Sam and his family. I would then introduce his family stating that beyond being a farmer and basketball star, he was first and foremost a husband and father. Photographer Rick Cassidy would then slowly zoom in on Sam's face as I began the interview.

When I asked Pratt how he handled his many roles, he responded as the humble hero that I thought he was, by giving credit to everybody but himself - his wife and kids, two farmhands, college professors, teammates, coaches and even his dog, "Forestor."

Rick suggested that I do two short standups, one for WFTW-TV Sports and another for CBS in case we made network . It went like this:

"Sam Pratt has a decision to make. Is it life on the farm or world of pro basketball? He could have both if he joins a nearby semi-pro team in Fort Wayne. This is Nick Cunningham reporting for CBS Sports in Huntington, Indiana."

I didn't think that the semi-pro team had much appeal to Pratt whose scoring records put him in a class with legendary figures like Oscar Robertson of Cincinnati and Austin Carr of Notre Dame. But, at just 6-5, and playing against small college competition, it was highly unlikely that Sam would generate any interest from the pros.

Rick did a great job of editing our story which came out to one minute and thirty-six seconds. After we ran it on the early news, news director Ray Gann stopped me in the studio before I went to dinner.

"Nick, your guy, Sam Pratt, is a small town hero that everybody can admire and relate to-and, I mean everybody from coast-to-coast. Plus, you and Rick made this a nice, tight, short piece of just over a minute and a half. I think we need to send this to Ed Doran at CBS."

Sure enough, Doran ran my story on the Friday afternoon newsfeed, complete with my standup that Rick suggested. This time, even KPIX-TV, the CBS network affiliate in San Francisco ran the story on their Saturday evening newscast, affording my friends and family back home a chance to see our story along with viewers from across the country. The fact that the story was "timeless" and ran on the Friday network feed really helped us get more exposure than usual. Many weekend sportscasters do not have the resources to produce their own local stories, and use network provided features to fill out their shows. We got letters and calls from many old friends and viewers who were inspired by this farmer/hoop star/husband/ father combo. I really should have done a follow-up report on the guy whose biography reads like a "good guy finishes first" story.

After graduating from Huntington, Pratt got a call from the Washington Bullets of the NBA who wanted him to play in the summer league for them in order to possibly earn a spot on their roster. It was now or never for Sam to chase his dream. He had an impressive summer for the Bullets followed by a strong pre-season playing against the best players on the planet; all the while his friends and family kept the farm going in his absence. Sam Pratt ended up being the team's final cut before the regular season, despite pleas to management to keep Pratt on the active roster by Bullets' all-star center Wes Unseld. Unseld and his teammates were impressed with Pratt's hustle and "team first" attitude. Washington coach K.C. Jones told him to remain in basketball shape in case a roster spot should open up due to injuries or trades.

Undaunted, Pratt returned to his busy world on the Huntington farm with multiple roles. He couldn't get basketball out of his system, and ended up building a dynasty as Huntington College's long–time head coach. "Little" Sammy junior, following in his dad's footsteps, gained fame as a local prep hoop star before becoming the point guard on his dad's college squad. Together they would win an NAIA (small college) national title.

More than 40 years after our Sam Pratt story I found an old ¾ inch video tape of the 1975 feature while cleaning out my garage. It was at the bottom of a box labeled WFTW-TV. I had it dubbed over to a DVD and took a look. Wow! The feature looked clear and crisp, as is it had been shot recently. I needed to get this to Pratt and his family. Using today's technology and social media, I found Sam still in his beloved Huntington and sent him a copy. To say he was appreciative and surprised to hear from me was an understatement. He called me immediately after receiving it.

"Nick, I'm overwhelmed and blown away that you have taken the time to track me down after all these years, and send this precious DVD to us. It is so timely. We're dedicating our new Huntington College basketball gym next month, and we'd love to show this on the facility's big screen. You just can't imagine how meaningful this is. Thank-you so much!"

Pratt told me that he was about to retire and be replaced as coach by his son, 45-year old Sam junior, the little boy from our video. He also said that the family basketball story wouldn't end there either as his grandson, Kelly Pratt, will join his dad at Huntington this fall, after leading his high school team to the regional championship in his senior year. To keep the family legend firmly in place the new Huntington gym was fittingly named "Pratt Fieldhouse."

Katie Mosher and Frankie Napolitano, Ray Gann's first hires as news director a year earlier, were making major contributions to our news team. Katie, who went by "Kate" on the air, was called upon to anchor our newscast for an entire week when Ray was called to a Corinthian news director's meeting in New York. Long time photographers Satterfield and Hartman both said they could not remember a female anchor ever doing the 6pm and 11pm news during the week. She handled the job like a skilled professional, and kept her cool during a "wardrobe malfunction" that could have been an on-air disaster.

On Katie's first night handling the anchor duties, she had one of her earrings fall on the set desk as she was doing a voice-over audio of a fatal shooting incident. Pow! The earring hit the desk sounding like a gunshot in the middle of the story. The viewer at home might have thought we had captured the shooting "live." Katie was flustered only briefly, fighting off laughter, while the rest of us in the studio were in muffled hysterics which was not helping her at all. I was immediately reminded of the studio craziness in Sacramento several years before. When director Steve Watson came back to her live on camera with only one large earring on her right side, we all feared the worst. Laughing through a fatality is a real no-no in the news business.

But she recovered and calmly went to commercial, which was not due for another three minutes. Then we all erupted in side-splitting laughter, including Katie, until director Steve Watson's voice came over the intercom:

"Settle down out there! We have sixty seconds before I come back to you TV news professionals who are laughing your asses off at a local shooting! Katie, you are doing great, but you either need to remove your right earring or add the left one. Nick, since we just took an unscheduled commercial break, I want you to throw another commercial break after the Komets' hockey highlights. That should put us back on schedule. Time to get serious everybody. Stand by in the studio!"

A well intentioned D.J McQueen was trying unsuccessfully to help her put her left earring back in place, but time was running out. Katie pushed him away and whipped off the right earring just in time as Steve put her back on camera to continue the newscast. Due to Watson's pep talk and his skillful last-minute juggling of our video line-up, we were able to complete the rest of the newscast without a hitch.

Frankie Napolitano, news director Ray Gann's other hire, was contributing top notch investigative reporting. In fact, in one of his reports he uncovered widespread fraud, collusion, and dishonesty among local auto repair companies and car dealers; several of whom ran commercials on our station. Before Napolitano's five-part series ran on the air, Frankie had to get the approval of General Manager Whitney Thompson, which really annoyed news director Gann, who had already okayed it. Thompson grudgingly allowed the feature to air, but he knew that running the series may cost him several car dealer clients, which would result in lost advertising revenue. That would not sit well with the Corinthian bigwigs in New York who owned us.

It turned out that the boys in New York were also unhappy with the latest rating book, which showed that we had slipped slightly in our battle with WKHG-TV, Herman Yates' station. They voiced their disappointment to Ray at the news director's meeting. It would be a great understatement to say that he was not a "happy camper" when he returned from New York in mid-April.

"Those meddling ding-a-lings don't have a clue," were the first words out of Gann's mouth when Tony Silva and I asked him about our Corinthian bosses on the East Coast. He then elaborated.

"They own five television stations in totally different markets, and they think one size fits all. They don't grasp the fact that the Fort Wayne viewers would rather watch the state high school basketball tournament than "Mash" or "All in the Family," or anything else for that matter. I tried to explain to them that the dip in the numbers coincides directly with the basketball tournament in February and March. We didn't lose any ground to the ABC affiliate, WPTV. In fact, we actually pulled away from them. If the assholes from the East leave us alone, we'll own the top spot in the fall ratings. I'm certain of it!"

Ray went on to explain, rather disgustedly, that Corinthian was going to be hiring the Magid Research Company out of Iowa to do a public survey in the summer months of our on-air personalities. Presumably, they wanted to see if we were "liked" by our viewers. This was a bit un-nerving to say the least. Gann insisted that our jobs were not at stake, and that he was more than satisfied with our work. Those were complimentary words from our news director, but Tony and I both worried about our fates if the survey was negative. I was reminded of some advice I was given nearly a decade ago by my college professors who said that job security in the television business, particularly for on-air personalities, is very rare.

But the more I thought about the survey, the less I worried about it. I felt I connected with my audience, and that the survey would actually help me negotiate a higher salary with the station. The management of WFTW-TV had not had any salary discussions with me in over a year.

PERSONAL APPEARANCES

I stayed with my plan to keep producing the best show I could, not actively looking for other jobs. With the help of Channel 18 personality D.J. McQueen, I was able to land a couple of personal appearances, which paid me between $100 - $250 each. They included a business skills competition, where I handed out trophies and cash prizes to champion typists and short-hand specialists. I was the ring announcer of the Fort Wayne Regional Golden Gloves boxing matches in 1974 and 1975. I also accompanied the Bluffton High School Orchestra, reciting the story of "Peter and the Wolf."

Safe Passage Guaranteed

One of my favorite gigs was announcing the local stock car races at the Steuben County Speedway. On one occasion I was asked not only to announce the "Nick Cunningham 50-lapper," but also to help select and crown "Miss Steuben County Speedway for 1975." I had coerced Rochelle to help me with this endeavor. After the race, seven young ladies lined up in their formal gowns and one contestant was clad in her racing outfit with her helmet under her arm. Lonnie Haygood, who finished third in the race, was also a nominee for speedway queen. Rochelle leaned over and whispered in my ear.

"You have to put a crown on the lady stock car racer. And you need to do a story on this real pioneer."

Lonnie was clearly the crowd favorite and was thrilled to be named "Miss Steuben County Speedway for 1975," although she told the audience over the race track microphone that she would have preferred to have won the race. That garnered laughs from the audience as well as a few "right on's" and "I told you so's." When I asked her what her goals were, she said to be the first woman to drive in the Indy 500. We would come back later in the summer and do a feature story on Lonnie Haygood. Unfortunately, she never got to compete in the Indy 500, but she did get to see Janet Guthrie become the first female to do it, along with the rest of us in 1977.

I interviewed the champion driver, Red O'Neill, on the race track mic, and he announced to the crowd of nearly a thousand folks, "What do say everybody? How would you like to see Nick take my car for a spin around the track?" With the crowd urging me on, I agreed to take Red's souped-up 1972 Chevy Camaro out on the banked oval track - something I had never done before. That car was so responsive that if I just touched the accelerator the Camaro would take off like a rocket. After completing one very slow and comparatively safe lap, I was encouraged by O'Neill, who now had the track mic, "Open it up Nick! Let's see what you can do!" I made eye contact with Rochelle who was shaking her head and mouthing the words "Don't do it!"

I gave the Camaro the gas and I was off like a shot as the crowd roared. The banked turn came up so quickly that I barely had time to react, slamming on the brakes causing the back end of the car to fish-tail on me. I screeched to a halt as my right rear tires literally skidded off the track. For a split second I thought I might wreck our local hero's special car, not to mention what that crash might have done to me. The large crowd didn't know whether to gasp in horror or laugh their butts off. Fortunately, I had sent photographer Howie Hartman home after I gave O'Neill his winner's trophy. I would have been totally humiliated if Howie had shot a video of this, and it would have ended up on the air. Finally, after dangling on the edge of the banked turn with a six foot drop off for what seemed like forever, I was rescued by the track's tow-truck crew, who pulled me to safety. On the ride home Rochelle couldn't resist voicing her displeasure.

"So, you think you're Richard Petty now, do you? I would have thought that you would have learned your lesson after getting beaten up by a bear in a crazy stunt. Now this!"

For a second I thought that I might be the 'Widow Cunningham' sooner than I expected.

"And that poor driver who lent you his car; he dropped his trophy and took off running down the track to save his prize possession when he saw you skid off the track. My guess is that he's going to be a lot more careful in the future about loaning out his powerful Camaro."

We both laughed out loud. I then added:

"If I would've wrecked Red's car the two of us wouldn't have gotten out of there alive!"

I seemed to be on a roll with personal appearances at auto races as the track announcer. Before my Indiana job I had seen just one auto race in my life when my dad took me to watch famed hometown driver Jimmy Bryan compete in the Phoenix 150 in 1959. Growing up, I never was the guy who had much interest in cars, whether it was high school or beyond. In early May, I was asked to be the grand marshal and track announcer of the Tri-State Grand Prix in Angola, Indiana-about 60 miles north of Fort Wayne. This was a souped-up go-kart 50 lapper around the campus of Tri-State College. The competitors were mostly fraternity members mixed in with several locals. It was going to be a big day for Rochelle and me as we had to get up early to be in Angola by 10am to help dedicate Tri-State's new tennis facility. Then it was off to the country club for lunch with the Tri-State tennis coach Bill Steckbeck and his wife Laura, before the parade and my announcing duties at the 3pm race. WFTW-TV Photographer Rob Satterfield was able to get some video footage for Tony Silva's 6pm sports segment. I roped Rochelle into joining me on this outing with the promise I would take her to dinner at Café Jonell in Fort Wayne, the fanciest and most expensive restaurant in town. By 4pm with the race just past its halfway point the skies opened up and sent us all scurrying for cover. Rochelle and I figured that the organizers may cancel the rest of the race due to the rain, but miraculously the clouds parted, and the sun came out in less than forty five minutes. We had come to understand how fast the weather could change in Indiana.

When the race finally ended at 6pm Coach Steckbeck invited us to the Tri-State evening festivities which included a dinner show put on by folk rock singer Jim Croce, one of my favorites. But unfortunately both Rochelle and I were exhausted and needed to make it to our 7:30 dinner reservation at Café Jonell. Looking back I wish we would have stayed to see Jim Croce as he tragically died in a plane crash several weeks later. Every time I hear one of Croce's hits like "Bad, Bad Leroy Brown," or "Time in a Bottle," I think back to that missed opportunity.

The Sons of the Summit City Foundation named ABC Sportscaster Chris Schenkel from nearby Bippus, Indiana as its 1975 Man of the Year. Schenkel, who was in the process of winding down his career as an ABC-TV football and golf announcer, was not a popular choice with my good friend A.D. Webster. At the end of one of our late night tennis matches he voiced his opinion to me in no uncertain terms.

"Nick, I've got nothing against Chris Schenkel, who seems like a nice guy. But the red-necked Sons of the Summit City Foundation really showed its ignorance by snubbing and disrespecting Indiana Pacers' Forward George McGinnis, the f—king 1975 American Basketball Association player of the year! There's never been an African American 'Man of the Year' and may never be, and what about a 'Woman of the Year?' Madame Curie and Mother Teresa wouldn't have a chance either, even if they were Hoosiers. It's a damn joke!"

A.D. had a very valid argument in the case of McGinnis who grew up in Indianapolis and played college basketball at I-U in addition to being picked to the all-ABA team three times and league M-V-P twice. Webster went on to explain that the Sons of the Summit City Foundation's snubbing of George McGinnis was not the first time that a deserving Black athlete was ignored by the organization. Perhaps the foundation's most glaring oversight was the omission of All-American halfback Johnny Bright of Drake University who went on to set the rushing records in the Canadian Football League, where he was recognized as the league's outstanding player in 1959. Bright had grown up in Fort Wayne where he was an all-state star in football, basketball, and track at Central High School. A.D. then mentioned Fort Wayne's Bobby Milton, also from Central High, who played basketball and coached for the Harlem Globetrotters from the late 40s until the early 60s. I got to thinking that there definitely was a "story" here, and I was going to pursue it.

While I really wanted to get the video comments of both Johnny Bright and Bobby Milton, I discovered that both no longer lived locally. The WFTW-TV news department, with its limited budget, was not going to fly me to Tulsa or New York City to interview these sports heroes. Meanwhile, George McGinnis was not an option as he was vacationing in Europe. I asked for A.D.'s help in finding a spokesperson for the African American community on this issue. He put me in touch with attorney Thomas Green, who was also the head of the Fort Wayne chapter of the NAACP. Green was soft-spoken and unemotional but got right to the point.

"If the Sons of the Summit City Foundation wants its 'Indiana Man of the Year' award to be meaningful to all the people of Fort Wayne and the state of Indiana, they need to be inclusive and consider people of color in all fields of endeavor, and of all genders. Over the last three years George McGinnis, a home grown Indiana kid, has dominated pro basketball, and brought honor to the state and the community. In our mind he's been ignored and 'snubbed' three straight times. We can only conclude by witnessing the 'plantation mentality' demonstrated by the Sons of the Summit City Foundation, that they should call their selection the 'White Man of the Year' award."

I then asked Green if there were any other local African American candidates that should have been considered for the honor. He didn't hesitate on that subject mentioning Fort Wayne natives Bright and Milton as well as NBA Hall of Famer, Oscar Robertson, who grew up in Indianapolis, and I had overlooked. Green then added a familiar name that caught me by surprise.

"I'll tell you who the foundation should consider, particularly if you factor in community service. Fort Wayne's Bobby Short was an all-state player at Central High and an All-American basketball player at New Mexico State, but more importantly he has changed the lives of countless youngsters-of all races and religions-with his inspirational summer camp and private mentoring sessions. In fact, you did a story on that Amish kid that Bobby helped last year. Short might be the most deserving of them all!"

I then needed to get a reaction from the Sons of the Summit City Foundation. I asked Whitney Thompson who was a member of that organization for a suggestion as to who would make a good on-air spokesman. Thompson, who asked to take a look at my story before it "aired," gave me the name and phone number of Ned Rollins, the owner of Rollins Dairy and long-time member of the foundation. Rollins agreed to come to the station and be interviewed on the subject.

When he arrived, I could smell the strong scent of alcohol on his breath. He and Whitney had gone out to lunch before the appointment and had a couple of cocktails, with the idea that the booze would make Rollins more relaxed for the interview. I figured that our general manager had prepared him for what was coming. When Rollins arrived, I brought him into the studio and showed him the video of Thomas Green's comments. His response was surprisingly combative.

"This is our tournament and we're going to select who we feel is the most worthy candidate. We're not going to be bullied by an organization that has its own agenda!"

I then asked him if the Sons of the Summit City Foundation had considered an African American for the honor, like George McGinnis for instance.

"We consider everybody from all walks of life, not just athletes, without regard to race, creed or color. We just felt that Chris Schenkel, with his local connection and legendary broadcast career, was the most deserving of the honor. Have you met Chris? He is a great guy who has done a lot for the Northeast Indiana community, plus he has broadcasted NFL and NBA games as well as pro golf and the 'Wide World of Sports' on ABC-TV. We'd be happy to consider McGinnis, Bright and others down the road, but they need to understand that this is our tournament, and we will decide who will be our 'Man of the Year.' "

I had my story. I would lead in with a background voice-over still shots of Schenkel, Bright, and Milton followed by some video of McGinnis, then I would go into the interview with Tom Green followed by Ned Rollins. The story was going to run close to two minutes, so I needed news director Ray Gann to give me the OK.

"No problem Nick. I think this story is more about local politics than sports anyway, but you need to get Whitney Thompson's approval before we run it, and he is out of town until tomorrow. Hopefully, we can get it on the news tomorrow night."

You could hear the disgust in Gann's voice. Sitting on this explosive story which we all had worked hard on really rankled him. Ray understood that the longer we waited the greater the chances that another news source could break the story before us.

Fortunately, Whitney returned the following day, and I showed him my story. He couldn't hide his disappointment in Rollins' performance.

"Wow, Ned sure didn't do himself or the foundation any favors with those remarks. You have done your best to be fair, so, while it pains me to say it, we need to run the damn story."

Thompson, a Sons of the Summit City Foundation member, knew he was going to face the wrath of his own organization as well as some of his paying sponsors. In fact, Rollins Dairy even had me pictured on their half-gallon milk carton when I joined the station in 1972. I admired my general manager's courage in letting the controversial story run even though he knew it could cost WFTW-TV some advertising revenue.

After we broke the story on both the 6pm and 10pm newscasts, I got a disturbing telephone call from a voice that I didn't recognize as I prepared to go home. I really should not have picked up the phone, but I really was curious about our viewers' reaction.

"Listen Cunningham, we have been doing things our way since 1946. We don't need some long-haired punk from California telling us how to run things. Make no mistake we have our eye on you and we know where you live!" (Click)

I didn't mind the "long haired punk" stuff, but the implied threat combined with knowledge of where I lived was chilling to say the least. I immediately contacted my "private body guard," trooper Fred Boomerhaus, who reminded me not to answer the phone after the newscast.

"Nick, you should know better than to answer the TV station phone late at night because most of the time you're hearing from drunks and nut cases. I should know because I am out here dealing with these people almost every night on my shift."

He went on to say that he would make sure to drive by both the station and my house for the next couple of weeks to see that Rochelle and I were safe. Boomer also reassured me that threats like these were rarely acted upon, and that whoever made the call likely had too much to drink. Even with Boomerhaus' soothing words I still was shaken, and would be constantly looking over my shoulder.

My drive home after the late news on Lindenwood Avenue going past the cemetery now got even more foreboding. I felt a little bit like Ichabod Crane in Washington Irving's tale of the "Headless Horseman." Frequently I would be stopped at the railroad tracks which bordered the cemetery on Lindenwood Avenue as I anxiously watched a long freight train pass by. On several occasions, cars would pull up behind me as we waited for the tracks to clear. Fortunately, the "Headless Horseman" or the threatening caller never used this opportunity to ambush me.

Most of the late night TV station calls would range from being bizarre to very funny, and they were not "G" rated or even "PG" for that matter. Most were of the "R" and "X" variety. In fact, WFTW's DJ McQueen, the station's prankster, thought it would be fun to record them all - illegally, of course - and put them on one audio tape which would entertain us at our annual Christmas party. We also had a collection of video outtakes and mistakes which we enjoyed at the same gathering. Getting the news team together to laugh at our accidents and mistakes was not only hilarious, but also a great "bonding" experience. To a certain extent, it made us all feel connected to one another like inmates at an insane asylum.

The Sons of the Summit City Celebrity Golf Tournament of 1975 gave me the opportunity to meet and interview several national and statewide sports personalities. Indiana University's football and basketball coaches, Lee Corso and Bob Knight, Purdue football coach Fred Akers and Boilermaker basketball coach Fred Schaus, legendary tennis player Bobby Riggs, and honored celebrity Chris Schenkel all were there and available for interviews.

Without question, the most informative and enjoyable interview was with Lee Corso who was warm and friendly. It was easy to see that he was going to have a career in broadcasting after his coaching days were over. ESPN hired him in 1987 and he has been a fixture there on "College Football Game Day" ever since.

The least enjoyable experience I had at this year's celebrity event was interviewing Bobby Knight, who I was warned about by I-U grad Tony Silva. To say Knight was surly and arrogant was a gross understatement. When I asked him a non-threatening general question like "How would you assess the Big Ten basketball race this year?" he turned on me as if I had insulted his wife.

"How should I know? That's for you media geniuses to figure out. Every year is different, and every team is different. I have a laugh every year trying to watch you people figure things out."

I didn't hesitate and fired another question at the dismissive coach.

"Coach, your team won 31 games last year, and you have several all-conference players returning this season. Isn't it safe to say that you will be the favorite to repeat as Big Ten champions?"

Knight looked at me for a long time without saying a word and then blurted out:

"You know-it-alls have it all figured out, don't you? So I guess we don't even have to play the games, do we?"

The coach then rudely turned around and walked away with the camera running. The viewers at home got to see the entire interview, including the "walk-away." At first, I took this incident personally, but I later learned from Tony that Knight treated almost everybody in the press with disdain. The exceptions, Silva explained, were a pair of fanny-kissing Indianapolis sportswriters who would write and say what the coach wanted to hear.

When I heard that I would have a chance to interview Bobby Riggs, I recalled a story my father had told me years before. The Cunningham clan had lived in Pasadena, California in the 1920s and 1930s, and my dad, his sister and two brothers had grown up competing against some great local athletes like Jackie Robinson, his brother Mack Robinson and Bobby Riggs. In fact, my uncle Jim Cunningham and his partner actually beat Bobby Riggs in the 15 and under doubles final of the Ojai Tournament in

Safe Passage Guaranteed | 167

1932, seven years before Riggs would become the world's top ranked amateur player and Wimbledon champion. I had to find out if Bobby remembered Uncle Jim, who was still winning senior tennis tournaments on the East Coast.

Riggs, who had recently regained fame by losing to Billie Jean King in the Battle of the Sexes tennis match of 1973, was in town to promote the opening of his new tennis museum in southern California. After a warm and cordial interview, I asked him off camera if he remembered my uncle and the Ojai Tournament of 1932. His whole demeanor changed in an instant.

"Yea, I remember Jim Cunningham. He and his partner got lucky at Ojai in '32. So what? That's ancient history!" Then the irritated tennis legend said to the other media representatives in the room, "Anybody else with a more relevant question?"

Dad had told me that he was sure that Riggs would remember Jim.

"Bobby Riggs probably would not remember all of his victories, but I can assure you he does remember all of his losses," my dad commented with a chuckle. "He came unglued when your uncle and his partner beat him in Ojai."

Not long after the celebrity golf tournament ended the WFTW newsroom was hit with the sudden resignation of news director Ray Gann, effective August first. I wasn't totally shocked because I could see Ray's growing frustration with the Corinthian ownership in New York which attempted to micro-manage every department at channel 18 from the general manger on down. Gann also had issues with the less than mediocre engineering department, and several whining photographers who were constantly complaining about being overworked and underpaid. To Ray's credit, he would not point to those issues as a reason for leaving.

"Nick, I got a great offer that I couldn't refuse from an NBC-TV affiliate in Albuquerque, New Mexico. They'll pay me almost twice what I was making here, and the station is locally owned. This is the best move for not just me, but for my family too. I promise you, if something opens up down there for a sports guy, I'll give you a call!"

I thanked him for all he had done for me and the rest of the news department, and wished him and his family the best of luck. I knew that the locally owned aspect of the new job was really important to Gann, particularly after he was constantly pestered here by the WFTW-TV owners in New York. Everybody in the news department, with the exception of the older photographers, was really disappointed at the loss of Ray Gann. In his time at Channel 18 he had hired some good people and put together a fast paced newscast that seemed ready to claim the top spot in the ratings. I also found myself feeling very envious of my outgoing news director, who was headed west to an exciting city where he was going to be paid almost twice as much. My frustration was compounded when I learned that Thad Copping, the sports director of our sister station at WIND-TV in Indianapolis, had been recently replaced by their weekend sports personality. I had hoped to be considered for that position when it opened up. Copping accepted a sports anchor position at an ABC-TV affiliate in Chicago, and gave WIND-TV just two weeks' notice before leaving. The change happened so fast that I never got a chance to apply, nor was I given an opportunity by WIND-TV news director Len Childs.

JOHN WOODEN

Being overlooked for the Indianapolis job combined with losing my second news director in three years hit me really hard in the summer of 1975, and made me think it might be time to leave Fort Wayne; this, despite my affection for our channel 18 news team, our close friends at the tennis club and our cozy new home. Who knows? The next news director could come in, clean house, and bring in his own team. Just when I started thinking about being more aggressive in looking for another job, or even changing professions, I got a tremendous early morning news tip from my good friend A.D. Webster. A.D., who forgot that I was on a late schedule and didn't get up until at least mid-morning, called me excitedly at 7am.

"Wake up Nick! I have a news flash for you! John Wooden will be in Kendallville this afternoon working with young basketball players at Coach Byron Hayden's Eastview High School youth camp. You're the only member of the Fort Wayne media that knows about this. Wooden, who's been a friend of Hayden's for years, wanted to help coach eight to ten year olds with little fanfare and media coverage so he could concentrate on the kids. Don't worry, I cleared it with my buddy, Byron; you're good to go."

I was still half asleep and wondered if I was dreaming, plus my caffeine driven friend was talking so fast that I asked him to repeat himself. When I finally grasped what A.D. was trying to tell me, I thanked him and got to work setting up a photographer for my 30 minute road trip to Kendallville.

The opportunity to interview the legendary UCLA coach, who had just retired after winning his record 7th national championship, would be one of the highlights of my career. Wooden, a native Hoosier who never forgot his roots, was an all American basketball player at Purdue as well as a head coach at Indiana State before going west to UCLA in 1948. His coaching style was based on discipline and preparation which was punctuated with clever phrases like "Be quick but don't hurry," and "Failing to prepare is preparing to fail." I wanted to think through what I was going to ask this iconic figure who was arguably the greatest basketball coach of all time.

When photographer Rick Cassidy and I arrived at the Eastview High School gym we found Wooden down on one knee showing an eight year old how to dribble a basketball.

I was taken with fact that the college coaching great could relate so well to younger kids, and seemed to really enjoy it. As we looked around the gym waiting for an opportunity to do an interview, we noticed that we were the only media people in the place. I suddenly flashed back to a similar situation five years earlier when Matt Stokes and I nearly had exclusive training camp access to the Oakland Raiders.

Eastview's Byron Hayden saw us waiting patiently, and advised us that he would bring coach Wooden to us at the next "water break" for the kids. When he arrived, my first question to the coaching legend was, "You've been coaching college kids for 29 years. What kind of adjustments do you have to make in working with the eight to ten year olds?" He studied me carefully as he collected his thoughts before finally answering.

"The game on all levels is about fundamentals. It's more basic with the younger kids, and gets more refined as you go up the ladder from youth leagues to high school to college and finally the 'pros.' I especially enjoy working with the young kids because you can make a real difference by coaching them on proper technique at an early age. It will make the adjustment so much easier for the youngster as he or she grows up, climbs the ladder, and faces tougher competition."

Then he laughed and added:

"You know, I am getting as much from these kids as they are getting from me. In fact, probably more. To see their enthusiasm and the discovery on their faces as they learn something new is such a terrific reward."

Safe Passage Guaranteed

I then asked Coach Wooden about his 1975 UCLA team that won the national title by upsetting favored Louisville in the semi-finals and favored Kentucky in the finals.

"I would have to say that they may not have been the most talented team I've ever coached, but they had the unique ability to play at or above their potential at the pivotal moments. They excelled at attacking their opponents' weaknesses with the full court press when the game was on the line."

He went on to explain how his trademark "full court press" evolved over the years from a man to man alignment to a disguised 2-2-1 zone, which would really confuse opponents. Then, before the coach excused himself to go back to work, he singled out one of his young students.

"The most complete player I've seen here today is ten year-old Brooke Robbins of Warsaw, the only girl in camp. If she stays focused, she has a chance to be a star, and you are going to be doing a story on her before long."

The "Wizard of Westwood," as coach Wooden was often labeled knew talent when he saw it. Brooke Robbins would go on to lead Warsaw High to the Indiana girl's state championship in 1983, become an All-American at Stanford, and earn a gold medal by being part of the United States Olympic Women's Basketball Team in Seoul, Korea in 1988.

Rick Cassidy and I put together a nice video piece on Coach Wooden for the six and ten o'clock news shows. I even sent the story to Ed Doran at CBS, but he didn't feel it was timely enough for the network. It had been almost four months since UCLA had won the NCAA basketball title and we were in the middle of the baseball season. But most importantly, I did not have the departed Ray Gann in my corner to promote my story to his old friend.

General manager Whitney Thompson, knowing the November rating book was only a couple of months off, quickly hired a new anchor to replace Gann. Rob DeForest came to us in mid-August of 1975 from Duluth, Minnesota where he had been part of a top-rated news team. Rob, with his good sense of humor and smooth on-air delivery, was a good fit for our news team from the day he arrived. To Rob's credit he was the first to say, "I'll be your news anchor but not your news director. I just don't think it is possible to do both jobs well at the same time." That still left us with a big hole to fill in the news room. DeForest's comments made a powerful impression on our general manager who was working hard to find Ray Gann's replacement.

Less than a month after hiring a news anchor, Whitney Thompson named Deforest's former boss from Duluth, 27-year old Sean Montgomery, the new WFTW-TV news director. Rob DeForest credited Montgomery with being able to turn around a last place newscast at WXDU-TV into Duluth's number one in less than six months' time. Apparently, an ownership change at that station prompted budget cuts and a mass exodus of top news personnel.

Montgomery, who was working as a handyman in Denver when he was hired, was a fascinating character. He was a whip-smart magna cum laude graduate from Notre Dame who grew up in Hibbing, Minnesota. What Sean lacked in experience, he certainly made up in hutzpah. If you played "Trivial Pursuit" with this guy, you would hardly ever get a turn because he would answer all the questions. Sean, who had longer hair than mine and sported an earring (shocking for the 1970's), had a great instinct for what the viewers would want to see, and how to present it. He was constantly telling us to "make our stories relevant and personal" so that the guy watching at home could identify with the subjects of our news features.

Sean also was able to convince our general manager to hire a full-time news producer/assignment editor. Micky Katz, another WXDU-TV refugee from Duluth, joined us three weeks later to fill that role. I was wondering how our new news director was able to convince Whitney Thompson to expand the news team and the budget as well. It turns out that Sean made a big splash in New York when he met with the Corinthian ownership group which, surprisingly, went along with the increased news budget. Montgomery, whose beer drinking prowess and sense of humor were legendary in Duluth, was skilled at "schmoozing the Big Apple boys," who thought he was a savant. Thinking back, they may have been right. As I got to know him, I could see that he was a likeable and charismatic leader. He was going to finish off what Ray Gann started, and that was leading us to the top spot in local TV news ratings.

JESSE OWENS

The late summer and fall were very busy times for me, not just with local news events, but for personal appearances as well. I got paid $200 to be the host of an evening with former Olympic great Jesse Owens, whose appearance at Hall's Gas House Restaurant was jointly sponsored by Coca Cola and the Fort Wayne Jaycees. My main job was to introduce Jesse to a group of 250 attendees who paid $50 a plate to hear his inspiring words about "overcoming obstacles in life."

This was a special opportunity for me to have dinner with perhaps the greatest track and field athlete of all time. I grew up in a family of former track and field athletes who idolized the Olympic hero. Jesse (he asked me to call him by his first name) and I spent over an hour together having dinner, and talking not just about sports, but about life in general. I had to pinch myself several times to make sure this was really happening. When he heard that I had eaten here before, he asked my advice on which salad dressing I recommended.

"Jesse, the Roquefort dressing is the specialty of the house. It's terrific!"

Jesus! I just told the greatest track and field athlete of all time what salad dressing to use!

It turned out to be as good as advertised, and Owens let me know it.

"Wow, Nick, you weren't kidding about the Roquefort."

We shared a laugh when I said, "Now I can tell my grandchildren that I advised Jesse Owens on which salad dressing to select."

It took forty-five years, but I was able to do just that after my 8-year old grandson read me an article aloud about a sports hero from long ago named Jesse Owens.

I spent some time researching the man before I prepared my introduction. Most everybody knows the story of the four gold medals at the 1936 Olympics, where Owens crushed Adolf Hitler's myth of Aryan superiority. I wanted to focus on a different chapter of his life - the 1935 Big Ten Championship Track Meet in Ann Arbor, Michigan where Jesse incredibly set three world records and tied another in just 45 minutes. I put that accomplishment in perspective for the audience as I concluded my introduction.

"Ladies and gentlemen, you received your cherry pie desert at approximately 8pm earlier this evening. It's now eight-fifty –in less than that time this man sitting beside me set or tied four world records. Let's give a warm Fort Wayne welcome to the great Jesse Owens!"

Owens then gave a thirty minute inspirational presentation that had the audience, including me, on their feet applauding. It was truly an unforgettable evening for those of us who were lucky enough to be there. Sadly, Jesse would pass away less than five years later due to lung cancer caused by a smoking habit he just could not outrun.

Another personal appearance that paid me well was the job of "ring announcer" at the Golden Gloves Boxing Tournament at the Fort Wayne Coliseum. This was something very new and different to me, but being a big boxing fan, I jumped at the chance to do it. The two night affair was a lot of fun, and very educational. It seemed like almost every young fighter, black or white, wanted to copy the style of the heavyweight champ, Muhammad Ali. Many of them got knocked senseless by their opponents as they tried to emulate the famous "Ali Shuffle," forgetting that they were in an "all-or-nothing" three round prize fight. In one instance, I introduced two middleweight fighters from different backgrounds and generations. One was an African American young man of about 18 who put on a display of shadow boxing and footwork that awed the crowd. The back of his golden robe said "Jerome 'Little Ali' Collins." His opponent was a much older man of 35 or 40 with little hair, a red goatee, a US Navy anchor tattoo on his forearm, and wearing a faded green robe that he could have found discarded in a public bathroom.

My first thought was that this was going to be a bloody mismatch. The youngster seemed to have too much style and speed for the old-timer. The bell rung and the fight began with "Little Ali" dancing all over the ring and throwing punches at imaginary opponents while his real opponent just watched with a wry smile on his face. This went on for about a full minute of the first round until the tattooed Navy fighter beckoned the youngster to come closer. "Little Ali" who must have thought he was in a dance contest on "Soul Train" because he STILL was paying no attention to the other guy. The cunning older fighter, a former Navy Seal, struck like a coiled cobra, and knocked out the youngster cold with just one powerful right hand to the jaw. The crowd was stunned and silent until "Little Ali" was lifted off the canvass by his handlers, and walked slowly to his corner. Many in the audience serenaded the victor by singing "Anchors Away." This was a mismatch alright, but not the one I expected.

ARTHUR ASHE

One of the most rewarding events I was a part of in 1975 was a tennis clinic that A.D. Webster organized for the inner-city kids on the dilapidated 40 year old courts at Fort Wayne's Lafayette Park. Rochelle and I, along with a number of members from our tennis club, joined A.D. for the big event. We brought a large stash of used racquets and balls for the boys and girls who showed up. It was a huge success and a lot of fun for all of us, as we introduced the youngsters to a sport that most of them had never played before. The event, with the help of our video, called attention to the damaged courts, which were in such bad shape that they were dangerous to play on. That was about to change.

In early November, legendary tennis player Arthur Ashe came to Fort Wayne with fellow touring pro Julie Anthony to play a charity fund-raising mixed doubles match at the Memorial Coliseum. In the main event Ashe would be paired with the city's women's champion, Donna Morandini, and Julie would have the men's champ Don Shultz as her partner. The preliminary match of the night would feature a TV station challenge pitting A.D Webster and the blonde bombshell weather anchor Terri Joe Tolan of WPTV against myself and WFTW news anchor Katie Mosher.

A.D. gave me a tip on when the pros would be arriving at our local airport, Baer Field International, so I could get the first interviews with them on the Friday 6pm news. They were scheduled to conduct a free tennis clinic Saturday morning followed by the feature matches in the evening. One of the exciting events at the clinic was the opportunity to play a point against either pro for $100. Several local companies like Lincoln Life Insurance, Magnavox, and International Harvester paid $100 each for their best tennis playing employees to have a shot at Ashe and Anthony. All the money raised by the two pros went toward upgrading the rundown tennis courts at Lafayette Park. It turns out that A.D. Webster had appealed to Ashe and his foundation for help through mutual friends after our clinic several months earlier.

I volunteered to do the play by play of this event as our newest WFTW-TV photographer, Todd Hamlin, another former WXDU-TV employee, shot the video. It made for good belly laughs as I poked fun at the locals over the public address system when they got clobbered by the pros. After my friend A.D. tried several times in vain to return Ashe's serve, I really gave him the business. Webster then came over, borrowed the microphone, and addressed the crowd.

"How many of you would like to see Nick Cunningham get his butt kicked by Arthur Ashe?" Webster bellowed as the crowd roared.

I could not say "no" to this proposal, and figured that this could be another video for my "Who Can Beat Nick" series. I was a decent club tennis player, but I had never hit a round with, or played with, a top-ten player in the world, and I didn't have 100 bucks which didn't matter to Ashe.

"You're getting a freebie, Nick, so get over there and serve 'em up!" were Arthur's encouraging words.

I faced certain humiliation, but I had already wrestled a bear and lost in this same arena. This can't be any worse than that. I hit a pretty good serve at him, and he gently hit it back to me. Arthur toyed with me as we rallied for about five or six shots. I then saw an opening and decided to try and hit a winner past him. My angled topspin backhand shot in the corner would have been a winner against almost anybody else. But Ashe suddenly went into fast-motion, took three quick strides, and hit an amazing backhand cross-court bullet in the corner sending the crowd into a frenzy. I dropped my racquet and "mugged frustration" to the camera. The tennis legend then waved his finger at me as if to say good-naturedly, "don't do that."

The evening matches were just as much fun and entertaining as the morning clinic. My doubles partner Katie Mosher spent the week before the event playing tennis every night at our club with Rochelle and T-V director Steve Watson. Katie was determined not to lose to Terri-Joe Tolan, who dubbed herself the "Tallahassee Lassie," and who boldly bragged about her athletic accomplishments at Florida State University. Our match turned out to be a straight set blowout as Katie was a much better player than Terri-Joe. The "G" rated family spectacle nearly turned into an "R" when the Tallahassee Lassie almost popped out of her revealing tennis dress while chasing down one of my partner's powerful service returns.

In the main event Ashe and Donna Morandini prevailed in an exciting 3 set thriller over Julie Anthony and Don Schultz. I had a feeling that Arthur was just having fun until he decided to go with his big serve and finish the match. The real winners of the event were the folks who would enjoy the renovated basketball and tennis facilities at Lafayette Park, which were scheduled to be completed in the spring of 1976.

Later in the month of November I joined the faculty of Dekalb High School located in nearby Auburn, Indiana as we played in a fund raising basketball game against members of the Chicago Cubs baseball team. The school was constructing a "state of the art" baseball stadium for its top-rated team, which consistently produced numerous college scholarships and even several pro signings. Among the Cubs players taking part were pitchers Rick and Paul Reuschel, catcher Steve Swisher and center fielder Jose Cardinal.

Cameraman Rick Cassidy came along to shoot the video and Channel 18 weatherman and afternoon movie host D.J.

Safe Passage Guaranteed

McQueen, an Auburn resident, joined us to do the commentary. News director Sean Montgomery, knowing we were in the middle of the November rating period, gave me the night off so I could possibly win some viewers living outside of Fort Wayne.

The game was not supposed to be a serious contest, but rather a light-hearted exhibition, with D.J. making fun of the participants and their lack of basketball skills. But the Dekalb faculty, led by former all-state point guard and current basketball coach Richie Blackburn, was determined to go all-out in an effort to win. The Cubs, led by the Reuschel brothers who were Illinois prep basketball stars before they were major league pitchers, were equally as determined to beat the home team. Besides the Reuschels, who were both about six-foot four inches tall, the Cubs brought a couple of minor league players I had never heard of who were good "ballers."

The Dekalb faculty started fast and jumped out to a 28-19 first half lead due in great part to the Chicagoans overconfidence. The Cubs even started centerfielder Jose Cardenal and catcher Steve Swisher, both of whom were not skilled basketball players.

My contribution came on defense where I stole the ball twice from struggling Steve Swisher; the first time I quickly passed it to Richie Blackburn who scored on an easy lay-up. The second time I took it away from the burly catcher, who just couldn't dribble, he was not a happy camper. As I tried to drive to the hoop Swisher, who outweighed me by about 50 pounds, ran me into the wall with him landing on top of me and whispering some choice words in my ear.

"Listen asshole, I came here to play a fun game of basketball not to get my pocket picked by a publicity seeking sportscaster!"

That was a very different tone from the guy who gave me such a cordial and articulate interview an hour earlier, so I had to respond.

"I'm playing to win Steve, just as I've watched you do against the Cards and the Reds, among others."

Before either one of us could say another word, the ref called a two shot foul on him. The referees then called both teams over and lectured us about rough play in what was supposed to be an exhibition. D.J. McQueen was having fun with the incident over the loudspeaker, comparing it to the World Wrestling Federation. I sank one of my two free-throws and took a seat on the bench for the rest of the game, which became less intense as the Cubs turned it on in the second half and beat us 58-45.

After the game, D.J. insisted that I join him for a beer at his favorite "redneck" bar, Julianne's Moonlight Saloon in Auburn. This popular historical hang-out, dating back to Prohibition times in the twenties and thirties, was even more "redneck" than I expected.

The place was packed on this late Friday night, and D.J. and I worked our way through the crowd up to the bar where I was introduced to the owner of the famed establishment, Julianne Burns. She was a red-haired lady in her mid-forties who had inherited a failing bar from her father ten years earlier, and had turned it into Auburn's "go-to" spot with several new on the market big screen TV's. Julianne, who had become a buddy of McQueen's, greeted us warmly and poured us a couple of beers "on the house". She talked to me as if we had known each other for quite some time, not having just met. I had found that was commonplace for somebody that was on television regularly. You appear on their TV sets at home, in their bedrooms and, in some cases, their bars. As such, they feel that they know you, and feel that they can carry on a conversation with you as if you have a history together. It was the price of being a celebrity, and most of the time I had no problem with this arrangement.

As we sipped our beers and chatted with the owner, we were watching an NBA game on the big screen featuring the Los Angeles Lakers and the Detroit Pistons. The Lakers were led by their new star, Kareem Abdul Jabbar, who they had just acquired from the Milwaukee Bucks in a blockbuster trade. On one of my shows I had referred to Jabbar as the "greatest basketball player of all time," touching off quite a fire storm of strong opinions in our audience. Many viewers felt that Pete Maravich, another fabulous player of that era, was better than Jabbar, who had changed his name from Lew Alcindor in college. The argument had racial implications as Maravich was white and Jabbar was black. When the television showed a close-up of the new Lakers' center, I heard a voice behind me trumpeting in my ear.

"There is that Alcindor or Jabbar or whatever he calls himself now. He ain't nuthin' but a big dumb N---er!"

I probably should have kept my mouth shut, but I could not help myself and responded matter-of-factly, without turning around.

"Jabbar did graduate with academic honors from UCLA, which is hard to do when you are playing college athletics."

Then I heard a different inebriated voice behind me join the conversation.

"Looky here, I think we have that hippy sportscaster who tried to f—k up the big golf tournament in Fort Wayne last summer."

I could hear more angry voices chiming in, but before the situation could escalate further, D.J. sensing a possible physical confrontation, jumped into the fray.

"Hey fellas! It's D.J.! You guys know me - I am your neighbor. Give Nick a break. He's just doin' his job. Meanwhile, what are y'all drinkin', cuz I'm buyin!"

As the crowd surged toward the bar, I felt a strong grip on my left arm pulling me away. It was Julianne, the owner.

"Nick Cunningham, I need to show you something right now in the kitchen. Come with me!"

Back through the bar and into the kitchen we went. She then led me out the backdoor and over to her new Porsche in the employee parking lot.

"It's not safe for you in here tonight, Nick. Your buddy, McQueen, will keep 'em busy while I drive you back to your car which I bet is at Dekalb High."

When we arrived at my car, I thanked her, and apologized for causing a ruckus at her establishment.

"Forget about it. It's I who should be thanking you for coming up here and helping out our high school kids get a new ballpark," she said. "This is a good town with mostly good hospitable country folk. Please don't judge all of us by what you saw from those two drunks who were trying to pick a fight. I'd better get back. D.J. is probably holding court and giving away all my booze!"

With that, she gave her Porsche the gas and sped away into the night. As I drove home over the thirty miles of country roads I thought about how lucky I was to have dodged a bullet at the bar. I should have ignored the comments by the two trouble makers just as Rochelle and trooper Boomerhaus would have advised me. No question about it, D.J. saved my butt on that night with Julianne's help.

WE'RE #1!

When the November ratings came in, we all celebrated because they showed us as a solid number one at both the early and late news. It validated what most of us at WFTW were thinking this whole year, that we had the best on-air news product in the market.

The Magid Survey which was done over the summer to see how well liked our on air personalities were didn't really matter, because the ratings would trump those results. Interestingly, we weren't given the results of the Magid Survey. It wasn't until the mid-1980's that Tony Silva would find them in a bottom drawer of a supply cabinet. The survey was a very positive report, and actually predicted our rise the ratings. Clearly that information was withheld in 1975 by the WFTW owners, Corinthian Broadcasting, because it would have given the on air personalities more leverage in contract negotiations.

Now I was going to ask for a meeting with general manager Whitney Thompson in order to state my case for a raise in salary, which was essentially the same as when I started in 1972. I had a base salary of $10,000, and with several commercials and paid appearances, I would make approximately $12,000. I did have "perks" that came with being a recognizable TV personality. The tennis club freebie was my favorite, and I could always get a dinner reservation at the best table at any restaurant in town. Occasionally the manager of the establishment would buy us a round of drinks. If Rochelle and I went to the local movie theaters, we generally were let in free if I got recognized by the manager. When I wasn't on WFTW-TV news business, however, I never went out of my way to publicly identify myself or wear my Channel 18 apparel. We never had any problems getting doctors' or dentists' appointments at oddball hours to match our late schedules. These all were nice additions to our life style, but they didn't pay the bills. Rochelle and I were now discussing having children of our own, so finances were going to be an issue, particularly if

Rochelle were to go on maternity leave. Her salary working only part-time was almost identical to my full-time TV income.

In early December of 1975, I took Rochelle out to dinner at the newest upscale restaurant in town, "The Wharf," which had a San Francisco theme. The Wharf was particularly meaningful for us because it was Rochelle's 28th birthday, and our first date was at Fisherman's Wharf in San Francisco in 1967. We had planned to talk about our future as possible parents, as well as looking back at the life we had made for ourselves in the last three years. Unfortunately as we walked to our table a "well-served" customer rudely shouts at me from across the room.

"Hey Nick, whose gonna win the Bears game this Sunday?"

I just waved and smiled. So much for the nice reflective evening we had planned. We were interrupted several times by friendly autograph seekers, and others who politely asked if they could take pictures with me. I accommodated all these requests as Rochelle patiently looked on. Her birthday dinner turned into an audience participation party when the entire restaurant sang the "happy birthday" song to her. When I made the reservation, I had told the manager that the occasion was my wife's birthday, which got me a good-natured scolding from Rochelle. But she did understand my predicament and forgave me for it.

"Nick, I get it. You can't have it both ways. If you want to be a popular local TV personality you have to expect situations like this and be responsive to your viewers' wishes."

Rochelle's compassionate words got me even more "fired up" to negotiate an increase in my salary. So, armed with the good ratings and new found confidence, I arranged for a private meeting with general manager Whitney Thompson the following week. This time I was prepared, and made an impassioned speech to Whitney about how much I liked the news team and wanted to remain at WFTW for the foreseeable future, but I needed a substantial raise. I explained that this was not an ultimatum, and that I was not currently looking at other job options, but that I might have to if I did not get what I thought I deserved. I went on to say that Rochelle and I were looking forward to having kids and making some long term plans. Thompson, with nearly 20 years of experience at channel 18, had probably heard the same story at least 10 or 20 times before my performance.

"Nick, I understand your frustration, and I wish I could increase your salary. But you must realize that the size of the WFTW news department has doubled since you joined us three and a half years ago. We have all been focusing on being number one in the market, including our Corinthian owners in New York, who authorized the hiring of all of our new people. Right now we're spread pretty thin, so I'm asking you to be patient. If we're solidly number one after the February books, we'll talk about this subject again. You can always use your visibility to get you more personal appearances and commercials, which can increase your income substantially. So, for right now, we can do a 'handshake' deal under all existing terms and conditions, and we want you to continue to produce the best sports show in town."

I was angry and disappointed to say the least because Whitney Thompson and the Corinthian boys were not ready to make a commitment to me. It was almost as if they were forcing me to look elsewhere. I was torn because I really felt part of a great team that could dominate the market for years. But if Rochelle and I were to build a family here long-term then I needed more of a commitment from management than just a handshake.

Within two days after my meeting with Whitney, I got a call from Jerry Stryker, a classmate of Tony Silva's at Indiana University. Stryker worked as an assignment editor for WKBQ-TV, the CBS affiliate in Detroit. He said his station was looking for a weekend sportscaster and that Tony had recommended me. Detroit was a top twenty market with possibilities, but after discussing the position with Rochelle we both decided not to pursue it. I wasn't thrilled with the idea of going to Detroit and being just a weekend sports anchor instead of an every-night guy, even if that was the price I had to pay to be upwardly mobile in the TV business. I thanked Jerry for considering me, and I also thanked my good friend Tony for the recommendation.

My next move was to call my former news director Ray Gann who was now working in Albuquerque, New Mexico. When I reached him late afternoon in mid-December, I was able to tell him that we now were number one in the ratings just as he had predicted. Ray, who was putting a newscast together, then asked if he could call me back at home the following morning. What he had to say surprised me.

"Nick, I made a real mistake coming here - it's a looney bin! I thought by going to a locally owned station I would be able to have more control over the on-air product, with less meddling from higher-ups. I couldn't have been more wrong. The owner of the station is in here every night telling me how to run my newscast; he's much worse than those bozos from Corinthian. Sure, I make a lot more money here, but this is a miserable and humiliating experience. I have my feelers out and can't wait to get out of here."

Gann laughed when I told him that I hoped he had a job for me. He added that I was much better off at WFTW than I would be at his place, and then offered another piece of familiar advice.

"This is a tough industry Nick. Job security is nonexistent, and it's hard to find a place with the right kind of work environment that pays you enough to support your family. I know the right job is out there and I'm going to keep moving until I find it."

I thanked Ray for taking the time to call me back and imparting his wisdom, but I found his words somewhat disheartening. If I was to continue in the business, was I going to be moving continually from one city to another? I wanted more stability for myself and my family.

Rochelle and I elected to take our two weeks of paid vacation around Christmas and New Year's, visiting our families in the San Francisco Bay area. This time away would give us a chance to reflect on our lives, and get some good advice from both sets of our parents who had lived through world wars and the Great Depression.

When we arrived at the San Francisco Airport three days before Christmas we were greeted by both sets of parents who were thrilled to see us. We also were able to enjoy sixty five degree temperatures and sunny skies, which was quite a contrast from the snowy twenty degrees we left at Baer Field in Fort Wayne. As was our usual custom when we came west, Rochelle and I split time between our families. Fortunately, Rochelle's family had their major Christmas celebration on Christmas Eve, while the Cunningham's partied on December 25th.

Because of the mild holiday weather, Rochelle and I got a chance to play tennis outside for the first time in two months. We went over to Woodside High School and began hitting around on the courts. Soon we were joined by another couple who began playing tennis on the court next to us. The guy who appeared to be about my age, looked very familiar to me, but I just couldn't place him. After retrieving my errant shot, he came over and introduced himself and his wife.

"Hi, I'm Gary and this is my wife Kathy. Would you like to play some mixed doubles?"

I answered "yes," and as I introduced ourselves, I suddenly realized that I was about to play against 1967 Heisman trophy winner Gary Beban of UCLA, a guy I idolized growing up. He was a legendary prep football player at Sequoia High School in Redwood City, California in the early 1960s, near where I grew up in San Mateo and Burlingame.

Beban was now a commercial realtor after a short and disappointing pro football career with the Washington Redskins. He and his wife were on their way to a ten year reunion party at UCLA for the 1966 Rose Bowl championship team. I wish I would have had a camera crew with me, but it was time to play tennis instead. Gary started the match by hitting his hardest and best serve at Rochelle, who proceeded to blister a cross court forehand return that the former Heisman trophy winner could only watch. That set the tone for a polite, but very quick match.

During some private moments with my dad, Doug Cunningham, I expressed my frustration with my job, as well as the plans Rochelle and I were beginning to make regarding having kids. My father was the manager of the Palo Alto branch office of Connecticut General Life Insurance, so he was quite familiar with the process of employee/management salary negotiations. I had kept my parents up to date over the years on the ups and downs of the broadcasting business. That might not have been such a good idea because they both had started lobbying for me to get out and come home, particularly when I didn't even get a chance at the Indianapolis job. I told Dad that my salary was essentially the same as when I started more than three years ago, and that my general manager would not consider giving me a raise until after the February ratings. I went on to explain that in that same three and one half year period, due to the efforts of the entire team, not just me, we had risen from number two to number one in the news ratings.

MY DAD THEN CUT LOOSE

"That's absolutely ridiculous! The station is going to make a lot more money on advertising because of the higher ratings, and the greedy owners don't want to pay the on air personalities who got them there. It looks to me that moving up the ladder in the broadcasting field is more about luck than skill. In the sales business, if you attract the customers you get rewarded for it, which is only fair. When you think about it, you're really a salesman when you're doing your sports show or representing WFTW-TV. You are attracting viewers who are actually customers for Channel 18, when you factor in the value of advertising."

My dad then went on to explain that I should consider residential real estate sales in the Bay Area. He made me agree to let him set up a lunch with his former employee and now successful home builder, Lyle Gibbons. Gibbons, who had worked at my dad's San Francisco insurance office in the late 1950s and early 1960s, was the CEO of LG Construction. In fact, "Uncle Lyle" was a long-time family friend who helped get me a summer job as a teenager in the 1960's at one his projects in Oakland. He made his pitch to me at Ming's Restaurant in Palo Alto shortly before New Years with my dad urging him on.

"Nicky, my boy, you're a natural born real estate salesman, and I would love to have you join our team. I've watched you grow up, and I know you've already received a lot of your sales training at home. The market's red hot and we have projects booked out for the next three years. We have buyers who are camped out overnight at our developments waiting in line to purchase our homes. I would be very surprised if you didn't make fifty grand in your first year!"

I was flattered that Lyle had made me an exciting offer, and Rochelle and I could not stop talking about it as we flew home to Fort Wayne. But was I really ready to give up on broadcasting at this point? What I didn't know as 1976 dawned was that the most exciting sports story of my career lay in front of me.

5

HOOSIER HYSTERIA

When we returned from vacation in early January, the Indiana high school basketball season was in full swing with several local boys' teams ranked in the state's top ten. In addition, Fort Wayne South Side and Norwell High School in nearby Ossian were ranked in the top ten for girls' basketball. Since I arrived in 1972 no Fort Wayne area team, boys or girls, had gone to the high school "final four" at I-U's Assembly Hall in Bloomington.

As we headed into the state tourney in late February local interest began to reach a fever pitch. I was having a lot of fun trying to select the winners on my prediction show, "Nick's Picks," even though my accuracy had tailed off significantly since I started the feature. My viewers, particularly the kids, really loved it when I was wrong and gave myself the "Clutch of the Week Award." It was supposed to be all in good fun, but some die-hards would never forgive me if I picked against their team. I even had somebody from the Elmhurst High School Class of 1974 track me down 30 years later to remind me how wrong I was to have picked against his team.

"Do you remember that you picked South Side to beat us 65-52 in the Summit Athletic Conference Championship game?" the viewer remarked. "You didn't give us much of a chance, and we won by twenty! Shame on you! You deserved the Clutch of Week-maybe of the year for that one!"

I politely reminded him that I did give myself the Clutch of the Week Award for that pick, and said contritely that I had underestimated his team. Those Hoosier high school basketball fans are a passionate group, even after 30 years.

By the middle of March the 1975-76 tournament had reached the final sixteen boy's teams, and just two of them would be considered to be local. The Fort Wayne "Semi-State" at the Memorial Coliseum would feature Fort Wayne Roosevelt, the city champs, against powerful Marion, the top ranked prep team in the state on Friday night. The other game on Friday would match Eastview High of nearby Kendalville against the number six team in the state, Anderson High. Both of the local teams were heavy underdogs to make the semi-state finals on Saturday night.

After my early show on Friday I was able to get over to the Coliseum to see the second half of the Roosevelt-Marion game. I plopped myself down at my assigned seat on "press row" and found myself sitting next to Dean Smith, the famous basketball coach from North Carolina. Smith, who was in the midst of his NCAA playoff run with the Tarheels, had flown in on his own private plane to meet with Marion High School's star point guard, Davey Prescott.

Prescott was Indiana's most highly celebrated "hoopster," and would go on to win the "Mr. Basketball" award given each year to the state's top prep player. This seventeen year old youngster had the following of a rock star. He reminded older folks in his home town of another outstanding Marion player from the late 1940's by the name of James Dean, who went on to become a famous movie star. Davey's facial resemblance to Dean was striking, although he was considerably taller than the five-foot-eight inch Hollywood icon.

The Marion Giants, led by Prescott's 21 points, five steals, and ten assists, beat our Roosevelt Bruins team 72-64, despite "Whip" Perkins' 25 points in a losing cause. After the game, Dean Smith got a commitment from Davey to attend North Carolina in the fall on a full- ride basketball scholarship.

In the other semi-final game on Friday night, Eastview High of nearby Kendalville was knocked off by the Anderson Indians 77-66, leaving the Fort Wayne area without a local team in the final four the following week. None of the local girls' teams made the state final four either, with Carmel High of Indianapolis emerging as champs. Marion would go on to win its second state boys' title in a row. But the strong showings of the local squads, led by juniors "Whip" Perkins of Roosevelt and Greg "Hops" Jordan of Eastview gave Fort Wayne area basketball fans hope that next year could be "the year."

THE KOMETS

Meanwhile, the Fort Wayne Junior Pepsi Komets hockey team, a squad of ten to twelve year-olds, was beating big city teams from Cleveland, Detroit, and Indianapolis with ease. The team, coached by Paul Katches with help from his wife Marianne, had a phenomenal record for the 1975-76 season of 16 wins, one loss and one tie. While the Pepsi corporate sponsorship was helpful, it only covered uniforms and equipment. The team had been invited to play in a June tournament at Schaumburg, Illinois featuring the top four youth hockey teams in the country. The Junior Komets needed to raise money to finance the trip, so the innovative coach Katches came up with an exciting fund raising plan. He got the local pro team to agree to allow them to play a short warm-up game before the "adult" Komets would play their regularly scheduled contest. Paul, a friend of mine at the Times Corners Tennis Club, asked me if I could put together a media team to play his youngsters.

When I told him that I could not ice skate and had never played hockey in my life, he laughed and said, "Don't worry, we'll get you some combat boots and you can play goalie! It can be another installment of Who Can Beat Nick?"

Why not? I thought about keeping this event "in house" rather than sharing the promotional value with other media outlets. I needed to see if there were any experienced hockey players at WFTW-TV, because I was going to be a team liability at goalie.

We didn't expect to win but we wanted to be competitive, and didn't want to get humiliated by the youngsters. It turns out one of our reporters, Frankie Napolitano, played a year of college hockey at the University of Wisconsin-LaCrosse. News director Sean Montgomery, Steve Watson and Tony Silva also had played some youth hockey as kids, and Katie Mosher had "mixed it up on the ice" with her hockey-crazed brothers while growing up in Pittsburgh. We added a couple Channel 18 salespeople and engineers to round out our squad of ten. DJ McQueen volunteered to be our coach and the team was complete.

We set up the game for mid-April at the Coliseum, after all the high school basketball was completed. The Channel 18 All-stars would take on the Junior Komets at 6pm, while the pro team would play its International Hockey League contest against Dayton at 7:30pm. We would play two twenty minute halves with a running clock, which would be more than enough hockey for the WFTW-TV contingent. The Fort Wayne Komets graciously agreed to donate part of the gate receipts to the Junior Komets tournament fund.

If I was going to play "goalie" for this team I needed to learn a bit more about both the position and the sport. Komets' goalie Bobby Steele, who had forgiven me for the bear wrestling incident, agreed to meet with me after practice and give me some much needed coaching. You'll recall, Bobby was the first guy that Victor the bear wrestled after I got the normally mild-mannered beast all riled up. Playing goalie in hockey is a bit like being a human target in a shooting gallery. Steele, who was about my size, loaned me his back-up practice jersey, mask, and equipment. I got some brief instructions from Bobby, put on Paul Katches' combat boots to complete the uniform, and let a couple of the Komets take "gentle" shots at me. The pucks came at me a lot faster than I expected, and made whistling noises as they hurled through the air, some bouncing off my chest and some going into the net.

Safe Passage Guaranteed

By 6pm on game night the Coliseum was nearly packed for our contest with the Junior Komets, who were determined to lay a decisive and popular butt-kicking on us. Our Channel 18 team received some polite applause as our squad was announced, but the crowd went crazy when the youngsters were introduced. The Junior Komets got off to a fast start when the coach's son, Gordie Katches, named after hockey great Gordie Howe, scored on a break-away just two minutes into the game. I went for the fake and the kid just beat me in the left corner of the net. Then the Coliseum lights flashed, the horn sounded, the youngsters celebrated, and the crowd went nuts just like it was an NHL game. I thought right then and there that this was going to be an ugly rout.

But as the game went on, we became more competitive. WFTW-TV's Frankie Napolitano skated through the entire Junior Komets team and scored just before halftime to tie it at 1-1. I actually made a couple of saves, or more accurately, I just happened to get in the way of two of the youngster's shots. One of the really difficult aspects of playing goalie is following the puck as the other team passes it from player to player, as they set up for a good shot. By halftime, I was sweating profusely in Bobby Steele's practice uniform and "slimy" mask with perspiration dripping in my eyes.

Napolitano scored again, with a great assist from Tony Silva, to open the second half, giving us a short-lived lead of 2 to 1. Then Junior Komets' coach Paul Katches made the adjustment of double-teaming Frankie, which essentially shut down our offense. The youngsters then scored two quick goals to beat us 3 to 2. Gordie Katches got the game winner when he took a rebound shot that bounced off my "combat booted" toe, and fired the puck over my right shoulder into the net-a true "top shelf" beauty. I actually heard it as it buzzed by my ear.

The money raised from the game allowed the Junior Komets to make the trip to Schaumburg, Illinois in June. The team, playing against some of the best junior hockey clubs in the country, finished second, losing only to the champion Schaumburg squad 4 to 3. I was able to get some video of the championship game involving our local team from my old pal Thad Copping, the former sports director of WIND-TV in Indianapolis, who was now a sports anchor at WJS-TV in Chicago.

After the Junior Komets returned from their tournament in early June, I got a call from coach Paul Katches. In our conversation he told me that he had played on the Marquette University Frozen Four hockey squad that lost in the national championship game to Boston University in 1956. Katches was an active member of the Marquette Alumni, which helped the university recruit local high school athletes of all sports. He told me unofficially that Marquette Coach Al McGuire was coming to town to visit with Roosevelt's junior guard "Whip" Perkins. Paul, as a thank you for my help in raising funds for his Schaumburg trip, agreed to pick up McGuire at the airport and bring him directly to the station where I was given an exclusive live interview with the famous coach. News director Sean Montgomery was going to give me a huge block of time in the 6pm news

When McGuire arrived at the WFTW-TV news studio he looked like he hadn't shaved in a week and had slept in his clothes. Clearly the coach, who had a reputation for being intense and well-prepared, was not aware that he was going on live television when he stepped off the plane. When our receptionist, Vivian, heard that McGuire was coming to the station she asked me if she could meet him. She was not just a fan of college basketball but of McGuire as well. To avoid an awkward situation, I suggested that I introduce Vivian as our makeup expert, which worked out even better than I had expected. The coach loved it when Vivian powdered his nose and put some pancake makeup on him.

"Thank you young lady, it's been a long day. Now, if you can fix me a double martini straight up with an olive, and get me my slippers, I'll be ready for my TV appearance," McGuire remarked with a laugh. I think Vivian thought he was serious and searched the entire studio for his slippers.

Al McGuire turned out to be a great interview, calling upon catchy phrases and "words to live by," in addition to all his basketball stories and observations. Here are a couple of my favorite McGuire-isms:

"If winning weren't important nobody would keep score."

"I come from New York where, if you fall down, someone will pick you up by your wallet."

"I had my moment on the stage. The trick in life is knowing when to leave."

The coach had some vivid memories of playing in Fort Wayne in the early 1950s for the NBA's New York Knicks when they would take on the home standing Zollner Pistons, who later became the Detroit Pistons.

"We played in the old North Side High School gym - a real bandbox," remarked McGuire. "And that gave the Zollner Pistons the biggest home court advantage in the league. The rowdy Fort Wayne fans were ridin' us right from the start, and the referees were intimidated by the hostile crowd. I think I fouled out of every game I played there, and got booed lustily each time. I swear those 'refs' must have been hired by the Pistons, because I didn't see them anywhere else."

The McGuire interview lit up our switchboard from the moment he left the studio that night. Many of the callers, and some of the letter writers, came to the defense of the Zollner Pistons and the NBA referees. Actually, one of the NBA referees who worked several of McGuire's games in the 1950s, Ben Booker, was retired and living in nearby Waynedale, Indiana. He called me and offered a response to the coach's criticism.

"As a player Al McGuire was a real whiner. He was always barking at teammates, opponents, and refs. I think he was the president of the 'I never committed a foul in my life club.' And, for the record, we were hired by the NBA and not the Zollner Pistons."

But Al would have the last laugh. He would guide the Marquette basketball team to the NCAA title a year later, in what would be his final season as coach. McGuire would then go on to be a very popular NBC-TV basketball analyst alongside Dick Enberg and Billy Packer. If there was ever a guy who was made for the bright lights of show biz and television, it was McGuire.

The Sons of the Summit City Foundation named Richard Luger, an Indianapolis native and former mayor, as it's "Man of the Year" in 1976. Lugar, who later that year would be elected to the United States Senate, was chosen by the foundation over basketball great George McGinnis, among others. McGinnis, to date, has never been named Indiana's "Man of the Year", even though he was named to the Naismith Basketball Hall of Fame in 2017. WFTW-TV general manager Whitney Thompson, a member of the Sons of the Summit City Foundation, elected to do a one hour special on the awards dinner, perhaps as a conciliatory gesture after he was criticized for allowing my investigative report to air the previous year. While I understood the politics of Whitney's decision to run the "special," I was irked by the fact that Herman Yates would be the emcee for this event which would air on "my" station.

The show, which was to consist mainly of Yates introducing Richard Lugar followed by Lugar's acceptance speech, turned out to be a disaster. Our remote equipment, possibly due to the heat, did not function properly, causing the lips of the speaker visually to not match the sound. Poor Steve Watson, our best producer/director, was given the job of trying to salvage the show - an impossible task. D.J McQueen, who did the voice-over lead-in, teased him about being the "captain of the Titanic."

In July, I met up again with Richard Lugar at the United States Track and Field Hall of Fame induction ceremony in Angola, Indiana. The former Indianapolis mayor, an avid track and field fan, was the emcee of the event, which attracted Olympic gold medal winners Wyomia Tyus, Harrison Dillard, and Greg Bell, among others. I got some great interviews and stories from all of them, even though I had heard many of the same stories from my dad in the 1950's and 60's. Bell, currently a dentist from nearby Peru, Indiana, won the gold medal for the long jump at the 1956 Olympics in Melbourne, Australia. He was America's second ranked long jumper behind University of California's Monte Upshaw, who had injured his knee before the '56 games and could not compete. I spent my early years in Piedmont, California where Upshaw was the local legend as a football star, and as the man who beat Jesse Owens high school long jump record. I grew up thinking (inaccurately, of course) that Greg Bell of Indiana University was the villain who stole my high school hero's gold medal. Here I was face-to-face with the guy who 20 years ago garnered the wrath of nearly the entire Piedmont community. I just had to ask Bell about Monte Upshaw.

"Monte Upshaw was the best in the world in the mid 1950's," Bell said with a deep sigh. "If he hadn't suffered that catastrophic knee injury, he might've broken Jesse Owens' Olympic record. It's also more than likely that the gold medal that sits in my trophy case would be his. Every time I look at that gold medal, I feel great pride, but also sadness when I think about how badly Monte must've felt about that lost opportunity."

Wow! It was hard to hate a guy with such humility and empathy. I couldn't wait to tell my family and Piedmont friends that Bell was no villain at all, but a humble hero who deserved the "gold" in 1956.

THE SUMMER GAMES

It was now July of 1976 and we have rejoined our story of our Saturday morning basketball game at Ben Geyer Junior High School, where I visited with two of the area's top prep hoop stars. William Isiah "Whip" Perkins of Roosevelt High in Fort Wayne's inner city and Greg "Hops" Jordan of Eastview High of Kendallville, a predominately white community, first met at Bobby Short's summer camp when they were 12 years old. Short had matched them up against each other because they were the two best players in their age group, and, at that time, they were both about the same size.

"But then 'Whip' shot up like a beanstalk and dwarfed me!" opined Jordan. "Whattaya now, 'Whip,' 6-6?"

"I think so, but I'm still growing. Been eatin' my Wheaties!" responded Perkins. "Why don't you tell the man why they call you 'Hops'?"

Greg Jordan, who was just under six feet two inches tall, was an amazing leaper. He would jump center for his basketball team against much taller players, winning the "tip" almost every time. When he set the school record in the high jump his sophomore year as a member of the track team, he was given the nickname of "Hops."

After a few minutes more of "getting to know you chit-chat," they revealed to me that they were planning to play a couple of practice games against each other during the summer months. The games would be just for the players; no fans, no parents, no coaches, and most of all, no press.

"Both of our teams just missed goin' to state this past year, and we both feel that we have a chance to win it all next season," explained Jordan. "Because it's so important to adjust to different

Safe Passage Guaranteed | 201

styles of play in the tournament, we felt we would really help each other by facing one another right now."

I jumped in with "Where are you going to play a game featuring a team of all black players against a team of all white players that won't attract a crowd, and possibly, I hate to say it, trouble?"

"We'll play one game at our place and one game at their place," added Perkins. "We'll keep the time and place secret until the very last moment, and we'll each guarantee the visiting team's safety."

"What was the phrase you used, Whip," asked Jordan. "Safe Passage Guaranteed?"

"That was it!" Perkins proclaimed.

I had to interrupt again.

"Guaranteeing each other's safety is going to be very difficult to say the least. How did you come up with the idea to schedule practice games?"

"We ran into each other after we both lost our games at the Coliseum last March", Perkins explained. "We talked about how preparation and hard work could get us to the next level. As seniors, neither one of us wants to walk off the basketball floor as losers in our last high school game. That's when the idea of putting a couple of summer exhibition contests together came up."

"We also felt that we might be doin' somethin' that other schools around the state won't be doin'," added Jordan. "That'll give both teams more confidence against unfamiliar competition. In the state tournament, you only get one shot at your opponent. You lose, you go home; like we both did last March, and that sucked."

Both players insisted that they were playing these games only because they each felt that their teams had a chance to win state, not to send any social, political, or educational message. This was just about "basketball." Both Perkins and Jordan felt that if this two game series became publicly known it would be misunderstood and politicized. The two teenagers also felt that if their parents were to hear about the series, that they might try to prevent it, due to its' inherent danger. The two of them made me promise that I would not expose this amazing story, which could have been so enlightening and instructive for a city, state and nation caught up in racial strife and confrontation. These black and white kids were showing us all that they had the same goals, and that their commonalities were much greater than their differences. This was the kind of a story that Walter Cronkite, John Chancellor, and Frank Reynolds, the major network news anchors of the 1970s, would include at the end of their newscast as a "feel good kicker" to balance the negative events of the day. It was killing me not to be able to tell this inspiring tale. If one of these squads were to win state in 1977 after their black vs. white summer games, you would have the makings of a Hollywood script.

I had to know how these games played out, so I gave each of them my unlisted phone number at home and private inside line to the WFTW-TV newsroom. They agreed to call me regularly over the next several months and fill me in on all the details, as if they were sports reporters themselves. I also asked them if I would be able to do a story on this event at some future date. The two of them looked at each other and told me they would talk about it. After an animated conversation in the corner of the gym, they returned. I was afraid I would be silenced forever.

"We think you can tell our story when we get really old, like say fifty," remarked Whip with a smile.

"Sure, I am O-K with that," Hops chimed in.

In the months of July and August of 1976 I must have talked to each of these teenagers at least four times. It was fascinating to hear the about same events from two different characters who had very similar perspectives and memories. There's no question that my relationship with A.D. Webster and our WFTW-TV intern Jackie Knight, a former Roosevelt basketball player, were the main reasons that these players felt comfortable opening up to me. I felt that both Jackie and A.D. knew about the black and white basketball series as well, but were also sworn to secrecy. Rochelle was my only confidant for this amazing saga.

"Nick, that is truly a story of a lifetime", she said as we lay in bed together before dozing off to sleep. "You need to write everything down so you can tell this tale accurately forty years or so from now. I'm sure it will be just as significant then as it is now."

Both Perkins and Jordan also gave me the names and descriptions of their teammates who took part in these exhibitions. The coaches of these teams, while not involved in the summer games, also had interesting background stories.

Whip, the younger of two sons of Wilma and Ike Perkins, was heavily recruited by at least a dozen top division one basketball programs including Marquette, Purdue, and Indiana University. His older brother, Woodrow, was stationed with the United States Army in Germany, while his two younger sisters, Jocey and Sidney, were both in middle school. Wilma worked as an emergency room nurse at nearby Parkview Memorial Hospital, and Whip's dad, Ike, a proud Korean War veteran, was the local handyman. His repair skills were so renowned that he was known in the neighborhood as "Mr. Fix-it."

Mike Huff, a burly six foot six inch senior center for the Roosevelt Bruins, worked as a bagger for the local Rogers Supermarket when he wasn't playing basketball or taking care of his younger siblings. His father was a construction worker, and his mom was employed by a local house cleaning firm. Both worked long hours to support Mike and his 2 younger brothers and two younger sisters. As a result, Mike had to play the role of parent and disciplinarian for his four younger siblings when mom and dad were away from home. His schedule was packed, and finding time for a road trip and a practice game was going to be difficult. A big senior year on the basketball court might earn Mike the scholarship he wanted so badly. There were "no-takers" yet.

Another member of the Roosevelt squad was six foot eight inch junior forward Maurice Brinks, the tallest member of a very tall Bruin team. Brinks, in great part because of his excellent grades in math and science, had already been offered a full ride basketball scholarship from Duquesne University in Pittsburgh. Maurice, who looked like a human beanstalk, wanted to work for NASA when his basketball days were done.

Dickie Patton, a five foot ten inch senior point guard, was a dependable ball handler and playmaker for the Roosevelt squad. He was the team's assist leader and let Whip, at the other guard position, concentrate on scoring. Dickie was the oldest son of a single mom who managed a local nursery where he would help out part-time after practice and during the summer. His mom would also work nights as a bartender in order to support her two sons and daughter. Patton, who also was a star shortstop on the Roosevelt baseball team, was often responsible for cooking dinner for himself and his two younger siblings. His dream was to play shortstop for the Chicago Cubs.

Senior James Townsend, at six feet two and over two hundred pounds, was the other forward on the Bruins. James, the youngest of three kids, had aspirations to be an actor in Hollywood. He resembled a younger version of his idol, Fred "the Hammer" Williamson, the former pro football player and current actor who starred in films like "Black Caesar" and "Three the Hard Way." James played Romeo in Roosevelt High's theater version of Romeo and Juliet. Townsend, whose dad was security guard at the bank and his mom was a cashier at Hook's Dependable Drugs, was the team's defensive specialist, using his chiseled body to intimidate opponents. His two older sisters, Destiny and Maggie, would help in that cause with a constant "trash-talk" dialogue during the games designed to distract and discourage the other teams.

Sixty year old Chet Dillard, who had more than three decades of basketball coaching experience, was in his fourth year as the head man of the Roosevelt Bruins. Previously he had coached some of the great teams of the 1960's at Central High School, featuring none other than local legend Bobby Short. Dillard, who was white, had a long and successful history of working with African American players. As a matter of fact, Chet was fiercely protective of his inner city kids when he felt they were being unfairly targeted by referees or hostile crowds. Bobby Short related a great story to A.D. Webster which was passed on to me. About ten years ago Dillard's Central High team went on the road to play a game at New Haven High, a school known for its cat-calling rowdy crowd. In the first half the raucous New Haven fans hurled a barrage of insults, some racially tainted, at the Central squad. By halftime, the coach had heard enough. As the teams filed into the dressing room at the break tied at twenty nine, Dillard grabbed the auditorium microphone and said:

"Ladies and gentlemen, to this point my players have acted like model citizens while you have been rude and insulting to them. This has to stop right now! If it doesn't, I'm going to turn my boys loose on you in the second half, and it won't be pretty!"

The New Haven crowd, due in great part to the visiting coach's admonishment, was mostly quiet in the second half. They had a reason to be just that as Central came out of the locker room breathing fire after a pep talk from Dillard, and beat the home team by twenty points. Chet, while intense as a tiger on the basketball floor, was a pussycat when he played with his four grandkids at his longtime Fort Wayne home that he shared with his wife Silvia.

On the other side, Eastview High School was led by its captain, Greg "Hops" Jordan, a six foot two inch senior guard, whose athletic exploits were legendary in the Kendallville community. He was a rare "four sport" athlete, competing in football as a wide receiver, baseball as a center fielder, track and field as a jumper in addition to his first love-basketball. If it weren't for Greg's mediocre performance in the classroom, he would have drawn more attention from college recruiters. He was the only child of Larry Jordan, another Korean War Veteran, who owned and managed a small plumbing firm in town. "Hops" had lost his mom, Hilda, five years earlier due to breast cancer, and his distraught dad had not remarried. In order to deal with the painful loss of Hilda both father and son threw themselves into projects that would help them move on with their lives, but would also draw them apart. For the younger Jordan it was sports twenty-four -seven, and for the senior Jordan it was building his demanding business. Unfortunately, because the father and son were so focused on their own activities, they never had time to talk about the tragic loss that gnawed away at both of them. In the mind of Greg "Hops" Jordan, the best way to honor his late mom would be to win the state high school basketball title.

Jeremy "Storm" Hendrix, a six-foot one inch senior forward for the Knights, lived in a nice single family home just outside of Kendallville with his parents and older sister. His dad managed a Marathon gas station in town and his mom worked on the assembly line at Lay's Potato Chips in Fort Wayne. Big sister, Lola, also worked at Lay's alongside her mom after her graduation from Eastview High in 1974. Jeremy was fascinated by the weather, particularly tornadoes which he would follow on television and his police scanner as the officers described them when they hit the area, usually in the late spring and early summer months. Hendrix was a solid player, and the team's best free throw shooter, but basketball would give way after high school to his dream job - working for the United States Weather Service as a "storm chaser."

Zack Yoder was a five foot eleven inch senior guard whose parents owned a music store in Kendallville, where he worked part-time. On the basketball floor Zack would do most of the ball handling and was the team's assist leader. His responsibility was not as a scorer, but to get the ball to the teammate who had the best open shot. Off the basketball floor, Yoder was a huge music fan, particularly of old forty-five records from the 1950's and 1960's. You could name a song from that era and Zack could tell you the artist, or the other way around. He also played guitar and put together a local rock and roll band that played at school dances. Yoder dreamed of going on tour as a national recording artist when his basketball days were over.

Jake Howe was the burley six foot two inch two hundred and twenty pound senior center, who was a star linebacker on his Eastview high school football team. He had been offered a football scholarship to Ball State University after his tremendous junior season. On the basketball floor, Jake was an intimidating force as a rebounder and defender, plus he had deadly short hook shot from either his left or right side. Jake lived on a farm just two miles outside of town with his parents, two brothers, and two sisters. The Howe family's farm featured corn, soy beans, pigs, cows, and horses. To make it run profitably, each family member had his or her own chores and responsibilities. Jake knew full well that his participation in sports represented a sacrifice by the entire family. He wanted to make them all proud by being the first to get a college diploma.

Cole Zeno was a six foot two inch senior forward for the Knights. Zeno was the man with the best outside shot on the team. Even though he was relatively short for a forward, he was recruited by several small schools who liked his work ethic, good grades, and most of all his jump shot. Cole lived with his single mom and two younger sisters in Kendallville, where his mom was the head librarian in town. Becky Zeno made sure her three kids read at least one book every month, and did their homework before they were allowed to socialize or play sports. To make ends meet, Cole helped out by working at the local Quik-Stop market as an evening cashier until 9pm during the week. After high school, the young man was ready to move on to the next chapter of his life on the east or west coast. He hoped that basketball might be his ticket to get there.

Forty-Two year old Byron Hayden was about to enter his tenth season as the Eastview head basketball coach. Hayden had grown up in Martinsville, Indiana, a small town just southwest of Indianapolis, where he was a high school basketball hero. He went on to play college ball at Purdue before an injured knee ended his playing career. Martinsville was also the home nearly 30 years earlier of legendary UCLA basketball coach John Wooden, who, like Hayden, attended Purdue University. It was no accident that a family friend put the two of them in touch with one another. Wooden, as Hayden's mentor, would have a huge influence on the young coach's career both on and off the court. In addition, the UCLA legend would conduct a youth basketball clinic every summer in the Eastview gym, known affectionately as the "Pit." The Knights, under Hayden, had only lost two games in five years playing on their home court, where rabid fans would fill the "Pit" to beyond capacity on game nights. In order to avoid safety violations, the Eastview Booster club would make sure that the fire marshall and local state troopers had good seats. Hayden, who was a hot college coaching prospect, seemed to be quite happy living in Kendallville with his wife Andrea, his high school sweetheart, and his two young daughters. Andrea was also a teacher and tennis coach at Eastview High.

Hops and Whip set up the first game for August 7th at William Henry Harrison Middle School on the outskirts of Kendallville. Both teenagers figured with the 3pm start on a hot summer afternoon at the school's outdoor basketball courts, that they would have the entire facility to themselves. The two five man teams would play 4 fifteen minute quarters with a running clock and a five to ten minute water break between quarters. Both teams agreed that they would not keep score and that they would call their own fouls, which sounds like a difficult task for two competitive teams. But that was a lot less difficult than finding a way for these ten players, with all of their different jobs and family obligations, to be able to "secretly" play this game. Somehow, they all found a way.

On game day, James Townsend was able to borrow his father's 1968 Oldsmobile Cutlass by concocting a story about taking his girlfriend out for a picnic in the park. He picked up his four other teammates at the Lafayette Park basketball courts and they were off to play the "hicks from the sticks," a nickname they gave the Eastview team. Hops Jordan had given Whip Perkins a map with detailed directions to the middle school courts located two miles west of Kendallville. He also gave Whip instructions to drive straight to the game site and not to stop anywhere along the way once they got off the interstate highway. The thirty minute car ride was going well until Townsend looked down at his gas gage which was on empty.

"Damn, gotta stop for gas guys. We're almost out," uttered a frustrated Townsend.

"I need a little help with a couple of bucks from my boys. Whip, this trip was your idea. You got any bread, brother?"

Whip pulled two dollars from his wallet and handed the bills to the driver as he turned into a Marathon Gas Station on a remote country road about three miles southeast of their destination. As Townsend pulled up to the pump Whip glanced in the garage to see a pick-up truck with a Confederate Rebel flag decal and a rifle in the window. Station attendant Toby Stevens, popped out from underneath the truck, and greeted his new customers.

"You boys are a long way from home, aint ya?" Stevens asked as he suspiciously eyed the five black teens. "Something I can do for ya?"

Townsend responded politely with "Two dollars' worth of regular, please," as he handed the bills to the surprised attendant.

"Two buck's worth!" exclaimed Toby. "Looky here, we have a real big spender."

An irritated Mike Huff mutters under his breath so that only his teammates could hear:

"That mother f-----g cracker needs to show us some respect!"

From the back seat Dickie Patton adds, "Nothin' that a good ass kickin' wouldn't cure, Mikey."

Whip Perkins immediately chimes in with, "You are stirring up shit, Dickie. Easy big Mike, we got a game to play. Let's get the F—k outta here!"

As the Roosevelt team pulled away, they could see that Toby Stevens went directly to the gas station office and picked up his telephone. Stevens immediately called Indiana State Trooper "T.J." Kluzewski in Kendallville.

"T.J., it's Toby out at the Marathon station. We just had a car load of colored boys stop here for two dollars' worth of gas, if you can believe that. They don't belong here. I just think they are up to no good, and I think you need to check 'em out. They're in a late 1960's dark blue Olds Cutlass with a broken left tail light, and they're headed your way."

James Townsend's car had to go through downtown Kendallville, right past the state trooper substation, in order to get to Harrison middle school. T.J. Kluzewski decided to follow the boys from a distance to see where they were headed, and what they were up to.

When the team pulled into the school parking lot the trooper pulled up quickly right behind them with his red light flashing. With his hand on his holstered .38 revolver, Trooper Kluzewski slowly walked up to the driver's side of the car and said to Townsend:

"Need to see your driver's license and registration, son."

James handed over the necessary documents to the trooper and added politely, "What did we do wrong, officer?"

T.J. quickly responded, "Well, for openers, you have a broken tail light which makes me think we need to take this vehicle into the station and do a complete safety check right now."

Suddenly, tempers started to flare in the car among the Roosevelt players.

Dickie Patton was the first to voice his candid opinion of the situation.

"Sheeeit! I knew this game in this place was not a good idea from the start. Whip, why'd we let you talk us into it?"

The normally quiet Maurice Brinks, a junior at Roosevelt who already had a college scholarship in hand, worried out loud.

"We might be so totally f—ked. I could lose my ride to Duquesne!"

As the Roosevelt players bickered, Eastview basketball team captain Greg "Hops" Jordan arrived on the scene, and addressed the state trooper.

"Hey Trooper Kluzewski, how are ya man?"

"Hops, what are you doing here?" a surprised Kluzewski responded.

"We invited these guys to play a friendly game of basketball this afternoon right here at Harrison," Jordan shot back.

Then the trooper said, "Well, I was just about to take these boys downtown for a safety check on this vehicle with a broken tail light."

Now it was time for Hops to take a stand or this game was not going to happen.

"Trooper Kluzewski, can we talk privately for a moment?"

The two of them wandered off, away from the Roosevelt players and the Eastview players who now had arrived at the parking lot to see what was going on. After a couple of minutes, Jordan and the trooper returned.

Kluzewski then announced to the Roosevelt team, "Ok boys, I'm gunna let off with a warning this time." He then turned to James Townsend and said, "Son, get that tail light fixed, ya hear!"

As the state trooper drove off, Whip Perkins grabbed Hops by the arm.

"Whew, that was a close one! My boys here were about ready to string me up. What didya say to that guy, Hops?"

Jordan winked at Perkins and said, "I just reminded him how much he liked his courtside seats for our home games at the "Pit." I also told him that this could be our year to go to state, and that if we wanted to be the best, then we needed to practice against the best."

"Do you think he can keep this quiet?" wondered Perkins.

"Yea, he's a good man and a big fan of Eastview High Basketball," Jordan said confidently. "Plus, if it ever got out that he let you guys go with just a warning, he could be in trouble with his bosses."

Just as both teams had hoped, they were alone on the blacktop playground on a hot August afternoon with no spectators or questions to answer. When the tall Roosevelt players got out of their car and began warming up, the shorter Eastview team members suddenly realized that they would be giving away three to four inches in height per man to their visitors. Zack Yoder, who had brought along an alarm clock that they would use to time the fifteen minute quarters, turned to Knights' teammates Jake Howe and Cole Zeno, and said:

"These guys are huge. We're gonna have to be quick, hit our shots, and run 'em."

"No shit, Sherlock!" remarked Hops Jordan after overhearing Yoder's comments.

"Now, let's do our thing and kick some ass!"

The Roosevelt Bruins' players had also noticed the big difference in size between the two squads; so much so, in fact, that they were getting cocky and confident as they warmed up by showing off several slam dunks for the Eastview Knights' players to take note of.

Six foot six inch Mike Huff looked over at the smaller Knights warming up and then turned to six foot eight inch Maurice Brinks. Shaking his head, Huff commented:

"We shouldn't have wasted our time coming all the way up here to play these guys. This isn't going to be much of a workout. We'll dust 'em quick. What was Whip thinking?"

In the first quarter the Eastview Knights jumped all over the surprised and overconfident Bruins. While there was no official scoring, both Hops and Whip acknowledged that the quicker and better prepared Eastview squad outscored their Roosevelt counterparts by five to seven baskets. Knights' center Jake Howe called on his football skills to neutralize a bigger Mike Huff of the Bruins, and Eastview small forward Cole Zeno stole the ball twice from Roosevelt point guard Dickie Patton.

The second quarter saw the Bruins wake up and play an even quarter with the Knights. The only controversy came on a blocking foul that James Townsend of the Bruins called on Storm Hendrix of Eastview.

"That wasn't a blocking foul, man!" protested Hendix. "That was clearly a charge; you led with your elbow."

Perkins and Jordan were prepared for this argument and agreed that the Bruins would retain the ball, and in-bound from mid-court. They both had explained to their teammates beforehand that these issues would pop up with no referees. That was also the main reason that Hops and Whip decided against keeping score, but all of these competitive athletes from both sides were keeping track in their heads anyway.

By halftime Perkins and Jordan reported that both teams were tired and thirsty on a hot ninety degree day with more than ninety percent humidity. Storm Hendrix, the resident Eastview "weatherman," had announced the climactic conditions just before game time hoping the heat would "get in the heads" of the Roosevelt kids. Both teams brought their own water jugs which were nearly drained by halftime. Fortunately, there was one working drinking fountain on the Harrison school playground, which all the players used. Interestingly, when the players lined up at the drinking fountain they did so in an integrated fashion, a fact that I called attention to when I questioned Hops and Whip on the phone. They were surprised that I brought it up, but both acknowledged that the phenomenon reflected hot weather and the spirit of the game. They both told me that I was "making too big a deal out of it." My college sociology instructor, Professor Marshall Umpleby, would disagree.

After an extended halftime water break, the Roosevelt Bruins began to assert themselves in the third quarter. They began to dominate the boards and block the shots of the shorter Knights. Perkins and Patton began to hit their shots from the outside, while Townsend, Huff and Brinks played shut-down defense. By all accounts from both sides, Roosevelt outscored Eastview by at least five baskets in a one-sided third quarter.

At the break between the third and fourth quarters the skies grew dark and gloomy. Storm Hendrix reminded both teams that the "lowering skies" meant that rain, thunder, and lightning were probably on their way. When Greg "Hops" Jordan huddled his Eastview team up, center Jake Howe was the first to speak.

"These guys are so big up front we're not going to get anything inside. That big 6-8 string bean even blocked my hook shot!"

Hops then came up with a new plan to try to confuse and exhaust the suddenly surging Bruins.

"Let's use that switching full-court press that Coach Hayden and Coach John Wooden showed us a couple of months ago. This'll give us a chance to see if it works against these guys like it worked for UCLA," instructed the Knights' captain.

The fourth quarter started with Cole Zeno of the Knights hitting a long jumper. Then the Eastview team immediately went in to a full court press which baffled the bigger Bruins. Zack Yoder of the Knights snuck up behind Maurice Brinks and stole the ball. He then fired a pass to Jordan who slam dunked the ball right over his fellow "game-arranger" Whip Perkins of Roosevelt.

Then Storm Hendrix of the Knights picked off James Townsend's pass intended for Mike Huff, and fired the ball to a wide open Jake Howe, who scored an easy lay-up for Eastview. The Knights put five quick baskets on the Bruins before Whip Perkins called a timeout for his team.

"Their press is gettin' to us; Coach would say we just need to settle down and find the open man," implored Perkins. "We need to learn how to handle this!"

"I can't figure out whether they're in a zone or a man-to-man press," proclaimed exasperated Bruins point guard Dickie Patton.

"Where are they comin' from? It seems like they have ten guys on the court," interjected confused Bruin center Mike Huff.

Perkins did rally his Roosevelt team with a couple of long range baskets, but the fourth quarter clearly belonged to a better conditioned Eastview squad. The alarm went off ending the game just as the thunder, lightning and rain hit the area. Players from both sides later acknowledged that round one of the Black-White series likely went to the home-standing Knights. As the teams collected their gear and ran to their cars to avoid getting drenched, Whip got Hops' attention.

"Hops, good game, man. But my boys are all dyin' of thirst. Is there someplace 'safe' near here where we can get some Cokes or Pepsi's?"

Jordan thought for a moment and then said, "Yeah, the Quik-Stop Market on the way back through town. It's on the right, about a mile and a half down the road. Be quick in there and keep movin' till you get home."

Perkins nodded as he jumped in teammate James Townsend's car, and the Roosevelt team sped off toward Kendallville. Eastview's Cole Zeno, a part-time employee at the same Quik-

Safe Passage Guaranteed

Stop market, overheard his teammate's advice to Whip, and quickly warned Jordan, who was preparing to drive home.

"Hops, old man McGlinchy, the owner of the place, keeps a shot-gun under the cash register. That "nervous nellie" Ricky Brannigan is the weekend cashier. When he sees five big black guys come in the store, he's liable to shit his pants and pull out the gun!"

"Oh, shit! Jump in with me, Cole. We need to meet 'em at the Quik-Stop! "

By the time Jordan and Zeno reached the Quik-Stop the Roosevelt team was already inside. Hops and Cole raced through the door just as the Bruin players were gathering up their soft drinks and putting them on the counter. Brannigan, the petrified cashier, had both hands on the shot-gun which was under the counter. Cole made eye contact with the cashier and said calmly:

"It's ok Ricky, they are with us. We've all been shootin' hoops."

Brannigan let out a sigh of relief and totaled up the purchases. As the Roosevelt team along with Hops and Cole left the store, Whip Perkins turned to Jordan and asked:

"Do we still need baby sittin'? What was that all about?"

Hops laughed and said, "Don't ask. We did guarantee safe passage, didn't we?"

The Bruin players overheard the exchange between the two and began chuckling. As James Townsend started to drive off, Whip rolled down his window and said with a smile, "See you in two weeks at our place?"

"We'll be there," Jordan responded. Then, as the Roosevelt team disappeared down the road, Hops turned to Eastview teammate Cole Zeno and said excitedly, "I think, if we were keeping score, that we actually beat those big guys today!"

"Yeah Man, we kicked ass!" responded Cole giving his teammate a high five.

The mood in James Townsend's car with the Roosevelt squad was much more reflective and somber.

"Right now boys, we're not very good," offered Whip. "Those little sons of bitches beat our asses today. If we don't learn to handle the press better, we're gonna get knocked out early in the state tournament."

"Come on Whip, this was just practice man. Now we know what to expect. Let's see what those white boys can do at our place," said a confident Dickie Patton.

"I'll tell you somethin," muttered James Townsend. "That guy named Hops can jump like no white boy I have ever seen. That cat can elevate!"

Perkins and Jordan set up the second game for 2pm on August 21, 1976 at the old run-down basketball courts at Fort Wayne's Lafayette Park. Those were the same courts that A.D. Webster got tennis stars Arthur Ashe and Julie Anthony to help raise money to renovate. That was nine months ago, and the summer was nearly gone. The money was all there, but due to political bickering and foot dragging no improvement work had begun on the old park.

The cracked concrete playing surface from the 1930's and the steel mesh nets around the basketball hoops at Lafayette Park were going to require quite an adjustment for the Eastview squad, who were used to newer and more pristine facilities. Whip and his Roosevelt teammates actually were elated that renovation work had not begun on their neighborhood courts. They felt this would give them a definite home court advantage over the "hicks from the sticks."

When game time arrived, the players had to deal with the hottest day of the year, ninety percent humidity, and stifling temperatures climbing into the mid-nineties. Whip gave Hops driving instructions to the game site just as Hops had done for Whip two weeks earlier. Perkins also had some advice for Jordan to share with his Eastview teammates.

"When you get into the hood, you have to look like you know where you're goin'. You can't look like five red-neck white boys joyriding in the neighborhood, huntin' for a rumble with the brothers. Don't make eye contact with anybody, other than each other, until you get here. When you leave, do the same thing. Got it?"

"Geez Whip," Jordan said with a deep sigh, "sounds like we're headed to a war zone."

"Listen Hops," responded Perkins. "Just be cool and follow my instructions, and everything will be fine. Safe passage guaranteed, right?"

On game day Hops had borrowed his dad's prized, almost new, 1975 Pontiac Bonneville with the cover story that he was going to visit his girlfriend and head cheer leader, Brittney Talbot. Instead, he picked up his Eastview teammates at the Quik-Stop market in Kendallville, and they were off to Fort Wayne for their second practice game of the Black-White series.

The Knights were feeling pretty confident after their performance earlier. They talked strategy during the thirty to forty minute ride to Lafayette Park. Center Jake Howe made a good point with his teammates in talking about his team's approach to this game.

"I think we should be careful not to show 'em too much of our Wooden full-court press this time around. No doubt we hurt 'em with it in the last game, and it helped us deal with their height advantage. But, if we end up gettin' them in the state tourney, we want this 'press' to be just as confusing to 'em then as it is now."

"You worry too much, Jake," commented Cole Zeno from the backseat. "They're not going to figure out our press after seeing it in a scrimmage without coaches."

Howe turned over his shoulder and responded to his teammate, "But we sure as hell don't want those big boys workin' for five months on how to beat it!"

When the Eastview team pulled up to Lafayette Park, they couldn't believe the poor condition it was in. Point guard Zack Yoder was the first to complain.

"Look at those courts! They're the shits. The concrete is cracked and the nets, if you can call them that, look like they're wire or some kind of metal. Do you guys really want to play this game?"

Whip fired back impatiently so everyone in the car could hear, "So Zack, are you f---ing in or are you f---ing out?"

As the rest of the team collected their gear and headed to the basketball courts, Yoder shrugged his shoulders and joined them.

"We got us a hot one today," Whip Perkins said as he greeted the visitors." Hope you guys brought plenty of water. We do have a drinking fountain here, but the water is gray and tastes like piss."

The Knights players laughed thinking that Whip had made a joke. That is, until they ran out of their own water, and had to use it later in the day.

The intense heat meant that the two teams had the park all to themselves, which was just the way they wanted it. This time the Roosevelt Bruins knew what to expect from their guests, and were ready for them right from the start. The Bruins dominated the first quarter, limiting the Knights to just three baskets while scoring seven themselves. The Eastview team was clearly bothered much more by the conditions than their Roosevelt counterparts. The Bruin momentum continued in the second quarter as the home team collected almost every rebound and played solid defense. Seconds before halftime, Knights' point guard Zack Yoder, normally a sound fundamental player, dribbled the ball off his foot. The Bruins Dickie Patton picked it up and fired a full court pass to teammate Mike Huff who resoundingly slam dunked the ball as the first half ended. Huff's dunk was so emphatic that the entire basketball standard shook from side to side. Both teams then took an extended water break to talk strategy.

"These guys are kickin' our asses," proclaimed a frustrated Hops Jordan to his mates. "We can't shoot, rebound or play defense worth a shit!"

Several Eastview players ranted about the heat and the conditions, but that only made Jordan more determined.

"Don't you think it's hot for them too?" inquired Hops. "Look, we beat 'em last time and we can come back and do it again. I've got an idea that may help us get back in this thing!"

Meanwhile, the host team was upbeat and even jubilant.

"We own these guys today!" Roosevelt center Mike Huff announced. "We're not shooting great, but we're stuffing their shots and grabbin' rebounds."

"Let's not get too cocky," warned Whip. "That's what got us in trouble two weeks ago. These guys can play, and we know it. Let's finish 'em off and send 'em home cryin' to their mamas!"

"Hey Whip" Hops yelled from across the court, "whattaya say that we shake things up a bit, and we play 'make it- take it' just in the third quarter?"

"You know that's our game," shot back Whip. He then turned to his teammates and said, "Guys, whattaya think? These boys want to play 'make it-take it' on the brothers' home court. Shall we give them what they want?"

All of the Bruins' players enthusiastically agreed.

"Make it-take it" in basketball is where the team that scores, gets to keep possession of the ball, and possibly keep scoring; thus, not allowing the other team to go on offense and score. It allows for teams to go on long scoring runs if they are executing their offense and shooting well. The make it-take it format is rarely utilized in organized basketball, but is very common in practice and pick-up games.

The Knights got the ball first, and thanks to long baskets by Jordan, Cole Zeno, and Zack Yoder, the Eastview squad suddenly felt that they were making a steady comeback. But when Jake Howe missed his hook shot, Maurice Brinks grabbed the rebound for the Bruins. The Roosevelt team then went on a five basket roll of their own, and eventually outscored their guests in a fairly even third quarter. By the end of the period both teams were hot, tired, and thirsty. All ten players lined up in an integrated first come first serve cue at the old Lafayette Park drinking fountain with its "Depression-era" pipes and fixtures. Together they consumed and complained about the gray, grimy, putrid water that oozed out of the fountain, a "bonding" experience, no doubt.

As the two squads took a longer than usual break between quarters, Hops Jordan noticed that three African American males had circled his dad's car, and were beginning to remove the hubcaps. He rushed over to the car, which was about one hundred yards away, shouting at the thieves as he ran.

"Get away from that car, you assholes! Don't touch those hub caps! What the f—k do you think you are doing?"

According to our WFTW intern Jackie Knight, former Roosevelt basketball player, Donnie Thorne, had fallen in with the wrong crowd. He was now spending time with drug dealers and small-time criminals, who were snatching purses and stealing hubcaps. Donnie, who was once a star player for the Bruins, had lost his starting job to Whip Perkins, then just a sophomore, in the 1974-75 season. Thorne, according to Knight, would not accept a backup role, and was so upset that he quit the team. He and his accomplices were now intent on removing the hubcaps on Larry Jordan's Bonneville.

Thorne saw Jordan coming toward him and immediately responded.

"What did you expect when you came into the hood you dumb-ass cracker? These hubcaps will be your parking fee!"

Hops was about ready to lunge at Thorne when Whip Perkins came out of nowhere to put himself between the two potential combatants.

"You and your boys need to back off, Thorny!" shouted Perkins. "We invited these boys to play some hoops here at Lafayette."

Donnie Thorne looked around to see that players from both teams were now surrounding the Bonneville.

"So that's how it is, Whip? You are now the white man's n----r, aren't you? If you can't beat this sorry assed group of five Opies from Mayberry, then you ain't shit."

"At least we're not quitters, like you, man," responded Perkins, who then pointed to the players behind him. "I count ten of us and but three of you, so you'd best be movin' your asses on outta here, now!"

Donnie nodded to his crew, and as they started to walk away, he turned and looked right at the Roosevelt captain with an icy stare.

"Just remember Whip, this ain't over. Me and the brothers will be back when the odds are more even, and we can settle things then," warned Thorne.

Hops checked to make sure all of the hubcaps on his father's car were securely in place before huddling his teammates during the break between the third and fourth quarters.

"OK, I know we are all gassed but I think we give 'em a taste of the Wooden Press," a determined Jordan told his teammates.

The Knights' press confused the Bruins, just like it had done two weeks earlier in Kendallville. Eastview's Storm Hendrix picked off a James Townsend pass and shoveled the ball to Jake Howe who scored an easy lay-up. Dickie Patton's inbound pass to Roosevelt teammate Maurice Brinks was picked off by Hops who slam dunked. Now the tired Bruins started bickering among themselves as they felt their big lead begin to slip away. The Eastview squad could feel that momentum had swung to their side.

But suddenly the game took an ugly turn as Hops Jordan tripped over a crack in the concrete playing surface, and fell head-first into the steel basketball standard as he drove to the hoop. Hops lay on the concrete surface clutching his forehead which was gushing blood, as both teams stood watching in stunned silence.

"Oh, Jesus, he's hurt! We got to do something!" screamed Knights' teammate Jake Howe.

"My mom's an E-R nurse at nearby Parkview Hospital," exclaimed Whip. "Let's get him over there right now! I'll jump in with you guys and get you there quick."

The Eastview Team quickly gathered up their gear and jumped into the Bonneville, with Cole Zeno behind the wheel, as the injured Hops Jordan clutched a towel to his bleeding forehead. It took Whip Perkins all of five minutes to guide the speeding car through the back roads of the inner city to the hospital.

Whip raced into Parkview's emergency room with the Eastview team close behind, including Hops who was holding a towel around his head that was now drenched in blood.

"I'm the son of Wilma Perkins, and we have a badly injured man here!" were Whip's first words to the startled receptionist. "He's lost a lot of blood and needs to be taken care of now!"

Fortunately, it was a slow day at the emergency room in the Fort Wayne hospital. There were several cases of heat prostration and dehydration, but most people stayed safely at home due to the record high temperatures. Wilma Perkins quickly appeared at the front desk to greet her son, and Hops Jordan with the bloody towel around his head.

"What's happened William? It looks like one of your friends has gotten hurt?"

Wilma steadfastly refused to call her son Whip. To her, he was always William. The E-R nurse then went over to Hops and quickly examined his wound.

"Let's get you in to see Doctor McGee right now, young man," she said to a visibly rattled Jordan.

Then she turned to the rest of the worried Knights' players and said reassuringly, "Don't worry, we're going to take good care of your friend. William, why don't you show these boys where they can get something cold to drink while they wait?"

Nurse Perkins ushered Hops into the examining room and Dr. Arthur McGee inspected the wound as Hops explained how he got the injury.

"We're going to need to get that forehead of yours stitched up and give you a concussion test before we can let you out of here," was the initial diagnosis by Dr. McGee.

"I was a little dizzy when I first hit my head, but I'm fine now," reported Hops. "When am I going to be back on the court playing basketball?"

"Well, assuming that you pass the concussion test, which I think you will, you can start shooting free throws as early as tomorrow," an upbeat Dr. McGee advised. "But you're going to have those six or seven stitches for about two weeks; so you're looking at about a month out of competitive sports involving contact."

Jordan started to object, but before he could speak nurse Perkins interrupted as she looked his driver's license, which Hops produced when he was checked in to the E-R.

"Gregory, I see here that you don't turn 18 until next month, so we need to call your parents or guardian to get you released."

Reluctantly, the young basketball star gave Wilma his home phone number as well as his father's business office number. Hops knew that he would have some explaining to do when his dad came to the hospital. Wilma made the call to a surprised and shaken Larry Jordan. She assured him that his son needed several stitches to his forehead and was going to be fine, but hospital policy required that minors be released to their parents in these circumstances.

Safe Passage Guaranteed 227

When Larry arrived at the hospital, he immediately noticed his son's teammates in the lobby of the E.R. As they all waited together for Hops to be released, the basketball players explained to the senior Jordan, without going into detail, that his son was injured playing basketball at nearby Lafayette Park. It was an awkward moment for the players who wanted to preserve the secrecy of the two-game series. Eastview's Jake Howe did introduce Whip Perkins to Larry as the "son of the nurse who took care of Hops in the emergency room." Just as Larry Jordan was about to ask why these Kendallville boys needed to come all the way to Fort Wayne in his car to play basketball, Hops accompanied by the doctor and nurse Perkins, came into the room.

Doctor McGee explained to Larry that his son had six stitches in his head, but did not have a concussion. He would be fine as long as he took it easy for a couple of weeks. A tired and groggy Hops then thanked the doctor and Wilma Perkins for their prompt care. He also thanked his teammates and Whip Perkins for getting him to the hospital so quickly after the accident.

"I would also like to add my thanks to all of you for your quick action in taking care of Greg," said a relieved Larry Jordan. He then looked over at the Eastview players and said, "Your parents have to wonder what's become of y'all cuz it's nearly dinner time. Go ahead, take my car and get on home. Greg and I will head back in my truck."

As the Knights' players filed out of the emergency room, Ike Perkins arrived to pick up his wife Wilma, whose Saturday shift was ending. The senior Perkins was surprised and concerned to see his son at the hospital standing beside his wife.

"What are you doin' here, Whip? What's going on? Did someone get hurt?"

Wilma then introduced her husband to the Jordan's and explained what had happened. Larry Jordan noticed that Ike

Perkins was wearing a baseball cap bearing the inscription "Korean War Veteran." Jordan, also a Korean War Veteran, then had to ask the question.

Larry pointed at the cap and said, "Korea, huh? I was over there too. Where were you?"

"I was at Inchon and Chuam-ni among others," responded the elder Perkins.

"Chuam-ni! I was there with the First Battalion, 9th Infantry trying to protect the supply line to Wonju," announced the elder Jordan.

"You don't say! I was in the artillery unit on the hill providing cover for you fellas," exclaimed Ike. "Remember when those thousands of Chinese soldiers came down from the north. I thought our goose was cooked."

"So did I," responded Larry with a smile. "But then the Brits and Indians came up from the south and saved our asses!"

"You got that right!" Ike said with a laugh.

"You war heroes can go down memory lane another time", interrupted Wilma. "This father needs to take his tired and hungry son home to dinner."

"Yeah, we'd better get going," responded a grateful Larry Jordan. Then he turned to Wilma and added, "Thanks again for all you did today. That includes you too, son," as he nodded to Whip.

Whip looked at Hops and said, "Safe Passage, guaranteed, right?"

A groggy Hops laughed and said, "Well, almost!"

On the ride home Hops told his dad the whole story about the basketball series with Roosevelt, knowing that probably Whip was having to do the same thing with his parents.

"I actually think the plan that you and Whip hatched was a good one, even if it was a bit dangerous," reflected Larry. "But lying to me and going with your teammates to the crime-ridden inner city of Fort Wayne was not a good idea."

According to Hops and Whip, both teams learned a lot from the evenly matched two-game series, and both teams hoped they would get a shot at one another in the state tournament. At the time, neither the Roosevelt Bruins nor the Eastview Knights knew or understood the significance of what had happened in August of 1976. They also didn't know that seven months later they would have another appointment with destiny. Their next game would be "for real", with a trip to the state finals on the line.

6

FATE AND DESTINY

After I heard about the injury to Hops Jordan on the courts at Lafayette Park, I could not contain my anger, but I felt handcuffed in my efforts to do anything about it. If I derided the city for its lack of concern and failed maintenance of the facility, I could end up exposing the story of the black/white basketball series. But I knew that WFTW-TV's Tony Silva had earned the trust and respect of Fort Wayne Mayor Ivan Christoff. I mentioned to Tony that no work had started on Lafayette Park even though the money was raised almost a year ago by Arthur Ashe's personal appearance. I also explained to him that I had heard that a couple of kids were injured during the summer while playing basketball on the run-down courts.

"Tony, I bet that Mayor Christoff doesn't even know about the delay in repairing Lafayette Park," I informed him. "You might be able to save him some embarrassment by calling the issue to his attention privately, before he gets blindsided by some reporter at his news conference."

"You're right," Silva responded. "Ivan has been so busy with the remodeling of the downtown bank building and the underground parking facility, that the Lafayette Park renovation has slipped between the cracks - no pun intended. He's going to be pissed when I tell him that no work has begun there, and that kids are being injured!"

Within ten days of my conversation with Tony, construction work finally commenced on the old courts, and by the end of a warm and dry October the job was done. Lafayette Park with its two pristine tennis courts and full court basketball playing surface looked shiny and new. Even the ancient drinking fountain with its' gray "piss" water was replaced, which proved to be a complicated job requiring all new pipes connecting to the city water supply. The city parks department planned a grand opening for the new Lafayette facility, complete with a ribbon cutting followed by a celebrity tennis match. The city asked A.D. Webster, who spearheaded the effort to upgrade the park, to be one of the participants. Webster declined, saying the new basketball and tennis courts were about the neighborhood kids, and not about him or any other local celebrity. A.D. suggested that the first ever match should feature the co-captains of Roosevelt High School's girls' varsity tennis team, Veronica Hughes, and Jasmine Pearson. It was only fitting as Veronica and Jasmine grew up in the neighborhood and enjoyed roller skating on the old Lafayette concrete courts as kids. I emceed the event, and the girls gave us a spirited match on a gorgeous fall day.

Finally, in October of 1976, at the urging of news director Sean Montgomery, WFTW decided to produce a promotional announcement for my sports show. Former news director Ray Gann and I had given the station a theme and script for the promo almost two years earlier. The thirty second spot would feature head shots of several of my news team pals saying, "Where's Nick Cunningham?" Then another news team member would say, "He's playing tennis." We then would cut to some video of me playing tennis. We would then do the same thing for baseball and basketball. The promo would show that I was actively involved in playing the sports that I reported on, which could separate me from my competition, namely the legendary Herman Yates. I was able to get our intern, Jackie Knight, to assist Steve Watson, Rick Cassidy, and I with the shooting. Jackie was a big help hitting me baseballs and tennis balls, as well as letting me drive right around him and score a layup on the basketball court at Lafayette Park. There's very little chance that I would score an easy layup on the six foot three inch former Roosevelt High hoop star in "real life." Jackie took a lot of ribbing from the "brothers in the hood" because of that scene. In order to help Jackie save face, I admitted, on my Friday night scoreboard show that Knight had actually let me score in the interest of showbiz. I really enjoyed having Jackie around, and his enthusiasm for sports was infectious. The Channel 18 management, at my request, even allowed Knight to adjust his schedule to be able to work on Friday nights so he could set up my high school scoreboard show. Studio director Steve Watson and I were lucky enough to attend Jackie's spectacular Southern Baptist wedding to his high school sweetheart, Darlene Joiner. The unforgettable ceremony was done almost entirely in song and music, with Steve and I joining in with our untalented singing voices. This was the closest he and I would ever get to feeling like we were actually in a "My Fair Lady" or "Porgy and Bess" type musical.

In November of 1976 Baltimore Orioles pitcher Jim Palmer, a future Hall of Famer, made an appearance in Fort Wayne on behalf of the Fellowship of Christian Athletes. I had always wanted to meet and interview Palmer because each of us had dated the same girl as teenagers in the early 1960's. In those days Nancy Spearman of Scottsdale, Arizona would spend her summers with her family on the beach at La Jolla, California. The Cunningham clan did the same, and the two families became good friends. I remember Nancy telling me back then that Scottsdale High had a pitcher named Jim Palmer who was going to make it to the major leagues. I couldn't wait to drop her name to him when we met.

The girlfriend coincidence was mildly amusing to Palmer, but there was also a second connection I had with the Hall of Famer. One of Jim's best friends on the Orioles was fellow pitcher Wally Bunker, who happened to grow up, like me, on the San Francisco Peninsula where he was a legendary athlete at nearby Capuchino High School. Bunker's prep statistics were off the charts with numerous no hitters, but there was one player who knew the secret of how to hit against the young phenom. Tom Finnerty, a light hitting shortstop from San Mateo High, would close his eyes as Bunker would go into his wind-up and count "One Mississippi, two Mississippi," and then swing. Finnerty, who knew that Bunker's control was so good that he wouldn't hit him, collected three singles, two doubles and a triple in ten at bats against the future big-leaguer. Bunker only gave up ten hits all season, which included Finnerty's six. When I told Jim Palmer that story, which was relayed to me by Tom's younger brother Bill Finnerty, the baseball icon doubled up with laughter and literally had tears running down his face.

"You need to write down that guy's name and school for me," a red-faced Palmer exclaimed. "Wally is a champion practical joker who has gotten me good me several times, and this will give me a chance to get him back. Can't wait for the right moment!"

Now I had a tale to tell my friends back home during the coming Holidays, especially the Finnerty brothers. Meanwhile, I got to do an enjoyable interview with the gregarious Jim Palmer, and it was easy to see that he was going to make a terrific broadcaster when his playing days were over.

When the November ratings came out in early December of 1976, the Channel 18 News broadcasts were solid number ones for both the early and late time slots. Frankly, I would have been shocked if we hadn't been in the top spot. Our news team had become a very close-knit unit, and we would spend our free time away from the station socializing with each other. The viewer at home liked to see that familiarity and warmth between on-air personalities which enhanced our ratings. News director Sean Montgomery's leadership and his ability to keep the New York owners from trying to micromanage us were also key factors in our rise to the top.

It had been nearly a year since I had my last conversation with Whitney Thompson regarding my salary. I had been so focused on my sports show and following the reports from my teenage correspondents on the Black/White basketball series that I hadn't given my personal income much thought. That was about to change as Rochelle turned twenty nine on December sixth, and the two of us agreed that it was time to start thinking about having children of our own. Rochelle had put her accounting career and her motherhood aspirations on hold, as well as move over two thousand miles from home so that I could pursue the TV broadcasting business. I knew the time was coming soon when I had to be prepared to financially support the family on my income alone, as maternity leave didn't become law until 1985. My dad had advised me to remain silent for the time being, and to let the station be the initiator of contract negotiations.

"You stated your case for a higher salary last year, and backed it up by being part of a top rated newscast in 1976," he said proudly. "You'll have more contract leverage if you let them come to you."

I appreciated my dad's advice and encouragement, but I wasn't that confident that Whitney Thompson would be offering me a pay raise anytime soon. The fact that we were now the top rated news team in town was both a blessing and a curse, as everybody on the team felt they should be rewarded. Recently, I had witnessed a steady stream of my co-workers head into the general manager's office probably in hopes of negotiating a better contract, just as I had done the year before. The penny-wise/pound-foolish ownership in New York was not going to reward all of us.

The possibility of being the sole supporter of a family of three, coupled with the fact that my income had remained essentially unchanged for four years, had made me become increasingly frustrated with the broadcast business. As much as I enjoyed my job and loved our terrific midwestern friends, I felt it was time to further explore job options in the San Francisco Bay Area real estate scene during our Christmas vacation visit.

One of my close friends from high school was a bright young Burlingame attorney by the name of Bob Kilpatrick, who actually was my college roommate for a year. He and I had remained in touch through the years, sharing our thoughts about careers and family. Bob encouraged me to come to Burlingame and look at his brother Bill's residential real estate firm. I was really impressed by what I saw - an office full of successful young salespeople and a hot market. Then I had another meeting with long-time family friend and home builder Lyle Gibbons, who said he had two projects coming up in 1977 that he felt would be a perfect for me. Gibbons said he needed to know in April if I wanted the job, which likely would open up in the summer. In the case of either real estate sales positions I needed to take time to get my license, which required classes and passing an examination. Both Bob and Lyle told me that they thought I could complete that process in less than two months. Both real estate jobs could pay me four times what I was making at WFTW-TV, depending on my performance. My parents and Rochelle's parents were both excited about the possibility of us moving back to California, but we made sure they understood that nothing was definite.

It was also great to visit with my two sisters, Gracie and Pat. Gracie introduced us to her affable new boyfriend (soon-to-be husband) Terry O'Keefe, while Pat and her husband Brett showed off their two adorable little girls. I could see the motherhood instincts in Rochelle's eyes as she got down on the floor and played with the two children. My sister Pat saw it too as she looked at me and nodded as if to say, "It's time for you two to start a family!"

When we returned to Fort Wayne in January of 1977, the high school basketball season was the talk of the town for sports fans trumping the NFL, NHL, and NBA as well as the local Komets hockey team. As expected, the Roosevelt Bruins had won twelve of thirteen games, losing only in overtime to third ranked South Bend Adams. The Bruins, on the strength of a strong non-league schedule, were ranked number nine in the state. Meanwhile, Eastview High School started the New Year with a record of thirteen wins and one defeat. The unranked Knights' only setback was a 64-60 loss to top ranked Lafayette Jefferson during a holiday tournament in West Lafayette. Even though Eastview gave the number one team in the state a real scare on the road in a hostile environment, sportswriters were not impressed despite a slew of thirty and forty point wins.

After hearing about the summer basketball series from Whip and Hops, I couldn't help but lose my media objectivity. I had become such an obvious fan that viewers would complain to me that I needed to feature other schools on my show besides Roosevelt and Eastview. Whip and Hops continued to stay in touch and give me telephone updates even after the summer games. Intern Jackie Knight brought Whip Perkins and Bruins' teammate Dickie Patton in to visit me and take a tour of the TV station, while I did the same for Hops Jordan of the Knights and his dad, Larry. I also arranged for Eastview's weatherman/basketball player, Jeremy "Storm" Hendrix, to meet our Channel 18 weatherman, D.J. McQueen, and help him with his forecast. My Friday night sports prediction and scoreboard shows would regularly include Roosevelt and Eastview news. I could always defend my bias toward these schools by saying that these were the two best high school teams in the region, and had the records to prove it. Following these two squads with great interest served another purpose for me. It gave me a distraction from the pressure I was feeling regarding the direction of my stalled broadcasting career, and whether or not I should take a real estate sales job in California.

For the time being, the distraction of the high school basketball season and being part of a top-rated news team helped me focus on my job. For the first time since I joined WFTW-TV, I felt that a Fort Wayne area team had a legitimate shot at capturing the state title.

As Roosevelt and Eastview kept on winning through the month of January and into February, I couldn't help but ask myself "what if they meet again?" The viewers at home would have no idea about the background or significance of such a game. It would appear to be just another collision between an inner-city black team and a country boy white team. The public would have no idea that these two basketball squads had already gotten to know each other on and off the court in the summer of '76. In addition to having two competitive practice games, the players together had experienced a near police confrontation and convenience store shooting in Kendallville, as well as a potential gang fight followed by a serious injury, and mad dash to the hospital in Fort Wayne. They had history with each other, and I was one of the very few people that knew it. I really wanted fate to bring them together again.

THE 1977 TOURNAMENT

The "draw" for the Indiana high school state tournament was held in late February with every school being eligible to take part, whether your squad was a league champion like Roosevelt and Eastview or a winless team like the Elkhart High Leopards. It was also an open tournament with all schools taking part in the same event whether its enrollment was three hundred students or three thousand. The tournament would commence on the last week in February and end in late March with the final four playing for the state title at Indiana University's Assembly Hall in Bloomington.

The unlucky Roosevelt Bruins matched up against the host team, Wayne High School in their sectional finals, a squad that took the Bruins into overtime in the regular season before falling to Roosevelt 62-59. In that game the Wayne Generals were paced by three-sport star Ronnie "Bad News" Barnes, who later would play linebacker in the NFL for the Detroit Lions. He got the nickname by being bad news for whoever he competed against in football, basketball, or baseball. The Bruins couldn't find a way to stop Barnes in the sectional finals either as he poured in twenty points in the first half. Roosevelt's Mike Huff fouled out as the third quarter ended trying to guard the Wayne star, leaving the

Bruins short-handed and trailing 46-40. Then Coach Chet Dillard brought in Tom Morehouse, a six-foot junior, to replace Huff. Before sending Morehouse on to the court Dillard had some special instructions for his versatile backup player.

"Tom, I want you to stick like glue on Barnes," Dillard instructed. "I don't care if you foul out in eight minutes. You go where he goes. I want you in this guy's jock strap for the rest of the game. Got it?"

Morehouse nodded as he took the floor and prepared to defend against the burley Ronnie Barnes of the Generals, who was three inches taller and sixty pounds heavier than the Bruins' super-sub.

A fresh Tom Morehouse did his job on the tiring Barnes, holding him to just five free throws the rest of the way, while collecting four fouls on the Wayne High star. Whip Perkins and Dickie Patton provided the offense as each scored three baskets and rallied the Bruins to a heart-stopping but unimpressive 59-57 victory. Roosevelt Coach Chet Dillard was very critical of his team during our interview after the game, despite their record of twenty four wins and just one loss.

"Nick, I know it's a long season, but we're going to have to play with more intensity than we showed tonight," Dillard told me. "Up until the final minutes of the game, our kids looked sluggish and tired. We have some hard work to do in practice before next week's regionals. If it wasn't for Morehouse's terrific defensive effort off the bench, that Barnes kid would've single-handedly ended our season tonight."

The Eastview Knights had a much easier sectional draw by being the host team, playing in their own gym called affectionately the "Pit," where they rarely lost. The Knights hammered Wawasee High School 94-60 in the sectional final with the entire starting five scoring in double figures. The only negative for the home team was the fact that center Jake Howe aggravated the ankle injury that he sustained during the football season. Coach Byron Hayden pulled his starters late in the third quarter with Eastview leading by forty points, as he wanted to keep his team rested and healthy for the tougher competition coming up at the regionals. Hayden told Channel 18's Tony Silva after the game that Howe probably would not practice all week to give his ankle a chance to heal.

Monday, February 26, 1977 was an unforgettable day for many reasons. For openers, a ten inch snowstorm hit northeast Indiana shutting down many businesses and closing schools. Because snowstorms of more than six inches were so rare, the city of Fort Wayne was not prepared to deal with so many impassable roads, leaving most of us snowed in. But the local news, complete with storm and prep basketball information, must go on. WFTW-TV sent out Frank the janitor, accompanied by intern Jackie Knight, on the company 4-wheel drive jeep to pick me up at home. I was told to bring food, a toothbrush, and a change of clothes in case I had to stay overnight at the station. Jackie talked my ear off about the Roosevelt–Wayne game, but I was distracted. I watched with trepidation as our driver Frank tried to keep the jeep on the road as he slowly navigated the icy streets, sometimes veering off the highway on to somebody's front lawn or parking lot, then back to the highway, all the while NEVER stopping or hitting anything. We learned that is how you have to drive on ice, because stopping and starting are so difficult, and the timing of street lights is a coveted skill. The drive from our home to the Channel 18 studios normally took me ten to fifteen minutes depending on the train schedule on Lindenwood Avenue. Today, that same trip was a forty-five minute white-knuckle affair.

When we finally reached the station at 1:30pm, news director Sean Montgomery assembled the news team to hear a special announcement from anchorman Rob Deforest. DeForest told us that he would be leaving Channel 18 as of April 15th to take the anchor job KTVM-TV, the ABC affiliate in Minneapolis. Rob made a nice speech thanking us all for accepting him into the WFTW family, and saying that if it wasn't for the fact that he had to think of his family's future first, he would be staying. The guy was a class act, and nobody at the station resented him for moving on to a larger market where he could make more money. That was the nature of the television business.

After the early news, my head was still spinning as I thought about the impact of losing our anchorman from our top rated news team. As I was trying to make sense of that, weatherman D.J. McQueen asked if he could talk to me privately between newscasts. He told me that he was leaving on May 1st to open his own advertising agency. D.J. explained that being a regular weather reporter on the WFTW-TV news kept him from being able to do on-camera commercials on competing stations. He also described his frustration in trying to negotiate a new contract with Channel 18.

"Whitney Thompson doesn't have much say in the matter," bemoaned McQueen. "It's all about those skin-flint New York owners who want the best but won't pay for it. Rob DeForest found that out too when he was promised a sweeter deal if the newscast went to number one. When they didn't deliver it, he said bye, bye."

When D.J. asked what my plans were, I explained that I was entertaining a real estate job offer in California, but that nothing was definite at this point. I added that I had hoped that WFTW would offer me a raise based upon the improved ratings.

"Don't count on that," McQueen advised. "These owners aren't into rewarding loyal on-air personalities. Look at Fran Bologna, who's been here for over 20 years. They're about ready to replace her show and her salary with a network soap opera."

After the late news ended, the roads had finally been cleared and I was able to hitch a ride home with Indiana State

Trooper Fred Boomerhaus, who was making his late night law enforcement rounds. Along for the ride was Jackie Knight, who had already put in a twelve hour day. The hard-working Knight was a frequent late night companion of Fred and D.J. McQueen, as he hoped to learn about both television production and law enforcement during the ride-along. Before we got to my home, Boomer turned to the young intern and asked him to tell me his big news.

"Well, with the help of you and everybody at channel 18, but especially you, Trooper Fred, I got accepted into the state trooper training program beginning in June," Jackie proudly announced.

I was absolutely thrilled for Jackie and gave him a congratulatory hug. I then looked at Boomerhaus and gave him a wink. All three of us sensed that times may be changing if a white Indiana state trooper can mentor and recruit a young African American to join him on the force.

What a roller-coaster of a day! What more can happen? As it turned out, the most unforgettable event of my day hadn't even occurred yet.

When I opened the front door, Rochelle was right there to give me a big passionate kiss and welcome me home. I thought the extra passion was due to the fact that she was relieved that I didn't have to spend the night at Channel 18.

"Welcome home Daddy," she said with a sly smile. It took me a moment to comprehend what she was saying, and then it hit me.

"Da, da, da Daddy?" I stuttered as my jaw dropped. I had left all my articulation at the office and was speechless. When I collected myself and tried to talk, nothing came out. Finally, after a long pause, all I could do was whisper, "That's great! I love you!" We danced around the room with no words or music, just enjoying the moment. This was poignant because we were never sure if we could have kids due to my vagabond profession and our late start; we both would be thirty in 1977. My news, which seemed trivial by comparison, would have to wait.

"I didn't want to say a word to you until I was sure," Rochelle said. "According to my due date, you will be a father on September 18th. That's it for me; how did your day go?"

I exhaled as I settled into the living room couch, and I tried to process the events of the day.

"My news isn't quite as exciting as yours, but not insignificant by any means," I said understatedly, doing my William F. Buckley impersonation. "DeForest is going to Minneapolis, McQueen is leaving to open his own advertising agency and my favorite intern is joining the Indiana State Troopers - all by June First."

Rochelle and I talked late into the night and next morning, as we discussed what impact the day's events might have on whether we were going to stay at WFTW or move to California. If we were going to take Lyle Gibbons real estate offer, we still had another month in which to decide. We felt that my value to the New York owners of Channel 18 might be enhanced because of the departure of my two on-air partners on our top rated news program. Rochelle and I agreed that "change was in the wind," and that we needed to let this drama play out a little longer before we made our career decision. Right now, the main topic of discussion was what to name our first child. If it was a boy, we liked Nathaniel, Nicholas, or Zachary. If it was a girl, we preferred Jennifer, Natalie, or Andrea.

WE SCOOPED HIM!

As the weather improved the interest and intensity began to build for the "Regionals" coming up on Friday and Saturday nights. Sixth ranked Roosevelt would have a short trip across town to play at the North Side High School gym where they would face the Allen County Athletic Conference champion Norwell Knights. Should the favored Bruins prevail in that contest, they would face the winner of the South Side-Carroll game in the Saturday final. Eastview, still unranked, would have a tougher match-up playing at Plymouth High in their regional games. The Knights would face rival Westview Friday, a team that they beat early in the season at home by just six points. The Westview Warriors, unranked because of a poor start to their season and numerous injuries, had won their last ten games in a row. They were led by all-state guard Gary Yoder, who happened to be the cousin of Eastview's Zack Yoder. If the Knights were fortunate enough to end Westview's winning streak, they would get the winner of the Plymouth-Warsaw High game in the finals. The 19th ranked Plymouth Pilgrims, with the advantage of playing at home, were picked by most sportswriters and broadcasters to win their own regional. My dream game was still alive, so on my Thursday prediction show, "Nick's Picks," I chose Roosevelt and Eastview to win their respective regional titles and make it to the Hoosier state's "Sweet Sixteen."

The exclusive live television coverage, with my competitor Herman Yates calling the action on channel 35, meant that we couldn't show any highlights of the game he was covering until at least one hour after the contest ended. That likely meant that we would have to concentrate on just post-game interviews rather than action highlights on our Friday and Saturday sports shows. But, since we knew that Yates and his crew would be covering the North Side High regional involving Roosevelt, we felt that we could gain more attention from our TV audience by sending a

Safe Passage Guaranteed

video crew to Plymouth. News director Sean Montgomery pointed out that by sending our crew there we would not be limited by Yates' exclusive broadcasting rights. The problem was that Plymouth was a 75 minute drive from our studio under normal weather and traffic conditions. With a 6pm start for the Eastview-Westview game on Friday at Plymouth, it was very likely that we would have video for the 11pm news. But Saturday's 8pm championship game start meant that getting coverage on the air by 11pm would be "iffy," requiring all of photographer Rick Cassidy's NASCAR-like driving skills.

Tony Silva, Sean Montgomery, and I came up with a plan for how to best cover the high school basketball regionals, given our limitations of broadcast rights and timing. Friday night Rick Cassidy and I would go to Plymouth, get video of the Eastview-Westview game including an interview with the winning coach, then shoot some early video of the second game featuring Plymouth and Warsaw before heading back to the studio. Tony Silva would remain at WFTW on Friday night to put together my show, and be prepared to do it if I did not get back in time. Intern Jackie Knight would assist him by putting together the high school basketball scoreboard using wire service and telephone reports. Also on Friday night, Katie Mosher and photographer Howie Hartman would be sent to the North Side Regional in Fort Wayne to get post-game interviews for the 11pm news. Hopefully that day would not feature another snowstorm or another major news event, as our Channel 18 news team was already stretched to the limit.

After I did the sports segment on the early Friday news, Rick and I headed directly to Plymouth where the game between Eastview and Westview was tied at 33 with just over twenty-five seconds left in the first half. The Westview Warriors were working the ball around in an effort to give star guard Gary Yoder the last shot before the break. With just five seconds remaining, Yoder got the ball and began to drive to the basket, and as the clock ticked down, he shot the ball just as he was fouled by

Eastview's Hops Jordan. The Westview fans erupted as the shot went in at the buzzer, and Jordan picked up his third foul. Yoder, who was headed to Cincinnati University on a basketball scholarship in the fall, hit the free throw to give Westview a 36-33 lead at the half.

Knights' coach Byron Hayden knew he had to make a defensive adjustment because he didn't want Hops Jordan, his best player, fouling out trying to guard Westview's all-state star.

"I got 'em Coach," volunteered Zack Yoder. "My cousin and I have gone one-on-one with each other hundreds of times on playgrounds and in our backyards. Gary is three inches taller than me, but I know all his moves. Please let me have a shot at 'em."

Hayden knew he had to get Jordan, his top scorer, going offensively in the second half. The coach recognized that Hops was so focused defensively on trying to stop the Westview star that he couldn't find his rhythm on offense, scoring only three points in the first two periods. Byron thought back to December when his team beat Westview, even though Gary Yoder dominated his smaller Eastview cousin. But this time, the coach could see the determination in Zack's eyes.

"OK Yoder, he's all yours," implored the passionate coach. "He got you the last time at our place. It's time for a little family payback tonight!"

The second half was a tight back-and-forth affair, with one team jumping ahead by five points and the other team coming back to take the lead. With the score tied at 71 and twenty seconds remaining, Zack Yoder fouled out trying to stop his cousin Gary from scoring an easy lay-up. Zack had done a great job in the second half on his cousin, holding the all-state guard to just 8 points, but now Gary had a chance to give Westview the lead at the free throw line. Eastview Knights' coach Byron Hayden inserted five foot nine inch junior Stewart Simons, a steady and speedy substitute off the bench, to replace Zack. Gary Yoder made the first free-throw, but missed the second, and Eastview's Jake Howe grabbed the rebound with 18 seconds left.

Coach Hayden immediately called time-out and huddled up his Eastview team, trailing 72-71. The coach wanted to work the clock down to give Hops Jordan a shot to win it at the buzzer. Jordan, with not having to guard Westview's best player, had gone on an offensive tear in the second half hitting 8 of ten shots and scoring twenty points. Byron also knew that Westview's bright young coach Karl Griepenburg was probably expecting Jordan to get the ball, and preparing his defense for that eventuality. Hayden said the Knights' back-up plan was Cole Zeno's outside shot from the corner. If Westview was going to double-team Hops, then Zeno was going to get the shot.

With time running out, Jordan got the ball with three Warriors closely guarding him. He leaped high in the air as if he were going to shoot a miracle off-balance 20 footer, but instead skillfully whipped a wrap-around pass to Knights' teammate Cole Zeno who was wide open. Zeno buried the shot from the corner at the buzzer, giving Eastview a breath-taking 73-72 victory. Wow! The dream was still alive, and we were the only TV station to get all the big plays on video. After the game I asked Coach Hayden about the final play.

"Nick, you gotta give the kids the credit on this one," the Knights' coach explained. "They improvised and made the play on the fly. Jordan was supposed to get the shot, but we knew they may be looking for that. Hops recognized instantly that with the Warriors' defense triple-teaming him that Zeno should be open in the corner. Cole got the great pass and hit the jumper, just like he does in practice every day. Big win for us, but we have a lot more work to do."

As we headed back to the station, we learned that Roosevelt easily defeated a game but out-manned Norwell squad 62-45.

The Bruins used a smothering defense and a huge size advantage to jump out to a ten point lead in the first period and never looked back. Whip Perkins led Roosevelt in scoring with 21 points and center Mike Huff pulled down 20 rebounds. WFTW's Katie Mosher got a quick comment from Bruins coach Chet Dillard after the game.

"Overall, we played a good game," a low-key Dillard explained. "We didn't shoot particularly well, but we played solid defense, and most importantly we got our intensity back right from the start. A definite improvement from last week."

We got back from Plymouth before 9:45pm, which gave Tony, Jackie and I just enough of time to set up our tournament coverage in the news. News director Sean Montgomery, who was also working overtime, felt we should lead the news with "Hoosier Hysteria," and our coverage of the heart-stopping Eastview-Westview game.

"We have the only highlights of the game of the night," remarked an effusive Montgomery. "A game that epitomizes everything that Indiana tournament basketball is all about. Herman Yates can take his WKHG-TV exclusive broadcasting rights and shove it. We scooped him tonight!"

Photographer Rick Cassidy put together a terrific two-minute highlight and interview package which I narrated at the top of the newscast. Then I returned with another three minute segment at the end of the show which included all the rest of the regional scores, video footage of Plymouth's 76-62 win over Warsaw, and Katie Mosher's interview with Bruins' coach Chet Dillard. It was a very exciting and satisfying night, to say the least. Rick Cassidy would later receive an Associated Press award for his video of the final seconds of the Eastview-Westview game, which was used by TV stations all over the state to promote the excitement of the tournament.

After Friday's 11pm show, news director Sean Montgomery said that he was approving overtime for the same crew to come back Saturday night for the regional finals. He also arranged for our best studio director, Steve Watson, to be available to work the Saturday late news. I was not going to be paid any overtime because of my contract, but Sean promised to get me a couple of days off as compensation for my extra work. I was into this tournament "hook, line, and sinker," and would have PAID THEM to let me work it. We all knew that getting back from the Plymouth-Eastview game on Saturday in time for the late news was going to be very difficult if we stayed to the finish, given the 75 minute "good weather" drive time. I really wanted us to be able to get the whole game, so I came up with an idea that might get us back to the station faster. I called Trooper Fred Boomerhaus, a big basketball fan, and asked if he could give us a police escort from Plymouth. Boomer said that if there were no incidents that would call him away, that he could link up with us just south, in Warsaw, on Highway 30 and lead us to Channel 18. Tony Silva would help coordinate the connection with the two-way radio at the station.

The home-standing Plymouth Pilgrims were solid favorites to beat Eastview in their regional final. The 19th ranked Pilgrims had played a much tougher schedule than the Knights, including a convincing victory over 18th ranked East Chicago Washington High School, and a narrow loss on the road to 10th ranked Indianapolis Cathedral.

The North Side High Regional final, which would be televised live by Herman Yates and Channel 35, would feature the Roosevelt Bruins against the South Side High Archers, a team they had beaten twice during the regular season. The Archers, who got to the final by dispatching Carroll High 68-61, would be a formidable opponent for the favored Bruins because of their size and rebounding ability.

When we arrived in Plymouth just before game time, we were very surprised to see that the packed gym was nearly half filled with blue and white clad Eastview fans. Knights' forward Jeremy Hendrix told me later that Eastview supporters were quick to obtain the tickets of the disappointed Warsaw and Westview fans whose teams lost the day before. Hendrix also told me that Eastview coach Byron Hayden had received a scouting tip from his good friend, Westview Coach Karl Griepenburg, after Byron's Knights eliminated Karl's Warriors. Griepenburg, whose team had lost to Plymouth by a single point during the regular season, said that the Pilgrims were not a good free-throw shooting team, particularly under pressure in the closing moments of the game. In December, Westview had come back from fifteen points down in the second half to nearly catch the Pilgrims at the buzzer. Hayden would remember this important tip from his good friend.

Plymouth took command early in the game, racing out to a ten point lead in the first period. The Pilgrims hit eleven of their first fifteen shots, most of them from ten feet and beyond, as they were consistently beating the Knights' zone defense. Eastview was shooting at a fifty percent clip but still could not keep pace with the home team. Plymouth led 39-29 as the briskly played first half ended.

In the second half, Coach Hayden decided to abandon the zone defense and go to a man-to-man. That meant Byron's players could be more prone to foul out and expose his comparatively weak bench. Eastview's only experienced substitute was Stewart Simons, while Plymouth could bring in four or five veteran players off the bench. Going into the final period the Knights were still trailing 57-49.

With two minutes and twenty seconds left in the game, Plymouth center Chad Morrissey was fouled by Jeremy Hendrix as he scored on a lay-up. When Morrissey converted the free throw, he gave the home-standing Pilgrims a nine point lead. Seeing that his team was tiring and needing encouragement, Eastview coach Hayden called a time-out and huddled his frustrated squad.

Hayden felt his desperate team needed more energy and change in strategy.

"Ok guys, it's time to give them the Johnny Wooden full court press," Hayden commanded. "Let's start with the man-to-man version and see how it works. Hops, I want you to call an audible and go to a zone press after the third possession. We don't want them figuring us out too early. I'm going to put Stewie Simons in for Jake Howe to start with, but stay close Jake, cuz you are going back in soon. This dream season has been so much fun, and I'm so proud of all of you. Let's not let it end here!"

The Knights' Zack Yoder quickly brought the ball up the court looking for Hops Jordan who was covered by two Pilgrims. Yoder spotted Simons, the open man, darting inside toward the basket, and hit him with a perfect in-stride pass for an easy lay-up. As Plymouth started to inbound the ball, the Knights went into the full court press, and fouled the first player to touch the ball. Pilgrim guard Jerry Hoskins missed the free-throw, and Howe, who had quickly replaced Simons for the Knights, grabbed the rebound, and passed it instantly to his teammate Hops Jordan. Jordan streaked down the floor and slam dunked the ball emphatically as he was fouled. He nailed the free throw, and the lead was down to four. Eastview coach Hayden again replaced Howe with Simons, who immediately intercepted the inbound pass. Simons whipped the ball to Knights' teammate Cole Zeno who canned the outside jumper cutting the lead to two, 75-73. The Eastview fans erupted as Plymouth called time out.

Before Plymouth inbounded the ball, Eastview's Hops Jordan directed his team to change to a zone press. The change didn't bother the Pilgrims, as the home team ran off twenty five seconds of game time before Morrissey scored on a short jumper giving Plymouth a 77-73 lead with 45 seconds left. Yoder again brought the ball up the court for the Knights, knowing that his best scoring option was Jordan, but he was double-teamed. The clock ticked down as Yoder tried desperately to find an open teammate.

His pass to Knights' teammate Jeremy Hendrix was picked off by Plymouth's Jerry Hoskins, who was immediately fouled by Simons of Eastview with 25 seconds left. Jake Howe replaced Stewart Simons for Eastview right before Hoskins again missed the free-throw, giving the visitors new life. Eastview's Howe grabbed another rebound and sent the ball down the court quickly to Knights' teammate Cole Zeno, who was fouled as he connected with his patented corner jump shot. Zeno's free throw cut the Plymouth lead to 77-76 with 16 seconds left. The rattled Pilgrims called time-out again as the revved up Eastview fans, sensing a comeback, roared with delight.

"Listen up guys," barked an instructive coach Hayden of the Knights. "We're gonna go back to a man-to-man press, but we're gonna make it look like we're in a zone. So we take the floor as if we are in a zone, and then when Hops shouts 'blue,' we switch instantly to a man-to-man press. Got it? They let us back in the game with missed free throws. Now, let's finish 'em!"

As his team walked back on the floor Hayden looked over at me at the nearby press table and said with a wry smile, "Hey Nick! How's your nerve, eh?"

I responded with "Right now Coach, I hope yours is better than mine!"

Eastview's Hops Jordan yelled "blue!" an instant before Plymouth inbounded the ball, making an apparent zone press actually a man-to-man version. The confused Pilgrims tried to loft a pass into their big center Chad Morrissey, but Jeremy Hendrix of the Knights knocked the ball away. It bounced off two players into the hands of Jordan, who immediately called timeout for Eastview. Miraculously, the Knights now had the ball and a chance to win it with eleven seconds left.

"Nice job on the press guys," said a surprisingly calm Eastview coach. "We're gonna run the same final play as last night except we're gonna go to Zeno first instead of Jordan. Cole, if your shot is open in the corner, take it. If not, pass it to Hops. I'm guessing that they saw the end of last night's game and are expecting Zeno to be the shooter. When we score, we need to abandon the press, and get back on defense. You guys can do this!"

The Plymouth Pilgrims came with their own man-to-man press as the Knights tried to inbound the ball. After a moment of indecision, Jake Howe fired a perfect inbound pass to Eastview teammate Zack Yoder who dribbled to the top of the key. With seconds ticking down Yoder faked a pass to Zeno in the corner, who, as expected, was double-teamed by two Pilgrims. Zack then saw Hops Jordan charging down the lane toward the basket and hit him with a bullet pass. As the clock ran out, Hops got a shot off that missed badly, but he was fouled by Morrissey of Plymouth. Jordan would have two free throws to win it for Eastview with no time on the clock, but before he got his chance the Pilgrims called time out to "ice him."

Knights' Coach Hayden pulled Jordan aside and said, "You know what you need to do, son. Take us home!"

After the time out, the referee motioned for the Eastview star to take his place all alone at the free throw line with the bellowing crowd noise. As Hops bounced the ball, he caught the eye of his dad in the stands right behind the basket. The moment came to a standstill as the two nodded at one another as if to say, "It's our time!"

Jordan, who was already the Knights leading scorer with 26 points, snapped back into the moment. He dribbled the ball twice, swished the first free throw tying the game at 77, and sending the Eastview fans into a frenzy. He then took a deep breath and looked straight up as he thought of his late mom, and how much he wished she was here for this moment. He dribbled the ball twice and calmly rattled in the second free throw, giving the Knights a thrilling 78-77 victory before getting mobbed by fans and teammates. My photographer Rick Cassidy and I quickly interviewed Knights' coach Byron Hayden as he was about to get swallowed by the Eastview celebration party at mid-court.

"You can call my guys the cardiac kids," shouted an exuberant coach above the crowd. "But we can't celebrate too much because we need four more wins to accomplish our ultimate goal!"

As Rick and I raced to the car, my "unemotional and impartial" photographer could not hold back his enthusiasm.

"Jesus! That was a crazy finish! I thought last night's game would be impossible to top. Guess I was wrong."

"That was a helluva game, just like last night," I responded. "And we're the only TV station with coverage, but now we have to find a way to get outta here and back to the station in time to get this on the air!"

When we pulled away from the Plymouth High School parking lot it was 10:10pm, so our chances of making the eleven o'clock news were ticking away. I got on the two way radio with Tony Silva who told us that Roosevelt High School, behind Whip Perkins twenty one points, crushed South Side 62-42 in the televised final of the Fort Wayne Regional. My heart skipped a beat knowing that my dream rematch game of Eastview versus Roosevelt was still a possibility. Tony also said to look for Boomer in his Indiana State Police car on Highway 30 at the Warsaw on ramp.

"Let him pass you with his lights flashing," Silva explained. "Then our favorite trooper says get right behind him and he'll get you to the station in record time."

I really wanted to make it back in time to get the footage on the air that same night, especially after our news director Sean Montgomery committed a lot of the station's resources and overtime budget to the Plymouth Regional. The fact that our games were much more exciting than those shown on live TV by our competitor gave us even more of an incentive to make the eleven o'clock news. Fred Boomerhaus was right where he said he would be, and he waved as he sped by us with his patrol car lights flashing. With other cars getting out of the way, Boomer was hitting speeds of 90 to 95 miles per hour. I wasn't sure the WFTW-TV news cruiser could keep up, but Cassidy put his foot to the floor, and we stayed right behind the patrol car. Tony and I planned that he would do the sports, with the exception of the Eastview-Plymouth game. They would budget three minutes at the end of the newscast for me to make an on-camera appearance and narrate the highlights. With our state trooper leading the way, we skidded to a halt in our WFTW parking lot at 11:15. The old news cruiser was spent, as the radiator was overheating even with an early March air temperature of 24 degrees.

There was not enough time for Rick and I to put together a full highlight report, so we decided to have me narrate the final two minutes and twenty seconds. Rick would cut out the breaks in the action so the story would run about one minute and forty-five seconds including Eastview coach Hayden's comments at the end. The value of video tape over film really became apparent to me that night. There was no way we were going to get this on the late news with film, even if the old processor didn't destroy our hard work beforehand. I made a note of all the plays I needed to describe, and Cassidy took the reel right into the control room so he could coach studio director Steve Watson on what was coming up. When we got to my segment we were running late, and we were supposed to show the 1936 hit movie, "San Francisco," starring Clark Gable and Jeanette MacDonald at 11:30pm. Watson came up with a brilliant idea to save time. He had the engineers in the WFTW-TV control room cue up the movie, but without our station stock introduction and commercial billboard. Watson explained to me during the commercial break before my segment that I was going to end the newscast by introducing the movie including an audio plug for the sponsor, and putting us back on schedule.

Our highlight package at the end of the newscast worked just perfectly as I narrated the action as if it were "live," just like I did in my college basketball play-by-play days at San Jose State with Hank Ramsey. Then it was time cue the movie.

"On behalf of the entire Channel 18 news team thanks for watching, and stay tuned for our big movie, 'San Francisco,' brought to you by Chuck Swift Chevrolet coming up right now."

As the opening credits for "San Francisco" hit the airwaves, our celebration party began with hugs and handshakes all around. Our fiery news director Sean Montgomery charged into the studio with two six packs of beer in his hands.

"All of you kicked ass again tonight," announced an enthusiastic Montgomery as he passed out cold Budweisers to the crew. "Where's Watson? Great maneuver on the movie intro. I want to kiss that guy! And Nick, you even got the Chuck Swift Chevy audio plug in, saving us money. Whitney and the New York boys will like that."

By taking the thirty second movie introduction out, we also lost a video sponsor logo, which would have required WFTW-TV to give the sponsor a refund or provide an equivalent video representation called a "make good." But, because our director had me do the audio plug instead, WFTW could make the case for no "make good" or refund.

It was a great night as I got to witness two walk-off victories: the first by the Eastview High basketball team, and the second by our WFTW-TV news team. I was also very excited because my dream game of Roosevelt versus Eastview was close to being a reality. But, as Tony Silva explained, the match-ups for the next weekend didn't favor my dream game ever happening. The Roosevelt Bruins would face Anderson Madison-Heights

High, the number eleven team in the state, in the first game of the Fort Wayne Semi-State tourney at the Coliseum on Friday. The underdog Knights would meet the number two team in the state, Marion High, in the second contest.

WHO'S GOING TO STATE?

The build-up for the coming Semi-State Tourney in Fort Wayne reached a fever pitch, with Hoosier Hysteria gripping the entire community in a more intense way than I had ever seen before. That week I visited the practices of both Roosevelt and Eastview, and got interviews with players and coaches. I was able to obtain video of the Marion and Anderson Madison-Heights teams from our friends at WIND-TV in Indianapolis in exchange for footage of Roosevelt and Eastview. I even got Marion's radio voice, Jim Drummond, another college pal of Tony Silva's at I-U, to narrate his team's highlights. After a very poor regular season of predicting high school basketball scores on my "Nick's Picks" show, I suddenly got hot in the tournament, thanks the success of my two favorite teams. Most of my viewers were not surprised that I picked the Knights and the Bruins to reach the championship game on Saturday night, with the winner going to the state final four the following week. Selecting favored Roosevelt to beat Anderson Madison-Heights was a no-brainer, but by predicting Eastview to upset highly favored Marion, I faced criticism from a local WOWO radio talk show host, Al Hershberg. He claimed that I had abandoned journalistic impartiality, and that I "let my heart control my head." My friend Al was 100% right!

I just felt that there was a powerful force, call it fate or destiny that was bringing the Knights and the Bruins together, maybe as a reward for the two teams reaching out to one another during the summer of 1976. If Roosevelt and Eastview were to meet in the Saturday final, I made it clear that I was not clairvoyant enough to pick the winner. Some of my viewers felt that my refusal to pick the victor of the championship contest was a cop-out, but I said that I didn't want jinx either team which faced must-win games on Friday. The truth of the matter was that I didn't want either team to lose.

I did my sports show on the 6pm news and immediately dashed out the Coliseum, along with photographer Rick Cassidy and intern Jackie Knight, to catch the end of the first half of the Roosevelt-Anderson Madison- Heights game. The Bruins were leading 33-25, but Roosevelt's Whip Perkins had collected three personal fouls while trying to guard Madison-Heights' 6-5 star forward Roy Traylor. Traylor sank two free throws in the final seconds to cut the margin to 33-27 at the break.

Madison Heights came out red hot in the third quarter, hitting their first four shots and tying the score at 35-35. To make matters worse for the Bruins, Perkins collected his fourth personal foul. Roosevelt coach Chet Dillard then had to send his best player to the bench, and bring in super-sub Tom Morehouse to replace Whip. Dillard went to a zone defense knowing that Morehouse, at just six feet tall, would not be able to guard the 6-5 Traylor of the Madison-Heights Trojans. Without Perkins for most of the quarter, the Bruins were lucky to be only down by two at 49-47 going into the final period.

Dillard made another adjustment at the start of the final quarter. In addition to bringing Perkins back into the game with four fouls, he switched back to his customary man-to-man defense, the key to his team's success all season. But rather than risk having Whip Perkins foul out trying to guard the Trojans' Traylor, the Bruins' coach assigned 6-8 junior Maurice Brinks to the Madison-Heights' star. The rested Perkins energized his Roosevelt teammates on offense by scoring four baskets, while Brinks held a frustrated Roy Traylor in check. When Traylor of the Trojans committed his fifth foul on Maurice Brinks with two minutes left, the Bruins were able to pull away and win 62-57. It was fun to see my excited intern Jackie Knight celebrate with his former teammates. After the game I asked Roosevelt coach Dillard about his team's comeback effort.

"I think what this win showed more than anything is that we're a team, not dependent on one player," said the exuberant coach. "Sure, I was nervous when I had to sit Perkins with his fourth foul early in the third quarter. But I knew Morehouse could deliver coming off the bench, plus we had key steals by Dickie Patton, rebounds by Mike Huff and solid defense by Townsend and Brinks. How about the job Maurice Brinks did on Traylor? Great stuff! I could go on, but we need to prepare for tomorrow night."

The Bruins were going to meet the winner of the second game between the Marion High School Giants and the Eastview Knights, who finally cracked the state top twenty at number 18. The second ranked Giants had only lost one game, a 79-77 setback to 7th ranked Muncie Central in January. The reigning state champ Marion High Giants may have lost" Mr. Basketball" Davey Prescott to graduation in 1976, but they still were loaded with size and talent. In fact, their line-up and style of play greatly resembled that of Roosevelt, a team the Knights became very familiar with last summer. The aptly named Giants' dazzling pre-game warm-up punctuated by slam dunks thrilled the crowd, but didn't intimidate the Eastview squad. The much smaller Knights had seen it all before, and felt if they could compete against a tall and talented inner city team like Roosevelt, then Marion was beatable. My dream game was one win away.

Eastview took charge at the opening tip, running off an early 15-6 lead over the stunned Marion squad, thanks to three baskets each by Hops Jordan and Cole Zeno. The first quarter seemed eerily similar to Jordan's description of the first game between Eastview and Roosevelt in Kendallville last summer. Marion made the same mistake the Bruins did in Kendallville by underestimating the Knights, who looked like a nondescript group of average sized white boys. The Giants discovered that the Knights were anything but average, as the quarter ended with Eastview leading 22-13. When his team came to the bench, I overheard Marion coach Bill Cardigan read his team the "riot act."

"What's wrong with you guys?" bellowed Cardigan to his starting five. "They are out- hustling and out playing you in every phase of the game. You should be ashamed of yourselves. Now get back out there and play with some damn intensity, or I'll get somebody in there who can. Do I make myself clear?"

In the second quarter the taller Giants began to assert themselves on defense and by dominating the offensive backboards. Eastview's Jake Howe and Cole Zeno couldn't stop Marion's 6-6 center Jacob Haderlein and 6-5 forward Mickey Bordon from getting easy tip-ins from close range. As the first half ended, the Giants had drawn even with the Knights at 38-all. But, in an effort to get more aggressive, the Giants' two top players, Haderlein and Bordon each committed three fouls, while Eastview fared much better in that department. Only two Knights, Storm Hendrix, and Jake Howe, had as many as two fouls. I sensed this was going to be a key factor later.

The Marion Giants continued to put their size advantage to good use, and raced out to a twelve point lead midway through the third period. Eastview couldn't stop Marion's Jacob Haderlein who seemingly was scoring at will on every possession. Any expectation of my dream game appeared to be slipping away. We needed our friends, "fate and destiny," to step in and rescue the Knights. Where were they? Just when it appeared that the Giants were about to go up by fifteen points, Haderlein committed his fourth foul. Marion coach Bill Cardigan had to take his big center out of the game to protect him from fouling out. Suddenly, Eastview had new life with Zack Yoder, Jeremy Hendrix and Hops Jordan all hitting outside jump shots on consecutive possessions. The Marion lead was down to seven points as the third period ended.

Safe Passage Guaranteed

The Eastview Knights had the momentum going into the final period, as a soft touch hook shot by Jake Howe narrowed the lead to just five points. Coach Cardigan of Marion then felt he had to roll the dice and put Jacob Haderlein back in the game to stave off the surging Knights. After the two teams went back and forth for the next five minutes trading baskets, Eastview coach Byron Hayden called timeout and huddled his team.

"Ok, we are down by five with two and half minutes to go. We've got 'em right where we want 'em," announced the confident coach. "We're going to get the ball to Jake Howe, and Jake, you're going right at Haderlein. I think you can get 'em to foul out."

Howe, who gave away four inches to the taller Marion center, was a fearless and clever competitor. He took an inside pass from Zack Yoder and drove toward the basket right by Haderlein, who let him go to avoid committing his fifth foul. After Jake scored the layup he brushed by his opponent and snarled, "Come on big fella, you can play better 'D' than that can't you?" After Haderlein scored again for Marion, the Knights came right back to Howe with the same play. This time the Giants' center couldn't resist engaging Jake Howe, and fouled him as he pulled up for a short jumper. When Haderlein fouled out and Jake made both free throws, the Knights were down just 81-78 with one minute left. Marion's Mickey Bordon inexplicably missed two free throws with thirty three seconds left, and Hops Jordan grabbed the rebound for Eastview. Jordan fired a behind-the-back outlet pass to Yoder of the Knights who threw a strike to a streaking Jeremy Hendrix. Jeremy scored on a layup, cutting the Giants' lead to 81-80 with twenty eight seconds left. Time-out Marion! The boisterous Eastview fans could sense another miracle finish.

"You know what time it is, guys," exhorted Eastview coach Hayden. "It's Johnny Wooden time! Let's make it a man-to-man press but make it look like a 1-3-1 zone. Hops, you call it out. We are putting in Stewie Simons for Jake on the press. Stay close Jake, cuz I may need you. We've got 'em rattled!"

The crowd was roaring as the Giants lined up to inbound the ball. You could feel all the momentum as well as "fate and destiny" were on Eastview's side. Marion's B.J. Walters looked over the Knights defense which was exactly what he expected- the 1-3-1 full court zone press. A split second before Walters inbounded the ball, Eastview's Jordan yelled "Blue!" and teammate Stewie Simons intercepted Walter's pass. Simons whipped the ball to Hops Jordan who drove right by a surprised Micky Bordon of the Giants. Jordan's lay-up gave the Knights the lead 82-81 with 25 seconds to go!

All of a sudden confusion took over the game as Marion's Walters quickly inbounded the ball to teammate Bordon, as his coach Bill Cardigan was screaming for a timeout. Apparently, the only people on the floor who didn't hear Cardigan's plea were B.J. Walters and the referees. Both teams were confused thinking that the action had been stopped when it actually had not. When Marion's Mickey Bordon caught the pass, he could have dribbled the length of the floor and scored for the Giants. It was a very lucky break for the Knights, who would have been caught flat-footed giving up the go-ahead basket with only seconds remaining. Instead Bordon dribbled to half court and called timeout, just as Cardigan had instructed, unaware that he had a clear path to the hoop. Both teams huddled around their coaches for what could be the final play of the game with nineteen seconds left.

"OK guys, we've been here before haven't we?" advised a calm and cool Eastview Knights coach Byron Hayden. "They're going to run the clock down to ten seconds and then they'll run their offense, with either Walters or Bordon taking the shot. Let's fall back to our man-to-man defense because they have to come to us. No easy shots or sloppy fouls. One more defensive stand and we beat these guys!"

The Marion Giants let the clock run down to the ten second mark just as Hayden had predicted. The Knights' Hops Jordan had given Marion's Mickey Bordon just enough space so that it appeared he would have an open shot, and that B.J. Walters would pass him the ball. At the five second mark Walters' eyes shifted to his Marion teammate, Hops anticipated the pass, darted in front of Bordon, stole the ball, and dribbled the length of the court, running out the clock. Little Eastview High School had upset the reigning state champion Marion Giants 82-81!

For the third game in a row the delirious Knights fans stormed the court in celebration. In the stands watching the game with interest were Roosevelt team captain Whip Perkins and his dad, Ike.

"Pop, tomorrow is going to be tough," remarked a circumspect Perkins. "Eastview has won three crazy games in a row, and they're on a roll. They think they can beat anybody, including us. Honestly, between just you and me, I would rather have faced Marion."

After the game, I asked Eastview coach Byron Hayden about the match-up with Roosevelt.

"We have a lot of respect for my friend Chet Dillard and his terrific Bruin Team, but I wouldn't trade my boys for anybody else's. We've won our last three games in the final seconds by a total of three points," proclaimed a proud coach, who then waxed poetically. "Nick, remember the children's book entitled 'The Little Engine That Could'? Well, we are that little engine, and we CAN!"

So the stage was set for my dream game, with very few people knowing the full background of it. To the casual fan this David and Goliath contest appeared to pit the big "run and gun" inner city team against the smaller and deliberate country squad. In actuality that description was only partially true. The much taller Roosevelt Bruins were not a run and gun unit, but rather a disciplined team that would slow down the action so they could take full advantage of their strengths - size and defense. The Eastview Knights, on the other hand, played at a much faster pace with high scoring games to make up for their lack of size. This was a match-up that I really wanted to see desperately, but I wasn't alone in that wish. The big school versus little school theme excites Hoosier prep basketball fans to the core as it brings to mind the Milan Miracle of 1954, where a tiny institution of 150 students won the state title, beating schools that were ten times its size.

It seemed like the entire town of Kendallville, clad in blue and white, caravanned down State Road 3 to the Fort Wayne Memorial Coliseum to support the Eastview Knights on Saturday night. Roosevelt High, the home team, had its rabid supporters as well, like my intern Jackie Knight, who was decked out in Bruins' orange and black. The sold-out arena could seat only about 8000 fans, but two times that amount of hopeful ticket purchasers were turned away. Play-by-play man Herman Yates of WKHG-TV would have a huge audience for his exclusive broadcast, and all I could hope for was getting some illuminating post game comments on the late news.

The starting lineups for the two teams, each with only one loss, were exactly the same squads that took part in the two summer games. Eastview would go with Hops Jordan and Zack Yoder at guards, Jeremy Hendrix and Cole Zeno were the forwards, and Jake Howe played center. Roosevelt lined up with Whip Perkins and Dickie Patton at guards, James Townsend and Maurice Brinks at forwards, and Mike Huff at center.

The Roosevelt Bruins were not about to underestimate their smaller opponents this time around. They controlled the slow paced first quarter, outscoring the Knights 15-9. Just as they had done at different times in the earlier contests, the taller Bruins dominated the backboards and limited Eastview to one shot per possession. By the end of the first half Roosevelt had pushed its advantage to 29-20. The Bruins' Whip Perkins led all scorers with twelve points as he was hitting outside jump shots over the Eastview zone defense. In the locker room at halftime Bruins' coach Chet Dillard reminded his team not to get complacent. Knights' coach Byron Hayden told his team that if they did a better job of rebounding and picked up the intensity, they could overtake their opponent in the second half, just as they had in the last three games.

The inspired Knights picked up the tempo and began to close the gap in the third quarter, capitalizing on Bruin turnovers and missed free throws. Eastview's Jake Howe, who would be playing linebacker in the fall for the Ball State football team, was giving a much bigger Mike Huff of the Bruins a good physical battle under the boards. At one point both big centers went after a loose ball and collided, with Huff's body check sending Howe to the floor. For a moment I worried that this would touch off an angry confrontation between the two squads. But Roosevelt's Mike Huff offered a hand to Eastview's Jake Howe and helped him up. The opposing players respectfully nodded at one another, and the intense game resumed. The Knights were led on offense by Hops Jordan, as he was consistently beating his defender, James Townsend of the Bruins. Jordan's three baskets and Cole Zeno's two brought Eastview within four points as the quarter ended.

In the Bruins' team huddle Whip Perkins lobbied his coach to have a chance to guard Hops Jordan of the Knights. Coach Dillard, who knew that Hops and Whip had a history together, originally stayed away from that strategy which could expose his star player to foul trouble. But now, with the Knights gaining momentum in the game, Chet felt it was time to go with "his best against their best."

Hops Jordan was having a similar discussion with Coach Hayden of the Knights.

"Coach, I know this guy," Jordan pleaded. "I've seen all his moves since we were 12 years old!"

"No, we're not going to change a thing," responded Hayden. "For now, I like our zone defense. We have momentum and they're feeling the pressure of our run at 'em!"

But after Whip Perkins gunned in two more jump shots over the zone giving Roosevelt an eight point lead, the Eastview coach changed his tune, and dropped the zone in favor of a man-to-man defense. It was the Perkins versus Jordan show in the fourth quarter, as the two star players put on a dazzling display in front of an excited Coliseum crowd and a captivated TV audience. Whip Perkins would score with a twisting left-handed lay-up for the Bruins, and Hops Jordan would respond with a driving slam dunk for the Knights. The low-scoring game of the first half had turned into a shootout in the final period. You could feel the intensity as players from both teams were diving for loose balls, contesting every shot, and crashing the backboards for rebounds. Because both teams had gone to man-to-man defenses as the tempo of the game picked up, both squads were suddenly faced with foul problems. Eastview's Jake Howe, Cole Zeno and Hops Jordan all had four fouls, while Mike Huff and Whip Perkins had four each for the Bruins. A lovely finger-roll in the lane by Perkins gave Roosevelt a 71-65 lead with just over a minute left, and triggered a time-out by Eastview coach Hayden.

"This is our time guys," explained a still confident Knights' coach. "Yoder, when you bring the ball down on offense, I want you to look for Jordan or Howe. They're being guarded by two guys with four fouls. When we score, we will go into the Wooden man-to-man press. Hops, you can audible to a zone depending on how they react. If we need to foul somebody, the guy to go after is number 55, Brinks. He's their worst free throw shooter."

Roosevelt coach Chet Dillard also had some instruction for his team. "We want to force 'em to go to somebody else other than Jordan. I want to double-team him with Patton and Townsend," coach Dillard said convincingly. "Whip, you have to back off with four fouls. When we get the ball, I want long possessions. Look out for their press which we prepared for all week."

Zack Yoder quickly brought the ball up the court for the Knights with seconds ticking away. He saw that Hops was double-teamed and fired a no-look pass to Jake Howe whose shot appeared to be cleanly blocked by Mike Huff of the Bruins. The referee blew his whistle and pointed at the big Roosevelt center, who threw his arms up in disbelief. The Bruin bench including coach Dillard exploded in protest knowing that Huff had just fouled out. The Roosevelt fans booed lustily as Dillard argued the call to no avail. Tom Morehouse, who was almost six inches shorter than Huff, replaced him in the Bruin line-up. When order was restored, Howe sank both free throws, cutting the Roosevelt lead to 71-67.

The Bruins' Dickie Patton surveyed the court as he prepared to inbound the ball. He fired a quick pass to Whip Perkins who made a nifty move to get free and beat the man-to-man press. Roosevelt spread out their offense and ran off 25 seconds before Eastview's Cole Zeno fouled Maurice Brinks of the Bruins. The desperate play meant that Zeno, the Knights best outside shooter, had just fouled out and was replaced by Stewart Simons. But Brinks, just a fifty percent free throw shooter during the season, missed both free throws and Jeremy "Storm" Hendrix rebounded for Eastview. There were less than thirty seconds to play as Zack Yoder brought the ball up the court for the Knights. His pass to teammate Stewart Simons was knocked away by Tom Morehouse of the Bruins, but into the hands of Eastview's Hops Jordan, who had eluded the defense in the momentary confusion. His left-handed lay-up narrowed the Roosevelt lead to just 71-69 with 23 seconds left. The rollicking Eastview crowd roared, anticipating a fourth straight comeback win. Bruins coach Chet Dillard quickly called timeout.

"There's no reason to panic," Dillard said reassuringly. "We worked on their man-to-man press and beat it on the last possession. This time I want Townsend to inbound the ball to Patton or Perkins, our two best free throw shooters. They're going to come after us and try to foul. Let's win it right now!"

In the Eastview huddle, Coach Byron Hayden had trickery up his sleeve.

"Guys, they look like they're prepared for the man-to-man press. Let's make them think they're getting it again, but quickly change to a zone press on Hops' command. If they're able to inbound the ball, we need to foul. When we get the ball back, we call timeout. Y'all got it? Let's go!"

Bruins' senior James Townsend looked out at the Knights' defense as he prepared to inbound the ball. Townsend saw what he expected, a tight Eastview man-to-man press. He knew that teammates Patton or Perkins would break free for his pass. At the last second, the Bruins' Hops Jordan yelled "Blue," switching the defense into a zone. The confused Bruin forward's inbound pass intended for teammate Dickie Patton was intercepted by Zack Yoder of the Knights. Yoder then passed the ball to Hops Jordan who dribbled away from traffic and called a timeout with 17 seconds left. The Eastview fans erupted.

Roosevelt coach Chet Dillard implored his team to keep their composure and to force the Knights to shoot a poor percentage shot from long range. Eastview coach Byron Hayden told his team to run down the clock, spread out the offense, and to get the ball to center Jake Howe or Hops Jordan for the final shot. His options were limited as his best pure shooter, Cole Zeno, had fouled out.

Safe Passage Guaranteed | 269

Stewart Simons of the Knights inbounded the ball to Zack Yoder, who played catch with Jeremy Hendrix as the clock ran down to the five second mark. Zack then passed inside to Jake Howe who drove toward the hoop, then pulled up and passed to Eastview teammate Hops Jordan who was doubled-teamed by Patton and Townsend of the Bruins. Jordan threw up an off-balance prayer shot between two defenders, as he fell backwards out of bounds. The ball bounded around the rim and went in at the buzzer, sending the game into overtime tied at 71!

My dream game had turned out to be everything I hoped it would be. Both squads had played their hearts out; I didn't want either team to lose. The Coliseum organist blared out the movie theme from "Rocky," and the crowd roared its approval. Everybody in the building and in the TV audience knew they were witnessing something special. What did "fate and destiny" have in mind tonight?

The overtime period saw both teams going back and forth exchanging baskets. Both Roosevelt and Eastview each had four players with four fouls, including Whip Perkins of the Bruins and Hops Jordan of the Knights. As a result neither team could be aggressive defensively. With 28 seconds left, and the score tied at 81, Bruins' coach Chet Dillard called timeout to set up for a final shot. His plan was to keep the ball in the hands of his best free-throw shooters, Patton, and Perkins, as the clock ran down. Jamse Townsend was instructed to set a screen for Whip, who was to take the shot as the clock ran out. But Eastview's Stewart Simons short-circuited that plan by fouling Perkins with 14 seconds left. Whip sank the first free throw giving the Bruins the lead 82-81. His second free throw rattled out and Jordan rebounded for Eastview. Knights' Coach Hayden called his final timeout.

"They're going to be looking for Jordan," proclaimed Hayden. "Zack, you and Hops run the clock down and look for Jake Howe in close. They won't be expecting that. Listen guys, we're going to win this game. We're better free throw shooters and they're missing their big man. This game is ours for the taking!"

Roosevelt coach Chet Dillard had his own strategic plan. "We're not going to let Jordan beat us, so let's stay with the double-team," Dillard announced. "They may go inside to Howe, their big football player. Brinks, that's where you're going to block his shot without fouling him. One more stop is all we need. Let's do it!"

Eastview's Zack Yoder and Hops Jordan exchanged bounce passes as the final seconds ticked down, knowing one more basket could win this epic game. With five seconds to go, Jordan zipped a bullet pass to teammate Jake Howe whose hook shot was blocked by Roosevelt's Maurice Brinks, but back into the hands of Hops. Jordan had an open ten footer for the win, but Whip Perkins of the Bruins came out of nowhere to block the shot. The deflected ball ended up in the hands of the Bruins' Dickie Patton, who dribbled away from traffic, and ran out the clock. Roosevelt had won a wild one 82-81 in overtime!

The Roosevelt supporters, chanting loudly "Bruins go to state!", stormed the court to celebrate with their team. I was able to get a couple of quick post-game comments from winning coach Chet Dillard about the last play of the game.

"Well Nick, the strength of our team all year long, as you know, has been our defense. It may not look flashy, but it's the reason we are 28 and one, and going to state. We knew they were going to go to Howe or Jordan, and Brinks and Perkins both rejected their shots with great plays. That was an awfully good team we beat tonight. Both squads left it all out on the floor - Hoosier Hysteria at its very best!"

Hops Jordan, who led all scorers with 33 points, sat all alone on the Eastview bench with his head bowed, tears streaming down his face. Whip Perkins, who tallied 29 points for the winning Bruins, came over to console him.

"Good game Hops! You guys were really tough tonight. Just like you were last summer."

A disappointed Jordan looked up at Perkins, shook his hand, and said, "Yeah, good game, Whip. Just go down to Bloomington and win it all, will ya!"

Larry Jordan, Hops' father, came over to congratulate Whip Perkins as he headed to his team's celebration. He then turned his attention to his distraught son and put his arm around him.

"Dad, I really wanted this tonight, not just for me but for you and Mom too," confessed the younger Jordan. "Right up 'til the final buzzer I thought WE were going to win. There was a force that was going carry us to victory tonight just like it has over the past three weeks."

"Son, you know this wonderful state tournament has one big drawback. Everybody loses their last game except one team," Larry said. "You ended the season for five teams before tonight including the reigning state champ, Marion. I'm so proud of you and the great effort you put forth tonight, and I know your mom was looking down with great pride too."

"God, I miss her," Hops said as he stood up and tried to regain his composure. Then he heard a familiar voice.

"Gregory, you are the best player on the best team we have faced all year. And you were brilliant tonight!"

There were only two people who called him Gregory - his late mom and his dad. For a moment Hops thought he was dreaming. Was his mother really calling him? The voice was actually that of Whip's mom, Wilma Perkins, who tended to him in the hospital last summer. The sight of Wilma, the sound of her voice, and the smell of her perfume reminded him so much of his own mother that he could not hold back the tears. As Hops was sobbing, the compassionate nurse who knew about Hops losing his mother, instinctively took him in her arms. Suddenly he was not a high school basketball hero who had just lost a big game, but a ten year old boy who was being comforted by his mother, after suffering the first of many coming-of-age heartaches.

As I watched this poignant encounter take place, I realized its importance to the story of these two teams. It was truly a crossover moment where the African American mother of the winning team's star player consoles the motherless star white player of the losing team. Was this going to be the final life lesson and the perfect final chapter of the Eastview-Roosevelt saga?

I raced back to the station to make it just in time for the late news headlines. I had my news "tease" all planned.

"I have just witnessed the greatest high school basketball game I will ever see, details coming up!"

By the time my show hit the air at 11:25pm, we were able to get the final four pairings for the state championship tourney, all to be held on Saturday March 19th, 1977 at Indiana University. Top-ranked and undefeated Lafayette Jefferson would face 9th ranked Carmel High School at 10:30am followed by 3rd ranked Fort Wayne Roosevelt against 5th ranked Jeffersonville at 12:30pm. The winners would face each other at 8:30pm that same night, a grueling task for the two teams making the finals.

I threw caution to the wind on "Nick's Picks", and predicted that Roosevelt would upset Lafayette Jefferson and win the state title, even though the two squads would have to win semifinal games in order to match-up. During the week I got a chance to visit the Bruins' practice, along with photographer Rick Cassidy and intern Jackie Knight. We collected several interviews with the players including Whip Perkins, who received his on-camera coaching from former teammate Jackie Knight. I also attended the Friday noon "send-off" rally for the team, where I read a poem that Tony Silva and I collaborated on extolling the skills of the mighty Bruins.

News director Sean Montgomery explained to me that he needed to be fair in providing overtime for the photographers, so he assigned me Rob Satterfield for the Bloomington trip instead of Rick Cassidy. Cassidy would have been our first choice, but I understood the difficult position that Sean was in. That would mean that I would be listening to the greatest hits of Buck Owens, Hank Williams, Charlie Pride, and other country artists for the three to four hour car trip each way. Tony Silva predicted that the "over/under" on me hearing Hank Williams sing "Your Cheatin' Heart" on the radio would be seven. Knowing that Satterfield would sing along with Hank's recording, I was really hoping for the "under."

THE 1977 STATE FINALS

Rob picked me up at 7am on Saturday morning which seemed like the middle of the night to me, but Rochelle's strong coffee gave me a shot of adrenaline and I was good to go. Fortunately, the weather was clear and mild, so we knew road conditions would be excellent. The month of March in Indiana could literally provide all four seasons of weather, and conditions could change quickly as we would later find out.

When we arrived at Assembly Hall on the Bloomington campus of I-U, the game between the Lafayette Jefferson Broncos and Carmel High School was already underway. The Broncos, led by Indiana's Mister Basketball, Eric "The Red" Svengaard's thirty points, took charge right from the start and defeated Carmel easily 81-62. Lafayette Jeff, guided by the Indiana High School coach of the year Walter Vorpahl, was a very impressive squad with no apparent weaknesses. In addition to the 6 foot seven inch two hundred and thirty pound Svengaard, who was headed to Notre Dame in the fall, the Broncos had plenty of other weapons. They boasted two dependable forwards in 6-4 Jaime Hodges and 6-5 Paul Snyder who could help Svengaard on the boards, as well as play-making guards Willie Strickland and Bobby Sands. Sands, a second team all-state performer, was a terrific outside shooter which opened up the inside game for Eric "The Red." They were going to be a tough match for the Roosevelt Bruins, should the Bruins be able to win their semi-final game with Jeffersonville. There was another factor working in the favor of Lafayette Jefferson High School. The Broncos, being the top-seed, were able to play in the early semi-final which meant that they would have more rest between games than the winner of the second contest.

It was also interesting to note that in addition to the live statewide television coverage, there were approximately 25 radio stations from all over the state doing live broadcasts, including Marion Giants' outstanding play-by-play man Jim Drummond. Jim told me that local sponsors would quickly buy up all the advertising on his final four broadcasts every year, even if the hometown Giants had already been eliminated. That meant that the Indiana High School Athletic Association was making a huge amount of money on broadcasting rights. So why didn't the IHSAA underwrite the two-day travel and lodging costs of the teams in the final four instead of just one? This should have been a two-day tournament, so that the finalists would not have to play two games in one day. It would take years before the IHSAA would make the change.

Roosevelt's Chet Dillard, like the other final four coaches, had to prepare his team for three opponents, one first-rounder and two second-rounders. Most of the time the final four squads knew very little about one another, as they often came from different areas of the state and had few, if any, common opponents. Such was the case with the Bruins first round opponent, Jeffersonville

High, a school located in southern Indiana near the Kentucky border. All Dillard and his staff knew was that the Jeffersonville Red Devils ran a high octane offense, and had a scoring average of over 80 points a game. They were led by 6-6 senior forward Willie Walker, a third team all-state selection along with Roosevelt's Whip Perkins. Ironically, both Walker and Perkins were going to be teammates on the Purdue University basketball team in the fall.

Roosevelt's methodical half-court offense and smothering defense proved to be very frustrating to Jeffersonville right from the opening tip. The better prepared Bruins began pulling away from the Red Devils in the second period and led 31-22 at half. By the middle of the fourth quarter Roosevelt had built a 55-39 lead, and Jeffersonville's top scorer, Willie Walker, fouled out. Bruins' coach Dillard then took out all of his starting five so they could rest for the evening title game. In the closing minutes, Roosevelt's lack of bench strength became very apparent as the Red Devils made a 15-4 run, making the 59-54 Bruin victory sound closer than it really was.

"I was really proud of our kids," said Chet Dillard. "We worked really hard this week, preparing more for Jeffersonville than anyone else. We felt that whoever controlled the tempo would win this game, and that's the way it worked out."

"Did you get an opportunity to see the Lafayette Jeff game and what do you know about the Broncos?" I asked.

"Yes, we saw a little bit of the first half of their game," Chet responded. "Obviously, they're undefeated and the top-ranked team in the state. We are going to have our hands full, but we don't know much about them, and they don't know much about us. I'm going to take our team back to the hotel to rest while my assistant coaches and I will come up with a game plan for tonight. It will be exciting to see how we match up."

I wished him luck as he hustled his team off the floor and into the locker room. After visiting with several of the Roosevelt school officials, I started to make my way up to the press room for lunch with photographer Rob Satterfield when I felt a tap on my shoulder. I was surprised to see Eastview High School basketball star Hops Jordan and his coach Byron Hayden. I told Satterfield to go ahead without me.

"We have some information about Lafayette Jefferson that we want to share with Whip and the Roosevelt team," proclaimed Hops.

"Nick, Hops told me about the summer games played by the Knights and the Bruins," added Eastview coach Byron Hayden. "What an amazing and heart-warming story connecting the two teams. We played the Lafayette Jeff Broncos early in the season. Our press really hurt 'em at the end of the game. We'd like to show Coach Dillard and the Bruins how it works. Do you know where they're staying?"

"They are at the Bloomington Howard Johnson's right off the freeway," I said. "I'd be happy to take you there in the Channel 18 news cruiser. It'll be a lot easier and faster for me to get back into the press parking lot than you trying to find a spot in the Assembly Hall public facility."

They agreed to the plan with the understanding that I would not bring my photographer, and that I would keep what I saw and heard at the meeting in confidence. I reminded both of them that I took an oath last summer to keep the Eastview-Roosevelt secret, and that I was not about to renege on my pledge. I found Rob Satterfield in the press room, and explained that I wanted to use the car to attend a coach's meeting where photographers were not allowed. He flipped me the keys, and resumed working on his huge roast beef sandwich, courtesy of the Indiana High School Athletic Association.

When we reached the Howard Johnson's, Coach Hayden had the front desk call the room of Bruins' coach Chet Dillard, who immediately came down to meet the three of us. It turns out that Hayden and Dillard had been friends for years since they worked together on several coaching clinics in the past.

"Byron, good to see you," said Dillard. "Are you going to lend me your best player for tonight's game?"

"Hops and I both wish he could play tonight," the Eastview coach said with a laugh. "But we have some information we'd like to share with you about Lafayette Jeff that you might find useful."

Then Dillard looked at me and hesitated, at which point I jumped in.

"Coach, I'm sworn to secrecy," I confessed. "I know all about the summer games between the Bruins and the Knights. I promised the players that I wouldn't go public with this story until they were at least fifty."

Chet winked at me and said, "Fifty, eh; I'll be dead by then. I was just testing you. The kids told me all about your interest in their story. Let's head up to my room and I'll gather my players and coaches."

Dillard packed his hotel suite with a standing room only crowd including his Bruin team, coaches, the three of us and a blackboard for Eastview Coach Hayden, who explained the "Wooden Press" to his Roosevelt opponents from the previous week. This was fascinating to watch as Hayden, with Hops' help, explained that the effectiveness of this pressing defense was based upon the last second switching between the zone version and the man-to-man version.

"Against you guys last week," Hops volunteered to the Bruin squad. "We would look like we were in a zone, then I would yell 'blue', and we would switch just as you inbounded. It worked against you, and it worked even better against Lafayette Jeff early in the season."

In the next 30 minutes the Roosevelt players and coaches peppered the Eastview coach and team captain with questions about what to expect from the state's number one team. Knights' Coach Byron Hayden explained that the Broncos' Eric Svengaard was a great player, but he would get frustrated if he felt he was fouled, and the referees didn't call it. He also pointed out that Lafayette Jefferson guard Willie Strickland was a terrific play maker, but seemed flustered by the "Wooden Press," and didn't shoot free throws well under pressure.

Before we left the hotel room, I was able to corner the two coaches and offer my thoughts about what I had just seen and the relationship between the two schools.

"You coaches have to be so proud of your players for organizing the summer games and the way they've performed all season," I said. "After hearing about the two practice games and the adventures that went with them, I just felt that fate and destiny would eventually bring the Knights and Bruins together on the court for real, and that the winner would take the state title. Good luck, Chet, to you and your Roosevelt team!"

Hops Jordan of Eastview had some final tips for Whip Perkins of the Bruins about how to play defense against Lafayette Jeff's "Mister Basketball."

"Svengaard is an ass-kicker who gets the jump on his opponents early because he is left-handed," advised Hops. "He prefers to go to his left, and does not dribble well with his right hand. At some crucial point in the game, overplay his left side forcing him to switch the dribble to his right side. That's when you do a full 360 degree pivot and steal the ball."

Jordan then demonstrated the pirouette move for Perkins.

Whip just held out his hand and said, "How can I thank you?"

"Just beat those cocky bastards, that's how!" retorted Hops.

On the drive back to Assembly Hall the three of us noticed that we were seeing light snow flurries hitting the windshield, after we had clear skies and mild temperatures in the morning. I drove into the press parking lot but was stopped by the security guard who said the lot was full. Apparently, a large contingent of the Indianapolis media, who didn't attend the earlier semi-final games, had just arrived for the title contest. So much for my plan of "easy in, easy out." I dropped off Coach Hayden and Hops Jordan at the entry gate, and spent the next half hour driving around before I finally found a parking spot in the far corner of the main lot. I hustled into the press entrance on the other side of Assembly Hall, hoping to get something to eat before the championship game. The complimentary food provided for the press had all been consumed by the newly-arrived Indianapolis media horde, but my photographer Rob Satterfield had rescued the last roast beef sandwich for me. God Bless the man! Satterfield might have me singing along with him to "Your Cheatin' Heart" all the way home if the Bruins could find a way to win.

The title game got off to a fast pace with Eric Svengaard of the Lafayette Jefferson Broncos scoring the first six points of the game and grabbing two rebounds. Svengaard appeared to be as advertised; a big strong man with touch and finesse, who could shoot free-throws. He was going to be a tough match-up for anybody that Roosevelt coach Chet Dillard selected to guard him. Dillard elected to go with a rotation of Mike Huff, Maurice Brinks and Whip Perkins to prevent an accumulation of fouls on one player. Chet also felt that mixing the defense up on Svengaard might confuse "Mister Basketball," and prevent him from getting in rhythm. The Bruins battled back with baskets from Perkins and Patton to close the gap to 18-14 after the first period.

The back-and-forth of the contest continued in the second quarter with Roosevelt making a run and briefly taking the lead, followed by the Broncos hitting three shots in a row to go back in front 34-30 at the half. Svengaard and his Lafayette Jeff teammates did appear surprised and frustrated by the Bruins' size and defense. Roosevelt, as coach Dillard had said many times, was not a flashy or impressive team on video, but in person they were aggressive and determined. Dillard dialed in on that very point when he addressed his team in the locker room at the break.

"These guys clearly don't think you belong on the same court with 'em," announced coach Dillard in referring to the Broncos. "Lafayette Jeff is the high and mighty number one team in the state. They fully expected to be playing somebody else in the final, and they're pouting because we are right there with 'em, making 'em work hard. This is about respect. Let's go out there and show 'em who we are!"

There was good news for the Bruins even though they trailed by four points. Nobody on the Roosevelt starting lineup had more than two personal fouls, while Lafayette Jefferson starters Willie Strickland and Jaime Hodges each had three. Broncos coach Walter Vorpahl had gone to his strong bench in the first half, with nine different players seeing action. Vorpahl knew he had the bench advantage in the second game of a long day of basketball. Dillard's lone experienced substitute Tom Morehouse, on the other hand, had only seen two minutes of service for the Bruins in the first two periods. As expected, the Broncos' Eric Svengaard led all scorers with twelve points at the break while Whip Perkins topped the Bruins' scoring with eight.

The third quarter started well for Roosevelt as baskets by Perkins, Mike Huff and Dickie Patton's three-point play gave the Bruins the lead briefly at 38-37. The contest see-sawed back and forth until a head-to-head collision between Roosevelt's Maurice Brinks and Lafayette Jeff's Paul Snyder stopped the game for nearly ten minutes. Both players were diving after a loose ball

Safe Passage Guaranteed | 281

when the accident occurred. Fortunately, neither young man was seriously injured, but both had to be helped off the court and would not return. While the ten minute break helped both squads catch their breath, the loss of the 6-8 Brinks to the Bruins was devastating. Any rebounding and defensive advantage that Roosevelt might have had was suddenly gone, and the Broncos raced out to a 52-42 lead at the end of the period. To make matters worse, the Bruins' Mike Huff just collected his fourth foul while engaging in a heated one-on-one battle with Svengaard of the Broncos. The two nearly came to blows earlier when "Mister Basketball" received his third foul as he retaliated after a perceived shove from Huff.

At the break, Bruins' coach Dillard knew he had to make a move to protect Mike Huff from fouling out which would put his exhausted team in a deeper hole. With Brinks out of the game and replaced by Morehouse, all he had on his bench were inexperienced sophomores. It was now or never.

"Listen up fellas," said the confident Roosevelt coach. "We're going to switch up on defense and put Whip on Svengaard. It may be early, but the Eastview folks said if they would have used the Wooden Press sooner, they could've beaten Lafayette Jeff. I know we haven't practiced it, but you have seen it used against you in three games, including last week. Whip's going to call the zone and man-to-man audibles, just as Jordan did for Eastview. This is where we turn this game around!"

The first two times the Bruins tried to use the Wooden Press the Broncos easily beat it. The Bruins were disorganized with some of the players in a zone and others in a man-to man defense. The third time they used it, Whip called a last second audible to the zone press and Willie Strickland of Lafayette Jeff mistakenly passed the ball to Roosevelt's Dickie Patton. Then the frustrated Strickland fouled out trying to stop Patton from getting an easy layup. Patton hit the free throw and the Bruins had new life, trailing by just seven with plenty of time on the clock.

After an exchange of baskets, Whip further confused the Broncos by setting up a zone press and calling an audible to a man-to-man press. Lafayette Jeff's Bobby Sands inbounded to teammate Eric Svengaard, who was called for traveling when he thought he was fouled by Whip Perkins. Svengaard exploded with anger, screamed at the referee, and got hit with a technical foul. Lafayette Jeff coach Vorpahl called timeout to calm down "Eric the Red," who had just committed his fourth foul. After Whip hit the free throw and James Townsend got a tip-in after a missed Tom Morehouse jump shot, the Bruins had cut the margin to just four points. The Wooden Press had definitely caught the Broncos by surprise, and given Roosevelt the momentum with five minutes left. But the amount of energy that the Bruins were spending on the Wooden Press was exhausting the short-handed Roosevelt team, and coach Dillard knew he had to make another strategy change.

"OK guys, we have these folks right where we want 'em," Dillard proclaimed. "We're going to slow things down a bit by taking off the press for now, and go into our normal man-to–man 'D'. Their big guy, Svengaard, is one mistake away from fouling out. Whip, I want you to go right at him on offense and defense."

With four fouls, Lafayette Jeff's Svengaard had to play very conservatively. On the next three Bruin possessions Whip Perkins drove right by "Eric the Red" to score every time, and give Roosevelt its first lead at 61-60 with two minutes remaining in the game. Bobby Sands, who finally got free from the suffocating Bruin defense, hit a long corner jump shot and put the Broncos back on top 62-61 with ninety seconds left. You could see the weariness and fatigue on the faces of the Bruins as they tried to use the game clock to their advantage with long productive possessions. Mike Huff and Perkins scored again for Roosevelt, followed by Svengaard's two free throws for the Broncos, leaving the Bruins ahead 65-64 with twenty-seven seconds left. During the time-out Bruins coach Dillard called for his best free-throw shooters, Whip, Patton, and Morehouse, to handle to ball and play "keep-away." The plan was for Perkins to drive toward the hoop with five seconds left, but it would be likely that the Broncos would elect to foul before then.

Lafayette Jefferson's clever coach Walter Vorpahl then had a surprise for the Bruins. He had his team set up for a full court zone press, hoping that Roosevelt might be confused and turn over the ball, just like his team had done earlier in the contest. With the crowd roaring, Bruins coach Dillard saw what was happening and tried to call time out, but it was too late. Roosevelt's Dickie Patton was caught off-guard by the press and hurriedly inbounded the ball to Whip Perkins who wasn't expecting it. As Whip caught the pass from Patton he stepped on the baseline for a turnover - Broncos ball! Now Lafayette Jefferson had a chance to take the last shot and win it. Chet Dillard called his final timeout, and tried to pick up his Bruin team which was now running on fumes alone.

"Listen to me," demanded Dillard. "That scoreboard says we're winning this game. They're going to run the clock down and get the ball into Svengaard in the closing seconds. We're gonna stop him and win this thing. Let's go with the tight man-to-man defense that has delivered us all year; a year, I might add, that has been the best year of my life thanks to you kids. I love every darn one of you. Now, just go out there and do what you have been doing all season!"

As Whip walked back on the floor, he suddenly remembered the defensive pirouette move against "Eric the Red" that Eastview's Hops Jordan had told him about at the hotel. He thought that this was the time to use it if he had the chance. As I looked on from my courtside seat, I just felt that fate and destiny were about to be heard from.

The Broncos worked the ball around, and ran the clock down just as the Bruins had expected. At the ten second mark it looked as if Bobby Sands was going to take the shot for Lafayette

Jeff, but as he rose up for the jumper, he passed inside to Svengaard guarded closely by Perkins. Just as Hops had instructed, Whip overplayed the Broncos' star to his left, forcing Svengaard to dribble with his less dominant right hand. In the blink of an eye, Perkins, mimicking a seasoned ballet dancer, made a full three hundred and sixty degree spin move and stole the ball cleanly. Whip dribbled away from traffic as the stunned Broncos looked on in horror. Perkins instinctively threw the ball high in the air as the clock ran out. The Hollywood dream ending that nobody would ever believe just came true. Bruins win it 65-64!

Pandemonium then reigned supreme at Assembly Hall in Bloomington! It seemed like the whole city of Fort Wayne rushed the floor to embrace its new favorite sons, and we recorded it all on video. Among the celebrants were Mayor Ivan Christoff who was bear-hugging Roosevelt coach Dillard, my friend A.D. Webster, basketball guru Bobby Short, plus Wilma and Ike Perkins, Whip's parents, who both looked emotionally drained. The Bruin players were actually late additions to the party, as Chet Dillard had instructed them to shake hands with the entire Lafayette Jefferson High School squad and its coaches. This was truly an unforgettable moment for me, and without question the highlight of my career. As I did my share of hugging and handshaking, I had to remind myself that I was there to do a job. My photographer Rob Satterfield videoed me interviewing just about everybody from the mayor on down.

"Nick, I don't know where to start," said an emotional coach Dillard. "I just think our team wanted this title more than anything, and we were not going to be denied. We were very fortunate to get a terrific scouting report on Lafayette Jeff from some good friends. But give the kids credit, they're the ones who performed under pressure and are now the state champs. You said something earlier about fate and destiny guiding this team, and you might be right."

As I tried to ask a follow-up question, the Bruin players stepped in and picked up their coach. Dillard waved to an appreciative audience as he got a victory ride on the shoulders of his delirious team. He also got a congratulatory handshake from Eastview coach Byron Hayden before Chet and his squad were given the state championship trophy by IHSAA commissioner Ty Eskridge.

Finally, as the celebration began to subside, we decided to pack up our gear and get ready for the long drive home. Before we left the arena, I noticed nearby that Whip Perkins was talking with Hops Jordan, and I overheard their conversation.

"Man, that spin move was magic," Whip said excitedly as he slapped hands with Hops. "The ball was right there, just as you said it would be! It just seems like every time I see you, I need to thank you for somethin'. Shit, if we didn't play those games last summer, I don't think we get here. And, if you and your coach didn't give us those tips today at the hotel, I'm not sure we woulda won tonight. Why'd you come all the way down here, anyway?"

"You know the answer to that question," Hops responded. "I came down here to see my second favorite team. And besides, you'd have done the same for me if you hadn't been so lucky to beat us last week."

Whip thought for a moment and said, "Ya know, I think I would've."

"You still owe me though," responded Hops. "How 'bout another game in Kendallville this summer? You get your boys and I'll get mine. Whattaya say?"

"I don't know," Whip said with a wry smile.

"Remember, what we agreed on - Safe Passage Guaranteed!" Hops announced as Whip helped him finish the phrase.

7

DECISION TIME

The Roosevelt victory celebration in Bloomington didn't end until shortly before midnight, and we were facing a long drive home. Rob Satterfield said he forgot to tell me that Mayor Ivan Christoff had announced to the Northern Indiana media between games that Fort Wayne was going to have a downtown parade at 3pm Sunday win or lose. The victory in the title game was going to make the parade another memorable day for the Bruins, and another exhausting but exhilarating one for me. Knowing we were going to be getting home much later than planned, I used the media courtesy phone to call Rochelle and let her know. At my photographer's request, Rochelle also called his wife Bobbie Satterfield, to let her know that Rob and I were running late.

When we walked out of the arena into the main parking lot, we were surprised to see that a white blanket of wet snow had covered the lot and all the remaining cars in it. To make matters worse, I couldn't remember exactly where I had parked the WFTW-TV news cruiser. Because we left on a mild spring morning, neither Rob nor I had packed our winter snow gear. This was my fault for being in such a rush to make the tip-off for the championship game, after I couldn't get into the media lot. Finally, after about a half hour of trudging through the snow in dress shoes and getting soaked, I found our car.

I think I heard "Your Cheatin Heart" at least six times on the radio during the ride home, and I sang along with Rob to the first two. It was five AM Sunday morning by the time I actually arrived home. Rochelle got up to fix me breakfast after she insisted I take a shower. Then I was able to get six hours of sleep before photographer Rick Cassidy called to say he would pick me up a 2pm, so we could cover the Roosevelt High victory parade downtown.

Indiana's fickle March weather was on full display that weekend. Saturday began with brilliant sunshine and temperatures in the 60s. It ended with snow and falling temperatures. By parade time at 3pm Sunday, the skies were gray and overcast with temperatures hovering around twenty degrees. The cold weather didn't dampen the spirits of the huge throng that crowded the streets to cheer on their state champs, the Roosevelt High School Bruins. I remembered basketball guru Bobby Short's quote when he compared a local team winning the state title to "Jesus Christ himself walking across the Maumee River." The people of Fort Wayne, irrespective of race, religion, age, or social standing truly felt that these were their kids, the real Sons of the Summit City, who had accomplished something very special. You really could feel the love and adoration in the air as the team slowly rode through the main streets of Fort Wayne on a fire engine with lights flashing and sirens blaring. These young men had genuinely brought a diverse community together. When they reached city hall, Mayor Ivan Christoff was there to give the Bruins the key to the city. But the memorable day was not over yet.

After the ceremony, the Roosevelt team asked if the fire engine could take a spin through the inner city neighborhood surrounding Lafayette Park, where most of the players grew up. As the fire engine circled Lafayette Park, the Bruins got a chance to wave to friends and neighbors who couldn't make the downtown festivities. The players made a special effort to reach out to the kids of the neighborhood. They asked the driver to stop briefly so that youngsters could get close to them and touch the state championship trophy. The uplifting message the Bruins were sending on their victory lap was "if we can do this, so can you!" As I watched this event, I realized how wise, beyond their years, this group of high school basketball players really was. If our future leaders would be coming from this Roosevelt team or the "never-say-die" Eastview squad, with whom they shared the secret 1976 summer basketball series, we have reason to hope for the future.

Rick Cassidy put together a superb video montage of the cold but festive afternoon which I narrated for the Sunday night 6pm news. News director Sean Montgomery called me at the station to tell me to go home and get some rest. He said he was giving me two days off to "re-charge my batteries." My boss could see that I really needed it because I was physically and mentally exhausted. I was back on the job by Wednesday to attend a special dinner at the Moonraker Restaurant, one of Fort Wayne's finest, honoring the Roosevelt Bruins and their families. I was flattered that the team invited me to the party, and asked me to be one the after dinner speakers. I think Jackie Knight, my intern and former Roosevelt player, might have had something to do with that.

"Your journey has had a huge effect on bringing our community together," I remarked to the Bruin family. "Years from now we will look back and say the 1977 Roosevelt Basketball team showed us that by making an effort to work together toward a common goal, that anything is possible. Reporting on your march to the state title was not only the most fun and exciting assignment of my sports career, but a memory that I'll treasure for the rest of my life."

Many people in the room knew that I wasn't just talking about the state title run, but the secret summer series of 1976, which likely made the 1976-77 dream season possible. Before I had to head back to the station after the dinner, I had a chance to talk privately with Roosevelt's Whip Perkins, who was named the Most Valuable Player of the Indiana State Tournament.

"Whip, you need to know that it was Hops who persuaded his coach to go to Bloomington and meet with you guys," I told him.

"I know, I could tell," remarked Whip. "Look, I think the best player I faced all year wasn't Eric the Red of Lafayette Jeff, it was Jordan. The guy lives, breathes and thinks basketball twenty-four seven. I wanna talk to Coach Schaus at Purdue about takin' a look at Hops. It'd be a lot more fun to play with 'em than against 'em."

Unfortunately, that would never happen as Hops Jordan was done with the classroom when he got his high school diploma. He would go on later to be a legendary amateur basketball player in the local recreation leagues, while at the same time eventually taking over his father Larry's plumbing business. Jordan's most intelligent career move, however, was marrying his high school girl friend, Brittney Talbot, who became his bookkeeper and partner. When the plumbing business began to flourish with Brittney's management, Hops got the opportunity to get back into basketball by replacing retired Eastview High School coach Byron Hayden in 1988. Since then, Jordan has guided the Knights to two Indiana state championships in the small school division. Hops got plenty of help from his son Larry Jr., first as a star player and later as an assistant coach. The state tournament was broken up into divisions after the 1996-97 season based on school enrollment. Sadly, the "David and Goliath" match-ups that the "dyed in the wool" Hoosier basketball fans truly craved, even if their team was not involved, became ancient history.

Whip would go on to Purdue where he would be selected to the All-Big Ten basketball team his junior and senior years, while at the same time earning his degree in journalism. I always wondered if I gave him his start in that department when I asked him to call me with reports on the summer black/white series of 1976. After a brief career in the NBA with the Cleveland Cavaliers, Perkins started a youth basketball program in the city of Atlanta, Georgia. Whip and Hops had lost touch with one another until 1997, when A.D. Webster brought them together again at the Roosevelt championship team's twenty year reunion in Fort Wayne. When A.D. introduced Hops as a surprise guest, the former Eastview star was welcomed by the Roosevelt Bruins with hugs and high fives, as if he was one of their own. Since that reunion meeting, Whip and Hops have each helped the other out every year by taking part in one another's basketball clinics in

Atlanta and Kendallville, Indiana. On several occasions the two of them would entertain the kids by re-enacting the final play of their classic 1977 semi-state overtime thriller.

The week following Roosevelt's 1977 state championship victory, WFTW-TV's versatile Tony Silva gathered up all the video we had on the Bruins' great season, and put together a terrific half hour tribute to the team in which he had me act as on-camera host. We had footage and interviews that the live telecast with Herman Yates never showed. We knew we needed to get it done, and on the air quickly while the Roosevelt story was still fresh.

We finished our taping Thursday night in hopes that the station would run it on Friday.

But Channel 18 refused to preempt the CBS special with Tony Orlando and Dawn.

Instead, the brain trust at WFTW decided to run our special, entitled "Bruins Go to State," the following Monday after the early news. That normally would have been a great time slot, but this time it was not. The Roosevelt special was scheduled to run on our station at the same time that the NCAA Basketball Championship game, featuring Marquette and North Carolina, was airing on NBC. Tony and I were furious, and both complained to general manager Whitney Thompson about the scheduling of what we thought was some of our best work.

This was a time before DVD and VHS recording, so the viewers at home only had one chance to see it. Thompson wouldn't change the original scheduling, but he agreed to a rerun the following Friday at 11:30pm before the Chuck Swift Chevrolet Big Movie, "The Great Escape," starring Steve McQueen and James Garner. Tony and I hoped that the Roosevelt team with its many fans, who, like most everyone else watched the NCAA title game instead of our special on Monday, would get a second chance to see "Bruins Go to State." We later gave the video of our show to the school, and it still sits in the Roosevelt High School trophy case to this day.

CALIFORNIA DREAMIN'

When the euphoria of the high school basketball season finally wore off in early April, Rochelle and I had come to our deadline to make a career decision regarding our California job offers. I had not made any effort to renegotiate my contract with WFTW-TV, nor had the station reached out to me on that issue. In addition, there were no other TV stations clamoring for my services. There had been two recent family developments which would ultimately have an impact on choices. My parents, who had lived on the San Francisco Peninsula since 1959, decided to sell their Menlo Park home and move to Rancho Santa Fe near San Diego. At almost the same time, my sister Pat and her family had elected to move from Orange County north to the East Bay community of Alamo. Pat's husband, Brett, had just become a medical doctor, and would be doing his residency at the nearby VA Hospital in Martinez. That would mean if I elected to take Lyle Gibbons offer to sell new homes in the East Bay communities of Fremont or Walnut Creek, we could live within 30 minutes of Rochelle's parents in Alameda or my sister in Alamo. With the baby coming in September and me starting a new job, I felt that having family backup close by was very important.

Rochelle and I used the two days off that my news director gave me to talk through this decision which I tried to put out of my mind during the state tournament. We agreed that my career in television had stalled, in part because we were very particular about where we wanted to live. The Detroit opportunity that we didn't chase after was a perfect example. Another avenue I wasn't comfortable pursuing was adding to my income by doing a heavy load of commercials at the expense of time spent on my sports show. We looked at our finances, and realized that Channel 18 would have to double my salary to make up for the loss of Rochelle's. When DJ McQueen reminded me of the stinginess of the station owners in dealing with Rob DeForest, I realized that getting a significant raise was very unlikely. Rochelle and I also felt that if we were going to make a career change, now was the time as we both were turning thirty in 1977.

After several sleepless nights following discussions of the pluses and minuses of staying in Fort Wayne, versus beginning a new career in California real estate, we finally reached a decision. Oddly, it was watching the PBS Sunday night mini-series of Charles Dickens' "David Copperfield" that helped me move forward. There was a scene where David had left England and was flying a kite in Germany. Suddenly the breeze stopped, and the kite drifted back to earth, signaling to Copperfield that it was time to return to his roots - England. That scene spoke to me, and it was time to go home to California. The bottom line is that I felt I would be a better provider for my family in real estate than in television. I was confident in my ability to be successful in real estate. That was due to the fact that my father, a long-time life insurance sales manager and trainer, had been subtly preparing me for this moment my entire life. Dad's mantra was that a good salesperson would "show up on time and tell the truth."

Rochelle, who had tried to remain supportive of whatever I chose to do, had a hard time controlling her enthusiasm about my decision.

"We have made lifetime friends here in Fort Wayne that we'll never lose touch with," she said with tears running down her face. "We're going to California to start a family, and you're going to be a top selling real estate agent. I'm thrilled beyond words!"

We contacted Lyle Gibbons in California on Monday morning to inform him of our decision to take his job offer. He excitedly told us that my sales position should open up in late summer, which should work out perfectly. Lyle explained that if we arrived in early June, that I would have plenty of time to get my real estate license before the Walnut Creek or Fremont projects were ready. That meant we would begin our trip to California on Sunday, May 28, 1977, which was Memorial Day weekend. Interestingly, we arrived on Memorial Day weekend of 1972, which seemed like a lifetime ago.

Both Rochelle and I felt overwhelmed with all the phone calls, arrangements, and tasks we had to address immediately. First things first, we called both sets of parents who were "over the moon," to use their words, that we were coming back home. My mom got so excited she sent us an LP of Al Jolson's 1930's greatest hits, featuring the hit song, "California, Here I Come."

After the emotional family announcement, it was time to go to the station to meet with the general manager and the news director to inform both of them that I was leaving. My first thought was that Whitney Thompson was expecting me to hit him up again for a raise. The general manager was very surprised when I announced that the May 26th 6pm news would be my last show.

"We're really sorry you're leaving, Nick," Thompson said solemnly. "You've been a valued member of our Channel 18 family for five years now, and we're sorry to lose you. But it looks like you have an offer in California that you can't refuse, and we want to wish you the best of luck."

I thanked him for giving me the opportunity to be the WFTW-TV sports director, and we shook hands. There was no inkling from him that I would get some last minute sweetened offer to get me to reconsider. I knew the discussions with co-workers Tony Silva, studio director Steve Watson and news director Sean Montgomery were going to be much more difficult.

Sean, who wasn't surprised by my decision, wanted to make it as easy as possible for me emotionally by calling a newsroom meeting. In that way I could make my announcement to everybody on the news team at the same time, although I knew I would have some private moments with nearly everyone, especially Tony and Steve.

Tony Silva was a native Hoosier who was always there to help me "fill in the blanks" on a local story, by providing historical background and perspective. I felt a real bond with Tony, as we were hired at the same time, and together we ushered in the "youth movement" that WFTW-TV desperately needed in 1972. He was the most versatile TV news person I have ever known. Silva could do it all - write, produce, and perform, plus he was a wizard with a camera in his hands, shooting film or video tape. Fortunately, the WFTW-TV station owners in New York finally recognized his talents in the mid 1980's. They made him the first Hispanic news director of a network affiliate in the state of Indiana. After broadcasting, Tony would go on to become a civic leader in the Fort Wayne community, serving on its school board and becoming the local director of the U.S. Department of Labor's Job Corps organization. Silva would marry Maureen Flaherty, the popular and talented emergency medical technician he met while covering fires and accidents as a Channel 18 news reporter.

Studio director Steve Watson was a true local boy, having grown up in Fort Wayne. What made Steve so talented as a TV director was his ability to "keep his cool" while others were losing their minds. I always felt when I was on the air that if I went off script or if we had a technical glitch, Steve could get in my head and get us back on course. He would eventually leave broadcasting in the early 1990s, and go into business sharpening medical instruments for surgeons. At the tender age of 49 he would finally meet the woman of his dreams; a pretty nurse from Kalamazoo, Michigan named Sharon Koppe.

Sharon, a competitive golfer and tennis player, was a single mother with two college-age sons. Her enthusiasm combined with her athleticism made Sharon the perfect soul mate for Steve. Rochelle and I were honored to act as their "best man" and "matron of honor" at their 1994 wedding in Kalamazoo.

Other members of our top rated news team would also move on from WFTW-TV not long after me. Our talented news director, Sean Montgomery, would end up being an Emmy award winning news producer in San Francisco, after brief stays in Tulsa and Houston. Katie Mosher landed in Phoenix, by way of Fresno, where she was a popular news anchor. Frankie Napolitano, after two years in Minneapolis, hit the big time at WCBS-TV in New York, where he was an investigative reporter. One of his big thrills was going up the elevator on a regular basis with Walter Cronkite. On a sad note, ace photographer Rick Cassidy, a Vietnam veteran, passed away in 1995 at the age of 48, due to the effects of "PTSD" and Agent Orange.

Telling A.D. Webster, another one of my closest friends, about our move to California was another painful chore. The same day that I announced my resignation at WFTW, I was also scheduled to play a late night tennis match with Webster at the Times Corners Racquet Club. After I told him our news, he gave me a hard time, as I expected he would.

"Cunningham, you can't leave now because we still have work to do here," A.D. said firmly. He always called me by my last name when he was very serious. Then he smiled and made me an offer.

"Here's the deal, if I win tonight, you have to stay. If you win, you're free to go."

A.D. Webster did beat me that night, but he also knew he would have to let me go to follow my dreams and destiny, just like I had to let him follow his. Webster would eventually leave his human relations job with the Fort Wayne school district in the early 1980's to become a full-time tennis instructor and high school coach. By the 1990's his high school teams had become so successful that he landed a small college coaching position in Kentucky, followed by a major college head coaching job in Florida. At every stop along his career path, A.D. continued his work of mentoring young people and furthering better relations among the races. He was so good "on the air" when he was interviewed by the media as a coach, that Webster was hired by ESPN in 2010 to be a color commentator for college tennis and basketball broadcasts.

As I look back, I can honestly say that A.D. Webster's contribution to the improvement of race relations in Fort Wayne in the 1970's cannot be overstated. He literally "moved the needle" in a positive way, by bringing people together to play basketball, or by organizing multi-racial meetings to address the issues of the day. I think Webster's impact on the community was clearly visible in 1977, when people of all races and socio-economic backgrounds in the city of Fort Wayne embraced the state champion Roosevelt Bruins, a team with an all-Black starting five. When I asked A.D. recently if he knew about the 1976 black/white summer basketball series, he smiled at me and said, "What do you think?" All along I felt that he knew, but we both were sworn to secrecy by the players of Roosevelt and Eastview.

During my final two months at WFTW-TV, I really made an effort to cover what I enjoyed most, local prep sports. I got to know my two new on-air partners, anchorman Mark Barrett from Wheeling, West Virginia, and meteorologist Pete Harris from Wilmington, North Carolina. Both seemed to be good fits for our news team, as they both were in their 30's with easy-going personalities. Harris, who was an avid tennis player, became a regular partner of mine during my final month on the job, as I introduced him to my friends and competitors at the Times Corners Racquet Club.

After my departure became public, I was touched by the fact that that I received numerous calls and letters from well-wishers. I even got calls from my competition, including WKHG-TV's Herman Yates, who always treated me respectfully, as I did him. Yates and I would connect years later when he played himself in the movie, "Hoosiers."

We exchanged several very warm and candid letters with one another shortly before he passed away in 2004.

One of the major chores that Rochelle and I faced before we departed for the West Coast was the selling of our house, which we had purchased two years earlier. D.J. McQueen mentioned to a friend, Bob Bender, at the local office of the U.S. Weather Service that we would be selling our three bedroom Times Corners home. Bob, who was looking for a small home in our neighborhood, called me and asked if he could see our residence. We set up a date and time for the following week, as Rochelle and I first had to come up with a price. After scouring the advertisements in the newspaper and visiting a couple of open houses, we decided on a list price of $28,900, which we thought was high, but would give us room to negotiate. Bender walked through our home just once, and asked about our list price. When we told him, he said, "I'll take it. When would you like to close?" Wow, that seemed too easy! I would later find out that we had grossly underpriced our home. Because of the influx of new buyers who went to work for nearby Magnavox and International Harvester, our area had seen great price appreciation over the past two years. If we would have had the good sense to use one of Floyd Cotton's top real estate agents, we would have sold it for much more, and netted more, even paying a full commission.

A week before our departure date I was asked by the Parent's Club of Huntington North High School to be their host for the Class of 1977's grad night. It would be an all-night affair paying me $200. This would probably be one of my last opportunities to interact face-to-face with local teens, who were my loyal viewers. It turned out to be a really fun gig, where I emceed a version of the dating game, introduced local bands like a radio disc jockey, and had my picture taken with literally everybody in the place. I hope the nice folks in Huntington enjoyed me as much as I enjoyed them. I had a warm feeling as I began my half hour ride home, with the sun coming up on what was going to be another gorgeous spring day. But suddenly it hit me, and I got emotional. This part of my life was ending, and I was going to miss it. Was I making a mistake leaving this community that I had become so attached to? After sleeping to early afternoon that Saturday, I needed Rochelle to help me again go through the reasons we needed to move forward with our California plans. With her help, I was able to overcome my second thoughts, and get back into planning our drive across the country.

My last week on the job was a blur as I tried to produce the best show I could, while at the same time winding up all the details of our move and the sale of our home. I dreaded my last show, which finally arrived on Friday. Sean Montgomery, my good friend and news director, told me to take all the time I needed in my show to say what I wanted to say to my viewers. I really wanted my words to be economical and effective, so I elected to put them at the start of my sportscast as opposed to the end. First, I thanked my co-workers at WFTW-TV, and then I thanked my viewers for the privilege of visiting with them on a nightly basis via their televisions for the past five years.

"I think what I'm going to miss most of all is covering high school sports in the Fort Wayne Area. Roosevelt's victory in the state basketball finals, and the Bruins great semi-state triumph over a terrific Eastview team were the most exciting and inspiring stories of my broadcasting career. I think you parents should know that your sons and daughters are being coached and taught by some of the finest people I have ever met. My wife Rochelle and I got a real estate offer we couldn't refuse, and are going home to the San Francisco Bay Area. We've made lifetime friends here, and we'll always think of Fort Wayne as our second home. Now, let's move along, and do the sports for the last time."

After I finished my show, I simply cued the commercial as I usually did at the end of my segment. I was afraid I would start getting emotional on the air if I dragged out my goodbye any longer. Director Steve Watson added a nice touch by asking Rochelle, who was nearly six months pregnant, to join me on the set for the final shot. As the news credits rolled on the screen, we both waved good bye to not only our viewers, but to my broadcasting career.

The next order of business was our Saturday "moving party" which we knew was going to be an all-day affair. We provided the beer and the burgers while our friends came to say goodbye, and help us load our U-Haul Truck. The first to arrive were our first Indiana friends, Tim and Joan Waters, who brought us donuts and coffee to help get us started at 9AM. It was a bittersweet day for Rochelle and me as we said good bye to our best friends as they all pitched in. Finally, at about 9pm we completed the job. The U-Haul truck, with the large red letters on the side saying, "Adventures in Moving," was packed to the top. Rochelle's 1965 Comet, which I was towing with the truck, was filled up completely, as was our Datsun. In the cab of the U-Haul I would also be joined by our television set and our baby's cradle, a one hundred year old family heirloom wrapped in bathroom towels. Steve Watson, who had become as close a friend to Rochelle as he was to me, was the last person to leave at around 11pm, after hugs and tears. Several years later I saw the final episode of the TV show, "Mash," with Hawkeye Pierce and BJ Honeycutt trying to find a way to say good bye in the final scene. I remember getting choked up because it reminded me so much of the final good bye with Steve. In fact, every time I see a rerun episode of "Mash," I think about how much our zany WFTW-TV news team resembled the crazy 4077th Mash Unit depicted on that show. We were constantly making each other laugh and playing practical jokes on one another, but when it was time to do the news, we were all business.

When moving day finally arrived, our neighbors, Al and Mayro Miller, prepared a sumptuous breakfast for us. We had either sold or given away most of our furniture, and all that remained in the house was the refrigerator and our bed, which we left for our buyer, Bob Bender. After more hugs and tearful goodbyes with our adopted Indiana parents, the Millers, Rochelle noticed the family heirloom cradle in the front seat of the truck. She insisted that it would be safer in the back with the rest of our belongings. With the help of Al Miller, we managed to open the back of the U-Haul, remove the vacuum cleaner and the dirty clothes basket, and replace them with the cradle. That would mean that I would have the TV set, vacuum cleaner, a basketball, and dirty clothes basket in the front seat with me. At long last we were ready to go, with Rochelle leading the way driving the yellow Datsun, and me with the U-Haul truck towing the Comet. Rochelle had never driven for more than two hours at any time in her life, and now my wife, who was nearly six months pregnant, was about to embark on a five day, twenty three hundred mile cross country automobile journey. She said she was inspired by Janet Guthrie, who had just become the first woman to compete in the Indy 500.

"If she can do it, then I can do it!" were her brave words.

I was so worried about Rochelle's long drive in her pregnant condition that I used our green stamps, which we had obtained from buying groceries, to purchase two battery operated walkie-talkies. These walkie-talkies would allow us to communicate during the trip if we were within a half mile of one another. The doctor had given Rochelle the "go-ahead" to drive provided that we stop every two hours. This was going to be a long car ride, with many stops.

ON THE ROAD AGAIN

As we pulled away from our house, I took one last lingering look at our happy home with all its great memories. In fact, I spent so much time looking and remembering, that I had to swerve at the last second to keep from crashing into Al Miller's pick-up truck parked by the side of the road. From there the trip seemed to go well for the first fifteen minutes until I followed Rochelle off Interstate 69 to the Highway 30 on ramp. I heard a loud "thump" as I hit the guardrail while guiding my truck with the Comet in tow. I looked in the rear view mirror and COULD NOT SEE THE COMET! As we merged onto to Highway 30, I flashed my lights indicating to Rochelle that I needed to talk.

"Rochelle, I bumped the guard-rail!" I blared into the walkie-talkie. "I might've lost the Comet. Can you fall back behind me to see if it's still there?"

"You lost the Comet?" she asked alarmingly.

Before I could answer, I could hear the relief followed by hysterical laughter in her voice when she told me that it was still there. The wide girth of the U-Haul apparently blocked my view of the Comet. When I practiced driving the truck the day before, we hadn't yet attached the towing rig with the second vehicle. This was going to be "on the job training for me."

The first day of travel had gone well in the morning as we worked our way toward Chicago. When we stopped for lunch, Rochelle told me that the temperature gauge was heating up on the Datsun. Even after a thirty minute lunch break the radiator was still very warm, and when I eventually opened it up, I found that it was nearly empty. That was not a good sign and another source of worry for me. A breakdown on the road would not only disrupt our travel plans, but also would be especially hard on my pregnant wife. After I refilled the radiator, I told Rochelle to keep watching the Datsun's temperature gauge as we made the turn west on

Interstate 80. By late afternoon, we had crossed into the state of Iowa and the skies suddenly got very dark. I turned on the radio to hear that a severe thunderstorm with tornado warnings was about to hit the area. I flashed the lights at Rochelle, and we both turned on our trusty walkie-talkies.

"Let's look for a place to pull off the main road," I said, doing my best to stay calm. "This storm could hit us any moment. Oh, and keep an eye out for funnel clouds cuz we have a tornado warning."

"What do you expect me to do if I see a tornado?" Rochelle inquired.

I was just about to answer when I saw her pull over on the side of the highway in the nick of time, as the storm hit with full force. I pulled in behind her as we got it all, thunder, lightning, wind, heavy rain, and hail, but fortunately no tornadoes. I could hear and feel the storm jostling the U-Haul as it blew through with increasing intensity. For a very scary moment I worried that the wind would topple us over. Rochelle came on the walkie-talkie saying that she was a bit shaken, and the baby was jumping up and down inside her. We agreed that the nickname for the kid, boy or girl, should be "Stormy."

After fifteen or twenty minutes the storm passed, and we were on our way again. By late afternoon, we made our way into Newton, Iowa where we discovered they had a nice Howard Johnson's resort with a pool. It also appeared that they had a large parking lot which would let me turn around without having to back-up. I was told when I rented the truck that backing up with a towed vehicle could uncouple or even break the tow bar connection.

Rochelle stopped at the front desk to check us in as I headed into the parking lot to find a good place to park my "rig" for the night. To my horror, I could find no place to turn around.

I was stuck! It was another lesson in "on the job training." I should have parked in the street and walked through the lot to see that I had plenty of room to maneuver. Rochelle found me in the parking lot trying to figure out how to turn my U-Haul around without uncoupling the Comet. As we discussed our options, I noticed two older men who were having a couple of drinks on their balcony. The two of them seemed to find humor in our predicament, which made me angry, and even more determined to solve our problem. With my adrenaline pumping, I made the decision to uncouple the Comet, turn the truck around, and push the Comet into place so I could reconnect it. The problem was that the two connections did not line up. When my friends and I put the rig together at home, four of us would lift the front of the Comet into place. I waved off Rochelle, who wanted to lend a hand, and took a deep breath. I gripped the front bumper and lifted with everything my amped up body would allow. I kind of stumbled backward as I pulled the Comet into place. CLICK! We reconnected our rig, and we were back in business. I really had to fight the urge to flip-off the drinkers on the balcony, who never offered any help or encouragement. Years later my orthopedic surgeon would trace the source of my back problems to that adrenaline powered lift. Rochelle and I were exhausted from a long day of travel. A cool swim, a prime rib dinner, and an early bedtime were just what we needed to recharge our batteries for the second day of our trip.

The weather the second day, which was actually Memorial Day, was sunny and mild as we made our way through Iowa, and across the familiar flatlands of Nebraska. The trip seemed to be going well until midafternoon when Rochelle flashed her lights indicating she needed to talk. I grabbed my walkie-talkie with one hand listened in.

"Nick, we're going to need to stop soon," she said with urgency. "The Datsun's heating up again!"

We got off the main highway in Kearny, Nebraska where we filled up with gas and let the Datsun cool down. The gas station attendant checked out our radiator, and told us that our problem could be a faulty radiator cap, which he couldn't replace. He also said that the nearest Datsun dealer was about one hundred miles down the road in North Platte, which just happened to be our second day destination. We filled our radiator up with water and headed back on the road, hoping to make it to North Platte without over-heating. We got about halfway there when the Datsun started to heat up again. Fortunately, we stumbled across a rest stop near Gothenburg, Nebraska where we were able to let the car cool off, and then refill our radiator. We finally limped in to the Motel Six in North Platte by 6pm. Before we checked in, I left my U-Haul on the street and checked out the parking lot to confirm that I had room to turn around. The motel accommodations including a convenient spot for our U-Haul worked out perfectly. Ernestine, the manager, told us that Cornhusker Datsun was right around the corner, less than a half mile away.

Ever since I lifted the Comet onto the U-Haul coupling 24 hours earlier, my back had been bothering me. I remembered that one of the last articles we packed in the back of the truck was the box with our hard liquor supply, including a bottle of Beefeaters gin. I think my parents bought it when they visited us in Fort Wayne several years back. Knowing a good martini would help me forget about my aching back, I opened up the back of the truck and began rummaging around in search of the gin bottle. Rochelle was not amused.

"Really?" she complained. "You're going to turn the truck upside down to find a lousy bottle of gin? You must be kidding me?"

"Not just any bottle of gin," I responded. "We're talking Beefeaters. Oh look, I found it!"

She just shook her head as I held up the half-filled bottle in my sweaty fingers. As I tried to extricate myself from our packed truck, I briefly lost my balance and juggled the gin.

"Look out!" I yelled at Rochelle as the Beefeaters bottle slipped from my fingers, and shattered on the concrete.

Rochelle, who was unhurt by the broken glass, went into complete hysterics as I looked at my broken bottle in agony. Finally, she regained her composure.

"That looked like a scene right out of 'The Three Stooges' comedy series," she opined; "with Curley trying to retrieve Moe's favorite bottled libation, and suffering the same fate. You got me laughing so hard I almost wet myself!"

She knew just how and when to turn my anger and frustration into laughter. I vividly remembered the scene she was talking about involving Curley and Moe. The look on my face must have resembled Moe's before he unloaded verbally and physically on poor Curley. I couldn't help but start laughing too. Maybe the same fate and destiny force that helped me lift up the Comet in Iowa decided to deny me a martini in Nebraska.

We both got a good night's sleep and were up early to visit Cornhusker Datsun in North Platte. Eddie, the assistant service department manager was there to greet us with his red baseball cap that had a large "N" for Nebraska on it. Rochelle and I noticed that everybody in the dealership, from the sales manager to the mechanics, all wore the same red hats. We explained our overheating problem to Eddie and told him we would be having breakfast across the street at the I-Hop.

"That sounds fine, Mr. Cunningham," he said reassuringly. "Give us an hour or so to check this out, and we'll have you back on the road in no time. Go Big Red!"

It seemed like everybody in this state would say "Go Big Red," instead of hello, goodbye, or see you later. This was an obvious reference to the famed University of Nebraska football program which had created one of the most fanatical fan bases in college sports.

I wondered if I was to drop the name of Nebraska football hero Johnny Rodgers, the 1972 Heisman Trophy winner, if it would get me a discount on my radiator repair.

When we returned from breakfast our car was parked in the visitor parking lot.

"You're all set," Eddie confidently announced. "It was a faulty radiator cap as you suspected, Mr. Cunningham. That'll be $36.50 total for the labor, pressure testing, and the new cap."

I felt very relieved, paid him with a traveler's check, and gave him a "Go Big Red" goodbye greeting before he smiled gave me one back. Knowing we wouldn't have an over-heating problem as we drove up the Rocky Mountains later in the day was a big load off my mind.

Rochelle and I agreed that we would stop for lunch when we got to the summit of the Rockies, which was about 8000 feet. Our drive went well until we nearly reached the summit when I noticed that the U-Haul gas gauge was on EMPTY! We had filled up in Nebraska, but I didn't realize that going up the steep climb of the Rockies combined with the pulling of the Comet consumed huge amounts of fuel. To make matters worse, we had just passed a sign that indicated that there were no gas stations until Laramie, Wyoming, nearly forty miles away. Desperate times called for desperate measures, so I elected to bypass the luncheon stop at the summit. I was going to try to make it, coasting if I had to, all the way to Laramie. I needed to use all the downward gravitational pull I could muster, which meant I coasted past Rochelle, who had no clue what I was doing.

Before we left on the trip, I showed Rochelle how to use the walkie-talkie microphone. I explained that you needed to keep it at least six inches from your mouth, and to speak in a normal voice or you could overmodulate, and not be understood. After all, I was the former professional television announcer. As I began my descent down the Rockies, I forgot all about the good microphone technique that I had preached to my wife. On the twisting mountain roads I had to keep two hands on the wheel, so my effort on the walkie talkie had to be brief, as I balanced it on the steering wheel between my fingers. I raised my voice as I got too close to the mike. I thought I told Rochelle that "I was out of gas and needed to coast to Laramie." What she heard were nothing but screeches and squawks.

It was all I could do to keep the big rig on the road as I barreled down the highway with Rochelle in hot pursuit. As I navigated the turns, I could hear nearly all of our earthly possessions rattle around in the back of the U-Haul, and I could smell the overtaxed brakes during my white-knuckle dash. Finally, after a roller coaster ride of about an hour, we were on nearly level ground. I spotted what looked like a gas station about 200 yards ahead on the left. The downward momentum from the Rockies had pushed me to 60 miles an hour, so stopping and turning into the gas station, which was across the highway, was not going to be easy. The Hudson station was set back about fifty yards from the highway on a gravel road. I pushed down on the brake gradually so as not to throw the rig into a skid or fishtail into oncoming traffic. With my tires screaming and my brakes burning, I made the turn onto the gravel road kicking up a nasty cloud of dust, gravel, and dirt.

"That's a helluva entrance Mister!" proclaimed Ricky, the gas station attendant, as he held his nose and put his hand over his mouth as my cloud enveloped him.

"Thanks," I remarked with a smile. "Where are we? Did I make it to Laramie?"

"Well, Mister, you're in the home of the brave and the land of the free, also known to most of us as Laramie, Wyoming," commented the annoyed attendant as he emerged coughing from the dust cloud.

Rochelle, who witnessed the entire wild ride down the mountain including my finishing slide as she followed me, was also annoyed until she heard my story.

"OK, I couldn't understand your walkie-talkie message, and then you passed me," she said. "My first thought was that your brakes had failed, and I was going to watch the father of my unborn child, with nearly everything we owned, careen out of control, and plunge off the side of the mountain. By the way, how'd you know there would be a gas station right at the base of the Rockies?"

I told her that I had no clue where the next gas station would be, other than somewhere in Laramie. It turned out that we were in the outskirts of the city, approximately two miles from downtown. We also discovered that our 30 gallon gas tank on the U-Haul still had several gallons left, even though the gauge had registered empty for the past forty miles. I learned later that the U-Haul people were tired of hearing from inexperienced truck drivers like myself, who got stranded when they ran out of gas. As a result, they set their gas gauges on empty when there are five gallons left. We ate a quick lunch at the gas station, and then hit the road again heading for Rock Springs.

Rochelle had remembered that Rock Springs had a nice Howard Johnson's Motel and a great restaurant just outside of town. I also remembered our adventure there five years earlier, complete with a late night stage coach ride after running out of gas. I also remembered Bronco Greenly, the rodeo star and gas station attendant who took time away from his annual celebration party to help us out. I was determined to see if he was still at that same gas station, so I could thank him again by filling our tanks.

It was late afternoon when we pulled into what was now "Bronco's Gas" just outside of Rock Springs, and a familiar face was there to greet us.

"Fill 'er up?" remarked the friendly cowboy.

"You sure can," I responded. "I have a U-Haul that'll probably take thirty gallons and a Datsun that may take three. Bronco, do you remember rescuing us when we ran out of gas five years ago?"

He took a long look at the two of us and then you could almost see the light go on in his head.

"Yes, I do remember you two!" he exclaimed with a smile. "You were that couple from California that Andy brought to me in the stage coach the night before the rodeo."

I told him that we were now headed back to California, and asked him if he or anybody else was able to ride the famous Bull named "Tarantula," which was the talk of the town the last time we came through Rock Springs.

"Yep, I was finally able to stay aboard that big devil two years ago, and won some money in the process," he said. "Sadly, it was discovered shortly after the rodeo that the bull was very sick with some form of cancer. We had to put 'Tarantula' down, and we buried 'em in the cemetery with all our other local heroes. There was no way anybody, including me, could ride that bull if he was healthy. But I was able to buy this place with my winnings."

As he filled up the U-Haul and then the Datsun, I asked him if the Purple Sage Country Club was still the best place in town for dinner.

"It ain't cheap, but yeah, it's still the best," he said without hesitation. Then Bronco directed my attention to the two front tires of the Datsun, which were nearly bald. I thought I had this car totally checked out by mechanics in Fort Wayne and again in North Platte, but nobody made mention of a tire issue. The real blame had to rest with me. I was so focused on the U-Haul, and then on the Datsun radiator, that I didn't check on my tires.

"You don't want your Misses driving to California on these two front tires?" he said emphatically. "The tire store in town is closed by now, and the nearest Datsun dealer is in Evanston, but I might be able to help you out."

Bronco had two Atlas tires that were not an exact match with the ones in the rear, but they were close enough. I felt I had no choice, and that I was lucky that my new best friend, Bronco, could rescue us for the second time in five years. He closed his gas station, and completed the tire installation in less than thirty minutes.

"Bronco, you've been our Wyoming guardian angel twice now," I reminded him. "Thank you once again and take care of yourself."

Even though we had just spent over one hundred dollars on gas and tires, we felt that we deserved a nice dinner at the Purple Sage Country Club. Before we settled in at the same Howard Johnson's Motel, we found five years ago, we made sure the U-Haul rig would have an easy exit spot in the parking lot. Clarence, the same inn keeper who greeted us in 1972, was on duty to check us in.

"I recognize you folks from several years ago," he said with a smile. "You were the couple that ran out of gas coming back from the Purple Sage and hitched a ride with the midnight stage coach."

"You have a great memory!" blurted out a surprised Rochelle.

Clarence explained that since Rock Springs Rodeo Weekend had just passed that he had plenty of rooms available. We picked the quietest one available, off in the corner, away from the pool and parking lot. After getting cleaned up and putting on some nice clothes, we headed up to the Purple Sage Country Club where we had another romantic dinner watching the sunset on the high plains. As we drove back to our motel, we figured that we could make it to Rochelle's parents' home in Alameda in two days if we averaged approximately 500 miles a day.

The drive the next day went very smoothly as we worked our way into Salt Lake City. Then we headed into the Utah high desert which was desolate and bare, followed by eastern Nevada badlands which were equally plain and flat. What sustained Rochelle and I on some of these long boring stretches were the chats we had on our walkie-talkies and the wonderful music on our radios. The spring of 1977 had some memorable songs like "Easy" with Lionel Ritchie, "Heard it in a Love Song" by the Marshall Tucker Band, and Kenny Rogers' "You Picked a Fine Time to Leave Me Lucille." Two other tunes really spoke to the two of us that trip - "Hotel California" by the Eagles because of our future living arrangements with Rochelle's parents, and Barry Manilow's "Looks Like We Made It" which became our trip's theme song. We didn't mind hearing those tunes over and over again because they helped us make it to the godforsaken town of Elko, Nevada, which was in the middle of nowhere. When we came through that little hamlet in 1972, we made the mistake of staying at a hotel which was also a casino. This time we pulled into a Motel Six across the street from a Denny's restaurant and not far from a school with outdoor basketball courts. It also had a huge parking lot for my U-Haul with plenty of room to turn around.

After Rochelle and I got settled in our room for our last night on the road, I grabbed the basketball from the front seat of my truck and headed out to the courts to see if I could get a game with the locals. I found three guys who looked to be either late teens or early twenties shooting around and looking for a fourth.

We played some two-on-two basketball for about an hour until it got really windy and dusty. The locals told me that early evening wind, dust and sand were pretty common for this time of year in Elko. It felt good to get a workout after all the driving of the last four days, even if it was just a short one.

That evening, Rochelle and I were focused on our last day of travel, so hunting for an upscale restaurant for dinner was not in the cards. Our dinner and breakfast meals at Denny's were serviceable, but not memorable like the Purple Sage Country Club in Rock Springs. We went to bed at 9pm, and were up early on the morning of Thursday, June first, because we had a big final day of driving in front of us. The truth is that we couldn't wait to get out of Elko, Nevada, which we agreed was an "armpit of a place," to use Rochelle's words.

CALIFORNIA HERE WE COME

The drive across Nevada was a smooth one and got more scenic when we reached Reno. We even enjoyed a laugh on the walkie-talkie as we discussed what our lives might have been like if I had gotten that job in Reno in 1971 instead of Fort Wayne a year later. Then we crossed into California about 1pm, and stopped for lunch at Donner Summit where we had a picnic in the woods. Rochelle got choked up as she pulled out a plastic bag with a withered poppy inside it.

"My mom gave me this poppy when we left California five years ago hoping it would bring us back," she said as her eyes filled with tears. "And, as the song says 'Looks Like We Made It.'"

An emotional Rochelle explained that she felt that she was in a scene from John Steinbeck's classic travel novel, "The Grapes of Wrath," as we started reflecting on our adventures during the trip. Our laughter turned into tears when we talked about the good times we left behind and the new life with our first child that was in front of us. Rochelle picked a small cluster of pine cones which she would turn into a Christmas ornament. That ornament has adorned our holiday tree every year since, reminding us of that special moment when we returned to California.

As we descended from the Sierras, we passed Sacramento, where we spent the first two years of our married life. I saw the familiar KCBG-TV studios from the freeway, and thought about my trusted former coworkers there like Mel Baker and Lloyd Brennan, who helped me make life changing decisions. I also thought about a future reunion with our good friends and former Sacramento neighbors, Mike and Joanne Ferris. The nostalgic lunch break had started my mind wandering alternately between the past and the future, especially as we drove by familiar landmarks.

When got closer to the Bay Area on Interstate 80, the traffic began to bunch up as we approached "rush hour." I knew our lives, like the traffic, would begin to be much busier and more stressful as Rochelle's due date approached and I would begin my new job. Rochelle and I planned to spend a couple of days at her parents' home in Alameda, before flying to San Diego to spend a week with my parents at their new home in Rancho Santa Fe. Then it was time to work on getting my real estate license, while both Rochelle and I would attempt to get part time jobs to make ends meet. We would be living with Rochelle's parents until we found a place of our own. The baby and my new real estate sales job would be just three months away. Holy shit, this is really happening!

Finally, the beautiful bay sprang into view over our right shoulders to the West, as we were literally creeping on the crowded freeway. Rochelle stuck her walkie-talkie antenna out of her window indicating she wanted to chat.

"There's the San Francisco skyline and the Golden Gate Bridge," she said enthusiastically.

I responded by singing "California Here I Come" over the walkie-talkie.

Then a trucker, who apparently was on the same radio frequency as our walkie-talkies, chimed in.

"Well done good buddy," he commented. Then he addressed the other truckers listening in. "Hey y'all, let's let these two-way communicators through!"

He then politely changed lanes so that I could be directly behind Rochelle. We had gotten separated in traffic.

"Thank you my friend," I responded. "We're moving back to the Bay Area after being away for seven years."

"Welcome back. I think you'll find it's a little more crowded now than when you left," he warned.

We inched along Interstate 80 until we made the turnoff to the Nimitz Freeway South (now called 880), which left us only a couple of miles from our High Street turnoff to Alameda. During the final half hour of our trip, my mind flashed back again to those boys from Roosevelt and Eastview High Schools, especially Whip Perkins and Hops Jordan, who chose to take a "leap of faith," and trust each other. I couldn't get them out of my mind, and I promised myself that I would tell their story someday. They were special kids blessed with good parents who helped them learn a value system that instilled honesty and fair play. Those youngsters truly inspired me as I began my real estate sales career. My dad had told me that a successful salesperson must believe in the overall "goodness of the human spirit." Until recently, I found myself having a hard time buying into that statement, particularly working in a television newsroom which can breed cynicism. But Whip Perkins and Hops Jordan showed me their hearts, and made me a believer in the "goodness of the human spirit" that my dad preached about. I felt empowered by that knowledge, which not only would help me in sales, but also in dealing with life's many personal challenges which lay ahead.

We got off the Nimitz on High Street, and headed west into Alameda's Bay Farm Island neighborhood. At last, we pulled up in front of the home of Albert and Pauline Wildi, Rochelle's parents. As I watched my pregnant wife dash into the welcoming arms of her mom and dad, I suddenly was reminded of Dorothy in the family-favorite movie, "The Wizard of Oz." Like Dorothy, I felt that I was also returning from the Land of Oz, where I learned a countless number of life's lessons from some unforgettable people. Instinctively I tapped my Adidas tennis shoes together and said out loud, "There's no place like home."

The End

About the Author

Pete Torrey was born in Hartford, Connecticut, but grew up in Northern California. He graduated from San Jose State University in 1970 with a B.A. degree in Radio and Television Production. After college, Pete worked for television stations in San Jose and Sacramento, California, before becoming a TV sports anchor in Fort Wayne, Indiana. After leaving broadcasting, he and his wife Jean moved back to California, and raised their two children in the San Francisco Bay Area. Pete has been a residential real estate broker in the East Bay for over forty years.

Made in the USA
Middletown, DE
22 June 2021